The White Orchid

The White Orchid

Book Three

J. L. Robison

For information, contact J.L. Robison at joanlrobison@yahoo.com or https://linktr.ee/j.l.robison

First edition
ISBN 978-1-7358382-8-1

Edelweiss Saga

Edelweiss
Winter Iris
The White Orchid
Beneath the Cornflowers

Learning to trust is one of life's most difficult tasks.

—Isaac Watts

I would like to dedicate this book to my family who (mostly) stayed patient while I spent countless hours writing it, and to my sister, Jane, who is one of my biggest fans. Thank you!

Chapter One

December 25th 1941

Eva sipped the coffee substitute, enjoying the sensation of the hot liquid as it went down. The cup was keeping her hands warm through the thin gloves that were insufficient for this weather. She found herself wishing she had brought thicker ones to help ward off the biting cold air.

The landscaped fields that surrounded the hospital were white as far as the eyes could see, with thick crystalline powder. The trees stood like ice sculptures lined in the distance, the snow sparkling in the early morning sun. It had snowed yesterday evening for the third time that week, then during the night, a misting rain came, freezing on top of the snow and the trees, covering everything in sheets of ice. Eva thought by now she would be used to this bitter cold, seeing how they had been here all winter on the Russian front, but how could someone ever get used to this brutal weather?

Sometimes Eva could not wrap her head around what was happening, that she was part of such a massive event in history. Three million Germans would invade Russia throughout this operation. It would be the largest invasion force the world had seen, even in her time; this enterprise would involve more men than any other theater of war. And it would escalate the war more than any battle in its entirety. Eva knew this area would see some of the world's largest battles and, sadly, some of the most horrific atrocities committed during the war. It would result in the highest casualties for the Soviet and the Axis forces, which worried her more than she could ever say. Gerhardt was constantly in her thoughts, and Sergei. She worried about him as well, and what would become of him? Germany would capture some five million Soviet Red Army soldiers, most of whom would never return alive. Would Sergei be amongst those who were caught? Would he never return home? These thoughts swirled in her head, disturbing every time they reared their ugly heads. But she could not dwell on them. There were too many people to worry about, including herself, Ingrid, and Dr. Möller.

She learned in her tenth-grade AP world history class of the *Hunger Plan,* implemented by the Germans to solve food shortages and exterminate the Slavic population through starvation. But the Slavic people weren't the only ones being starved by the Germans. They deliberately starved to the point of death over three million Soviet Prisoners of war or just straight up killed them.

2

This was a side of the war she wished never to see or be so close to. It was an extraordinary part of history to read about, not experience. Germany achieved notable victories and occupied many of the most important economic areas belonging to the Soviet Union, mostly in the Ukraine. But in doing so inflicted heavy civilian casualties as well as sustaining heavy losses themselves. Despite their early successes, the German offensive stalled outside of Moscow. When winter came, the Germans were wholly unprepared because they had not equipped their troops for the cold. They also failed to provide enough food and medicine for the soldiers fighting on the frontline, but the situation would only grow worse. On December 6th, the Russians pushed the Germans back, almost to the Belarus border, and now the Germans were bombing their own supply trains so they wouldn't fall into the hands of the Russians. The German soldiers had to stand by and watch their food, clothes, rations, and other necessities blown to pieces and could do nothing about it. It weighed heavily on Eva's mind, so she could only imagine how it must be for the soldiers.

Just a few weeks ago, a war was raging to re-secure the town of Smolensk, which they achieved. And again, from history, she knew that the Germans would launch another offensive in the summer of 1942 in the south and southeast toward Stalingrad. She also knew that this would be the Germans' furthest geographical expansion. The Germans' hope of a quick collapse of the Soviet resistance as they had in Poland obviously didn't happen, and the Russians being... well Russians, absorbed the German Wehrmacht's strongest attacks and slowed them down in a war of attrition, something else the Germans were unprepared for. And so, they had to retreat towards the Baltic states.

If only the Germans knew what she knew, that the subsequent operations to retake the initiative and drive the Soviets back into their own territory would also fail. Case Blue in 1942 and Operation Citadel in 1943 were lost before they even began, which caused the Wehrmacht's collapse, and thus the end of the war.

Someone draped a blanket around her shoulders and Eva looked up at Ingrid's face. Her eyes a vibrant blue in the bright morning sunlight, and her pale round cheeks a deep shade of pink from the cold.

"You shouldn't be out here with so little to keep you warm," Ingrid told her.

"I wasn't planning on being out long."

Ingrid sat beside her on the steps of the hospital with her cup of coffee substitute. "You are up early. Is everything alright?"

"It's Christmas morning, and I'm here freezing my ass off in Russia with barely enough to eat while I watch men die like the poor creatures on a fox hunt because we don't have the room, proper medical equipment, or medicine to keep them alive. I want nothing more than to be with my family right now, sitting on the living room floor drinking eggnog while listening to Christmas music and opening presents."

"I miss my family, too. We never had much, but my parents always made sure that my three brothers and I had something for Christmas."

"I didn't know that you came from a poor family." Eva's parents by no means were wealthy, but she and her brother never wanted for anything. They grew up in a modest home in a lower-middle-class neighborhood and always had nice clothes to wear and food to fill their bellies.

"Yea, we grew up on a small farm in rural Germany. I couldn't wait to turn eighteen, so I could be an army nurse and get out of that place where nothing happened."

Eva glanced at the side of Ingrid's face as she stared off into the distance, trying to gauge her mood. "You know, I thought as you do once. I felt like nothing ever happened in my hometown and that my life was going nowhere. And like you, I couldn't wait to leave and go somewhere different. I thought all the exciting things in life always happened somewhere else and never where I lived. But now, I would give anything to go home. To see my family again and the place I tried so hard to get away from."

Ingrid focused on Eva, clearly confused. "But it is different for you. This isn't your country, and your family isn't here."

"Doesn't matter. It's still the same. We think we want something different because we don't understand and appreciate what we have. I understand wanting to escape the mundane, slow pace of life for a while. That is all I wanted. But for me, it has been more than a while. It has been years now. And in those years, I've had some time to reflect, and I realized life was slow because things were good, peaceful, and that isn't a bad thing."

"I know it's not, but life can get stagnant if nothing ever happens and things never change."

"Well, things are happening now, and a lot has changed," Eva said, struggling to keep the sadness from her voice. "And it will continue to change, and not necessarily for the better."

"I know. But how will I ever find a husband if I stay in that little town? I don't even live in the town. I live on a farm out of town."

"I think we find the people who are supposed to be in our lives when we are not trying to find them."

Ingrid blinked, fluttering her impossibly long lashes. "You sound like you speak from experience. Do you?"

Eva ignored her question. "I think we better go in. I'm freezing, and our shift starts soon."

"Sure." Ingrid stood and pulled the blanket from Eva's shoulders, tucking it under her arm.

Eva followed her inside, and they went to the nurse's quarters, showered, and dressed for the day ahead. The last couple of days had been slower than usual, maybe because it was Christmas, maybe not. Eva didn't really know the reason.

"Good morning, girls," Dr. Möller said when he walked into the room they used as a patient wing. The building they were using as a hospital wasn't originally a hospital. It had been a school. As they moved along the front lines, they had to use what they could find, what was accessible to them.

Eva gave him a warm smile. "Good morning, doctor."

"Good morning," Ingrid chimed.

"And what do we have today?" he asked, flipping through papers on a clipboard.

"No one new. I believe a few will be sent back to the front today, though."

He looked up from his clipboard. "Correct." He scanned the room. "Poor boys, nothing in this world could have prepared them for what they face out there."

Eva surveyed the faces of the wounded young men. "You are right. I can only imagine what it must be like for them."

"Well, let's get these patients on their way so we can prepare the critical ones for the move. Home by New Year, right?" His tone suggested that he didn't wholly believe it.

"That is what they said. I guess we will see if it actually happens. Five months here; what is another few days?"

Eva was to help with the discharge of the patients, which was usually a smooth procedure. Bringing them their clean clothes and signing paperwork was the bulk of what was done before they departed. She would help them into their uniforms, then explain how to care for their wounds. Today the discharges were going as usual until she got to the fourth patient and pulled the blankets back to give him one last check. She paused, perplexed. His bandage was missing, and it appeared the wound had been torn open with a blunt instrument. The skin was mangled, and fresh blood trickled out, soaking into his shirt and the sheets.

Eva gazed down at the wound, trying to figure out what happened. She glanced around the room to see if anyone was watching them but didn't notice anyone looking in their direction. She leaned over and spoke in a low voice. "Did you do this?"

The young man turned his bloodshot eyes to her, brimming with tears. "You don't know what it's like to fight on the frontlines. One night you are eating and laughing with the guys, and the next day you watch them blown to pieces. You build a bond with them while in the foxholes and from the shared experiences. We sleep together, eat together, and fight together, but it is more than just that. The horrors you see will haunt you when you sleep, and every day you worry it will be your last. The Russians are cruel and heartless, and there is no honor in how they fight. They don't even seem to care about their men. They would sacrifice a hundred of them just to kill one of us. It was so tragic watching them get cut down the way they were. Every time I pulled that trigger, someone died at my hands. Bloodied and mangled, they fell to the ground, one after another, piling on top of each other like stacked wood. Only they were bodies. I don't want to go back there. Anything would be better than that." He gripped tightly to the blanket as he spoke, twisting it in his hand.

Eva didn't need to ask him to explain. She understood why he did it and how cruel the Russian army could be. "You think being shot for cowardice would be better?" she asked him.

"They won't shoot me. They will imprison me. I know it will be awful, but it won't be anything like this."

Eva knelt beside the bed and put a hand on his arm. "No, they won't. They will kill you for this. You will never succeed. If your superiors don't find out about what you did, they will just send you back to the front as soon as you are well, and if they do learn of it, they will try you, and the court will find you guilty. There is no doubt of that."

He wiped the tears from his face with the back of his hand. "You really think they will shoot me?"

"I know they will." She looked around the room again, checking to make sure they were still alone. "Here is what we are going to do. When the doctor comes, I will tell him you moved and tore your stitches."

"Do you think he will believe it?"

"He will believe me," Eva assured him. "But I need to make the wound look like you tore it while moving and not from whatever you used to do this." Dr. Möller's voice echoed in the hall. "We better hurry." She took a piece of gauze in one hand and some forceps and scissors in the other. "I am going to cut the thread and pull some of it out to make it look like you tore it. Let's hope this works. Here, take this." She held the gauze out to him. "You dab the blood as I cut." He took the gauze from her but didn't say anything. She heard Dr. Möller's footsteps getting closer. "Try not to make any noise." She began clipping the thread and pulling random pieces out as she went along. He winced and clenched his jaw but didn't make a sound. "Dab, hurry," she instructed. With the gauze he patted the wound, then she went back to cutting the thread until reaching the fresh wound he gave himself. "I think that will do." She hid the bloody tools, thread, and gauze in the pocket of her apron just as Dr. Möller entered the room, coming straight toward them.

"How is our patient?" he asked when he was almost to them.

She gave the young man a quick glance before looking back at the doctor. "Not well, actually."

He furrowed his brows and glanced at the clipboard. "According to this, he will go back to the front today."

"Yes, he would have, but when he was trying to sit up, he turned wrong and tore his stitches, pulling most of them out and re-opening his wound."

Dr. Möller eyed the tow of them, skeptical. "Let me take a look." He lifted the man's shirt and inspected the wound. "You did this by sitting up?" he asked.

Eva glanced at the man, her eyes pleading with him to keep calm and stick to their story. "Yes, Sir, that is how it happened."

"Hmmm, well, let's get you stitched back up. You will have to return to the front a little later." Dr. Möller's expression was of disappointment.

While Eva assisted Dr. Möller, she continuously glanced at the man, making sure he was alright.

"After you get this cleaned up, meet me in my office. The replacement doctors and nurses are already here."

"Already?" She could hardly believe their luck.

"They arrived early."

"Well, that's good for us, then."

"Yes, we can get on the road sooner. See you in a bit." He tapped her on the shoulder and walked away.

Eva nodded. Once Dr. Möller was out of earshot, she turned back to the patient. "You are not to speak of this to anyone, ever. Do you understand?"

"I do. So that's it then. I'm still going to go back to the front?"

"Yes, I'm sorry. But at least it won't be for another week or so. That's something." She tried to sound encouraging. "It gives you a little more time away from all of that."

10

"A week, maybe two. I don't want to go back in a week. I never want to go back to that hell."

"I know, but you aren't left with many options. If you get arrested by the Gestapo for being a coward, you will most certainly die, but if you fight the Russians, there is a chance that you will survive and get to return home someday. The choice is yours." He languidly nodded in understanding. "Ok then." She gathered the tools and bandages and started to leave but stopped, turning back to him. "Good luck."

"Thank you. Will you get into trouble for this?"

"They won't find out, but even if the doctor who was here does, he won't do anything."

"He seems like a good doctor."

"He is, and a good person. He usually does the right thing." She looked at the door, then back at him. "I have to go now. The convoy is readying to leave, and I need to be on it."

"Are you going home?"

She huffed. "Home, no. I'm going back to Berlin."

"It's still better than here."

She considered everything that happened while she was living in Berlin. "That depends on who you ask. Take care of yourself." She turned and left the room. Dr. Möller and the convoy were waiting, but she had reservations about returning to Berlin, and didn't know how to feel about going back. After being gone for five months, there was no way of knowing what being back in Germany held in store for her. Was Bauer still there? Was the resistance still in operation, or had they all been arrested, and was that what awaited her when she returned? She didn't know the answer to any of it, but she couldn't hide on the Russian front forever.

Chapter Two

December 28th 1941

They traveled west for two days but were only halfway through Poland. The snow, the size of the convoy, and the wounded made for a slow journey. They had camped just outside of Tódz, a town in the middle of the country. Frequently, the convoy had to pull on the side of the road to allow an eastbound company of soldiers to pass, no doubt to prepare for the upcoming summer attack and lend assistance to the companies still holding Russian territory.

Eva hadn't opened her eyes yet, but could tell it was already morning. The recently built fires crackled as boots crunched on the frozen snow around her, and the aroma of cooking food filled her nostrils. She rolled onto her side, and instantly the pain shot up her back from laying on the hard ground. Sleeping outside in winter was not something she would have done under most circumstances, but the trucks were full of patients who needed the bedding and the warmth the trucks provided. They needed it more than her.

She let out a whimper and sat up in her makeshift sleeping bag, which was really only two blankets she rolled up in. *I'm going to be feeling this the rest of the day,* she thought.

"Eva, you're up." Ingrid lowered herself on the frozen ground, holding out a steaming cup of the coffee substitute.

"Did I sleep longer than you?" Eva glanced around, searching the camp. Most of the others were already packing up, preparing to leave.

"It's alright; most of us just got up too. Dr. Möller says we will leave soon."

"I better hurry and drink this, then." Eva took a sip of the steaming black liquid and cringed as it went down. "I always forget how awful the taste of this is."

"You get used to it," Ingrid said, peering into her cup. "That was nice of you to let the driver sleep in the truck last night."

Eva looked at her. "He's older. The cold would have been harder on him than me."

"Dr. Möller would be upset if he knew you slept outside."

"That's right. If he knew, but he doesn't. Where did Dr. Möller sleep?"

"Outside. He told the nurses to sleep in the trucks, that the doctors would sleep outside."

"Well, that doesn't surprise me. He would do that." Eva regarded the flurry around them. "I think we are ready to leave. Did you get something to eat?"

14

"I ate a little, but you didn't eat anything. You should get something before we head out."

"I'm not hungry. I can eat when we stop again." She dashed the remaining black liquid to the side and stood. "I'm going to step into the woods and pee. I'll pick the blankets up when I come back."

"Alright, don't be long."

Eva smiled. "I'm fast, as quick as a man."

"I don't doubt that."

Eva narrowed her eyes at Ingrid jokingly, then walked into the trees until she could no longer see the convoy. She pulled down her pants and squatted, her breath coming like a cloud in front of her. She finished and got ready to stand when twigs breaking nearby echoed through the trees. Her butt and legs were growing cold but she remained frozen, unsure what to do. Should she wait in the squatting position or hurry and pull up her pants? The crunching of twigs and leaves stopped, and voices were now what traveled through the trees, one of a man and one of a woman.

Eva focused on the whispering but couldn't make out what they were saying. Then there was laughing and giggling. Because of how lout it was, Eva knew that they were close, maybe a tree or two away. She quietly stood and pulled up her pants, trying not to make a noise. Normally, she would wear a nursing uniform but opted for women's trousers while traveling.

She put her hands on the tree for support and peered around it, trying to see the people. She couldn't see them, but could hear the sounds they were making, the smacking of kissing lips and heavy breathing that accompanied it.

Engines roared to life, echoing in the distance; then the people exchanged a few words and the girl giggled. Then multiple footsteps moved quickly over the frozen earth and the people finally came into view. Dr. Hoffmann led Ingrid by the hand as they briskly made their way through the forest, stopping only for a quick kiss, then continuing out of the trees. Eva couldn't believe what she saw. How could Ingrid be so reckless as to get involved with one of the doctors?

Once they were out of sight, Eva hurried through the woods, back to the convoy, and climbed into the front of the truck Ingrid was in and closed the door. Only now did Eva remember she had not picked up her blankets and hoped that someone else did.

Sitting next to Ingrid and not being able to say anything about what she saw was eating her up. She understood that Ingrid was old enough to make her own decisions, but questioned if she was mature enough, because Ingrid always seemed to make bad ones when it came to men. Although she was one to be talking when she too continued to make poor choices with relationships.

Eva continued to give Ingrid side glances, but most of the time she didn't seem to notice. Occasionally though she would make eye contact with Ingrid.

"Alright, what is it?" Ingrid demanded, irritation seeping through.

"What is what?"

"Why do you keep looking at me?"

"I will tell you when we stop."

"Why can't you just tell me now?"

"Trust me. You won't want me to."

"Why?"

Eva gave her a look that spoke volumes. "It's about my bathroom trip into the woods this morning, and what I saw there."

Ingrid gaped at her for a fraction of a second, then turned to face forward again. "I don't know what you are talking about."

"I could smile and pretend I don't know the truth, but I'm not going to."

"We will be taking a break for lunch soon, and we can discuss it then," Ingrid finally agreed.

"That is what I thought."

When the convey stopped for a break, Eva took Ingrid's arm and pulled her to the side, out of earshot of anyone else. "What are you thinking, getting involved with a doctor?"

"I like Dr. Hoffmann, and he likes me. He can see me for who I am."

Eva let out a frustrated laugh. "Oh, I can see that, but it's not your personality he likes. It's what you do with him."

"You only say that because you are jealous."

"Jealous of Dr. Hoffmann? No, I most certainly am not."

"No, I mean jealous that I have someone and you don't."

This gave Eva pause, as well as a twinge of pain along with guilt. Pain that she no longer had Gerhardt in her life and regret that maybe part of what Ingrid said was true. But she cared for Ingrid and didn't want to see her get hurt or into trouble for fraternizing with a doctor. "No, Ingrid, he is older than you and a doctor."

"He is not as old as the others."

"I know, but he is still quite a bit older than you. Has it ever crossed your mind that maybe he is just using you to escape the loneliness of being here?"

"I'm sure that is part of it for both of us, but it is more than that. I have real feelings for him, and I know he feels the same way about me."

"Has he told you that?"

"He doesn't need to. I see it in the way he treats me. Besides, being with him makes me feel secure."

Eva opened her mouth to say something but decided against it. "Ingrid, you know I care about you. I don't want to see this turn bad. I would hate for you to get hurt because of it."

Ingrid took one of Eva's hands in both of hers. "I won't. Let this be our secret?" she asked, the innocent smile on her face reminding Eva so much of a child's, so she nodded. "Thank you." Ingrid gave her a quick hug, then let go. "We should make it to Berlin today. We have averaged a little over six hours a day, and the driver said this morning we were about seven and a half hours from Berlin. Isn't that exciting?"

"Maybe." Eva forced a smile. She honestly didn't know if it would be exciting, at least the right kind of excitement.

"You better go eat before we take off again, or you will be starving."

"I'm going to." Eva went to the back of the convoy and took some rations out of the truck, then sat on the bumper to eat.

"I haven't seen you all day. How are you holding up?" Dr. Möller asked as he came around the side of the truck and sat next to her.

"Doing fine. I just decided I better eat before I become angry from hunger."

"Well, none of us want that," he said, teasing.

Eva swallowed. "Exactly. I'm like a bear if I don't eat." She then took another bite.

"Maybe of the cotton stuffed variety."

Eva laughed, almost choking on her food. "No, like the big, angry, wild ones who live in the forest. You've just never seen me starving."

"Angry like a bear, no, I haven't seen you like that." He checked his watch. "The convoy better get back on the road. We are only three hours from Berlin, and I want to make it there before nightfall." He stood but paused next to her. "I was wondering, do you know where you will stay when we get to Berlin?"

"Oh, at my old apartment, I guess. I hadn't really thought about it. I just assumed that is where I would go."

"Have you been in contact with your old roommates?"

"Yea, we write letters back and forth. They are still in the same apartment."

"That's good. If anything changes, let me know. If need be, you can stay with me until you find a place."

His concern touched Eva. "Thank you. I will."

She finished her food and loaded up with the others, then the convoy continued its crawling journey towards Berlin.

It was late when the convoy pulled in front of the hospital. Their hopes of arriving before dark were shattered when one patient had a seizure just eighty miles from the city. The convoy had pulled off on the side of the road, and Eva stood by as Dr. Möller and Dr. Hoffmann tried to stabilize the man but ultimately failed. They wrapped his body in a blanket and placed it back in the truck to take him home so he could have a funeral.

Eva stepped down out of the truck and stretched, taking in the view. Seeing the hospital again brought back so many memories, some good and some not so pleasant. The chill in the air was nothing compared to the cold in Russia. It didn't cut through you like a thousand tiny knives. It was strange being back, and frankly, it made her a little uncomfortable.

"Let's get the patients unloaded so we can go home," Dr. Möller called from the front of the convoy.

They moved the wounded inside quickly and out of the cold, handing them off to the night shift staff at the hospital. When they were done, Eva got her suitcase and purse, told Ingrid bye and that she would see her later, then found Dr. Möller. "Do you think you could give me a ride to my old apartment?"

"Sure. There is a car waiting to take me home. I'll just inform the driver that he will take you home first."

"Thank you."

"It's not a problem." He slipped on his military uniform jacket and buttoned it down the front, then took his cap from the desk and pulled it down on his head. "The car is out front."

Eva followed him outside to a black car. The orderly was standing beside it, waiting. He opened the back door when he saw them, and Dr. Möller slid in after Eva.

"I can wait in the car if you want, just in case they aren't there."

"I think I will be alright."

"If you're sure."

Eva appreciated his fatherly concern. "I am."

The car dropped her off in front of her old apartment, and she waited outside until it disappeared. Being chased by the resistance and her fleeing the apartment was the first thought that ran through her mind when she looked up at the simple brick structure. *It won't be like that now,* she thought. She took the key to the apartment that she had held onto and unlocked the front door, and climbed the stairs to her floor. Eva decided it might be good to knock first to see if Liesel or Heidi were home instead of unlocking it and walking in. She brought her hand up and tapped a few times on the old, familiar brown door. Footsteps creaked on the other side then the door opened, and Heidi stood staring at her, surprise evident on her face.

"Eva… oh my God. What… why are you here?"

"It's my rotation. I'm back in Berlin for a while."

Heidi took Eva in her arms. "We weren't sure you were going to come back."

Eva pulled away and looked at her face. "You thought I was going to die?"

"Not necessarily that. We didn't know if you wanted to come back to Berlin."

"Well, as of now, I have nowhere else to go. I have a job here and a place to stay, so there is no reason for me to go anywhere else."

"I guess it makes sense that you would come back." Heidi turned back to the open apartment door. "Liesel, it's Eva."

Liesel came out of her bedroom, a bright smile spreading across her face when she caught sight of Eva. "I can't believe it's you. It has been so long." She embraced Eva. "I am happy you are back. Are you here to stay, or will you return to the front?"

"I don't know. Right now, nothing is decided."

Liesel picked her bag up off the floor. "Let's go inside."

Eva followed them into the apartment, hanging her purse and coat on the rack near the door, then sat on the couch. It all seemed so familiar to her, and yet something was different, missing, like a strange empty feeling.

"So, how have you guys been? What has happened in Berlin while I was gone?"

Liesel and Heidi sat on the couch next to her. "Well," Liesel said, "not much has changed. A few bombings a week, and Frau Wagner is still her old self."

Heidi shook her head in agreement. "Yea, nothing much."

"What? I can't believe this. So, no boyfriends or anything like that?"

Heidi laughed. "Liesel dating, not likely."

Liesel smiled. "She is right. I won't date until this war is over."

"I can see the logic in that," Eva said. "I'm sorry to cut the evening short, but I'm utterly spent."

"I'm sure you are," Heidi said understandingly. "Your room is just as it was when you left."

"Thank you, guys." Eva took her things to her room and fell onto the bed. It felt so good to lie on an actual bed again and not a cot. She closed her eyes and drifted off to a dreamless sleep.

Chapter Three

January 1st, 1942

After days of spending time with Liesel and Heidi, Eva decided it was time to figure out what she should do next, although she was fairly sure she was going to go back to the front. There she could do the most good, even though it took a toll on her most days. Witnessing all that death day after day was hard, but it kept her mind off the constant fear of being arrested by the Gestapo or the deep-seated pain of Gerhardt.

Eva walked along the river, and although she was back in Germany and away from Russia, it was still a harsh winter's day. The collar of her coat was up to help shield her face from the bitter wind. She decided to go by the little shop where the resistance always met, wondering what became of them. The thought that someone in the resistance might spot her was concerning, but she also worried that the Gestapo got to all of them. If the Gestapo had arrested the entire Berlin resistance, did that mean they would come for her now that she was back? She needed the answer to these questions, and she thought the best way to get them was to start with their meeting place.

She was almost at the shop when she stopped in her tracks. She stared across the street at the destroyed building. All the windows had been blown out, and the front was blackened from a fire. The whole right half of the roof sagged. It looked like someone had tossed grenades inside. "Noo…," she breathed. Immediately she knew the Gestapo had done this and that it meant they probably had everyone in the resistance already. Eva decided against going anywhere near the building because it might look suspicious. She didn't look at it as she walked on, pretending to be indifferent.

Am I just a dead woman walking? She wondered. *Are they going to come for me next? Have I just been pretending that I was fine while at the Russian front and not truly knowing how close I've been to my own demise?* The uneasy awareness returned. She could not stay in Berlin if this was what it was going to be like.

She went back to the apartment and locked the door. She knew that Heidi and Liesel were both at work, which was good because she needed time alone to think. She paced back and forth in the living room with one hand on her hip as she bit the thumb nail of the other. "What am I going to do… what am I going to do?"

The phone rang, making her jump out of her skin. She went to the wall, resting her hand on the receiver for a moment while catching her breath before finally answering.

"Hello?"

"Is this Fräulein Abrams?" a woman's voice said on the other end.

"It is. Who is asking?"

"I am calling from Oberst Heinrich Schmitt's office. He wanted me to find out if you were free to see him today. Is there a time that is convenient for you?"

She sighed a breath of relief. She couldn't believe Heinrich Schmitt wanted to see her, and then wondered why. "I have nothing planned for today, so anytime is fine."

"Let me ask the Colonel what time he will be by to pick you up. Hold on." The other end the phone made a crackling sound from being put down, then footsteps clicked in the distance. After about a minute, the woman returned and picked up the phone. "He says he will be there to get you in an hour."

"That would be fine. Tell him I will wait." Eva hung up the receiver but didn't move. What could he want? She found it odd that Heinrich wanted to come and see her, and that he even knew she was back in Berlin. *Maybe he just wants to visit me after all this time. He has always been kind to me and enjoyed my company,* she thought, smiling.

She tidied up the apartment while waiting, trying to find anything to keep herself occupied until he got there. Finally, came the much-awaited knock. She hurried to the door and pulled it open. A man in a low-ranking military uniform greeted her from the hall. "Oberst Heinrich Schmitt is waiting in the car. I am to retrieve you."

Eva figured he must be Heinrich Schmitt's orderly. "Of course. Let me just get my things." She grabbed her coat from the rack and put it on, then her hat, gloves, and scarf. She got her purse off the floor and followed the orderly. As she walked beside him, she couldn't help but feel a little uneasy, although she didn't know exactly why. Her heartrate was elevated and her palms had started to sweat.

When they got to the car, he opened the back door for her. She slid in next to Heinrich Schmitt, and then the orderly shut the door and went to the front. She gave Heinrich a bright smile as their eyes met, but it quickly faded when he didn't return it, and didn't speak until the car pulled onto the road.

"Eva, why have you come back to Berlin?" The expression on his face was weighted as he took her in.

She swallowed hard. "I'm on rotation. It's my break from the front."

"That's not what I mean. You should not have come back here."

She tried to gather her thoughts. "Why should I not have come back?"

He took hold of her arm. "Eva, do not play coy." He looked in the front of the car and spoke to the driver. "Pull over here and wait outside."

"Yes, sir." The orderly pulled to the curb, turned the engine off, then got out and stood dutifully on the sidewalk with his hands clasped in front of him just a few feet away.

Heinrich let go of her arm. "Because you were in the resistance."

Eva couldn't hide the shock and horror on her face. Did she dare deny it? "How do you possibly know that? Do you work for the Gestapo?"

His expression was confused but then turned to comprehension. "No, I do not work for the Gestapo. So you don't know?"

She was growing frustrated. "Know what?"

"The person passing information from the inside was me, Eva."

Her jaw dropped. "You, you were the spy on the inside?"

"Yes, that is what I'm trying to tell you."

Eva had so many questions she didn't even know which one to start with first. "So that is how you know I was in the resistance?"

"Yes."

She shook her head, still trying to comprehend. "Then why are you still here?"

"They are not suspicious of me. My cover is solid. Yours is not. No one ever saw my face. I would drop the information at specific locations, then leave. The notes I would hide always had the next drop location. We changed it every time, and I was the one who chose them. Before placing the letter, I would stake the location out to make sure it had not been compromised. We always did dead-drops. It was the safest way."

"But how are they on to me?"

"Because they caught all of them, except two, one of whom fled to France. And I'm sure it is just a matter of time until they catch you. Did you not know this?"

The faces of the others appeared unbidden in her mind. A knot formed in her throat. "No… I didn't know."

"If you don't get out of Berlin, you will pay for it too."

28

"Trust me. I've already been paying for it."

"This time, it will be different. I would be surprised if one of the others didn't give you up, but even if the Gestapo isn't aware you were involved, they will find out eventually."

"Did you always know I was in the resistance?"

"Not when I first met you. It wasn't until I looked into your file the day you asked me to get you a pass. Do you remember?"

"I do."

"That was the day I figured it out. One thing that still puzzles me, though. With the extensive file they have on you, I'm surprised you are not already in prison or dead. It doesn't add up."

Eva shrugged. "I don't know either."

"There were also parts of your file that had been blacked out and some sections left blank that should have been filled out."

"Blacked out?"

"Parts that had been hidden on purpose, by who or from who I don't know."

"Is that bad or good?" Eva still didn't understand.

"I don't know."

"Do you think a high-ranking Gestapo officer would know what it said and why it had been blacked out, or maybe have access to the missing information?" she asked.

"I suspect someone does."

She looked at her hands, debating if she should ask her question or not, finally deciding she would. "Do you think it could be SS Obersturmbannführer Bauer who had it done?"

"Was he the Gestapo officer who survived the bombing?"

"Yes, he is," she said.

"I'm sure it's possible, but I don't know why he would."

"He is the one who put the travel ban on me."

"Now that you mention it, his name was on the paperwork that day I looked. But it still makes little sense that he would hide information about you."

"No, it doesn't, but nothing he does makes sense, at least to anyone but him."

"I would have to disagree with you there. There is nothing that man does that doesn't have a purpose. I don't personally know him outside of seeing him in the hall or attending some of the same meetings, but I have heard plenty about him from others. He is not one to trifle with. Eva, make sure he doesn't find you if you want to survive this war."

"Is he here in Berlin now?"

He thought for a minute. "He had been in France, but I believe he is in town this week for meetings."

She remembered Jon's letter, his words about Bauer being the one that could help her, but that seemed to fly in the face of what Heinrich was telling her now. Nothing made sense. She felt like she was being pulled in two different directions, but which way did she choose? "Heinrich, I don't know what to do. Tell me, and I will do it?"

He took her hand. "I can only tell you that you need to leave Germany and hide somewhere. I will help you if I can, but I'm not even sure if you can get a pass to leave."

"This will sound strange, but I think that SS Obersturmbannführer Bauer might be the one person who can help me."

"Are you out of your mind?" His voice rose in pitch. "You obviously do not know who he really is. He isn't someone you can trust. He is not your friend, and people like him are not the kind you want to deal with." He looked out the window at his driver. "We cannot leave him out there forever. Just find a way to get out. And remember, you can't trust anyone in the Gestapo. They are the ones after you. And I will say it again, he is not your friend, remember that." She reached for the doorknob when he took hold of her hand. "One more thing. The name of the traitor in the resistance was Lina."

Eva's eyes widened. "Lina?" she said through clenched teeth.

"Yes."

"Somehow, in my gut, I knew it was her. She was always such a bitch, and now I know why. And where is Lina now?"

"She is still in Berlin. She is the other resistance member who got away, but it was intentional. Apparently, she was asked to infiltrate the resistance by her lover, a high-ranking officer, but I guess he just used her. She did all of this because she thought he loved her, then he told her he didn't after."

"Good. She got what she deserved. Is she the reason they know I was part of the resistance?"

"I don't know. Because of all the blacked-out paragraphs, I'm not even certain they know."

"It might be a while before I can leave."

"I understand, but you need to as soon as you find a way, and it needs to be sooner rather than later."

"Can I contact you if I need help?"

"Only if it is absolutely necessary. If it isn't, we should not be seen together."

"I will only contact you if I'm desperate."

"Let's get you back to your apartment. And if I were in your shoes, I would start coming up with a plan tonight." He knocked on the window, then waved at the driver to return to the car.

Chapter Four

Eva sat on the bed, her head spinning from the information dump she had just received an hour ago. Why would Jon tell her to go to Bauer for help if Bauer was the one after her? It sounded plausible, though, that Bauer was who he was talking about. But, as far as she knew, he still despised her. Eva wished someone had some advice to give her on what to do, but no one was here now to help her. Maybe she would go ahead and ask Bauer for a travel pass, and if she were lucky enough to get one, she would try to cross the channel somehow or maybe go north to a neutral country. Or, hopefully, there was still the option of returning to the front and escaping that way. "I know what I'm going to do," she muttered. "I'm going to go back to the front. I think that will be the easiest way for me to escape."

The following day, she made her way to the hospital to talk with Dr. Möller, who had already gone back to work the day before. She suspected that he, too, would return to the front in the next few weeks. She walked down the familiar path following the trees to the hospital. Once she was inside the foyer, she ran up the steps two at a time and turned left down the long hall. She was going to Dr. Möller's office first to see if he was there, and if he wasn't, she would start checking the patient wards.

"Frau Abrams, what are you doing here?" Frau Wagner asked, stopping as Eva passed her.

Eva halted and turned around to face her. "I'm just here to see Dr. Möller. I need to speak to him about something."

"About what?" Frau Wagner asked suspiciously.

"Something about work."

"Is it something I can help you with?"

Eva pursed her lips and shook her head. "No, I don't think so."

Frau Wagner's cold gaze bore into her. "He is in patient ward C, but make it quick."

"Thank you." Eva quickly walked away before Frau Wagner detained her longer with more questions. She climbed the stairs to ward C and scanned the room for Dr. Möller. She spotted him at the far end next to a patient's bed and hurried through the room past the rows of beds toward him.

He looked up when she got close. "Eva, what brings you here today?"

"I wanted to talk with you about something when you have a minute."

"Give me a second, and I will be done here."

"I'll just wait over there," Eva said, pointing in the general direction of the hall.

"I shouldn't be long." He smiled at her, then turned back to the patient.

Eva leaned against the hall wall as she waited, but wasn't there long when he walked out. She straightened and came towards him. "You went back to work quickly?"

"You know me," he said, holding his hands out to the side. "This is my life."

"Yes, I know it is."

"So, what did you want to talk about?"

"Well, a couple of things, actually. Were you planning on returning to the front?"

"I was thinking about it."

"Do you know when that will be? I mean, if you decide to go back."

He put his hands on his hips under his white lab coat, pushing it back with his arms as he looked at the floor, obviously thinking about what she asked. Finally, he spoke. "Maybe in a week or two. Why do you ask? Is it because you want to go back too?"

"It is. I think that is where I need to be."

"Eva, I hate to tell you this, but I received a list of names yesterday of the nurses who are cleared to go this next rotation, and your name wasn't on it."

"What…?" Her brain was scrambling for an answer as to why this might be. "Is it because I was just there?"

"I don't believe so. Some of the nurses on the list just got back as well. But Ingrid wasn't on there either, so I don't think it has anything to do with you."

"If I ask to go again, do you think they will let me?"

"It's possible, but they have not issued you a pass for this time, so you would need to request one."

"I can do that. Just don't be too hasty to leave, okay?"

He squeezed her arm. "Don't worry. I won't leave until we know if you can go."

"Thank you."

"I have to get back in there."

"I'm going to try to get a pass today."

"Let me know." He gave her a quick smile, then returned to the patient ward.

She took a deep breath, and let it out in a loud exhale. She turned the options around in her head. *How am I going to get a pass? If I just ask for one, will they tell me no, or could it be that easy? I think I will try. The worst that will happen is they say no.* She turned on her heels and hurried out of the hospital to the tram stop. She got off at the stop closest to the Reich Main Security Office. It never ceased to make her hair stand on end every time she saw this building. She hadn't been in here in almost half a year, and now she wasn't sure she could make her feet move. Her heart was thumping loudly in her ears, and the same pins and needles pricked her body as it always did when the adrenaline was high. She curled her fingers, pressing them into her palms, and mentally berated herself for being such a coward. *You can do this, Eva. You have to.* She put one foot in front of the other. Her feet felt heavy like she was wearing lead shoes. She entered the building and headed to the front desk. *Oh no,* she thought, spotting the same woman from last time sitting in the chair staring down at something in her lap, the same woman who tried to have her escorted from the building. Eva considered if she should come back later or try her luck with the woman. Maybe she wouldn't recognize her. Eva could only hope.

She slowly approached the desk, focusing on the woman the whole time. Even when Eva was only inches away, the woman didn't bother to look up.

"Can I help you?" she asked disinterested with a hint of annoyance, but still didn't look up.

This made Eva happy. She could use this to her advantage. "Can you tell me where I need to go for a travel pass?"

The woman slowly looked up, eyes narrowing as soon as she saw Eva, and it was obvious the woman recognized her. "Those are obtained at the Civil Affairs office. It's down the hall to the right."

"Thank you." The woman continued to glare and didn't reciprocate the thanks.

Eva followed the long corridor until she found the door that said *Civil Affairs* written in gold lettering on the frosted glass window. She turned the knob and stepped in, seeing yet another desk at the end of the room, but this one was smaller. Eva wanted to hurry and get this over with, so she went to the desk. The woman there looked up at the sound of her approach. "Is this where I get a travel pass?"

"It is," the older woman said. She had her hair in a tight bun on top of her head and wore a uniform and side cap, unlike the woman at the entrance desk. She put a piece of paper and a pen on the counter in front of Eva. Fill this out and bring it back with your ID.

"Thank you." Eva took the paper and sat down to fill it out. This was the first time she had to fill one out herself. Gerhardt had done the paperwork for the first few, and Bauer had for the last one. She paid close attention to the information they wanted. It asked for her name, country of origin, address, age, marital status, occupation, the reason for her travel, and where she was traveling to. She was nervous about the questions they wanted, and she also noticed that it required a signature by an officer at the bottom, along with a stamp. There was no way she could get out of answering, so she filled them out, then brought the paper along with her ID back to the desk and handed them to the woman. "How long do you think it will take?" she asked.

"The paperwork will be filed quickly, but I can't guarantee you will get a pass today. It could take a few days." The woman looked down at the paper and Eva's ID, and when she saw Eva's nationality her demeanor changed. "Take a seat, please. I will give you your ID back when they are finished processing the paperwork."

Eva took the chair in the corner of the room and slumped into it. She had a bad feeling about this. The look on the woman's face told her something wasn't right.

Eva kept checking her watch as she tried to find things to keep herself busy. She had already been here for over half an hour. She got out of the chair and went back to the desk. "Will it be much longer?"

"That is not my department, so I honestly can't say."

Well, she is less than helpful, Eva complained to herself in annoyance. She went back to the chair and sat down, crossing her legs as she tapped one foot on the floor. More than fifteen minutes passed when a man in a uniform finally came out of the office and said something close to the woman's ear.

She looked up at Eva. "Fräulein Abrams."

Eva stood quickly and went to the desk. "Follow me, please," the man told her.

She planted her feet firmly on the floor, not wanting to go anywhere with him. "Go with you where? Why?"

"It's about your travel pass." He extended his hand towards the door. "This way, please."

She hesitated, but he continued to stare at her expectantly, so she went, wearily following him up the stairs to the third floor, taking in the surroundings as he led her down a hallway lined with office doors. It reminded her of the floor Oberst Heinrich Schmitt's office was on, but the atmosphere here was unsettling. He stopped at a door and lightly rapped on it.

"Come in," a voice sounded from the other side.

Eva froze. *That voice, no, it can't be?* She thought, panic rising. Subconsciously, she backed away, and the man turned to her, noticing her retreat.

"Fräulein, he is expecting you."

"I…" The rest of the words failed to come out. Her mouth was dry, as painful thumping pounded against her ribs. He opened the door and gestured for her to enter. She had no choice but to do what he wanted. Forcing one foot in front of the other, she stepped into the office and stopped just on the other side of the threshold, almost getting hit with the door as the man closed it behind her.

"Have a seat, Miss Abrams," Bauer said in an even tone, focusing on her as he held the phone to his ear. She walked to one of the two brown leather chairs by his desk and lowered herself into it.

"I don't care what you have to do. I want it on my desk by this evening," Bauer said into the receiver. "You know he will. Just do what you have to." He hung up the phone but never took his eyes off Eva. She noticed her ID and the paperwork she filled out lying on the desk in front of him. He picked the paper up and held it in his hand. "You are not going back to the Russian front." He laid it back on the desk again and looked at her.

"Why?" The word almost a squeak.

He opened a drawer of his desk and pulled out another piece of paper, tossing it in front of her. Before she could even read it, he spoke. "You are going to Dieppe, France. There was a bombing near the hospital there, killing many of the staff, and they desperately need more doctors and nurses."

She looked down and read the words on the paper. It was a pass to France. There had to be some other reason he wanted her to go, and it couldn't be good. Maybe he was afraid she would escape if she returned to the front? In France, he can watch her, seeing how he is the Gestapo officer over the country. She pushed the paper across the desk back towards him. "No. I'm not going to France. They need me at the front." She met his gaze and trembled involuntarily at what lay behind those greenish, hazel eyes.

He was still for a long moment, but his anger was palpable. When he spoke, his voice was low and dangerous. "You will go to France," his voice was like ice, a trace of bitterness that was surprising, and the darkness in his gaze frightened her. What made this encounter with him different from all the others?

"Because I don't have a choice..." she said, more a question than a statement.

"How astute you are," he said like he was mocking her.

"Can I ask a favor?"

"You don't deserve any favors, Eva."

She honestly couldn't understand why he thought that. Why was he meaner to her now than when she left for the front? He was almost nice to her before, almost. "I guess it's more of a suggestion. I might be able to get a few other doctors and nurses to agree to go. If I do, is that acceptable?"

He leaned back in his chair, rubbing the already visible five o'clock shadow with the tips of his fingers. "I suppose you can ask a few people."

"When do I tell them I'm leaving?"

"We head out in three days."

Eva took notice of the word 'we.' "What do you mean, we?"

"You will travel with me, and I return to France in three days, so that is when you will leave also."

"May I ask why I am to travel with you?"

"Because I don't trust that you will go if I don't personally escort you there myself. Then once we are there, you are free to do as you like, within reason. I'm sure you know that you will still need a pass to travel within the country?"

"I am."

"So just stay put in Dieppe unless you have permission to do otherwise. That will be all." He laid her ID on the paper in front of her. "Don't forget the pass." He took a cigarette from an ashtray and inhaled deeply.

She lifted her head, forcing a brave face as she picked up the pass and ID, then stood, her legs feeling unstable beneath her. She started for the door when he called out to her. "Oh, and Eva, I'm leaving early in the morning, so make sure you are packed the night before. I don't appreciate being made late."

Of course, you don't. You're German, she thought with disdain.

Chapter Five

January 5th, 1942

Eva had learned that 'early' meant six in the morning by way of Bauer's orderly, who had stopped by two days ago with that information. All her luggage was stacked next to the front door as she waited on the couch for the car to arrive. The sun wasn't up yet, and it was a frigid January morning. It had snowed that night, covering everything in two inches of white powder.

Eva surveyed the room, nostalgia settling over her. In the pit of her stomach was an uncomfortable twisting, a sense she would never live in this apartment again or with Heidi or Liesel. She had asked them if they would go with her, but as she expected, they both said no. They informed Eva how much the hospital needed them here, which was true. Ingrid, though, said yes when she had asked her, almost giddy at the thought of getting to go to France. Eva asked Dr. Möller as well, and he told her he would think about it. He assured her that if he didn't go, he would write to her often. She also visited the priest and went to see Oberst Heinrich Schmitt, letting him know what was happening. He told her she could use this to her advantage. That she would, after all, be living on the coast of the English Channel.

A knock on the door broke the silence. She stood, going to the door. "Fräulein Abrams, SS Obersturmbannführer Bauer, is waiting in the car. I will help with your bags," Bauer's orderly said when she opened the door.

"Thanks, they are just over here." He followed her to the three suitcases that were sitting near the door and picked up two. She put on her coat, gloves, hat, and scarf, then draped the strap of her purse over her shoulder, picked up the remaining suitcase, and followed him out into the hall, turning back toward the apartment one last time. Would she even like Dieppe? She had no idea what it was like there, how big it was, or where she would live. The only thing she knew was that it was on the west side of France, nestled on the coast of the English Channel. Perhaps this would be the break she was looking for like Oberst Heinrich Schmitt suggested, and she could somehow escape across the channel. She could only hope.

They put her bags in the trunk, then the orderly opened the back door. She slid in, the cold leather of the backseat stinging her legs. Bauer was sitting on the other side, next to the door. He was in a black suit instead of his uniform, his legs crossed, looking at papers in his lap. She wondered why he wasn't in uniform.

44

"Good morning, Miss Abrams," he said when the orderly closed the door, not looking up from the papers.

"I don't know that I would say it is good. Why are we leaving so early?"

"Because I want to make it to Metz by dinnertime."

"Metz, I thought we were going to Dieppe?"

He lifted his head from the papers and shot her a swift upward glance. "Yes, but Metz is where we are stopping for the night."

"How far are we from Dieppe?"

"It's over seventeen hours. Now, do you see why we are stopping for the night?"

"Yes. So, how far is Metz?"

"Roughly ten hours."

"Right." She leaned back in the seat, trying to figure out what she was going to do in the car for the next ten hours.

They pulled onto the road and headed out of Potsdam, and Bauer had gone back to his papers. Eva wished that Ingrid was here with her now and not traveling in two weeks by train, but Bauer had not given Ingrid permission to ride with them even if she was leaving today. Part of her found it odd that Ingrid had agreed to go. She knew Ingrid was involved with Dr. Hoffmann and believed he loved her, so why would she leave him? Eva planned to ask Ingrid about it when she got to France.

Eva laid her head on the window and watched the buildings pass by until the urban landscape gave way to the country. The sun was rising now but still hung low in the sky, cascading orange and pink hues across it. A few large, white clouds lingered in the pale, washed-out blue in the distance, and a few scraggly trees and some bushes dotted the sloping fields. The road they traveled on was mostly empty, save for one or two cars that passed, and occasionally a farmhouse. Every so often they would pass through a small village.

Even though it was no longer dark, Eva was having a hard time keeping her eyes open. She was up late packing and was awake by four that morning to make sure she was ready when Bauer came to pick her up. She lifted her head from the door and peered sideways at Bauer. He had a pen, marking on the paper in his lap as he read over it. They had been on the road for well over an hour, but he hadn't talked to her once except when she first got in the car, and that was only to say hi and briefly explain their travel plans. She laid her head back on the window and closed her eyes, listening to the sound the tires made on the road and the rumble of the engine.

She reached to scratch her face as she came out of sleep, brushing the back of her hand on something soft. She was momentarily confused, remembering she was leaning on the door with the left side of her face pressed against the window, but the glass didn't seem to be there anymore, and the soft thing was touching her right cheek. Slowly, she opened her eyes and lifted her head, trying to register her surroundings as she blinked away the blurry dryness. She blinked a few more times, then turned to the right. Bauer's shoulder was only inches from her face as her body slumped towards his. Realizing how she had been sleeping, she bolted up right in the seat, trying to think of what to do, but her brain was still foggy from sleep.

"Did you have a nice nap?" he asked.

"Oh, I am so sorry!"

"You didn't drool on my shirt, so it's fine."

She glanced over at his shoulder, the material of his crisp white shirt didn't have a wet spot on it but was a little wrinkled, and that is when she realized he was no longer wearing his jacket but had draped it over her lap. She dropped her eyes to the black suit jacket covering her legs. "I don't remember you putting this on me."

"It was when you were resting your head on the back of the seat before you slid against me. You had your arms crossed over your chest and your legs pressed together. You looked cold, and your dress doesn't seem like sufficient clothing for January."

"No, it's not." She pulled the jacket off her legs and held it out to him.

"You can use it while we travel. I don't need it."

She could already feel the cool air on her bare legs and wanted the warmth of the jacket, but didn't want to use it because it was his. "It's alright. I'm good." She laid it on his lap and scooted back to the other side of the car next to the door. He didn't say anything but laid the jacket in the middle of the seat between them. "How long was I asleep for?"

He looked at his watch. "You were out for almost an hour."

"And how long had I been leaning on you?" she asked, embarrassed.

"Probably forty minutes."

She put her hand over her eyes and squeezed her temples. Why could she not have ridden in the front with the driver instead of in the back with Bauer? "I'm sorry," she said again.

"Eva, stop apologizing, for heaven's sake. Why do you constantly feel the need to do that? Do you honestly think you did something wrong?"

"Not wrong, just without asking first."

"You were asleep. You hardly needed to ask permission."

"True, but if it happens again, wake me."

"No." His voice was clipped.

"Why?"

"Because you are being ridiculous."

"Did you ever stop to think that you might be the last person I want to lay my head on, Ober-sturm-bann-führer Bauer?" she said, pausing at every syllable on purpose.

He laid his papers on the floor in between their feet, then leaned back, angling in the seat so he could look at her easier. "Are you afraid to say my name?"

This seemed to come out of nowhere, bewildering her. "No, why would I be?"

"Because once you do, it humanizes the person. It is no longer a formal address but an intimate one."

"Intimate?"

"I mean two people who know each other well enough to be on a first-name basis."

"But you call me Miss Abrams all the time."

"Yes, I do when we are in public or a professional setting, but when we are alone like now or when you would come to my home, I would call you by your first name often, but you have never called me by my first name."

Eva thought about that, realizing that he was right. She had never called him by his first name. "I haven't, so what?"

"Say it. I want to hear you say my name."

She opened her mouth, but only a squeaky 'uh' came out.

"We still have a long way to drive." His hazel eyes penetrated hers.

"What about those papers on the floor?" she said, feeling like she had him.

"They can wait."

"Fine, Wilhelm. Happy now?"

"No, but satisfied." He picked the papers off the floor and laid them back in his lap.

Oh, how she wanted to slap him right now. Bauer had a sinisterism and a charm, which was hard to find in one person. "Why do you think we know each either well enough to be on a first-name basis?"

"Eva, the things that escape you. Well, let's see, it was years ago we met, we have had many encounters with one another, not always pleasant, I will admit. You have helped me, and I have helped you. That, in itself, connects two people. You have been to my home, eaten my food, befriended my mother, slept in my bed, seen me naked, and practically touched my penis. I am beyond caring if you sleep with your head on my shoulder, and frankly, a little surprised that you seem to care at this point."

Eva glanced in the front seat, very much aware that the driver had to be listening to their conversation. What he said was true. In some ways, she had more connections with Bauer than Gerhardt and more experiences, but as he said, not all of them good, but a shared history nonetheless. It was also true that they helped one another. She saved his life, and he no doubt saved hers, too. She didn't exactly know why, but she didn't want to admit to him he was right. But if she continued denying it, somehow it was not true.

"When are we going to stop and eat? I need to get out of this car." More like she needed to get away from the person in the car.

He glanced at his watch. "Soon."

"How soon? Plus, I have to go to the bathroom."

He looked at the driver through the rearview mirror. "Stop at the next village," he told him. The driver nodded.

Eva leaned forward, closer to the driver. "How far is the next village?"

"I'm not sure, Fräulein, maybe ten minutes."

"Alright." She leaned back in her seat and peered out the window again. The drive seemed endless; they had been on the road for five hours, but it passed like days.

The driver pulled in front of a small café and shut the engine off. Eva had the door open before he was even out of the car and rushed into the building. She asked an employee at the café where the toilets were, and the woman pointed to the back corner. Eva hurried to the bathroom, shutting the door and locking it. She was happy to finally get to use the bathroom and be away from Bauer for a while. *I can't believe I'm stuck in the car with him for five more hours today and another seven tomorrow,* she mentally grumbled.

50

Finally, she came out of the bathroom, spending much longer in it than she needed. Bauer was at the counter ordering food and hoped that he was getting it to go, because she wanted to trip to end as soon as possible. Eva came and stood beside him. "Are we eating in the car?"

"Yes, we need to make good time."

"Alright, I'll order my food when you are done."

"No need. I already ordered you something."

"What? You don't even know what I want," she protested.

"Do you like sandwiches?"

"Sometimes."

"Do you like ham?" he asked, snidely.

"Yes."

"Then you will like it." She pulled some money out of her purse and held it out to him. "Don't be ridiculous," he told her. "I don't want your money."

"Well then, what do you want?"

"From you…?" He left the question hanging as piercing eyes locked on her.

She crammed the money back into her purse and clasped it shut. "I think I will ride up front with the driver when we leave."

"You will distract him, and it is not appropriate."

"How is that not appropriate?"

"When women ride in government cars, they never sit in the front seat with the orderly. They always ride in the back."

"That is a stupid rule."

"Stupid or not, that is how it is done."

She promptly turned and walked out of the café, going to the car and leaning against the side. He was insufferable and she needed a breath, and time to collect her emotions.

He came out shortly after with the food. "Get in the car. It's time to go."

The orderly came around and opened the back door for Bauer, then closed it once he was in. He went to the other side and opened Eva's door for her. She hesitated for a second, then slid in, and he shut it. Bauer set a paper bag with food on her lap and handed her a small, Giara Swing Top Bottle. She turned to him, glaring, but didn't take the it, so he laid it on the seat next to her, and it rolled into her leg.

"We will eat dinner seated at a restaurant. Sorry for having to eat on the road."

"It's fine. I did it all the time on the front."

He unrolled his paper bag and took out the sandwich. "How was the front?"

"Bloody, sad, and cold. Anything else you want to know about it?"

"Maybe more detail." He took a bite of the sandwich, the lettuce crunching between his teeth.

"Like what?"

"The morale, the living conditions, and how was it for you?"

"The morale was low when I left. I had to burn bodies every few days on the front. That smell gets burned into your brain and you can't believe you are burning what used to be human beings. And the living conditions were awful most of the time, but I'm sure you know that already."

He took another bite of his sandwich. "I do."

"Then why did you ask? You know more about what is happening on the front than I do, even though I was there."

"Because I wanted to hear about it in your own words. And only you can tell me how it was for you."

"It was terrible, and I was miserable most of the time, but I would rather be there than here."

"No, you wouldn't." He pointed to the bag in her lap. "Eat your food."

She saluted, then took the sandwich from the bag and bit into it, turning away from him to the window. She did not want to look at him right now.

When they arrived in Metz, they booked three rooms, then looked for a place to eat. They found a quaint little restaurant in the middle of the city. The sitting area was small and could only fit eight tables with two chairs each. The restaurant wasn't busy, only a few of the tables occupied. They were seated in the corner near the back of the building. Next to their table was a round metal fireplace with a smoke pipe leading up into the ceiling, and a large crackling fire was already burning, warming the air. The table was of bare wood, no table cloth covering it, and a tealight candle flickering in the middle.

Bauer pulled the chair out for her and pushed it in as she sat. Then he went to the other side and took his chair. "This place isn't too bad," he said, glancing around the lounge.

"No, it's nice."

She couldn't help but notice the similarities of tonight's events to a date, making her uncomfortable. Eva ordered quickly, not wanting to be fussy about her food tonight. She then wondered who was going to be paying for dinner. No doubt Bauer would insist on paying for hers again.

"So, will you be staying in La Chapelle?"

"No, Paris."

"That is where the Gestapo Headquarters is located for France, right?"

"Correct."

Eva was racking her brain to figure out how close Paris was to Dieppe, but because she wasn't sure of the exact location of Dieppe, she had no way of knowing. She hoped it was far away, but knowing that it was on the west side of the country, she suspected it was closer to Paris than La Chapelle was. She also didn't want to ask about the distance between the cities. There were only two things he would think about that question. One that she might hope to be close to him and that sure wasn't the truth, and second that she wanted to be as far from his as possible, which was the truth but would only anger him.

"We will need to find you a place to stay when we get there. I'm sorry I haven't had time to do that yet," he said, pulling Eva out of her thoughts.

"Oh, so where will I stay in the mean time?"

"Well, if you want, you can stay at a hotel until we find an apartment."

Eva could not afford a hotel room for more than a few nights. "As long as it's only a couple of days, I don't want to go broke."

"I will be in Dieppe for a while before I return to Paris. I'll be staying in a house that was abandoned at the start of the war. No one else is living there, it will only be me. If you want, you can stay in one of the rooms until we find you an apartment?"

Just me and him living in a house together for who knows how long. That sounds like a disaster waiting to happen. There is no chance of anything going wrong with that arrangement, Eva thought, surprised he even offered. The only thing she could think of was that he wanted to keep an eye on her and make sure she didn't try anything. She honestly couldn't afford to live at a hotel, but she didn't want to stay alone with him.

"Umm, I don't think so."

"Do you have a better idea?"

"Yes, staying at a hotel like you first suggested."

"I will remind you that you said you couldn't stay at a hotel for long."

"I can afford a few days."

"I'm sure you can, but how do you know it will only be for a few days?"

"I don't," she admitted.

"You are a grown, single woman. You can do what you want. The offer still stands if you find you don't want or can't keep paying for a room."

She smiled uncomfortable. "I will."

The waiter brought their food, and they didn't talk for a while. She stared at the flickering flames that caressed the side of the fireplace as she ate and thought about how nice it would be to lie on the floor in front of it and fall asleep. It was so warm and inviting.

"Lovely, isn't it?" he said, noticing her staring into the fireplace. "The fire, I mean."

"Yes, it is." She needed to change the topic. She didn't want to do casual talk with Bauer. "What time are we leaving in the morning?"

"Seven."

"Well, that is a little better than six."

"We don't have as far to drive tomorrow, so we don't need to leave as early. You are more than welcome to sleep in the car again."

"Thanks. I didn't know I needed permission."

He laid his fork on the plate. "No matter how much I try to be civil to you, you continue to be hostile towards me, and you say that I am the awful one. Maybe you should take a look at yourself."

"Did you ever ask yourself why I act that way towards you?"

"Yes, I have, actually."

"And what conclusion did you come to?"

"That it's you and not me."

There was no way he believed that. "Are you serious? How could it be me? Look at all the shit you have put me through. And you wonder why I treat you the way I do. You have a reputation for being a bad person. You should hear the things people say about you."

He leaned back in his chair and studied her face. "I don't have to ask myself why. I know why. What I do is just a job. It doesn't define who I am. And I know what people say about me."

"It absolutely does define who you are."

"I'm nothing if not a soldier, but that doesn't make me inhuman. I'm sure there is no one that has hurt you like I have. Most things that happened to you over the last few years was because of me, but that is not to say that you didn't deserve a lot of them. You speak of the things I have done, but what of the things you've done? People like you don't care about what is right or the natural order of things."

"I care about the natural order of things. But it is people like you who will kill twenty innocent people just because someone killed one German. That should not be the natural order of things."

"You must understand, Eva, it's not easy being in my position. These attacks are hopeless and serve no greater good. When they attack, they aren't just killing German soldiers; they put civilian lives at risk too. And if people like me, as you say, don't stop them, they will continue to kill innocents as well as members of the German military. Sometimes tough decisions must be made for the common good. If you do not punish those who break the law, they will continue to break it, encouraging others to do the same. When these people attack, I have to retaliate in a way that hits them the hardest. I am left with no other choice."

"You have the choice to look inside and see if maybe you have a heart. And if you do, use it."

"I do. You just choose not to see it."

"Let's say for argument's sake that I was in the resistance," Eva said, looking him squarely in the face. "If you murdered someone I loved or even just innocent townspeople because of an attack, it would not make me stop. It would only serve to anger me further. I would want to kill every German I saw because of it. It would be like pouring gasoline on the fire."

"You should be careful, Eva. You start off playing a role, and then you realize one day it doesn't feel like acting anymore. I remember everything you have said about me, about how Germany operates. If I were you, I would be more careful in the future when speaking ill of those with the power to hurt you. Don't be so vocal about your opinions."

"Is that a warning or a threat?"

"A warning. If you think this was bad," he said, touching the tip of two of her fingers, "then you do not know what the Gestapo are capable of." She tensed at his touch, and he sensed it, pulling his hand away.

She swallowed, trying to regain control of her nerves after his stern dictates that battered her already wavering emotions. "I do have an idea. I know how you are, inside and out."

"I understand you want things to be different, but that is just a flight of fancy. In a perfect world, it would be different, but we don't live in a perfect world."

"You don't think I know that?"

"Honestly, I'm not sure. Sometimes I think you live with your head in the clouds, which is not realistic."

His words genuinely surprised her. His directness always took her off guard, but she was becoming accustomed to the lack of empathy in his words. "I don't live with my head in the clouds. It's just unlike you; I choose to show other people compassion."

"As do I, like I have shown you on so many occasions." She started to disagree with him, but he spoke before she had the chance. "It is later than I thought. We really should get going," he interrupted, looking at the clock on the wall.

Eva glanced around the room, realizing they were the only ones left in the restaurant. How had she not noticed the passing of time? "I agree. We should go."

Neither of them spoke in the car on the way to the hotel, and she was glad of it. As they climbed the stairs and walked down the hall, he still didn't speak to her, not even to say goodnight. Once she was alone in the room, she sat on the edge of the bed, happy to finally be away from him. She could feel the fatigue fogging her brain and wanted nothing more than to crawl under the blanket and fall asleep.

Chapter Six

The last leg of the trip was quiet so far. Bauer read his work papers and didn't talk to her, and even though it was boring, she wasn't about to strike up another conversation with him. Besides, she was sure he was upset with her after their conversation last night. Since then, he had treated her with indifference and didn't speak to her unless he had to.

Eva tapped her fingers on the windowsill as she peered out, trying to find anything to keep herself occupied, wishing she had brought a book. She was exhausted but would not let herself fall asleep. Not only because he had given her permission to, and she felt the need to defy him in some way, but she would not risk sliding over into him again.

"Would you stop that?" he said, his voice sharp with annoyance.

"What else am I going to do, then?"

"I don't know, read something."

"I didn't bring anything to read. Maybe you would be so kind as to share?" she said, sarcasm oozing from every word.

Obviously, he would not let her read any of the papers, nor did she want to, but she had to make her point.

He sifted through his papers, and in the middle was a newspaper. He pulled it from the stack and held it out to her. "Here, now you have something to read."

"I don't want to read a German newspaper. I'm aware of what is happening around me well enough."

"Suit yourself." He put the newspaper under the stack of papers, then returned to what he had been doing, and they fell into an uneasy silence.

This is ridiculous, Eva thought. *I don't want to talk to him, but I also don't want to sit in silence the whole drive.* She waited a few minutes, then spoke. "Why were you in La Chapelle?"

He looked up from the paper. "What?"

"If the Gestapo's headquarters for France is in Paris, then why were you in La Chapelle?"

"Because I had business there."

"For that long?"

"Yes." He looked back down at the paper in his hand.

It was so obvious that he didn't want to talk to her. She didn't care, though. He made her move to Dieppe and forced her to travel with him, so the least he could do was talk to her. "So, what was it?"

"What was what?"

"The business you had to do there."

He laid the paper down and sighed. "What do you want, Eva?"

"To know what you were doing there. I want to know what took up so much of your time that you had to spend months there, in a little town of barely a hundred people? You are the Gestapo officer overseeing France. Didn't they need you in Paris?"

"I can't tell you why I was there, and you know it. And I am not the only Gestapo officer in France. I can't be everywhere at once. I have a handful of officers under me stationed in different parts of the country. So, though I oversee other officers, SS soldiers, and the country, I am still needed in the field sometimes. I have a job to perform."

"OK, then tell me something else. Why are you mad at me?"

He turned to her. "I'm not mad at you." His voice held no emotion, and Eva couldn't make out if he was telling her the truth or not.

"Yes, you are," she insisted.

"Alright, fine, I am mad at you."

"Why? Is it the conversation we had last night?"

"In part."

"What else have I done?"

"I made that very clear last night."

"What, that I don't reciprocate your supposed kindness?"

"All I ask is that we are civil to one another, but apparently, that is asking too much of you," he snapped back.

"Do you remember when I tried to help you and attempted to be nice to you in the hospital, but you rejected it?"

"I do."

"So, doesn't that make you a hypocrite to say I am rejecting your attempted kindness?"

"Maybe, but doesn't that make you one, too?"

"Touché," she said, biting the inside of her cheek to lessen the sting of embarrassment.

"So, Miss Abrams, should we not meet in the middle?"

"Depends on what the middle is."

"Well, I am trying to repay you for saving my life and being kind to me while I was in the hospital by returning the favor and being nice to you. That is me meeting in the middle, and how you can meet me in the middle is to accept my offered kindness. And no more of this hateful attitude you direct at me."

"Then you have to do the same."

"That is exactly what I have been trying to do, but you resist it."

This was new and uncharted territory for her. She never imagined she would find herself on this neutral ground making a truce with Bauer, and honestly, it made her a little afraid. She did not know what this was going to look like. "Fine, I will try to accept your kindness."

"No, and no. Meeting in the middle is you accepting my kindness, not trying to. It's a conscious decision, not something you have to work at," he said.

"Alright, I will accept it next time you offer."

"Good. You can start with the offer I made last night."

Her head shot up, horrified. Well, she made her bed, and now she had to sleep in it. "You mean for me to stay with you until I find a place?"

"That was the offer. I was hoping you would accept with a smile instead of the expression you are giving me."

"I… suppose, and it hadn't crossed my mind that you would circle back to the offer you made last night."

"Eva, I know you can't afford to live at a hotel until you find a place. And you wouldn't be able to pay for the rent once you found it because you would have spent most of your money on the hotel. I honestly offer to help you out. You didn't have a choice in moving here, so the least I can do is assist with your transition."

"I appreciate the help. Although I think it will be awkward?"

"Why would it be?"

"Um, because it will be just the two of us."

"We will have our own rooms, and I will be gone most of the time, and once you start work, you will be gone a lot, too. I doubt we will even see much of each other."

She nodded. "What about things like dinner and cleaning? How is that supposed to work?"

A smile broke at the corner of his mouth. "I actually didn't think about that. My mother cleans the apartment in Berlin, and I have a maid in Paris. When I am staying in other parts of France, I'm usually billeted with someone."

"Can you even cook?" she asked, wondering if it was a silly question, but so many men in this time couldn't.

"Um… well—"

"That means no," she said, interrupting. This was the first time she ever heard him at a loss for words.

"You are right, no. Growing up, my mother always cooked for me, and at university, my roommate cooked, and since I've been in the military, there has always been someone to do it for me, or I go out. I only know how to cook a few things."

"How about this? I will do the cooking, and if you aren't home, I will leave it in the fridge, and you can heat it up, but you have to do your own laundry, and we can share the cleaning."

"I hate to tell you this, but I won't have time to clean. I work long, crazy hours. If you can't or don't want to do it, I can employ a maid."

Eva chewed on her lip, thinking about how complicated this had become. "No, that seems like a waste. I can clean while I'm there, but you still have to do your own laundry."

"I'll just have it sent out."

"It's settled then, and I will start looking for a place tomorrow."

"Yes, and you should go to the hospital too. They will let you know when they need you to start work."

"I will. So, if I was not going to be staying with you, how would you eat? Were you going to hire someone?"

"Yes, that was my plan. What I mean by that is the military would have someone sent over. I don't personally hire them."

"I see. Well, look at me, saving the military money."

His lips at the corner pulled up even further, widening the smile, exposing his teeth. "And they thank you."

It was just past 3:00 PM when the car pulled in front of a small cottage nestled against the beach overlooking the Channel. Eva couldn't believe how beautiful it was, not just the cottage but the entire city. It was so different from La Chapelle; it was larger, on the coast, hardly any trees, and flat comparatively.

She stepped out and looked at Bauer from across the top of the car. "Is this the house we are staying in?" She couldn't hide her delight at the sight of the cottage and the location.

"I take it you like it?"

"Yes, I do. Did you know this is what it looked like?"

"No, but I knew it was on the beach." Bauer turned and said something to the driver, who then went around to the rear of the car and retrieved their suitcases, setting them on the ground. "Let's get our bags and go in."

"You already have the key?"

"Yes, it was sent to Berlin over a week ago." He pulled a brass key from the pocket of his pants, then picked up his suitcase. Eva got one of hers, and the driver took the other two. They carried them to the house, and Bauer unlocked the door, stepping over the threshold into the entryway. The cottage was dark and cold, and Eva shivered as she followed Bauer inside. "I know. It's cold in here. I'll build a fire in a minute," he said, noticing her shiver. "I have to be at the office tonight, so you will be alone most of the evening."

"Oh, OK." He wasn't kidding. He did work a lot. He wasn't even taking time to rest after the journey. The driver said something to Bauer, then left, closing the front door, leaving them alone in the dark. Bauer set his bag on the floor and flipped on the light. "Is there any food here, or do I need to go to the store?" she asked.

"No, the fridge and cupboards should be stocked." He walked into the tiny living room, flipping the light on in there as well. He took some wood from the neatly stacked pile next to a fireplace and placed a few in it. Then took some twigs from a copper bucket and broke them into smaller pieces, tucking them under and around the logs. He reached his hand up into the fireplace, pulling the damper open, then took a box of matches from the mantel and struck one. He held it to the wood until the ends of several twigs caught fire, then he placed the box back on the mantel.

Eva stood in the living room doorway, watching him the entire time. It was so odd, all of this. Here she was waiting nearby as Bauer built a fire in a house they were sharing. He walked past her to the kitchen, bringing her back to the moment. She followed him, not sure what else to do.

He washed the black from the damper handle off his hand, then picked up a dishtowel to dry them before turning to Eva. "The house should warm up soon. Don't forget to put more wood on the fire."

"Is there any other source of heat in the house?"

"No, it is very old, and small, so it only has one fireplace."

Eva was a little unsure about what to do with the fire when she went to bed. She didn't want to fall asleep with it burning if it didn't have a gate, but then the house would get cold. She had never lived in a house with a real wood-burning fireplace. "What do I do when I go to bed? Should I put it out?"

"I don't see a cover for it, so we will need to unless one of us is going to sleep down here with it. I will have to get a cover for it later."

67

"Ok, I'll make sure it's out."

"I'm leaving now. Don't worry about making any food for me. I'm going out to eat with some of my men."

"Alright."

He went to the door, then paused, his hand resting on the knob. "There are two bedrooms. You can have whichever one you want."

"Thank you." He gave a faint smile, then was gone. She looked around the now empty house and sighed. It still felt like it was freezing, so she went into the living room and sat on the couch. The fire crackled and popped, and the heat from it was divine. Suddenly she felt utterly drained and a little sick from the exhaustion. She stood, put some more wood on the fire, and then sat back down. She glanced around, taking in her surroundings. It wasn't a big room, with only one window behind her overlooking the road. The walls and ceiling were made of white plaster, and across the ceiling were four dark wooden beams that ran the length of the room. There was the couch she was sitting on, two chairs in opposite corners of the room, and a side table between them. She noticed a blanket draped over the back of the couch and pulled it off. She took the only pillow on the couch and laid down, poking it under her head. Then she wrapped the blanket tightly around her and closed her eyes.

Chapter Seven

Eva thought she could hear noises coming from the foyer and opened her eyes. Her lids felt heavy, and her vision was blurred from sleep. The house was now veiled in darkness, the fire no longer burning, and she wondered what time it was. She sat up, resting on one elbow, and looked through the entryway of the living room into the hall. There was a soft thud on the tile near the front door, then another. She squinted to try and see better in the darkness. There was virtually no light coming through the windows because the city was in darkness because it was past curfew, just the dim light from the moon and the glow of the embers in the fireplace. A dark shadowy figure walked past the entryway, startling her, and she bolted upright on the couch. The sound of the stairs creaking under someone's weight was loud in the silence. She didn't know why this unnerved her because it was probably Bauer. The thought of being alone with him in the house still made her uneasy, but if this wasn't Bauer, then she had bigger problems. Should she call out to him or try to sneak into the hall to see who it was? She wasn't sure. She sat for a second considering her options, then decided to call out, assuming it was Bauer and not some intruder. But then she would have to call him by his first name, and she was still trying to get used to that recent development. *Screw it,* she thought and cleared her throat lightly. "Wilhelm?" she called, her voice echoing in the house. The footsteps ceased on the stairs, then retracted, coming back down. The figure stepped into the doorway. Then the lamp was flipped on, illuminating the room in a wash of yellow light. Eva squinted from the brightness, trying to let her eyes adjust.

Bauer looked at her, taking in her current state. Then his eyes drifted to the dying fire and then to her suitcases that were still sitting in the living room. "Have you not even gone upstairs?"

She brushed the hair from her face that had fallen out of her bun while sleeping. "No. I laid down on the couch to nap, but I slept longer than I had intended." She pulled the blanket off her legs and draped it back over the couch. "I haven't picked a room yet, sorry."

"It's fine. You can choose when we go upstairs. The fire should be burned down enough now." He picked up her two suitcases and started up the stairs, not waiting for her to follow.

She hadn't even taken off her coat or shoes. She slipped out of the coat and hung it in the closet near the door along with her scarf that was on the floor next to her purse. She stepped out of her shoes, put them in the closet, then picked up her other bag and retrieved her purse, turned out the light, and went up the stairs, finding Bauer standing in the hall waiting for her. He was serious about letting her choose a room. It was not a long or wide hallway, and there were only two rooms to the left of the stairs and one to the right. "Are these the bedrooms?" she asked, looking down the hall to the left.

"They are, and the bathroom is just at the end of the hall to the right."

It just dawned on her he said, 'bathroom.' "There is only one bathroom?"

He seemed confused by her reaction. "Yes, it is just a small cottage, not a big house."

Even houses this size in her time had two bathrooms or at the very least a full bath and a half bath. "I know, but… that means we will have to share it."

"Unless you want to bathe in the sea."

How did she know he would be insensitive about this. "OK, do we need a schedule or something?"

"No, I'll just let you know when I'm going to shower if you are home, and you can do the same. If the door is closed, it will be obvious that someone is in there."

"I guess that will work." She walked past him to the first bedroom, flipping on the light. It was a tiny room with a twin bed against the wall, a nightstand with a lamp next to it, and an armoire for a closet. She hoped the other room was larger and that he wouldn't care if she took it. After all, he told her she could choose. She went to the room at the end of the hall and flipped the light on, peering in. It was about one and a half times the size of the other room, and it had an actual closet and not just an armoire. The bed was still a twin, but it wasn't pushed up against the wall, which allowed you to walk on both sides. It, too, had a nightstand with a lamp next to it. She turned to look at Bauer, who was intently watching her from the other bedroom doorway. "Can I take this one?" She thought she saw the hint of a smile at the corner of his mouth that he quickly concealed.

"I said you could choose." He picked up her two bags and carried them into the bedroom, setting them on the floor at the foot of the bed. "I have to be up early tomorrow, so I'm going to shower while you get settled."

"Alright."

He went back into the hall and got her third bag, and brought it in, setting it next to the other two. Without saying another word, he walked past her and got his bag from the hall, carrying it into the other bedroom. She closed her door and then went to her bags, sitting one on the bed and opening it. *What time is it?* she wondered. She looked at her watch. It was a quarter past eleven. *Oh wow, I didn't realize it was so late.* She hurried and hung her dresses in the closet and put her underclothes and pajamas in the small dresser in the corner of the room. She slid her suitcases under the bed, then sat on the comforter, listening to the shower running. She hoped he didn't take long, but he didn't strike her as the type to indulge in long, hot showers. After what seemed like only minutes, the water shut off, and the shower curtain slide on the metal rod. She laid back on the bed with her legs hanging off the end as she waited. There were a few cracks in the plaster on the ceiling, and it looked like it could use a fresh coat of paint.

Finally, the bathroom door open and the dull patter of bare feet on wood echoed in the hall. She sat up and slid off the bed, going to the dresser and retrieving her toiletry bag, a clean pair of pajamas, and the underwear she had laid out. When his door closed, she quietly opened her door and tiptoed down the hall to the bathroom. She stepped in and closed the door, making sure it could lock. To her relief, it did, so she turned the latch and laid her stuff on the toilet. Only one hook on the wall had a towel hanging from it, and it was damp. "Where are the towels?" She whispered, looking around the bathroom to see where he got that one from. There was a small cabinet above the toilet. She opened the two doors, happy to see three clean towels folded inside. She pulled one out, then quickly stripped, stepped into the tub, and pulled the shower curtain closed as she turned on the water. The warmth felt nice and made her realize how tired she was. No wonder she slept so long on the couch.

She showered quickly, then stepped onto the mat and dried off. She hung her towel on the empty hook, brushed her teeth, combed through her wet hair, then got her stuff and tiptoed back to her room, noticing the light was out in his room. That, for some reason, made her happy. She gently closed her door and looked around for a hamper but couldn't find one, so she laid her clothes on the floor in the corner, pulled back the blankets on her bed, and crawled under them. The temperature in the house had already dropped, and the cold sheets made her shiver. She was going to have to look for another blanket tomorrow. Then the thought that maybe Bauer needed another blanket crossed her mind. She might need to look for one for him too, but she didn't know if he got cold as easily as her. Perhaps it didn't bother him. She pulled the blankets to her chin, then reached up with one arm and pulled the chain on her lamp.

When Eva woke to the sun's dim light shining through her window, she realized how quiet it had been last night compared to Berlin. There wasn't the constant air raid sirens blaring through the city, the explosions from the bombs, sirens from the ambulances and firetrucks, or just the general cacophony produced in populated areas. It was nice not having the clamor and the commotion all the time.

She sat up in bed and picked up the twin bell alarm clock on the side table. "It's already past seven. Shit," she said aloud, remembering that she agreed to cook, which meant breakfast as well. She threw off the blankets and hopped out of bed, grabbing a pair of socks and pulling them on before opening her door and sprinting down the stairs in only her nightgown. When she reached the kitchen, she discovered it was empty and still dark from the early morning. *He can't still be asleep.* She looked in the sink for any dirty dishes but saw none. She was puzzled. She climbed back upstairs, lightly knocked on his door, and waited, but there was no answer, so she put her hand on the knob and slowly turned it, pushing his door ajar. She peered in and saw that the bed had been made and he wasn't there. *He must have left early. I wonder why he didn't wake me and why I didn't hear him leave?* She returned to her room, dressed, put her hair into a bun, and then went back downstairs to make herself breakfast. She took the milk jar and a couple of eggs out of the fridge and set them on the table. In the middle was a piece of paper with something written on it. She wondered how she missed it. Reaching over, she picked it up.

Eva,
It is not even six, and I am leaving for work. I didn't expect you to get up and cook for me this early, so don't think that I am upset. When I have early mornings like today, you don't have to cook. Most days, I leave around seven, just so you know, but if I am to leave earlier, I will let you know the night before. Make dinner when you are hungry, and don't worry about me. I can eat leftovers when I get in.

-Wilhelm

"OK, good to know," she said, laying the paper back on the table. She cooked her breakfast and ate fast, wanting to leave soon and see the city. She also needed to go to the hospital and see when they wanted her to start work. She washed the dishes, put them on the rack to dry, then got her coat, gloves, scarf, and purse and stepped out the front door. She realized then that she didn't have a key to the house. She would have to ask Bauer about it tonight if she saw him. She also remembered that she didn't know where his office was or the hospital. She took a pen out of her purse and wrote the house's address on her palm. She needed to make sure she could find her way back.

She asked around and was pointed in the hospital's direction. It didn't take long to get there, and when she saw the building, one of the first things she noticed was its size. The structure before her was much smaller than the hospital in Berlin; it was a modest, white structure. She walked up the three front steps to the wooden doors, pulled one open, and entered the building. The familiar smell of the bitter antiseptic mixed with undertones of the artificial fragrance contained in soaps and cleaners that was used in hospitals filled her nostrils. On patient floors, the smells become more intense and diverse, sometimes combining with the scent of the sick and dying.

At the desk near the front were two nurses standing behind it, chatting. Eva went to the desk and placed her hands on the top. "Excuse me, I'm one of the new nurses from Berlin and wanted to know who I need to talk to?"

"Nurse Moreau is the one you need to speak with. She is in her office. Go down the hall, and it's the first door on the right," the taller nurse said.

"Thank you." Eva walked down the hall to the first door on the right and knocked.

"Come in," came a high-pitched, jarring voice. Eva twisted the knob and opened the door, stepping into the room. The woman looked up from her desk and smiled. "Can I help you?"

This woman was nothing like Frau Wagner. She was short and skinny, not tall and robust, her voice was high, not deep, and she had a convivial personality. Her hair was black and piled in a neat bun on top of her head, and she wore wire-rimmed glasses that rested on the bridge of her nose.

"Yes, I'm here from Berlin. I'm one of the new nurses."

The woman pulled the glasses from her face and leaned forward on her desk. "Oh, I wasn't expecting you for two more weeks."

So it wasn't the hospital that wanted her to come early. "Oh, I guess there was a mix up. It's the other nurse, Ingrid Braun. She is the one who will be here in two weeks."

The woman pulled two brown folders out from under a stack of loose papers and flipped open the top one. "It says here that you were also supposed to arrive in two weeks. But no matter, you are here now." She gave Eva a warm smile and closed the folder.

"When would you like me to start?" Eva asked.

"When did you arrive in Dieppe?"

"Yesterday."

"Why don't you start in two days? That will give you a little time to relax before you start adjusting to a new position."

This sounded so strange to Eva. The hospitals in Germany were always so busy. They would have had her start work probably that day. Eva raised an eyebrow. "You don't need me to start sooner?"

"No, this is a small hospital on the far west side of France. The patient count here is low unlike the hospitals in Germany or the ones farther east. We typically only get a dozen or so patients in per day, and most don't even need to be admitted."

Eva was stunned. "That is all?"

"Ahh huh," the woman said, viewing Eva's surprise with amusement.

"Alright then, I guess I will see you in two days. What time?"

The woman placed the reading glasses back on the bridge of her nose. "Eight would be fine."

Eva left the hospital feeling disappointed. What was she going to do for the next two days? She decided to walk the streets of Dieppe for a while and familiarize herself with the city. Eva looked through the shop windows as she weaved up and down the narrow streets. The town's layout was confusing, unlike the other cities in France she had been to. One good landmark to follow was the coast. If you ever got turned around, all you had to do was find the water, and you automatically knew which way was west.

Eva's feet hurt from walking on the cobblestone streets. She had strolled through miles of the city and seen a lot of Dieppe, except for the Château de Dieppe, the castle on a hill overlooking the town. She would have to see it another day. It was already one o'clock, and her stomach cramped from hunger and her mouth was dry with thirst. She decided to return to the cottage and eat, then plan the rest of her day.

She turned and headed down the hill back to the cottage, wondering where in town Bauer worked and thought it might be a good idea to learn. She was getting ready to cross the road to the house when she looked up, then stopped. Bauer's car was parked on the street in front of the house. Why was he home? *Oh no, maybe he came home expecting lunch,* she thought. She hurried across the street to the house but paused, her courage faltering at the door. She went to the living room window and peered in. She couldn't see anyone inside, the house was dark. *Maybe he isn't home?* she wondered. She opened the front door, stepping lightly on the tile, pulling it closed behind her. She walked to the kitchen but he wasn't there or any sign that he had been. She returned to the hall and tiptoed up the stairs, glancing down the hall at the bathroom, but the door was open and the light was off. She turned left and walked down the hall towards the bedrooms. To her surprise, his door was open, and the room was empty.

Well, this is strange. She thought. *Why would his car be here if he wasn't home?* She went to her room and unwrapped the scarf from around her neck and tossed it on the bed, then went to the hook on the wall near the window so she could hang her coat. She glanced out at the choppy water battering the shore and caught site of a figure standing on the pebbled beach facing the sea. She paused, not removing her coat, then walked to the window, resting her hands on the windowsill as she put her face close to the glass to see better. She could tell it was a man and that he was wearing a trench coat. The breeze blew his hair out of place and the trench coat behind him as it flapped in the wind.

Eva moved her face even closer. "Is that Bauer?" She turned from the window, grabbed her scarf off the bed, and wrapped it back around her neck, then hurried down the stairs. She went through the kitchen and out the backdoor, following the narrow trail that led to the beach. The house was only about thirty feet from the edge of the gravel, but the beach was large, so it took several minutes to get to the water.

Her feet pressed into the loose pebbles as she walked, crunching as they sank down. This was the first time she had been to the beach since they arrived. She was too tired yesterday and hadn't had time today until now. As she got closer to the figure, she tried to assess who they were from the back of them. They were roughly the right height and build as Bauer, and their hair was the same color.

"Wilhelm?" she called from a few feet away.

The man turned his head and part of his torso towards her, and she could see the side of Bauer's face, standing there with his hands in the front pockets of his pants. He didn't smile, but his expression was not harsh either, simply unreadable. "Hello, Eva."

"If you came home expecting lunch, I'm sorry I wasn't there to make it. I was at the hospital."

"It's alright. I'm home for the rest of the day."

Eva blinked against the wind as it made her eyes water. "I thought you were working today?"

"No, I had to go in and take care of a few things before tomorrow when I start work."

"Then why did you leave so early?"

"I don't like to have things hanging. I want to get them done early."

German efficiency, she thought. "Do you want me to make lunch?"

He stared down the length of the beach. "Maybe in a little while. I think I'm going to check out more of the coast. Would you like to come?"

"On a walk?"

He pulled his brows together. "Yes… on a walk."

"Umm…." She looked up at the house briefly, then back at him. "Sure, I guess," she agreed, uncertain as she wrapped her coat around her torso, pulling the belt tight. She stuck her hands in the deep pockets for extra warmth. She walked beside Bauer, occasionally glancing up at the side of his face. They didn't talk, and Eva admired the view and appreciated the silence, inhaling the salty air that came off the sea. "It would be much nicer if it weren't so cold," she said, finally breaking the silence.

"Yes, you are right. It is pretty cold out today."

Wow, we are really talking about the weather, she thought. "So, have you ever been to Dieppe before?"

"Yes, several times."

"Really, why?"

He peered down at her. "Because it is my job. They need the Gestapo in all parts of the country with a large military presence. These areas are targets for the resistance, as well as England and their allies."

"Makes sense, I guess. So, there is no Gestapo presence in Dieppe when you are not here?"

"Of course there is. Eva, do you not know that the Gestapo recruits from each country it occupies? We could not successfully function without local help. There simply aren't enough of us from Germany to do it. Here in France alone, there are over thirty thousand Carlingue members who work on behalf of Germany. They mostly work independently, but still have to report to Germany, which then comes back to me."

"But if they are here, then why do you need to come here?"

"To help when they need, and sometimes to oversee operations."

"Thirty thousand is a lot. Why are there so many in France?"

"Because this is where the resistance is the strongest." He stopped walking. "We need to turn back now."

"How come?"

"Because civilians are not allowed any further." He points up the beach to an area where the beginning of a brick wall is visible. "There are areas guarded by batteries with machine guns."

"I suppose I don't want to get shot today." He gave her a side glance, then turned and started back in the direction they came. "What other cities in France do you go to often?"

"If I'm not in Paris, I go to Brest, Lorient, Saint Nazaire, La Rochelle, and Bordeaux."

"Why those cities?"

He stopped walking and looked at her. "Why are you asking me these questions?"

"Because I'm trying to have a conversation."

"It sounds like you are fishing for information."

Eva was surprised. That was not at all what she was doing. "I'm only trying to get to know the person I'm going to be living with for the next few weeks."

"I go there for work. There is no more to say about it."

Eva creased her eyebrows in concentration. She tried to remember what was important about those cities during the war. She knew they were all on a coast. *Maybe it has something to do with their navy? That's probably it,* she thought.

When they got back to the cottage, Eva went to make a fire before removing her coat because it would take a while for the house to warm up.

"I can do that," he said, squatting down next to her.

"It's OK. I think I can handle making a fire."

"I'm sure you can, but maybe you should make lunch while I do this."

"Oh, now I see the real reason," she said jokingly.

He gave her a side smile before she left for the kitchen. She searched the cabinets for food that would be suitable for lunch and settled on making sandwiches. She set his plate and a cup of water on the table in front of one of the empty kitchen chairs, then sat down with hers and took a bite. She could smell the wood smoke coming from the living room and wondered if she should tell him that his food was done. "Your food is ready," she called into the living room.

"Alright." He walked into the kitchen and peered down at his plate. "Should we eat in the living room where it's warmer?"

"Oh, I didn't think about that. I would prefer to eat where it's warm."

He picked up his plate and cup of water and carried them into the living room, and Eva followed. She waited for him to sit, noticing that he took the spot on the couch farthest from the fire so when she sat down, she would be closest to it.

"Are you sure you don't want to sit here? You made the fire, after all."

"I'm alright here. You sit there."

She sat down, putting her plate on her lap and placing the cup on the floor at her feet.

"This is good. What all did you put in it?"

"Thanks, but it is really simple. It's just ham, tomatoes, cheese, lettuce, and mustard."

"It's good."

"Well, aren't you easy to please?" she jested, trying to lighten the mood. He stopped chewing and looked at her. He seemed confused by her comment as his eyes bore into hers. "It's just a joke," she said. "I mean that you like simple, easy to make food." He nodded, then went back to eating.

After Bauer had finished his lunch, he disappeared upstairs, leaving Eva alone in the living room. When she was done, she brought her plate to the kitchen and went to the sink to wash it, noticing that Bauer had cleaned his plate and cup because they were sitting on the counter drying. She smiled to herself because they had talked about who would do the dishes, and he had told her he had little time to.

After cleaning the dishes, Eva went upstairs, noticing when she reached the top that his bedroom door was closed. She walked down the hall to her room and sat on the bed, trying to decide what to do now. Maybe she would sleep, but she wasn't that tired right now. She had already gone on two walks and the house was clean, so that left little for her to do.

She could read, but there weren't any books in the house; she would have to get some. Then she remembered she had The Wizard of Oz Gerhardt gave her. She went to her dresser and slid open the drawer, pulling the book out from under her pajamas. She smiled at the sight of it, but it also caused a pang of sadness.

She brought the book downstairs to the living room, drug one of the armchairs in front of the fire, then took the blanket from the back of the couch and sat down, draping it over her legs. She opened the book to the first page and, seeing English written on it, a lump formed in her throat. She rubbed her fingers over the words, wishing she was back home and that all of this was only a bad dream. She sighed, knowing it wasn't, and started reading, devouring every word, even though it was a book meant for children. Just getting to read in her language was comforting, and it reminded her of Gerhardt. Eva just got to the part where Dorothy met the scarecrow when she heard Bauer's voice behind her.

"Can I sit with you?"

She turned in the chair to look at him. He was standing in the entryway of the living room, watching her. "Of course."

He made his way into the room, picked up another log, and tossed it in the fire, causing tiny embers to flutter above the mantel. Then he pulled the other armchair beside hers and sat down. "What are you reading?"

She closed the book on her thumb and held it up so he could see the cover.

"The Wizard of Oz. Interesting choice. Where did you get that book?"

"It's not one of Germany's banned books if that is what you are thinking."

His brow creased. "It's not what I was thinking, and I know it's not. I was just wondering where you got an English book; if maybe you brought it with you."

"No, a friend gave it to me a long time ago." She wasn't about to tell him it was Gerhardt who gave it to her.

"Is it good?"

"It's alright. It's a children's book."

"I gathered that from the cover."

"Would you like to read it?"

"No, that's alright."

"Are there any foods you don't eat?" she asked, thinking about what she would do for dinner, redirecting the conversation.

"Not really. Because of my upbringing, I eat just about anything."

She hadn't really given his past much thought in relation to food, but now that he mentioned it, it made perfect sense. "That's good. I wish I could say I was to that point." He glanced from the fire to her, then brought his eyes back to the flames. *He is hard to talk to tonight,* she thought.

She pulled the corner of her mouth up in a private smile. "Have you heard of the game twenty questions?"

He turned his head to her, raising a brow. "Twenty questions…?"

"Yea. It's where I ask you twenty questions, and then you ask me twenty questions." That wasn't exactly how it was played, but she wasn't going to tell him that it was supposed to be yes or no kind of questions about another person other than the ones playing.

"No, I have not heard of this game."

"Well, we're going to play it. I'll go first," she said, feeling strangely in control. "What is your favorite color?"

"Blue."

She thought she could hear agitation in his voice. "Alright, now your turn."

He took in a breath, blew it out, then turned in the chair, facing more towards her than the fire. "What is your favorite color?"

"Red, but I also really like white." She rubbed her chin. "Hmmm... OK, were you ever married?"

His nostrils flared. "What if someone doesn't want to answer a question?"

"Nope, they have to answer all of them. Don't worry; it applies to me too."

"Alright, no," he said reluctantly. "You?"

"No. Were you ever engaged?"

"No," he said, the word coming slow and deliberate. "Were you?"

"No." She smiled at his obvious discomfort at her intrusive questions. "What about a girlfriend?"

He tilted his head to the side, narrowing his eyes into a glare, his apparent hesitation making her wonder if he did. "No," he said finally. "I haven't had time for a woman. Now I know you were with Gerhardt, so asking if you have a boyfriend seems pointless, and I'm sure you have had them in the past, so I'll ask a different question. Do you have any children?"

His question took her by surprise. "God, no." His expression shifted at her response, but she couldn't read it. She cleared her throat. "Do you have any children?"

He shook his head. "No, not that I know of. Judging by your response, I guess you don't want children?"

Eva thought carefully about her answer. "Well… actually, I'm not sure. I know I don't want any right now, during the war. In my opinion, this is the worst possible time to be having kids. But I think I will worry about finding someone first before I even think about having children. Having a baby affects the mother's life so much more than the father's. I don't want to quit work or have something interfere with my plans of finishing my degree. What about you? Do you want kids?"

He looked away, gazing into the fire. "I don't know."

"So, having kids during the war concerns you, too?"

"Sure, but there is no right time to have kids."

"True, but there are definitely times that are better than others. Who's turn is it?" she asked, losing track of who asked the last question.

"I believe it is mine." The lightness in his expression was gone, replaced with a more severe look. "Do you love Gerhardt?"

Her cheeks flushed to a dark shade of pink, and her mouth opened slightly, and he gave her a 'you said we have to answer' look. She was happy the only light in the room was from the fire. "Of course, I do."

"But he is a German?"

"What, I can't love someone because of their nationality?"

"Sure, you can, but I thought you would want to be with an American."

"It doesn't matter where someone is from."

"Yes, it does."

"No, it doesn't. You wouldn't be with someone because of their nationality?" she asked, honestly unsure what his answer would be.

"As a member of the Nazi party, I am supposed to marry a German girl, not a foreigner."

"Are other nationalities so offensive to you?"

"It's not that. It's what Germany expects of me. It's my duty to."

"And what of your heart? What if it doesn't align with your duty?"

"In the scheme of things, it doesn't matter what my heart feels. It's politics."

"You are the kind of person who would go along with an arranged marriage."

"No, I get to choose my wife. She is just expected to be a loyal German."

"Is this how it is for all the officers?"

"Yes, they expect it from all of us, especially those who belong to the party."

"That is the most ridiculous thing I've ever heard." Part of her wondered if that was why Gerhardt chose his fiancé over her. Even though he was not a member of the Nazi party, maybe he felt like he had to marry a German.

"It's not. Let's change the subject. Your turn. Ask me another question."

"OK. What is your favorite flower?"

"The cornflower."

"The cornflower? That is a flower you don't hear of often. Why that one?"

"Because it is the national flower of Germany."

She gave a nod. "Of course."

"What is yours?"

"I've always had a strange attraction to the orchid, particularly the white ones, but recently I have also liked primroses."

"Why is that?"

"Do you remember the little girl in La Chapelle, Sabina?"

"The one who died?"

"Yes. It was her favorite flower."

"Ahh, so that is why you like that flower now?"

She squeezed the fingers of her left hand between her thumb and index finger. "Yes."

"So, how do you think your parents would feel if they knew you were with a German, now that our countries are at war?"

"My parents?"

"Yes, I can imagine your dad wouldn't approve."

My God, he is just like Gerhardt in that way, thinking I need my dad's permission to do things, she thought. "For starters," she told him. "My parents wouldn't care, and second, my dad's opinion isn't more important than my mom's." He eyed her, unconvinced. "We don't live in medieval times, Wilhelm. Things are very different in America than they are here."

"Oh, I am very aware of that."

She couldn't tell if he was just agreeing with her or if he meant it condescendingly. "Well, I'm sure we have reached our twenty-question quota. Should I make dinner?"

He checked his watch. "I am getting hungry, so I think that would be good. Do you want me to help?"

She lifted a brow. "You want to help?"

"Sure, why not. Let's make dinner. Maybe you can teach me something."

"Only if you are an excellent student."

"I'm sure I will be the epitome of the model student."

"We will see."

He followed her into the kitchen and Eva looked for an apron and found three in a bottom drawer, and tossed one to him. "Put that on." She put her on as she watched him unfold his and put it over his head. As she tied the apron in the back, she couldn't suppress a smile. He looked so funny in a cooking apron, out of place. It was probably the least intimidating she had ever seen him, except for when he was in the hospital.

He glanced at her. "Why are you smiling?"

"Nothing. It's just this," she waved her finger in a circular motion in his direction, "is something I never thought I would see."

"Well, don't get used to it."

"I don't plan on it."

Together, they made a meatloaf, and Eva put it in the oven to bake. He only chopped the onion and crushed the bread into crumbs that she had baked dry, and she did the rest while he watched. He went to the cabinets and started opening them. "What are you looking for?" she asked.

"I'm looking to see if we have any wine."

"Oh, I think I saw some earlier in that cabinet." She pointed to a door just to his right.

He opened it. "Here we are." He pulled out a 1940s-style bottle with a flip top, filled with red liquid, then retrieved two glasses from another cabinet. He set them on the counter, poured both glasses half full, then handed one to her.

She took a sip, held the liquid in her mouth for a few seconds, then swallowed. She did not know what kind of wine this was, but it was dry. She coughed and put her hand on her chest. "Wow, that is a really dry wine."

He sipped his. "It is, but it's good. Do you not like dry wines?"

"Not usually, but this is fine for now."

"I can look for something else?"

"No, this will do." The timer sounded, so she set her glass on the counter and went to the oven, pulling the meatloaf out, placing it on the stove. "It's done. Grab some plates." He took two plates out of the cabinet and set them on the table. She carried the meatloaf and an extra hot pad to the table and set the meatloaf on it, pushing it to the middle. "Bon appétit," she said.

"I'm sure I will."

They sat at the table and Eva watched his reaction as he took a bite. He appeared to like the meatloaf. "I don't start work for another day, so I thought I would look for an apartment tomorrow. Ingrid will be here in less than two weeks, and I need to have a place before she arrives."

He took a sip of the wine, swallowing his food with it. "That makes sense."

"I think I'm going to try to find a place close to the hospital. What part of town do you work in?"

"We work out of an old hotel on the east side of the city."

"Where does your orderly stay?"

"In a little apartment a few blocks from the cottage."

"How come you didn't have him stay here with you? Wouldn't that have been more convenient?"

"He doesn't want to stay with me, plus I wouldn't put up with his antics."

She frowned. "What antics?" He looked up from the plate with only his eyes. Eva drew in a breath. "Ohh, I see." She now felt stupid for asking.

"Tell me about your home, Eva?" He put another fork full of meatloaf in his mouth.

"My home?"

"Yes, the part of America you are from and your family."

"Alright, umm, it's a dry place. It's on the west side of the country and is considered a high mountain desert state because the lower areas are like a desert, but we have large mountains near by that get snow."

"Sounds interesting. I have never been to a place like that before. The closest to that description would be when I was in Spain. And what of your family?"

"Well, my parents are still together, and they live in a different city than my school."

"What are the names of the cities?"

"I live in a city called Salt Lake. That is where the university is I go to, but my parents live in a city called Provo which is made onto Salt Lake."

"Is that where you grew up, in Provo?"

"It is. I spent my whole life in the same house."

"Sounds nice. And you have a brother if I remember correctly?"

She eyed him. "I do. He is my older brother."

"And is he fighting in the war?"

"No."

He paused, focusing on her. "How is that? I'm not so misinformed as to think that the US isn't doing a draft after the Pearl Harbor attack. When I was in the hospital, you told me that he was a musician, but he is surely in the military now?"

"The US is probably drafting, but sometimes men can get out of it."

"Is there something physically wrong with your brother?"

Eva's eyes grew wide. "No."

"Then what could keep him from service?"

Eva didn't want to have to try and think up an answer to this question. "It is personal."

"I don't mean to be offensive, but how can a young, perfectly healthy man not step up to serve his country in its time of need?"

She stood, taking her plate to the sink. "That is none of your business. I know that you have some skewed concept of loyalty and duty, but that is you. Not everyone is like that."

"German men are."

"Well, then there is something wrong with all of you."

"I will say no more about your brother. Anything else at this point would be indelicate."

"You mean the cruel things you want to say?"

"I said I will say no more." He picked up his plate and came to stand next to her at the sink.

"You don't seem to care that I am not regretful that I can't step up to fight for my country."

"That's because women don't fight, so they do not expect it of you."

"Yea, and that is stupid. If you asked my brother, he would agree with me."

"I'm sure he would," he said with disdain in his voice.

"Think whatever you want of my brother, but you couldn't be more wrong about him. Thankfully, he will never have to explain himself to you." She forcefully took the plate from his hand and began washing it.

"I will wait with the fire until it burns out. You can go to bed if you want."

"I think I will." Truthfully, she just didn't want to be around him right now.

Chapter Eight

Eva woke to pale sunlight that sifted through the curtains, covering the low arched windows of her bedroom. She slipped out of bed and went to the window, pulling the curtain aside. A white blanket of snow covered everything in a shimmery brilliance. She frowned, peering down at it in the pre-morning dawn. *No, I was going to look for an apartment today,* she thought disappointedly.

It was just past six, and she needed to hurry and make breakfast so Bauer could leave for work. Eva patted downstairs in her nightgown and socks and turned to the right, peering down the narrow hall into the kitchen. The main floor was dark, and she wondered if he was still in his room. She went into the kitchen and fried the last of their eggs, mentally noting to pick up some more today while she was out. Then she made coffee, real coffee, not the nasty substitute. It didn't surprise her that he could get the real thing. She had not had real coffee since being in this time. She toasted some bread, took some cold cut meat and jam out of the fridge, and set them on the table.

The sound of boots on the stairs echoed in the house, then creaked on the hall floor boards. Bauer appeared in the kitchen entryway as he pulled his suspenders over his shoulders.

"I could smell that upstairs. What did you make?"

"Just eggs, toast, and coffee. Nothing grand."

"It smells delightful anyway." He took the plate from the table and stood near the stove as he ate.

"Why don't you sit? There is no need to stand."

"I don't have a lot of time. If I stand, I will eat quicker."

His constant need to hurry didn't surprise Eva. Not only was it a German thing, but it was so characteristically Bauer. Soon she would be alone again and did not know what she would do with her last day off.

"Do you have plans today?" He eyed her as he sipped coffee.

"Not really. I thought maybe I would go for a walk."

"Perfect. I have some free time later today. I thought you would like to see Chateau Musee after dinner."

"Is that the castle on the hill?"

"It is."

His offer pleasantly surprised her. Eva had actually considered going there on her walk. "Yes, I would like to see it. What time?"

"I will come by the house when I'm done, and then we can walk there together. Probably around six."

"Oh, does that mean you will not be home for dinner, then?"

"No, I will eat there today."

Eva nodded and watched him finish the last of his breakfast in silence. He put his plate in the sink and left without even a goodbye. She finished her food, then did the dishes before going upstairs to change. Even though she was going to walk to the Chateau Musee with Bauer later, she decided on a walk by herself first.

She pulled the collar of her coat up around her neck to help guard against the strong January winds that carried the cold off the Channel. She was seriously reconsidering her walk with Bauer, knowing that it would be even colder tonight than it was now. The fear of upsetting him is all that kept her from changing her mind.

She walked through the town, familiarizing herself with the streets so she could navigate the city better, and ended her walk at the coast. Standing in the tall brown grass atop the hills that overlooked the Channel, she peered out over the stretched beach and the aquamarine-colored water. Her hair freely whipped around her face as the wind tugged at it. She now regretted not putting it up that morning.

She looked longingly at the Channel, knowing that England lay just on the other side, so close yet not attainable. Her freedom, her old life, Jon, and everything she once knew lay just over this body of water. Never had she been so close since leaving for France, and now she was here, and brought here by Bauer, of all people. She didn't know how, but she would find a way to cross it. She would go home, even if she died trying.

Footsteps crunched in the dry grass behind her. She turned, scanning the surrounding area. To her surprise, she didn't see anyone, but there was no way she had misheard. There had been someone there, walking in the grass not far behind her. The hair on the back of her neck stood on end, and she had the distinct feeling of being watched, but from where she couldn't tell. All she could see was the brown grass dancing in the wind from where she stood. A strange sense of déjà vu overcame her, and she turned, hurrying down the hill back towards town.

She went to the cottage and locked herself inside, not knowing if someone had followed her. She took off her coat and scarf and then went to light a fire. This was the first time she had built a fire since living here. For some reason, Bauer had always been the one volunteering to do it. She broke the kindling, putting it in the fireplace, then a few small logs. Once the fire was burning, she sat on the couch, covering up with the blanket, watching the flames lick the brick around them.

She peered at the small grandfather clock that sat in the living room corner. Its second hand was ticking away, bringing the hour hand ever closer to the six. She didn't have long to wait, so she picked the Wizard of Oz off the side table where she had left it the night before and opened it to the bookmark.

She had almost finished it now and was at the part where Dorothy learned that Oz was just a man and not a wizard. It made her think how you can believe someone is one way, only to find out they are nothing like they appeared on the surface. You have to find someone at their most vulnerable to truly see them for who they are. When all their armor, lies and pride have been stripped away, all that is left are their raw emotions.

The front door opened, and Bauer's boots squeaked on the tile, the footsteps in the hall growing louder as he came into the living room entryway and stopped, peering at her.

"Are you ready?"

She laid the book back on the side table. "Let me get my coat and put my shoes on." Once she was bundled up, she followed Bauer out the door into the chilly night.

Eva poked her hands deep into her coat pockets as they walked the streets. The clicking of their shoes on the pavement echoed off the buildings loudly in the deathly silence of the city. Eva knew it must be past curfew, but she was allowed out because she was with a German officer.

"Have you been to the castle before?"

"Yes. The last time I was here. It is a beautiful structure. You can really feel the history there."

Eva did not know how old the castle was or its story. "So do you walk at night a lot?" she asked, curious about what he got up to when she wasn't around.

"Sometimes. I find the silence relaxing. I'm with people all day, so it is nice to be alone, and I don't have that luxury when I'm at work."

"I can understand that. Sometimes all I want is to be alone."

"You have had quite a bit of alone time in the last few days. And you go back to work tomorrow, so I imagine you will be glad of the company."

"Yes, and no. It is a new place with people I don't know, so it will be a little strange and stressful at first, I think."

"It can't be as bad as the hospital in Berlin or the Russian front. This one should be a slower pace for you."

"Sure, but still different. As strange as this might sound, I think I will miss the intensity of it. Always knowing where you will be, having something to do every minute, and saving someone's life every day."

"That doesn't sound strange at all, I understand. You like the adrenaline, the constant need for the rush."

He made it sound like an addiction. "I mean, I enjoy feeling useful."

"You will be useful here, too."

"I suppose."

"We're here." He stopped, gazing up at the extensive structure nestled in the shadows.

"Do we just go in?"

"It's empty. There is a walkway that takes us to the entrance. You have to be careful once we are inside, though, so you don't trip. We can't use a flashlight because of the lights out."

Eva wondered why he took her there at night if they couldn't use flashlights. "Maybe we should have come when the sun was out. Maybe we should come back tomorrow or another day."

"We can come during the day again if you want, but it's much more fun to explore at night."

Eva was questioning his choice at this moment. She could not quite figure him out, and his actions seemed odd to her.

She followed him up the ramp that led to the castle, then under an archway that opened into a stone courtyard. "Where is the door?"

"Just over here," he said. "Can you see alright?"

"Sort of. I can make out the surrounding walls, and I can see you. If I have to, I will feel with my feet."

"Alright then." He started towards the front of the castle, and she trailed after him.

It was funny to her because Gerhardt would have taken her hand and led her to the door and through the castle, but not Bauer. He was more than content to leave her to feel her way on her own. Not that she cared, because she didn't need his help, nor did she want it.

He stopped in front of a large door, but she couldn't quite tell what it was made of because it was too dark to see. He pulled on the handle, and the hinges made a high-pitched squeal, breaking the silence that surrounded them. It was an odd, eerie sound, like a creature crying in the night. He stepped over the threshold, not waiting for her, and she could no longer see him. She walked through the doorway and stopped, trying to let her eyes adjust to the added darkness. As her eyes focused, she could make out a large room, maybe a ballroom or something similar. She had no idea where Bauer had gone, but she felt strange calling out to him. She took several steps to the middle of the room, trying to see which way the exit was. "Where is he?" she whispered into the empty room. It was so dark inside the castle, and the atmosphere was unsettling. She wasn't particularly fond of the dark, and this was setting her nerves on edge, and she could feel the fear creeping in.

There was a section of the wall that looked black with no defining details, and she figured it must be the doorway out of the room. She strode over to it and put her hand out to make sure that it was actually the entryway. When her hand went through it, she was relieved and continued through. Now she had to decide which way to go. She turned to the left and saw a figure standing at the end of the hall, and jumped, startled at the sight of them, but when she moved, the figure did as well. It was then she realized that it was only her reflection at the end of the hall. She placed a hand over her still pounding heart and let out a small sigh, feeling silly for scaring herself. No longer wanting to go in that direction, she turned to the right, only to collide with a figure standing behind her. Tumbling a few feet backward, she screamed, instinctively putting her hand in a defensive position. Without warning, the figure stepped towards her, putting one hand on the back of her head and clasping the other over her mouth.

"Eva... it's me." When Bauer's voice came, it was low and austere.

Panicking, she pulled at his hands, trying to remove them from her head. It took a few seconds to register that it was Bauer and that he had spoken to her. When she stopped struggling he released her.

"What the hell! I thought you were behind me, but when I turned around to tell you we were going to go up the stairs, you weren't there. Where were you?"

She fought to catch her breath, her words coming out labored. "I couldn't find you, and then I saw my reflection, and it startled me, then immediately I turned around and ran into you."

A chuckle escaped his lips. "You scared yourself with your own reflection?"

The anger pushed through the fear. "Do not laugh at me. Anybody would have been startled by that." She was upset by his obvious lack of sympathy.

"I would not have."

"You aren't like most people. You aren't normal." She had always been afraid of the dark. It had started with the movies that scared her as a child and then getting lost in the Belgium woods had turned it into an irrational fear. She could not tell him that, though.

"Normal…? How many grown men do you know that are afraid of the dark, or women, for that matter?"

"I didn't say I was afraid of the dark. I said seeing someone there when I wasn't expecting to startled me, that is all."

"I'm sure half of Dieppe heard you scream. Here, give me your hand?"

She hesitated at first but then held it out. Bauer closed his fingers around hers, pulling her hand down to his side. This was unexpected, and a strange sensation coursed through her hand and up her arm. His hand felt nothing like Gerhardt's, even though it was just a hand. It wasn't so much the actual feeling of his hand that was different, but the feeling it gave her was different. She couldn't identify what it was exactly or the strange sensation. She had the sudden urge to pull her hand away, but she didn't want to get lost from him again, so she let him keep hold of it.

He guided her up the stairs to a landing, then up another flight. It led them onto a balcony that overlooked the city and the Channel. "This is what I wanted to show you. Look how pretty it is. You can even see the stars because most of the city is dark."

She looked at the shapes of the buildings below. The city was shrouded in darkness, and to her left was the flat surface of the water that reflected the sky like a mirror. It was like a sea of stars, a dark blue hue with hundreds of diamonds gleaming off its surface. It was one of the most beautiful things Eva had ever seen. "Wow, this is amazing. You have been up here before at night, then?" she asked, leaning over the balcony wall for a better view.

"I have."

"Do you and your buddies come up here often when you're here?"

"No. I have only been up here by myself."

"Oh." There was a strange twisting in her stomach. She wanted to quickly move on from the awkward silence that now hung between them. "It would be even nicer up here if it wasn't so cold." She automatically pulled her arms tighter around her chest.

"It is a chilly night. Do you want to go back?"

"That might be better."

"I can show you the castle during the day if you still want to see the inside?"

She honestly had to think about that. Did she really want to come back again with Bauer, just the two of them? The last few encounters with him played through her mind like a reel. So many times, he had been ruthless towards her. But not these last few. She wouldn't call them pleasant, but they were different. He always had something up his sleeve, and she was sure his change towards her wasn't any different.

"I didn't think that question was going to stump you," he said, breaking her silence.

She couldn't see his face well, but she could hear the obvious annoyance in his tone. She laughed, but there was a difference to her laughter. Nothing was funny. It was more of an involuntary laugh out of sheer nervousness. She didn't know quite what to say. Frankly, he scared her most of the time. Not only from what he had done in the past, but she didn't think he realized just what a formidable person he was. "I… um…."

"Is it truly so hard to answer? I was expecting a simple yes or no, but obviously, there is more to this than meets the eye. Perhaps you can explain to me why such a simple question is so difficult for you?"

"I thought it would be pretty clear why. You and me, here alone at night together, us living together. This is so wrong. You know it, and I know it."

"Your casual use of the word 'wrong' is interesting. I'm a firm believer that in war, you need to remain strong, which is why you should not fall in love. But one of the worst things about being a soldier is the loneliness. A person would do just about anything for a small bit of comfort."

Was this a confession that he enjoyed her company? Or was he using her to ease some inner turmoil, smiling at her with masked civility, all the while condemning her because her beliefs and mindset differed from his own? She was certain he felt he was better than her. "You had me tortured, and now you are using me for your own personal comfort. Is there no level you won't stoop to?"

"Of course, that is all that comes to your mind when you think of me. I don't blame you, really, I don't, but I am not just using you for my personal comfort. And if you are afraid that what happened in the past will happen again, I hope you believe me when I say I will not harm you now. You have my word."

"You mean like you have already done so many times? And I'm not just referring to when you had me tortured. I'm talking about how you treat me and the mean things you always say. Words can be very hurtful too." She glared at his dark figure in the starlit night—unshed tears welling in her eyes.

"I know you won't believe me when I say that I'm being cruel for your sake. This world is worse than you can imagine, and if you can't face the hard facts of reality, it will eat you alive. You have to toughen up. Life isn't always going to be easy on you and give you what you want."

"And you are helping me, is that it?"

"This will be hard for you to swallow, but I'm not the scariest, most dangerous person out there."

Eva knew that this was true, but right now, he was probably the most dangerous thing in her world. "I don't know what you want me to say."

"We have been out here for a while now, and the temperatures have dropped below freezing. Why don't we go back to the house? I will build a fire, and we can talk about it then?"

He wasn't wrong about the freezing temperature. She felt the cold had gone to her bones. "Fine." She agreed, only so they would leave.

An odd silence hung in the air as they walked along the dark, deserted streets. He didn't speak to her or even look in her direction, but to be fair, she didn't talk to him either. She hung back, following a few feet behind, not wanting to be close to him.

Coming up the street were headlights and the roar of an engine. It surprised her at first, but soon it was clear that it was a patrol vehicle. It pulled to the side of the road, and two men jumped out of the back, guns drawn, and made their way across the street towards her and Bauer. She couldn't help but tense at this, the memory of all the times she was taken by the Gestapo overtaking her. This time she did not distance herself from Bauer but instead took a few steps forward to stand beside him, knowing he was the only thing standing between them and her. It was funny how things worked.

"It is past curfew. Why are you out?" a large, stern-faced German asked in broken French.

"I know it is past curfew," Bauer said to him in German, barely containing the anger that was brimming just under the surface.

The man looked momentarily confused. "You are a German—"

"Yes, I'm German, damn it. And the next time you speak you will address me as SS Obersturmbannführer Bauer or Sir." The man stared at him without speaking. Bauer gave him a once-over, narrowing his eyes. Eva had seen him do this to people before. There was a very condescending look on his face as he held the mans gaze.

"Sir... I didn't know—"

Bauer held up his hand. "Just go." The two men hurried to the truck, the one saying something to the driver before he crawled in the back.

Eva watched the truck pull back onto the road, and out of the corner of her eye, she noticed Bauer had already started walking away. His interaction with the two men just confirmed that he wasn't easily intimidated. She followed, and they fell back into the same awkward silence as before.

Large white flakes gracefully fell from above with little warning, sticking to Eva's hair and lashes. She blinked a few times and wiped her face with the back of her gloved hand. The water on her face from the melted snow made her cheeks even colder. She picked up her pace, now walking beside Bauer instead of behind. But of course, he didn't even glance at her when she came up to his side.

When they were back at the cottage, Bauer pulled out his key and promptly unlocked the front door. Once they were both inside, he closed the door and flipped on the light, then shrugged out of his coat. It was dampened by the snow, and the white flakes were still in his brown hair. When he turned to hang his coat and scarf in the closet, she noticed his face and how it was drawn and weary. He looked tired.

He walked into the living room without a word and started making a fire. She came and sat on the couch, covering up with the blanket, and watched him break the twigs and place them in the fireplace, then the logs. He lit a match and held it to kindling until small flames danced up from them. Finally, he stood and turned to look at her, staring down with an unreadable expression, then came to sit beside her on the couch, folding one leg over the other as he draped his left arm over the back.

He stared at her for a protracted moment before finally breaking the silence. "You may think you know me, but you don't. I have seen more of hell than most people could dream of and lived through more than a lifetime's worth. I have stared it in the face and come out the other side. Has that made me a harsh, callous person? Yes, but I am better for it. It has taught me to be resilient and not care about people's whims and opinions. And when shit happens, it doesn't knock me down because I don't let my feelings get the better of me. My motivation is my duty, and I am good at my job because I am mentally and emotionally strong."

"Emotions? Feelings? What emotions? What feelings? You don't have any. You are empty and hollow inside. That is why things don't get the better of you because you feel nothing. It doesn't bother you to torture someone or watch them be tortured. That is why you are good at your job. If you saw me drowning, you wouldn't even offer your hand; you would just watch. I know the kind of person you are. You don't fool anyone. Do you know how much pain you have caused me?" She could no longer hold back the tears, her voice cracking as she spoke.

"I don't show my emotions often, but you bleed yours."

"You never show them, and nothing you ever say is real, except the part about you being a callous, harsh person." She had learned that Bauer kept his emotions under ruthless control, rarely revealing a chink in his carefully maintained armor. He was the personification of grace under fire.

"You want me to tell you something real?"

"That would be nice for a change."

"I am a calculated person, but I follow my heart, and when I speak, I speak my mind. I dream of a simple life when this war is over, to find the girl that I will make my wife. I say after because that kind of life doesn't happen when you do what I do for a living. This I am aware of. But who knows how this war will end, or what it will be like when it does."

"You have barely even touched the surface of who you are. And, of course, we don't know what will happen at the end of the war." She did, of course, but she couldn't tell him that.

"You think you deserve to know more?" he said, a note of challenge in his tone. His dark eyes burned a hole in her.

She swallowed hard, feeling slightly faint as her heart thundered in her chest. "Yes. I think you owe me something for what you have done."

111

"Maybe an apology, but not a description of my private life or the inner working of my mind."

She would not let him do this again to put her in a situation where he has all the control and power, and she has none. He learned a little more about her with every encounter, but she still knew nothing about him. It was his turn to feel vulnerable. She took a deep breath, and feeling bolstered by her newfound anger and courage to confront him, she locked eyes with him, and with a tremulous voice, she spoke. "Tell me something you've never told anyone."

His carefully controlled anger finally flared. "You paint me out to be this monster capable of doing terrible things, but that is because you have no idea what I've been through and what is required of me. So, I will indulge you in this. Let me tell you what I know from one of my experiences. When my sister died, I never thought I'd be alright again. I cried for weeks; I blamed myself, and I blamed everyone and everything around me. And then I realized all that sadness was swallowing me up. I eventually had no more options left open to me, so I made the choice that I would not let it eat me up from the inside. That was one of the few times I have allowed myself to lose control and my emotions to take over. Not that I don't feel them, it's that I have learned to control them and have chosen not to show them to the world."

"And you have closed your heart after that day, which is why you are the soulless shell of a person that sits in front of me now."

His expression changed, some of the anger fading to a more unreadable look. "It has made me guarded, not unloving.

It is true that apart from my mother and sister, I have never really known what it is to be loved and had not known what it was to love."

She could sense a note of sadness in his voice. "So you have never been in love before?" Eva thought it was tragic, and found herself feeling sorry for him, Bauer of all people.

"I have been with plenty of women, but I've never been in love with any of them."

This gave her pause. Were women only things that he used and then disposed of? Was he using her now? It occurred to her that she didn't even know why she was here, in France, living with him. "What am I doing here, Wilhelm?" She knew that was a loaded question, so she braced for what would come next.

He looked at her pointedly. "I think there is a reason we keep meeting."

"And what is the reason?"

"I don't know, but it's like we are in a vice, being pushed together since the first time we met. I don't suppose you'd care to tell me why?"

This triggered a panic deep inside. "I'll tell you why. It's because you are a… mean person who keeps trying to punish me for something I didn't do. So you are always there, waiting for me to mess up."

"The only reason you are alive now is because of me. You realize I could have had you tortured and shot so many times?"

Eva swallowed hard. No matter how much she wanted to deny it, he was right. "I realize that," she forced out.

"Do you think you would have fared better with Gerhardt if I hadn't been around?" he asked, resentment thick with every word.

"He did save me."

"But at what cost to him?"

"I don't know what you mean."

"Yes, you do." She stared at him, honestly confused. "Russia, the front. Does any of this ring a bell?"

Her jaw dropped. What he was saying couldn't be true. He was trying to make her feel awful, yet again. "No, that is not why he went."

"Come on, Eva, let's be honest. Did you actually think what he did in France would go unnoticed?" She didn't respond, so he continued. "I had been asked, among many of the other men stationed in La Chapelle at that time, if he warned you before the residents of the farm were rounded up and questioned. You know what our answer had to be. There was no way it could be concealed."

Tears streamed down her cheeks freely now, and she looked at him with such contempt. "So he is there because of you?"

"He is there because of you, Eva."

Those words were like a sharp knife stabbing her in the heart. "Why am I not in jail or dead, then?"

"I told you why."

"If you really are the reason I am not in jail or dead, then why are you still here and not on the Russian front, like Gerhardt?"

He was quiet for a few seconds before responding. "Because he doesn't have access to the things I do or the same authority. I am a Lieutenant Colonel of the Gestapo, and he is a captain in the Wehrmacht. There is a big difference."

Eva couldn't believe her ears. If what Bauer said was true, then she is the reason Gerhardt was sent to the front and not safely behind a desk in Berlin. "Why would you do that for me?"

"I don't know." He paused, staring into the fire. He was silent for a long while, but when his words came, they were soft and low. "Perhaps I am in love. You are always in my thoughts. I think about you all the time. Isn't that what someone does when they are in love?"

Eva was stunned. In her whole life, nothing had surprised her more than this. The only thing that compared was learning time travel was real. For a few seconds, she couldn't speak. All she could do was look at him with an astonished expression frozen on her face. She didn't quite know what to say or how she was supposed to feel.

Noticing her silence, he turned away from the fire and gazed at her. "I would be afraid to ask if you loved me too because I know it's not the same for you."

"You are a powerful man from the country that is dominating the world, and you are afraid of me?"

"What we work for and what we live for aren't always the same thing. I have put most of my energy into this war. There wasn't much else that was important to me until recently. I will always be a soldier. That is who I am, and it is my duty to fight for my country, but I think there can be more than one thing worth fighting for. I'm hoping I never have to give one up for the other. I'm praying a time doesn't come when I am asked to decide which one is more important to me, which one I value more. Yes, I have lied for you, kept things from my superiors, and in doing so deceived my country, but I think it is possible to do the wrong thing for the right reason."

Eva shook her head in exaggerated motions. "No, none of what you say is true."

"I'm surprised you can't see that what I did was out of love for you."

"Do you expect me to believe you loved me since France?"

"No, I didn't even like you when we first met in France. It wasn't until Germany that I realized my feelings for you. I'm not completely sure when they began, but I noticed them in Germany or acknowledged them then. That is when things started changing."

Butterflies knotted in her stomach. "How can you love me?"

"In the way that I understand love."

"But I always thought you hated me?"

"I do."

"What…?" Eva thought her ears had tricked her.

"I was foolish and let down my guard. I'm in love with you now because of it. I allowed myself to feel sorry for you, to take pity on someone who should have been imprisoned. I think that makes me hate you even more because I love you."

Eva's thoughts were in turmoil. She couldn't comprehend what he was saying, and she wondered how much he knew about her and her involvement with the resistance. She was afraid to ask, but knew it might come to that. "You said 'that is when things started changing,' what did you mean?"

"I will not tell you that you have changed me or that I am a different person and a better man. None of that shit. I am still the same person now that I was before. I think the same, and I act the same. The only thing that has changed for me is you. You, Eva Abrams, are the one thing that made me tap into the emotions I so carefully keep hidden away. I used to use this war, my anger, and my duty to try to force you from my mind. It worked well initially, but every time I saw you, it would get a little harder until not even those things were effective. Then we would meet, or I would catch a glimpse of you, and my world would crumble."

She searched for a response to these revelations. "I want you to know that I respect your honesty. But I will lock this knowledge away forever and forget that you ever said it. You have to understand that it is impossible for me to ever love you. You were right. I don't feel the same way about you. I don't know if I could love you even if I tried. How could I have those kinds of feelings for the person who has been so cruel to me, a man so undeserving of my love? And your confession of love rings false in my ears because how can you love when you have no soul?"

"I told you how I feel, which was difficult for me to do, and this is how you respond? You say I am heartless, but that was one of the coldest, most callous responses I think anyone could have given. Even though I wasn't foolish enough to imagine I ever stood a chance with you, I expected a kinder rejection." His eyes bore into hers, so full of fury and hurt. He stood up from the couch. "I am going to bed. Make sure the fire is out before you go upstairs." He turned and walked away from her without another word.

She looked around for a quiet place to retreat and recover her composure. The emotional roller coaster she had just been on with Bauer, and the verbal lashing he gave her before leaving, was more than she could take. For reasons unknown to her, she felt the need for darkness, so she went into the kitchen and sat at the table. The tears flowed like rivers down her face, and wiping at them with the back of her hand proved insufficient, so she stopped trying and let them fall. She didn't even know why she was crying exactly and why inside felt so turbulent. Her mind was flipping through thoughts rapidly like channels on a television. She didn't know what she felt, what she thought, or what to do next. She had never been as confused about anyone or anything as she was about Bauer. She went from thinking he was the most insufferable, awful, vile person she had ever met to finally reaching beneath some of his layers only to see one of the most complex and frustrating people she had ever met.

That night she lay in bed, replaying that evening over and over in her mind. Leave it to Bauer to find a new way of turning her world upside down. How had she missed that he was in love with her? It hadn't crossed her mind, not even once. She never was suspicious and felt confident that he despised her, as she did him. Or was it as she had, past tense, because her feelings shifted? She didn't know anymore.

Chapter Nine

January 12th, 1942

Eva had been working for days now, trying to learn the ropes of the new hospital. There weren't a lot of patients, but they did things differently here. The strangest thing was working under French doctors and alongside French nurses instead of German ones. Ingrid would be here in a week, which made Eva extremely happy.

She mindlessly cleaned the instruments, thinking about Bauer. She had not been able to get him out of her head since that night. She had barely seen him since, and he hadn't spoken more than ten words to her. For the last four days, he had left before she was even out of bed and didn't return to the cottage until long after she was asleep. She knew it was deliberate, and was still trying to decide if it was a good thing or a bad thing. The one time yesterday that they were both home at the same time and not sleeping, he wouldn't even look at her. She tried talking to him, but he just gave her an icy glare. His callous indifference towards her was upsetting and unsettling somehow. Now that he was pissed at her, Jon's words kept coming back. That she needed him to keep her alive; if she ever needed him again, she doubted he would help. He was more than angry, and he would not be generous with her again. He had been there for her, and she couldn't even see it. She was blind to what was right in front of her, to more than one thing.

"Nurse Abrams," a short, fair-haired nurse said as she came into the operating room. Eva looked up from the tools, barely remembering even washing them. "Nurse Moreau wants to see you in her office."

Eva frowned. "Is something wrong?"

"No, I don't think so. It didn't seem like it. I can finish those for you." She reached out for the forceps still in Eva's hand.

Eva laid it in her palm, giving her a faint smile before walking past and out of the operating room. She followed the long corridor, feeling the radiated warmth coming in through the windows that ran along the south side. Eva wondered what Nurse Moreau wanted. She couldn't think of anything she had done wrong, so maybe she just had another job for her to do.

She knocked on the closed door of Nurse Moreau's office and waited to be told she could enter. "Come in." Eva turned the brass knob, pushed the door open, and stepped inside. She closed the heavy white door behind her and came to stand by the desk. "Have a seat, nurse Abrams." Eva sat in the small wooden chair across from her. "First, I would like to say that you have been doing a fine job, but that is not why I have called you in here."

Eva looked at her questioningly. "Thank you. Is that why you have asked for me?"

"No. There is someone here to see you."

Eva's breath caught in her throat. *Bauer,* she thought. The shape of someone appeared in her peripheral. She turned to see a man in an officer's uniform coming up on her right. Instantly, she could tell it wasn't Bauer. This man had a different shape. She raised her eyes to his face, gasping. She put her right hand over her mouth and tried to hold back the tears that threatened to escape.

"Hello, Eva."

"Klaus..." She practically jumped from the chair, wrapping her arms around his chest. "I can't believe you are here. What... how... I mean, why—"

"I came to see the hospital and the state they were left in after losing some of their doctors and nurses. You said they were in need, so I came to see for myself."

"Are you transferring here?"

"You asked Ingrid and me if we would like to join you in France, and she said yes, but I left you hanging. I've had a lot of time to think about it, and I decided it would be a nice change, at least for a while. I know things are slower here in France, and you and Ingrid are here, so what reason did I have to say no? Working here will practically be a vacation for me, well, for all three of us, compared to what we have been through on the front."

Eva felt lightheaded. She couldn't believe he was here. She quickly wiped the corners of her eyes and cleared her throat. Finally, releasing him from the embrace. "When do you start?"

"In a few days."

"I have to say, you being here is the best thing that has happened to me in quite some time."

"Why don't you take the rest of the day off," Nurse Moreau said, looking between Eva and Dr. Möller.

"Don't you need me to finish sanitizing the tools?"

She chuckled. "I'm sure we can manage."

"Thank you." After Nurse Moreau dismissed her, she went to the nurse's lounge and gathered her things, then followed Klaus out to the street.

"So, where are you staying?"

At this Eva wasn't sure how to explain or if she wanted to tell him at all. How could she disclose to him that she was living with a man? Not just any man, but the German officer who had her arrested? "Um... just a small cottage by the sea. It is temporary, though. I have been looking for a place for myself and Ingrid to stay these last few days."

"Why not stay where you are now?"

"Well, it's just that the person I'm staying with doesn't want any more renters."

"Maybe Ingrid can find a place of her own or stay with me until she does if you are already settled."

"No, I mean they want me to move out soon and don't want any more renters. They are only letting me stay until I find my own place."

"Hmm, well, I can help find a place. Why don't you show me where you are staying, and we can have some tea or that black sludge they call coffee?"

She smiled, looping her arm through his. She couldn't tell him no, that she didn't want to take him back to the cottage for fear of Bauer being there, so there was no reason to wait. She doubted Bauer would be there this time of day anyway, so at least she could relax a little.

As soon as the cottage came into view, Eva searched for Bauer's car. It wasn't there, and she breathed a sigh of relief. When they reached the house, she took the key from her purse that Bauer finally gave her and unlocked the door. She hoped that there wasn't something of Bauer's that would give away who she lived with.

They took off their coats and shoes and went into the living room. Dr. Möller sat on the couch at the behest of Eva. She insisted she could build the fire without his help. Once she got it lit, she came to sit beside him.

"So, how have you been? How is it in Berlin?"

"I am doing well. And Berlin, it is the same. The bombings have picked up again, so it's good that you are not there now." Eva was saddened that the bombings had continued, but she knew they would. He looked around the room. "This is a nice little place. It is too bad that they want you out."

She let her eyes roam the cozy sitting room. "Yes, it's a shame." He couldn't be more wrong.

"So, where are they now?"

"Work," she answered quickly.

"And you live with a couple?"

"Uh, no, just a single person." She needed to divert his attention. Even though she wanted to tell him about Bauer and how he professed his love for her, she couldn't. "Speaking of single, have you found that special someone yet?"

He gave her an aporetic side glance. "We both know that will never happen. Whatever happened to that young man at the ball?"

Her breath hitched in her throat, and she swallowed hard. "He is… on the Russian front."

"I am sorry to hear that. Have you heard anything from him? Do you know how he is?"

She shook her head. "No, and I don't think I will. Where are you staying?" She wanted to change the topic from her.

"At a hotel in the center of town."

"Oh, that must be expensive."

"Not for me. The army pays for it." He laughed at the look on her face. "I'm an army officer. They don't make me pay for housing when stationed abroad."

"Sorry, I always forget that you are in the army. You aren't like the others to me."

"You know, they aren't all bad, Eva."

"Not all of them." Talking about the Germans was a sore spot for her. "So, do you know how long you will be stationed in France?"

"No. For a little while, though, I imagine. What about you? How long will you be here?"

Truthfully, she had no idea. What Dr. Möller didn't know was that it wasn't up to her. Everything about her foreseeable future was in the hands of Bauer. "I'm not sure. I guess I will play it by ear. I might hate it here and decide to leave."

"Where would you go?"

"Truthfully, I don't know. But I have a feeling I will be here for a while. How have Ingrid, Liesel, and Heidi been? I miss them."

"They miss you too. I hadn't suspected that you and Ingrid would become so close, but I'm glad you have each other. It's not the same there without you," he chuckled. "I think even Frau Wagner misses you, but she would never admit it."

"Why do you think she misses me?"

"We got some new nurses in last week, and she compares them to you. I once heard her say that you were a good nurse, smart and hardworking, and that it would be hard for them to live up to your reputation, but that they better try."

"She really said that?"

"She did. It surprised me as well. She is a stern woman, but I think there is good somewhere under all that hard exterior." He patted her on the knee. "Well, I better be on my way and let you get on with your day."

She usually would argue with that, but she didn't want Bauer coming home while Dr. Möller was there. "We should get together tomorrow, maybe for dinner or something," she said.

"I would like that. I'll come to the hospital. What time do you get off?"

"I work the early morning shift, so I'll be off at three."

"I'll pick you up, but in a car. It is too cold to be walking."

"It is rather cold, isn't it?"

"It is colder than I had expected." He hugged Eva, then left.

She watched him from the window, missing him already. But she was so happy he was here. She turned around and sat back on the couch, crossing her arms over her chest to guard against the cold, and stared into the fire. Her stomach rumbled, and she realized it must be later than she had thought. She glanced at the clock. It was a quarter past six. "I better make dinner." She stood and headed for the kitchen. She would make something small and easy, then probably spend the rest of the evening in her room.

She started preparing the food when she heard the front door open and close, then the familiar sound of boots on the tile. She froze, hovering the spoon above the bowl, waiting to see what he was going to do. This was the first time he had been home around dinner time since their talk. The boots creaked on the hardwood floor as they came down the hall towards the kitchen. She listened to him enter the room and sensed his presence behind her, but she didn't turn around. The awkward silence in the air was growing, and she couldn't stand it any longer. She had to say something.

"Do you want some dinner?" She didn't turn to look at him.

For a long moment, the kitchen was silent, then he spoke. "What are you making?"

"We have a small piece of pork left and some potatoes, so I was going to cook them up before they went bad. There isn't a lot, but I think it will be enough for the two of us."

"Fine."

His footsteps retreated, and when they creaked on the stairs, she finally turned. He was so curt and cold towards her.

In some ways, she couldn't blame him. He told her he loved her, and her only response was that she would try to forget he ever said it and that she couldn't bring herself to love a monster. She remembered how rejected she had felt when Gerhardt told her they couldn't be together because he was back with his fiancé. He wasn't mean about it and even admitted that he still loved her. He reciprocated her love and let her know that she would always have a part of him. Bauer had no part of her, not her love, passion, or body, and she had no commitment to him. But, if she was being honest with herself, the way she had felt about him in the past had changed. No longer did she hate him, that much she knew. She wasn't even sure she still disliked him. But, she didn't know how she felt about him or thought of him. She couldn't deny he had done a lot for her and that she more than likely owed her life to him. But what feelings do you direct towards a person who had been so cruelly calculated to you in the past but nice to you in the present? She no longer felt the searing hatred and loathing or the fear when she thought of him, but it wasn't love either. It was like a blank canvas. Nothing was there, and she could paint it however she wanted from this moment on. Although she couldn't paint it without him, and he had once again closed himself off to her, probably for good. But how could she have known what he had done for her? He wanted her to think that he hated her, perhaps because he was trying to convince himself that he did, and it would be easier for him if she thought so as well.

I can't worry about him now. I have too many other things to think about. I do not need another man in my life, especially that one. She sliced the potatoes into cubes, more forcefully than was necessary, and tossed them in the pot of boiling water. She didn't hate him, but she was furious at him for putting her in this situation. She couldn't help but feel that it would have been better if he had kept his feelings to himself.

She set two plates and two cups on the table, the plate with the pork and a bowl with the potatoes in the middle. She sat down in one chair to wait for him, but when it was clear he wasn't coming down now, she ate without him. She wasn't going to go upstairs to tell him that the food was ready.

She dipped some potatoes onto her plate and took one of the small pork slices. She bit into the salty meat and savored the flavor. Above her, the floorboards creaked, and she tensed in anticipation of him coming downstairs. Part of her wanted to talk to him about the other night. But she didn't know if she should or if he even would. The heavy footsteps descended the stairs, and after a few seconds, Bauer appeared in the kitchen entryway. He looked at the food on the table and then at her. Without saying a word, he came to the table and pulled out the chair across from her, its legs screeching on the tile, then sat down. He dipped out some potatoes and took the last piece of pork.

For a while, they ate in silence, not looking up from their plates. Eva knew it was now or never. If she was going to have an opportunity to speak to him, this was as good a time as any. "Is this how it will be between us now?"

"No. Because you will be moving out."

Eva knew immediately that he wasn't just referring to the fact that she was looking for an apartment but that she had no choice. He was going to make her leave. "OK. Is this going to be how it is until I move out?" He glanced up, then looked back down at his plate and took another bite of potato. "Look, I'm sorry. You took me by surprise."

"Don't, Eva. You knew exactly what you were saying and meant every word. You know how I feel now, but you will never hear those words from me again. I'm over it, and eventually, I will be over you." He abruptly stood up, taking his plate and cup to the sink. "You need to find an apartment soon because I'm leaving for Paris in a few weeks, and the house will be locked back up."

"Paris? Why are you going to Paris?" The feeling she had at him returning to Paris confused her.

"Make sure you have a place to stay before then," he said as he left the kitchen.

She was convinced now that there would be no reconciliation between them. Whatever he felt for her was dying, and there was nothing she could do to stop it. She jumped when the front door slammed. She was mad now. Angry with him and upset with herself. She put her dishes in the sink and went to the closet in the hall to retrieve her coat and shoes. She would wash the dishes later because right now, she needed a walk to calm down and clear her head.

The frozen snow crunched beneath her shoes as she walked, fighting against the chill of the night air. Her scarf was wrapped around her nose and mouth and over the top of her head to cover her ears. She wasn't walking in any particular direction, just aimlessly wandering the city. It was dark and quiet, even though curfew hadn't started. She was happy to be alone, hidden in the darkness.

Her thoughts raced, her head hurt, and her stomach was unsettled. Nothing in this time had been what she had expected or could have ever imagined. She was lost in every sense of the word. There wasn't a single thing that was clear to her anymore, not her thoughts, feelings, place in the world, purpose, absolutely nothing. She was drowning in this ocean of confusion and fear. She wanted to be anywhere but here, anywhere other than Europe. She knew everyone gets scared, but she felt like her constant worry and loneliness were consuming her.

The movement of something to her right caught her attention. She looked across the street to see a man walking in the same direction as her. He looked at the ground, his hat low on his head and his collar pulled up high around his neck, covering most of his face. He did not alarm her at first, but when she noticed the presence of someone behind her, the hair on her head stood on end. Eva glanced over her shoulder and locked eyes with the man who was following seven or eight feet behind her. Like the man across the street, his hat was low on his head, and he looked to the ground, walking with his hands in his pockets. At first, she wasn't sure if they were following her or if it was just coincidental, so she turned down the next street, and the man behind her did the same. The man across the street also turned down the same road as her but stayed on the other side. Her heart spiked, and her breaths were rapid. She wasn't sure what to do because she didn't know who they were or if they knew where she lived, or even why they were following her. Her eyes darted around, searching for another person or a means of escape, but she didn't see either. She turned down another street, and so did the men. She decided her only option now was to run because she couldn't fight both of them, and she wasn't about to risk them catching her. If she could get back to the cottage, maybe she stood a chance of escaping them. She bolted into a full sprint, praying she didn't slide or fall on the ice. She could hear their shoes in the snow behind her, just above her labored breathing. She ran faster, pushing her legs and lungs to their limit. She dared a glance over her shoulder. The two men were gaining on her. Their flat shoes allowed them better traction and speed. She wondered if screaming would help, but she was afraid she didn't have the breath for it.

She knew they were closer to her now because she could hear their breathing; it was almost as loud as her own. She focused on the snow-covered road ahead and tried to push herself harder. She could see the street the cottage was on, only yards away now. She didn't slow when turning right onto the street, and her feet slid in the snow, then she fell forward onto her hands and knees. Quickly, she got to her feet and tried to run, but her feet slipped back and forth on the slick, compacted snow on the corner of the sidewalk. The two men rounded the corner, also sliding on the frozen snow. The first man caught himself on the brick wall of the building while the other man grabbed onto the back of him.

She finally gained a little traction, but when she tried to run her high-heeled shoes slid around on the ice, almost making her fall again, and she, too, used the wall for support. Just then, a hand grabbed onto her coat, pulling her backward, down towards the sidewalk. Her head hit with a dull thud as the back of it contacted the pavement. For the first time, she screamed and pulled at the hand that now had hold of her hair, prying at the fingers as they twisted tighter. The other man came to stand over her, kicking her in the side. She curled into a ball on her side to protect the more vulnerable parts of her body and covered her head with her arms. The man drew his foot back and kicked her again, then rolled her onto her back and stood over her, bending one knee down into the snow. He took a gun from the inside pocket of his coat and went to cock it. Eva lifted her leg just as the hammer was pulled back, kneeing him in the groin as hard as she could. His face contorted before he fell onto his butt, holding himself with his hands, dropping the gun in the snow. She took advantage of his temporary delay and hurried to her feet, but the other man lunged for her, and she yelped as they both went down. He landed on her back and she grunted, emptying her lungs as he knocked the breath out of her. He struggled to his knees and she twisted, jabbing him in the jaw with her elbow, a popping sound coming from it. She crawled from underneath him and ran, crossing the street, the cottage now in view. She broke into a cold sweat, the adrenaline and fear taking over as she ran, her legs numb from the exertion and cold. Her lungs were starving for air, but she couldn't stop now because the cottage was only a few hundred feet away. Even so, she wondered if she would make it.

Headlights blinded her as a car turned down the street she was on. It pulled in front of the cottage, and she knew it was

Bauer coming home for the night. She could only think of one other time she was this relieved to see him. Eva was so focused on reaching him that she didn't even want to scream or call out. She needed to get to the car, and soon. The back door opened, and Bauer stepped out, facing her direction. The driver's door also opened, and Bauer's orderly got out of the car, leaving the engine running and the headlights on. She ran at him so fast that she almost slid past him, but Bauer grabbed onto her, almost taking them both down, but only she slid and fell. His face was unreadable and set like a stone. He let go of Eva, turning to the men who had been pursuing her. The two men slid to a stop, then turned to run back the other way when Bauer pulled a pistol from his side holster, aimed it at the man closest to him, and pulled the trigger. Eva instinctively covered her ears when the shot echoed loudly off the buildings as she stared down the street. The man fell face down on the street, the snow around him turning red as blood slowly trickled out of the hole in the back of his head. Bauer was now aiming for the second man. His orderly had also pulled out his gun and aimed it down the street at the fleeing man. They both took a shot but were aiming lower, hitting the man several times in the back of his legs. He collapsed, screaming, and held onto his left leg. He then. let go, rolled onto his stomach and tried to pull himself along the road.

"Get him. Put him in the car, and I will make a call," Bauer told his orderly. His orderly nodded. "Come with me." Bauer roughly pulled Eva to her feet by the upper arm and led her to the cottage. He unlocked the door and escorted her inside, slamming it behind them. He led her into the living room, shoving her on the couch. He then went to the phone that hung on the wall at the end of the hall. The dial turned, there was a few seconds of silence, and then he spoke rapidly in German, giving orders for some of his men to come and retrieve the body in the road and the man his orderly was holding outside.

While Bauer talked on the phone, Eva looked down at her shaking hands and realized that her palms were bloody, the hose on her right leg was torn, and both of her knees were scraped as fresh bruises turned an angry shade of black and purple. She held her hands out in front of her and focused on the sticky red that covered them. They trembled uncontrollably, as did her legs, and without warning, her stomach churned, and she vomited on the floor at her feet. He hung up the receiver and stepped into the living room entryway, his arms at his sides as he focused on her. She turned her head towards him, wiping her mouth with the back of her hand. They stayed this way for a while, neither of them speaking when finally he turned and went into the kitchen. Pouring water was the only sound in the house. It ran for a few seconds, then stopped and he returned with a wet dish towel and a cup of water. He sat the cup on the side table and held out the towel for her. She slowly reached for it, locking eyes with him, taking the towel from his outstretched hand.

"I will give you a few minutes to compose yourself, and then you will tell me why those men were chasing you." His voice was stern but controlled.

She wiped her mouth, then cleaned the vomit off the floor with the towel the best she could. She took it to the kitchen and tossed it in the sink. She would take care of it later. She returned to the living room and drank some of the water Bauer had brought for her, holding the cup in her lap. Bauer was sitting in the chair across from her, legs crossed, hands resting on the armrests. He stared at her contentiously, waiting for her explanation. His expression was stern and heated. "I have never seen those men before."

"But you do know who they are?"

"No. I told you I have never seen them."

He took a deep breath, nostrils flaring, having to work harder now to contain his anger. He uncrossed his legs and leaned forward. "You will not lie to me. If I even think you are lying or holding something back, I will have you brought in along with the man I shot. Do not think for a second I won't."

Eva felt like she might vomit again. She took a deep, shuttering breath to calm herself. This was it. She was going to have to tell him more than she thought she ever would. But what would he do with this information? "Wilhelm…," she said. "I want to tell you the truth, I want to trust you." Wilhelm remained quiet. "I don't know who those men are, that is the truth, but I think I know why they are after me." He didn't say anything, just motioned with his hand for her to continue. "I think they are with the resistance."

"Why would the resistance be after you?"

She wondered if he already knew the answer to that question. "They approached me years ago when I was in Paris with Madame Blanc. They wanted me to join them, but I didn't. I think they believe I am a collaborator, so they want me dead. I guess I am a collaborator. I'm in love with a

German, and I live with a German. The people I associate with the most are German. I think the French people hate the collaborators more than they hate the Germans. I can only imagine what they do to collaborators."

"And nothing more than a suspicion would warrant them hunting you? I think a part is missing in your story," he said, a clear warning in his voice.

"I don't fully understand it either. There is obviously something I am missing, too."

"There is a lot I am missing. I am giving you this opportunity to tell me, here, in the cottage, right now at your leisure, where you are safe and unharmed, but Eva, I cannot go easy on you. If you do not tell me everything, I will have to bring you in and get the information another way." He paused and looked away, fighting with some unspoken emotion before turning back to her. "As I look at you, sitting there in the state you are in, bloodied and vulnerable, I feel sorry for you. I want to help you, but I can't if you don't help me. Do not think that we are on good terms. Part of me wishes they had killed you because when I think of you, my mind is in a fury of rage and anger. But if they had killed you, your death would haunt me for the rest of my life. I could never forgive myself for letting it happen. Do you see the dilemma I am in? And those are just some of the things I am grappling with, and I still have my duty to uphold. All these things are fighting each other, competing for my loyalty, but they cannot all win. If you do not tell me what is going on or what you are mixed up in, I will be forced to choose my duty over you, no matter the outcome or how I wish it to be. I will never abandon my duty to Germany, but I think I can do both. Help you, and remain loyal. But if they conflict, I will have to decided which one is more important to me. Ideally, I won't have to choose, as long as I keep one secret and separate from the other. But I can't keep saving you, especially if you are unwilling to cooperate."

He was going to leave her with no choice. He had finally given her an ultimatum. She dropped her gaze to the floor. "What do you want to know?

"Everything."

"This is hard. It has never been easy for me. I am alone here, stripped of everything I once knew. I feel vulnerable, and it frightens me because you hold all the cards."

"You are at the end of your rope, Eva."

"I know." The only part she could leave out now was that she came from the future because of course he didn't suspect that. "A man in Paris approached me and offered me the opportunity to fight the Germans. I decided I didn't want to take the risk, and I was going to tell him no when we met again. He never showed, though, and I don't know why. But after Sabine died, I decided I wanted to be in the resistance, so when I got to Germany, I found ways to let the resistance know I was willing to help, and they found me." She looked from the floor to him. He was deep in thought as he sat quietly, his expression giving nothing away. He didn't even ask follow-up questions. She drew in a deep breath. "A spy that had infiltrated the resistance betrayed me, but the resistance thought it was me who betrayed them and tried to have me killed. I was being chased by them the night I showed up at

137

your apartment and fainted. It was them who broke into my apartment."

In some way, she was relieved he knew now. Telling him lifted a weight off her shoulders, but now she needed to tell him about her involvement in the attack on his life, only she didn't quite know how to say the words. She had been afraid to face the fear of what he would do with this information. The knowledge that she helped in almost killing him was sure to nuke what little remained between them. She stood from the couch and moved to the fireplace, feeling as if she was embarking on an irrevocable course.

"The attack, the one that almost killed you. I was there because I helped. I was in the car." She didn't want to turn around, but she had to. She needed to see his face, to try to understand what was going on in his head after her confession. She slowly turned her back to the fireplace; his calm, collected expression vanished and was replaced with anger. An anger so intense, a look so frightening she couldn't help but back away, bumping into the mantel. She knew his anger was inexorable.

He stood from the chair, his gaze taking her in for a long moment, fire blazing in his eyes as his demeanor filled with rage, boiling to the surface. He abruptly walked toward her, and she held her breath, pressing her back to the stone beside the fireplace. His hand rose, balling into a fist as if he was going to strike her. She winced, squeezing her eyelids closed, preparing for the blow, but it never came. Instead, he punched the wall next to her head, and she flinched. She felt as if maybe she would have deserved it, deserved whatever punishment he threw at her for what she had done to him.

"Get out of my sight!" he hissed, low and venomous. "I can't look at you right now without wanting to put my hands round your neck and squeeze the life from you," he said through clenched teeth. He stepped back away from her, both of his hands balled into fists firmly at his sides, his breathing slow and deep. A heavy silence hung in the air, and she could feel his irate energy. He always had a predatory nature, but it had never been so apparent before. The only other time she had ever seen him looking so wild and dangerous was when she watched him fighting in the ring.

She hurried past him without looking in his direction and up the stairs to her room, closed the door, and slid to the floor.

Chapter Ten

Eva didn't know how long she had been sitting on the floor when finally she stood and laid on the bed. She didn't understand what she felt outside of being terrified of Bauer. His fierce eyes would haunt her in her sleep. She was aware that he was still downstairs and a part of her wanted to go back down and talk to him, for reasons she failed to understand, but didn't dare leave the bedroom. "How the hell did you end up here?" she asked herself. Jon said Bauer would save her, but how could that be true? How could this brute downstairs be her savior? As a child she believed in fairytales, that prince charming always rescued the princess, but maybe he wasn't a prince at all. Perhaps he was actually the monster disguised as the prince? She felt like her whole life she has needed people for stability, like pillars to hold her up. Had she let Bauer in because he was her pillar now, the first person in this time strong enough for her to lean on? If he was a prince, she was in his kingdom now, and prince charming, and beast were the same man. Was it not possible to get her happy ending unless she loved both men in her life? But loving Bauer would mean loving all of him, the man, and the monster inside the man. She didn't really have a choice anymore, he was now her anchor, protecting and caring for her.

Hadn't she wanted this, though? Didn't she want him to rescue her, even if that meant being loved by him? Hadn't she asked for all of this? She sat up on the bed. "Didn't you ask for this? Huh, didn't you ask for it?" she whispered. "I am so stupid!" She pounded the bed several times with her fists, silently screaming inside. *Do I need to say now that I love him and that I can live like this, live here in this time? Should I say anything except the truth about the doubt hiding behind all my clouded emotions? But what if I don't love him? What if I can't love him?* she thought. Was welcoming his love the only way she was to survive this war? She was aware of the conflict that was now beginning to encircle her. Would loving him be moving from propriety? She could only imagine what sins he kept hidden from the world. She was sure there were many. *What cruel jokes God plays on us,* she thought. *My only option is to find sanctuary in the home of the enemy.*

She looked around her dark room, staring into the nothingness. When a car door slammed outside, she jumped. The front door opened, and voices downstairs echoed through the house, then the front door opened and closed again and the house fell into an empty silence. She stood and went to her bedroom door and opened it crack, listening for any noise in the house. There was nothing but a deathly silence, so she opened her door all the way and quietly made her way down

141

the stairs. She looked out the front window, but the street was dark, and Bauer's car was gone. This was possibly the most scared she had ever felt for so many different reasons. Bauer just might have her shot this time; no matter what he says his feelings are for her.

Out of nowhere, exhaustion overtook her, and she could hardly keep her eyes open. Whatever was going to happen would happen no matter where she slept, so she pulled the blanket from the back of the couch and laid down, closing her eyes. Her sleep was restless, and dream after dream of Bauer and the men chasing her played in her mind like a horror movie. In one dream, Bauer actually punched her. In another dream, the men chasing her caught her, and she didn't get away like in reality. Telling Bauer, she helped in trying to kill him played on repeat. But one dream was different from all the others. Bauer had her arrested and brought to the jail in the middle of town. Two men pulled her outside to an enclosed courtyard and shoved her against a wall. She now faced a firing squad of eight men, and Bauer stood off to their side, hands clasped behind his back, and the evilest smile spread across his face as he eyed her. He told them to aim, and all the guns went up, pointing at her as she stared down the barrels. She didn't think she could stay standing any longer because her legs shook violently. "Fire!" he yelled.

The loud echo off the brick walls from the simultaneous firing jolted Eva from her nightmare. She blinked, staring into the flickering flames in the fireplace. She watched them gently caressing the inside of the fireplace. She fought the exhaustion as she replayed the dream, when she had a realization. *I didn't build a fire,* she thought, trying to make sense of it. She scanned the room with her eyes and caught sight of a man sitting in the chair across from her. She bolted upright on the couch, the blanket sliding off her torso, fear the only thing keeping her seated. Bauer calmly watched her from across the room, his face emotionless, completely unreadable, all the while her emotions were written all over her face and in her body language. She remembered her last dream and wondered if it was a glimpse of what was to come. "Are you here to arrest me?"

"I had seriously considered it, but no."

"So what now?" Eva honestly did not know how to move forward because she didn't know what he would do, and it all rested on his decision.

He pressed his fingertips together and tapped his thumbs. "Tomorrow, you will be moving into an apartment across from the hospital."

"Why tomorrow?"

"Because you cannot stay here. I told you that already. We can no longer live together. I am not speaking of decorum either. Besides, I killed one of the men who was chasing you and captured the other one, but there are more, and I don't know who they are. I have been trying to infiltrate the French resistance for a long time now, but they are smart and careful. They know where you live and will not hesitate to come after you again. How did you get away from them?"

"They grabbed me, knocking me to the ground, then one straddled me and pulled a gun. And I kicked him in the... well, you know."

"Yes, I do. You will not always get a chance like that. Do you know how to fight at all?"

"I've never been in a fight if that is what you mean."

"I mean, do you know how to defend yourself if it came to it? You can't carry a gun, so you need to learn how to use your body as a weapon and be as lethal as you can. I can't keep saving you."

"To fight someone one-on-one, no, I don't think I would win."

"Well, we need to change that. I will vow to you that you will not come to harm by my hands."

"Because you love me?"

His eyes darkened. "No, Eva. I opened that door for you once, but it has since closed. I still have to go to Paris soon, but in the meantime, I can teach you to fight. But not for a few days until your hands are better."

She glanced down at the dry blood still on her palms and knee. She reached around and touched the back of her head, her fingertips rubbing against the crusty scab matted in her hair.

"I will help you with that, too. Then we need to go to bed. I have an early start tomorrow, and you need to pack." Without waiting for her to answer, he left the room and went up the stairs. After a few minutes, he returned with some alcohol, a roll of gauze, and a bowl of water with a rag floating in it. He placed the things on the nightstand and sat beside her on the couch. "Give me one of your hands." He more demanded than asked. She held out her right hand, and he took it in his, pulling it towards him without ceremony, then reached into the bowl and rung out the towel. He gently wiped at her palm, but never did he look at her face.

She didn't know why the tenderness of this action hit her so hard, but that combined with the stress of the day, and the roller coaster of emotions finally steamrolled her. She started to cry, the tears falling onto her lap. Somehow, him being here now helped numb the pain she was feeling. How many times had he helped her get through a challenging situation? More than once, that was for sure. She hadn't realized until recently that she had gotten used to him caring for her. But he pulled the rug from underneath her with his comment about that door now being closed.

He stopped wiping her hand and lifted his eyes to her. Something flashed in them, but in a second, it was gone. He brought his attention back down to her hand and resumed cleaning it. He took the alcohol from the table and poured some on her palm. An instant burning pain filled her senses, and she instinctively tried to pull her hand back, but he held on tightly, not letting her pull her hand free. He laid her hand on his knee, picked up the gauze, and wrapped some around a few times, then tied it. "Give me your other hand." Without a word, she stretched her other hand out to him, and he did the same to it. When he finished he laid her hand in her lap. "Turn around so I can clean the blood from your hair," he instructed.

"No. I can wash it out in the shower."

"How, you have bandages on your hands?" She was too tired to argue, so she turned, facing her back to him and waited. She could feel him taking her hair out of the partial bun that somehow remained, even after being attacked. One by one, he took out the pins and fingered the matted knots of hair away from the wound, then dabbed at it with the damp towel. She winced from the pain, but he still said nothing. She was dying to know what he was thinking, but she didn't believe he would ever open up to her again. She was floored that he was helping her, even after she confessed to assisting in the attack that almost killed him.

"Why are you helping me now that you know what I did?"

"I had time to think about everything, and I realized that the attack would have happened, whether you were there or not. I think you felt guilty about the part you played, which is why you chose to save me. If you had not been there, you never would have felt that guilt and would not have saved my life. My existence now is born of that guilt."

She turned to face him. "I don't understand what any of this means."

"You don't have to understand."

"I think I do. You hate me, then you love me, and now you hate me again. Sometimes you are nice to me, like now, and other times you are so unkind. I know you have a heart in there, but where do you keep it?"

"Hidden away."

"Why?"

"Because love can be so very cruel and dangerous. Or should I say, the object of one's love can be."

"So you choose to keep your heart locked away?"

"I had, but I failed at that, apparently."

"But don't you think something good can come from our experiences of pain?"

"I'm sure it happens occasionally."

"Love isn't supposed to hurt. It should bring joy and happiness."

He made a low chuckle to himself. "It's not called gently stepping into love. It's called falling in love. Falling in love could be as painless as falling off a chair, or it can be like falling off a cliff. With you, it's the latter. We are done having this conversation. Now turn back around so I can finish."

She did as he told her, and he meticulously cleaned the dry blood out of her hair, then dabbed some alcohol on it. When he finished, she turned back towards him, and he looked down at her knee, the blood now dry, gluing her stocking to the skin. His eyes met hers, the question clear in them. Eva couldn't help but feel that it would be awkward for him to clean the blood from her leg. It somehow felt too intimate a thing to happen between them. "It's alright. I can clean it myself." With that, he stood and started for the stairs. "Thank you," she called. He gave her a curt nod, then disappeared out of the room. She couldn't have realistically expected a warmer response from him.

She didn't sleep well that night. Her hands and head throbbed as a dull pain radiated from her right knee, and she intermittently cried throughout the night. When her alarm went off, she sat up in bed feeling groggy. She threw off the covers and planted her feet on the floor, the cold wood instantly sending a chill through her body. She hadn't showered or bathed in over a day, and it was a must before she went to work. She peeled off yesterday's clothes she had slept in, dropping them to the floor, then removed the bandages from her hands, looking at the angry scrapes that covered her palms. It brought back the memory of last night and how meticulously gentle he was in wrapping them. How tender he was in the way he wiped the sores, the softness of his grip, the way he cared for her. She stepped into the shower, continuing the monologue in her head. The things he has done recently seemed so contradictory to his usual demeanor. He confounded her in a way no other person ever had.

She carefully rinsed the shampoo from her hair, so she didn't aggravate the sores on her hands further. She turned off the water and stepped out of the tub, the chill in the air making goose pimples form on her skin. She dried off, dressed, re-bandaged her hands, then tended to her knee. Her body was sore all over, but the real pain was inside. Her feelings were bruised. Not just her feelings, but her pride and her righteous indignation had been thwarted. He had finally broken down the only weapon she had against him. The idea that she was in the right, he was in the wrong, and that she was a good person, but he was an awful human being. That idea is what kept him separate from her. The divide between them that she felt was essential. She needed that clear, defining line between the good and bad sides, America versus Germany, her against him. But there was no line anymore. It wasn't even clear who the bad one was anymore. Not the countries, that was still obvious to her, but it was muddled when it came to her and him. Was he truly as bad as she had always thought? It was clear to her now that she had to reassess him. She had to consider everything. Not just how she observed him on the surface, but how he treated other people, ones he knew and ones he didn't, and how he treated her. His behavior towards her was different than it was for other people. She knew this. She didn't doubt his sincerity in his feelings for her, but she was sure he was now trying to kill those feelings. The question was, did she let him diminish them, and to what end? If he succeeded, what did that mean for her? Would he let the resistance have her, or would he finish her off himself? The thought was horrible. But, if she encouraged his feelings, and they blossomed, did that mean she had to give herself to him? Both outcomes were almost equally terrifying.

She quickly ate breakfast, then made her way to the hospital, trying to keep warm as she maneuvered the city streets. She remembered that she was supposed to have dinner with Dr. Möller after work and that he was going to pick her up. How would she find time to pack? She knew Bauer would be pissed if she wasn't packed when he got home.

She passed the hours at work in a blur, trying to force a solution to her most recent predicament into her mind. But she came up short every time. She really felt like she was only left with choices and no answers, and those were to let Bauer love her or to drive his hatred further. He had said that he hated her even more because he loved her. Perhaps he was using that to fuel his feeling for her now.

"Nurse Abrams, someone is here for you."

Eva turned to see nurse Lavigne standing behind her. She was a tall, slender, busty brunette woman. Eva guessed her to be in her early twenties and thought she looked like a movie star. "Thank you." Eva knew it must be Dr. Möller waiting for her. She finished taking inventory of the medicine cabinet, stamped her time card, then met Dr. Möller in the lobby.

He smiled when he caught sight of her, but it quickly fell when he noticed her hands. "What happened to you?" Concern was etched on his face.

"Nothing. I fell on some ice yesterday while I was on a walk. It was stupid really, just me being clumsy." She was happy her hair hid the sore on the back of her head. "I have a favor to ask."

"Sure."

"Can we eat at my house? I have to move out today and haven't even had time to pack."

"You have to move out today?" He furrowed his brows and stared as if he had misheard her.

"Yes. They informed me yesterday. It's OK because I have an apartment just across the street from here."

"Well, that was an unkind thing to do."

"I guess they had their reason." She hoped Dr. Möller and Bauer wouldn't meet, but she didn't know how it could be avoided now. She wasn't sure which apartment Bauer was referring to, and she didn't have a key to it, anyway. She would, unfortunately, have to wait for him to get home before moving out.

"The car is just outside," Dr. Möller said.

She followed him to the large, black Mercedes Benz that was waiting out front. As she slid into the back, she wondered how often she had ridden in a military car with German officers. It was a strange realization that it felt normal to her now. She watched the buildings pass by as the car made its way through town, knowing this would probably be her last time in the cozy cottage she had shared for a short while with Bauer. She wasn't sure how she was supposed to feel about it. She did feel a sense of relief that she wouldn't have to live with him anymore, but at the same time, there was an unfamiliar feeling of sadness and loss in the pit of her stomach. It wasn't like the loss she felt with Gerhardt. This feeling was alien to her.

"Eva, are you alright?"

She turned away from the window and looked at Klaus, forcing a small smile. "Yes. Why?"

"You seem distant. Like something unpleasant is occupying your mind. Is it?"

She wrung her hands. "Sort of, but I can't tell you about it now. Maybe soon."

"I hope you know you can tell me anything, anytime. Day or night."

"I know. And I would tell you if I thought you could help, but you can't. This is something I have to do on my own." His expression was tight as he looked at her. It was obvious he thought she was in some kind of trouble, and of course, she was. He turned away from her and looked forward, staring out the windshield, his arms crossed over his chest.

When the car pulled to the curb, she stopped breathing. Bauer's car was parked right in front of them. Why was he home so early? He was seldom home this early.

Dr. Möller looked at her, then back to the other car. "Are you expecting company?"

"No... I'm not."

"Is there a reason the Gestapo would be visiting the owner of the house?"

She turned in her seat to see him better. "He lives here." It took all the courage she could muster to tell him that.

His head snapped towards her. "You live with a Gestapo officer?"

"I do, but not after today."

"You didn't tell me the owners of the house were boarding you with him."

"No, Klaus, no one else lives here. The military owns the house now. The people who used to live here fled before the Germans invaded."

He narrowed his eyes, squeezing his brows together. "I'm sorry, I don't understand. You live alone with a Gestapo officer?"

"Yes, but it was only temporary."

"How did this happen? I'm not criticizing; I'm just trying to understand."

She looked at the house. The faint glow of the fire could be seen through the window. "We sort of have a history. I was coming here too, so he offered me a place to stay until I found an apartment of my own."

"Why is he making you leave now, then?"

"Well, he is leaving for Paris soon, so he needed me out of the house."

"That doesn't make sense. Why would he need you out of the house? It would not be an inconvenience to let you stay even when he was gone."

"I don't know, but he said he does, so I'm leaving. He is the one who found my new apartment."

"Eva, what is going on? There is more to it than that, but you're not telling me. You understand that you are crazy living with this man, whoever he is?"

"I suppose I am. We should go in and get my stuff."

"Yes. Let's get you out of this house and away from this man."

He followed her to the front door while his driver waited in the car. She hesitated for a second before opening the door and stepping across the threshold. She didn't bother to remove her coat or shoes and went straight into the living room. Bauer was sitting in the chair he always did, reading papers in his lap. He turned to look at her, and surprise registered on his face when he saw Dr. Möller follow her into the room. His hat was on the side table, and his jacket was unbuttoned, showing his white shirt and suspenders. He laid the papers on the armrest and stood, buttoning his jacket. It was strange for her to think that he was a lieutenant colonel and Dr. Möller only a Major, given the age difference. Dr. Möller gave him a perfunctory salute, and Bauer gave him one back.

"Eva tells me you were kind enough to offer her a place to say while she found an apartment?"

Bauer's eyes flashed to Eva, then back to him. "Yes, I did. But she is moving into her apartment today."

"So I heard. I see that you are in the Gestapo. Are you stationed here? You look familiar?" He did not know who Bauer was because Eva never told him. And she never mentioned that he was the officer who had her arrested all those times. She was happy this was their first time meeting.

A smile broke at the corner of Bauer's mouth, and he glanced at Eva, understanding she had said nothing to the doctor. "I'm stationed here, yes. I am the head of the Gestapo in France. I look familiar to you because you treated me some time ago. I was in the hospital you worked at in Berlin. I was one of the wounded from the attack on the German high command. You operated on me."

Dr. Möller focused a little closer on him, and recognition registered on his face. "I do remember you now. I am glad to see that you are doing well. I'm thankful that you have been so generous to Eva."

"Thank you. Yes, I have been quite generous with her." He gave Eva a knowing look. She didn't know why, but she blushed, turning her head away.

"We are going to go upstairs and get her things now," Klaus told him.

Bauer nodded once. "I will help you carry it to the car, and then you will follow me in my car to the apartment. I have the key, and I will help bring her things up."

"We won't be long." Dr. Möller climbed the stairs behind Eva then to her room. Once they were inside, he closed the door and took her hand, pulling her to the bed. He sat her on the edge and focused on her face. A disbelieving, horrified expression was set into hard lines on his usual calm, gentle face. "Are you out of your goddamn mind? Do you understand who this man is? If he is telling the truth about his identity, which I'm sure he is, then you are an idiot. I don't know him personally, but I have heard of him. There is a reason the rest of the army doesn't like the SS." Dr. Möller pointed to the bedroom door. "This officer is an extremely dangerous man and very good at camouflaging it. If he commands the Gestapo in France, then he is someone to be avoided. You do not know the kind of things I've heard that these guys do over here. Maybe I should tell you to strike a little fear into you."

She felt like a disobedient, petulant child being disciplined. "I know the kind of things they do."

"But yet you chose to live with him. What has gotten into you to contemplate such a thing?"

Her eyes watered, and she was afraid they would spill over any minute. "Because there was no gracious way to refuse."

Dr. Möller sat on the bed beside her and put an arm around her shoulders as a father would. "I didn't mean to upset you, Eva. I'm trying to make you understand the seriousness of the situation."

Eva wiped the corner of her eyes with her knuckle. "I understand that part. I'm sorry. I seem to cry a lot these days." She wanted to tell Klaus everything. Her involvement in the attack on Bauer, his reaction when he learned of it, having had her arrested in the past and almost tortured, and his confession that he loved her. She hoped she would comfortable enough to tell him one day.

"It's all right. Let's pack up your things and get out of here." She stood and peered down at him, the sorrow in her eyes hard to miss. She went to the side of the bed and pulled out her two suitcases. They quickly took her clothes from the armoire and the things from her dresser and put them in her bags. She then went to the bathroom and retrieved her toiletries, putting them in her small tote bag. They gathered her last remaining things, then carried the bags downstairs, sitting them by the front door.

"We are ready. We will put the things in the car and wait for you there."

"No need, I'm ready now," Bauer said. He was already in his trench coat and had his hat and gloves on.

She put the strap of the small bag over her shoulder along with her purse and reached for one of the suitcases. She wrapped her hand around the handle, only to have it pulled from her fingers. She looked up in time to see the back of Bauer, carrying her bag out the open front door. Dr. Möller followed Bauer with her other suitcase, and she watched through the open from door as they put them in the trunk. She regarded the room one last time, then stepped out into the snow and shut the door.

She slid into the backseat with Dr. Möller and watched as Bauer got into the backseat of the car in front of them. "There is something unsettling about that man," he said.

She glanced at the side of his face. He was focused on Bauer's car through the front windshield. "I'm sure he has his demons."

When they arrived at the apartment, Bauer helped carry her things up to the second floor but said little and only stayed long enough to drop off her stuff. He gave Eva a key, bid them adieu, and left. She was relieved that he did.

"Do you want me to help you unpack?"

She surveyed the small, already furnished apartment, then turned to him. "No. I think I've got it. Sorry that I didn't make us dinner."

"Well, seeing how you don't have any food in the apartment, why don't we go out and eat as we had originally planned?"

"That would be great, actually."

Dr. Möller took her to an upscale restaurant near the city center. She would not have gone there for dinner on her own. The price of her meal would have cost her a couple of days' pay. She felt terrible that Klaus was paying for her food, but there was no convincing him otherwise.

"Really, I would have been just as happy with the sandwich I was going to order as I am with the Au Poivre."

"Nonsense. I'm paying, and we are going to have a nice dinner."

She smiled, and her heart swelled as she thought of him. He was so like her father, which was bittersweet. She was happy that she had this wonderful man here that was like a father figure, but at the same time, it made her miss her actual father that much more. She knew she would leave Klaus one day, and the thought was almost incomprehensible to her.

"So, are you going to tell me now what is going on?"

She slowly cut through the pork on her plate with the knife, not looking at him. "I thought I did."

"If you think I believed what you told me was the entire story, then you must not think I'm very intelligent."

She leaned back in her chair, laying the white napkin on the table beside the plate. "Can I have some time? I will tell you."

"How about I tell you what I think is going on, and you nod if I'm right and shake your head if I'm wrong? Would that be easier for you?"

"Maybe. I'm willing to try."

"Alright. I'll start with an easy one. You are in love with the man that was at the dance?" She nodded. He thought for a second. "You being arrested, did that have something to do with that Gestapo officer?" Again, she nodded. "He is monitoring you. Is that why you were living with him?"

"Sort of," she answered.

"But there is something else. Is there more to it than that?"

"So much more," she said as she thought about all that had happened between them.

"I don't think I need to ask, but because I don't know him personally, I will call it infatuation instead of something else." She didn't answer. "Is it mutual?"

She looked at him. "Certainly not."

"My advice to you would be to keep it that away. And you should stay away from him."

"That is something I already know. I will say, however, that it's not going to be easy. I don't believe he will allow it for several reasons."

"What reasons?"

She waited for the waitress to pass by their table before answering. "He doesn't trust me, but it's not all unwarranted. So he will probably always keep tabs on me."

"I see. And the other reasons?"

"It seems he is keeping some information about me from Berlin. I heard secondhand that some papers are missing from my file, and some things have been blacked out. I don't know how much information is being hidden though."

He puzzled over what she said. "I'm going to ask you a question, and I want you to answer it honestly. Has he ever given you a reason to think that he is in love with you? Or has he ever said something to you of that effect?"

"Yes," she answered shamefully.

"Have you encouraged him in any way or led him on?"

"No. When he told me he loved me, he admitted that he knew I didn't love him. I have always made my dislike for him known, so I can't possibly think of what I've done to make him love me. But I believe I would be in prison now or dead if it wasn't for him. He is the devil who loves me. I'm in trouble, aren't I?"

"The SS is ruthless. The Gestapo is made up of heartless men who will stop at nothing to get the people they are hunting. They live in the grey area to get away with whatever they want, not like Berlin cares anyway. They are killing machines. When they are spoken of or seen on the streets, they strike fear in the hearts of the bravest men because they are murderers. If he fell in love with you, that would explain why you are sitting here in front of me now." He looked her squarely in the face. "That love saved you. Do you love him?"

"No!" Eva's voice rose in hurried denial.

"Loving a bad person doesn't make you a bad person, but love makes you stupid, and it can make you do stupid things."

"But I don't love him. I don't believe I could even if I wanted to." She had to tell Klaus what he wanted to hear, not what she was feeling inside.

"I'm glad to hear you say that. It's unfortunate that I say that about my own countrymen. Most of the German military comprises good men, but not all of them are. Sadly, in war, innocence is lost. Don't let this man take yours."

"I know, and I won't."

"Do you even know him?"

"I'm not sure anyone knows him, really. I mean, can you truly know someone like that? Trying to figure him out is like stumbling your way through a labyrinth, but I have managed to navigate through some of his complicated paths. He is single-minded, without pity. He is unable, or maybe he is just unwilling to see or even consider the worth of someone unless it is someone important to him. I believe, even then, that his feelings could change from an all-consuming love to murderous hatred with no trouble. I don't believe he thinks like other men. He is so unpredictable, which I'm sure serves him well. He doesn't wear his feeling on his sleeve, but I think underneath that callous exterior, he has depths no one understands. I think anger is one of his dominant emotions, but instead of yelling and going into fits of rage as some people do, he uses his anger intelligently." She watched Klaus as she told him these things.

"That explains why he is in the SS. Stay away from men like that, Eva. Like you said, no matter what his feelings are for you now, they could change in an instant, so you need to be careful. And remember, the Gestapo can arrest anybody at any time for anything and for any reason."

"I plan on avoiding him in the future."

They finished their food, and Dr. Möller took her back to her apartment. "Thank you again for dinner."

"It was my pleasure. I'll see you at work tomorrow."

"I'm glad you'll be there." He gave her a warm smile and walked away. She shut the door, went to the window, and watched his car drive away.

Chapter Eleven

January 16th, 1942

Her conversation with Klaus wouldn't stop dominating her thoughts, even though it was a few days ago. She was thankful that he hadn't broached the subject of Bauer with her again. As her mind went to Bauer, it fixed on the fact that he had not been by her apartment since the day he helped her move in. He said he would teach her self-defense, but he never specified the details. He didn't say where or when it was to happen. She didn't necessarily want him to teach her, but she had to admit that she didn't exactly not want him to either. She knew it would be good for her to learn, and he would make a fine teacher.

She decided to take her ration card and buy a little more food that afternoon. On her first trip to the market, she had only bought the bare necessities, but now she needed more food if she was to make any kind of proper dinner. It was her day off, and she wanted to relax, so she planned a pamper day. She was alone in the apartment for another week before Ingrid arrived, and she wanted to enjoy her alone time while it lasted.

When she returned to the apartment, she put the food away, made dinner, then ran a bath. She was going to soak in the hot, soapy water, then sit in bed while reading a book as she sipped the wine she splurged on. She took off her clothes and stepped into the tub, lowering herself down into the steaming water. She laid her head on the back of the tub and closed her eyes. The gentle glow of the candles made the atmosphere perfect. It was relaxing and would calm her nerves and anxiety. The tips on her hair were getting wet as they hung down from her messy bun, but she didn't care. She laid her arms along the side of the tub, watching the steam slowly rise from her skin and off the top of the water. Sighing, she closed her eyes again and let herself drift in and out of shallow sleep, feeling more relaxed than she had in a long time. Her thoughts went to her family and home, and then the vacation to Bear Lake when she was thirteen. She remembered making sandcastles, taking the boat out on the crystal water, and falling asleep on the beach with her brother. She and Thomas woke to sunburned bodies that peeled for days. It was a happy memory for her; collecting wood with her dad so he could take it home for his woodshop, her brother playing his guitar at night around the campfire as they sang a duet.

She thought she heard a knock come from the front door. She opened her eyes and listened closer, but it didn't come again. She shut her eyes and returned to her thoughts, but the wrapping was there again. "You have got to be kidding me. Talk about bad timing." She stepped out of the tub and put on her robe, tying the belt tightly around her waist. She opened the bathroom door and peered into the dark apartment. She took one of the candles from the side of the tub into the living room so she wouldn't trip, turned on the light, and then sat it on the end table. She hesitated for a second before cracking open the door and peering around it. Her breath caught when her eyes fell upon Bauer standing in the hall, alone, wearing civilian clothes.

"I was beginning to wonder if you were asleep," he said.

"No… um, I was in the bath." She quickly looked behind her into the apartment, then back at him, not opening the door any farther than the inch it was at. "What are you doing here?" she asked in a whisper.

His relaxed demeanor faded. "To start teaching you to defend yourself."

Her eyes widened. "What, now?"

"Yes, now."

The thought unsettled her. "No. I just got out of the tub. I'm only in a robe, and it's late."

"This is when I'm not busy. I would have been by sooner, but I have had little free time." She gaped at him with her mouth ajar. "Eva, open the damn door." She took a step back, pulling the door further open to admit him. He walked past her, and she closed it. He looked at the lit candle on the end table, and then his eyes drifted to the open bathroom door with the glow of the candles visible. "You better go change unless you want to practice fighting in that." He gestured towards her robe.

Her eyes widened at that thought. She had nothing on under the robe. "Yes, I'll change." She blew the candles out in the bathroom, pulled the plug in the tub, then went to her bedroom and closed the door, making sure it was shut tightly. She looked for appropriate clothing but wasn't sure what to wear. She didn't own any pants, so she opted for a knee-length dress. She wished she had sweat pants, but they hadn't been invented yet. She walked back out into the living room, and when Bauer turned to face her, she lifted her arms then put them back down to her side in a gesture saying, this is all I have.

"You don't own any pants?"

"No, but I guess I should get some."

"I would recommend it."

"So, how are we going to do this?"

"Well, first we need to move the furniture. Grab that end table and lamp and move it over there." He pointed to the wall that separated her bedroom from the living room and kitchen. She slid the table across the room while holding the lamp. Bauer shrugged off his jacket, tossed it on the couch, then rolled up his sleeves, revealing the dark hair on his arms. Then took off his tie and undid the first few buttons on his white shirt. He bent down and pushed the couch up against the wall next to the table. "There, I think that is good enough." He walked to the center of the room. "Come here and stand in front of me." He motioned with his fingers for her to approach.

165

She was feeling extremely nervous about tonight because she didn't know what was going to happen precisely. She took a few steps towards him, stopping a few feet away. "Will this be like when I watched you boxing?"

The left side of his lip curled. "No. This is more like street fighting or bare-knuckle fighting. They both require many of the same skills, but while boxing can help you channel aggression, this is more for defense. I will also teach you things that aren't allowed in the boxing ring. Both fighting styles are raw and violent, and both require hard work and dedication, but in the end, one is more of a sport. Alright, let's get started."

Eva stood still, arms at her sides. "What do I do?"

"First, ball your hands into a fist." She held her hands in front of her, wrapping her fingers around her thumbs. "No, not like that." He closed the distance between them, unfolding her fingers. "Never put your thumb inside your fingers. You run a higher risk of breaking a bone that way. You want to put your thumb on top of your fingers and press your thumb to the second knuckle of your index finger. Like this." He took her right hand and rolled her fingers back into a fist, then pressed her thumb down on her knuckle. "Do you see?"

She looked down at her hand. "I never knew which way was right."

"Now you do. OK, hold your hands back out." She correctly placed the thumbs on both hands and held them in front of her again. "You want to balance your punches," he continued. "Every punch should be relaxed, hard, fast, and accurate. But, if you are too relaxed, your punches become lazy and leave you open to counters, and punching too hard takes a lot of energy, leaving you tired too quickly. If you punch too fast, you are not as accurate, but if your attention is only on being accurate, it takes a lot of focus, leaving your defense open. You don't want to always be on the offensive either and become overly passive. Remember this; not all punches are equal."

Eva blinked, wondering how she was going to retain everything he was saying. "How am I supposed to remember that?"

"With time."

His knowledge of fighting and things regarding survival was like a door to the unknown thrown open. "You need to teach me how to do all of that," she said.

Wilhelm flashed her a look of approval. "I will. There are four kinds of punches we will learn. The jab, which is the one used most of the time. The right cross; the second most used, the left hook is the third most used, and the uppercut is the least used. Someone who knows how to do a good jab can keep his opponents from ever using any of the other punches most of the time. What I'm telling you now is from boxing, but even though street fighting is dirty, this will help you too. A lot of what I want to teach you is defense, because if you ever need to use what I'm teaching you, chances are your opponent will be bigger than you. A woman fighting who knows the proper techniques and remains calm and in control of her body and emotions, can overpower a larger stronger man."

Her first instinct was to take offense to his comment about a woman remaining in control of her emotions, but she understood he was not trying to be sexist, but that he was saying women need to remain more in control than the man because of the body size and physical difference between her and him. She needs to use that to her advantage.

"It doesn't matter how tall or big someone is," he said. "You still have vulnerable parts like your throat, chin, nose, eyes, ears, back of your head, back of the knees, and all your opponent needs to do is strike at these spots with precision. You might find yourself in a situation where you can't simply run, and you will need this. Also, remember that defense is not about not getting hit. Defense is about not getting hit while moving into a position to hit the other person. It's also about not getting hit after you have already hit them. Never try to have an unbreakable defense or attempt to hit the other person two times in a row. It's not going to happen. Another important thing to remember is endurance. Everybody gets tired, but the question is, who will tire first? There are two answers to this. Which person is in better shape, and which one is a more efficient fighter. The simple thing is, don't waste energy. You also have to work with what you have. I'm speaking of body size. They match you up by body size, weight and skill in the ring, but if somebody attacks you, it most likely won't be equally matched. This is why it's good to remember that all the power doesn't come from the muscles, but also from the ground and how you pivot, move your hips, and the rest of your body, depending on the strike you are planning to use. Your power is going to be the force you use with the proper technique unlike strength, but to move effectively and correctly you need to train consistently. If you train often your ability to fight increases, and your confidence if you come up against a bigger, stronger opponent. You won't be as afraid to face them."

"So, if you are smaller than the other person, how do you win the fight?" she asked.

"Technique, endurance, being a better fighter than them, and luck. Techniques that are in martial arts use others strength against them, which a lot of the time is more important than brute force. If you are fast and know where to hit, immediately immobilizing your opponent, then you have a chance of beating a far larger, stronger person. This is especially true when it comes to self-defense, which is all about using fast, effective techniques, and then getting yourself out of reach of your attacker. It isn't about long, sustained fighting, where each side will inevitably strike the other, and the strength of those strikes take all its importance away from the skill. In this situation, a trained woman can often beat an untrained man. But, if you let him get a blow in then he can get the upper hand. It's not only about punches thrown, it's about damage done. A blow a man would deliver is going to be far more painful and do more damage than the blow you give him. He will break your jaw or cheek bone before you break his. Remember, I mentioned that earlier about taking a shot and then moving out of the way. See, it's easier to punch down than it is to punch up. Men are generally taller than women, and if you are swinging in a downward direction it enables you to punch with a hell of a lot more force." He met her fixed gaze. "The taller person has the advantage in a fight."

"It sounds like you are telling me I don't have much of a chance."

"No, I'm telling you what the reality will be if you go up against a man and you are not trained. That's why I'm not just going to teach you boxing which would be harder for you to win at."

She nodded her head.

"Alright, I'm going to start by teaching you defense. I want you to come after me and try to punch me in the face."

Eva looked at him, shocked. "But... I don't want to actually hit you."

His lips curled into a smile. "Don't worry. You won't."

This confused her until she realized he meant she wasn't good enough to actually get a punch in. She frowned, then came at him, swinging her left fist to the side, trying to hit him in the jaw, but he dodged her attack.

"That is possibly the worst swing I have ever seen. Let's do this. I will hold up my hands, and you will punch them, so you get used to the feel of it."

"Won't that hurt your hands?"

"No, you won't be hitting them that hard. All right, come on." He held his palms out in front of him. She took her right hand and punched it into his right palm. "Do it again." She did the same with her left hand. "Again. This time harder," he said with authority. He made her do it over and over until she was sure his palms hurt. "Now I'm going to come at you, and I want you to block me."

She swallowed hard and held her fists in front of her, hoping she was ready. His fist came towards her face, and she drew in a rapid breath, squeezing her eyes shut.

"Never close your eyes! That is a sure way to lose. Fight back!" Wilhelm growled. "Fight back against my thrall!" She opened her eyes and looked at him just in time to see his fist coming at her face again. She flinched, bringing her hands in front of her face to shield the blow. His arms dropped to his side. "I'm not going to hit you, Eva. Now let's do it again." He slowly moved his fist towards her this time. "Put your arm up, block me." She lifted her right arm, blocking his fists. "That is how you do it," he said, straightening.

"I see that now. Sorry, I'm so bad at this."

"It's alright. You haven't had practice. We'll work on punching some more another time.

"Can I try coming at you as you did me just now?"

He thought about that for a second. "Sure."

She noticed that he didn't lift his arms in preparation for her swing like he told her to do. She lifted her arm suddenly and swung it at him, her fist contacting the side of his head. She could feel all the knuckles in her hand pop and instantly dropped it, cradling it in her other hand. She cried out in pain.

He came to her side and took her hand to inspect it. "It isn't broken, just sprained."

She gritted her teeth as he moved her fingers. "Did I hurt you?" she asked as she looked at his head.

"Well, it didn't feel good. But you hit my skull, not my jaw or nose. You seemed to miss all the vulnerable places on the head. Why don't you sit down for a minute, and then we will continue if you feel up to it?" He led her to the couch, and she sat down, massaging her fingers. They were already feeling better. How could he enjoy this, getting hit and hitting someone else?

He let her sit for several minutes as she tended to her hand, but finally, he spoke. "The chances of someone getting ahold of you is likely, so I'm going to show you how to get out of their grip. Are you up for it?"

She nodded. "I'm sorry I hit you. I thought you were going to deflect my swing."

"I didn't think you were going to swing just then, and if I'm being honest, I didn't think you would actually make contact with my head."

She was annoyed now. "I'm not that uncoordinated."

He gave her a side glance with a half-smile. "Come here." She stood and walked over to him. "Turn around with your back to me." She did as he said. "Now, I'm going to come up from behind and put my arm around your neck." He was close behind her now, his chest touching her back. The closeness made her tense. He wrapped his arm around her throat, and she instinctively wrapped her hands around his forearm. "Put your chin down," he said quickly. "You want to keep the person's arm from touching your neck so they can't choke you, and you do this by keeping your chin down. The next thing I want you to do is take a step to the side." She stepped to the right. "Most likely, the person who has you will be a man, so I want you to take your left arm and swing it back like you are hitting me in the groin."

She pulled away, breaking his hold. "What? No." She could feel the heat on her cheeks.

"You're not going to be hitting me. You won't be touching me at all. Now get back here." She reluctantly turned her back to him, and he came behind her, wrapping his arm around her again. "Remember to keep your chin down and step to the side." She did and waited for the next move. "Swing your arm back as if you are going to hit me." She swung her arm back, making sure she didn't hit him. "Now come up with your elbow to hit me in the face." She bent her arm back, her elbow stopping at his jaw. "Very good. Sometimes the person will pick you up by the neck, and you can't step to the side to punch them in the groin with your hand, so you would have to use your leg. You just bend your leg back at the knee as hard as you can." He had her kick her leg back several times. "Alright, now I'll show you how to flip someone over your shoulder. I want you to come behind me and put your arm around my neck like I did you. She stepped behind him and reached up as she stood on her tiptoes, wrapping her arm around his neck. Their height difference made it harder for her to do it to him. "I'm going to flip you over my shoulder now, but you won't hit hard because I won't do it fast." He took her arm with his one hand, stooped, rolling his shoulders forward and his hip to the side, pushing it into her stomach, and then she was in the air, going over the top of him.

Her dress flew over her head as she contacted the floor. She hurried to her feet, her dress falling back around her legs as she stood. Her face was beet red. "You knew that would happen," she spat at him, unable to hide her anger and the embarrassment.

"Yes, that is why I asked if you had any pants, but you said you didn't. If you don't want this to happen next time, I advise you to wear some. That anger you have now, use it."

"Yes, I want to punch you in the face right now."

"If you dare, step a little closer." He baited her. She lunged at him, swinging, but he caught her wrist, pulling her towards him, then kicking her leg out from underneath her, but holding onto her as she went down so she didn't hit the floor hard. He let go and looked down at her, then held out his hand. She stood up without taking it. "Use your anger wisely, not stupidly," he said.

She was so flustered with him that she didn't know what to say. She hated that he was so much better at this than her. "Why don't I flip you over my shoulder this time?"

"Alright." She came and stood in front of him, and he put his arm around her. "Take a step to the side and turn your body," he told her. She did as she remembered him doing. "Pull on my arm at the same time you roll your shoulders forward and push towards me with your hip." She gripped his arm tighter, rolled her shoulders forward as she bent, and pushed back. But unlike her, he did not go over her head. She only succeeded in bending him down with her, leaning him over her back as her butt pushed into his groin. She quickly let go of his arm and stepped away, horrified by what had happened.

A slight smile played on his lips. "Well, if that's what you wanted, Eva, all you had to do was ask, and I would have obliged."

"You bastard. I don't want to do this with you anymore."

"Why? Because you can't win? You only get good at it by doing it. Don't be a quitter because it's hard. It's funny because I haven't even been tough on you yet. If you don't want to learn how to defend yourself in case you are attacked again, then I will go, but if you do, stop bitching and let's get on with it."

"You could just give me a gun."

He shook his head. "That's not going to happen."

She glared at him with her hands on her hips, her heart racing in her chest. She pointed a finger at him. "You have to behave."

"I thought I had been."

"You thought no such thing."

He just smiled and motioned for her to come back to the middle of the room. She walked across the floor and stopped right in front of him. "You chose what we do. But don't blame me for the outcome like last time."

"Wrestling," she said.

"Wrestling?"

"Yes. It might be good to learn how to get up if someone gets on me." She remembered how the man had her on the ground while straddling her.

He thought about it. "You said the two men had you on the ground, so I suppose that would be good to learn. Alright, how do you want to do it?"

175

"I'll hold you down, although I'm not sure how to do that."

"Well, there are several ways. The person can be on their stomach or back, for starters."

"Ok, you lay on your stomach." He laid down on the floor. "Now what?" she asked.

"Take my right arm and bend it into a chicken wing, then put your leg on the back of my knees." She took ahold of his arm, bending it towards his lower back, then put her bent leg across the back of his knees. "That's about the gist of it."

"Can you get up?" She was so hoping he couldn't.

"I'm not going to try."

"Why?"

"Why don't we switch places," he suggested, intentionally not responding to her question.

"Fine." She moved off him, and he stood up.

"Lay down." She lowered herself onto the faded carpet face down, and he knelt beside her. "I'll show you a different method." He put her left arm in front of her, took her right arm, bent it behind her back, then straddled her, sitting on her legs. "This is a more effective way."

She had not expected him to sit on her. He had all of his weight on her, completely pinning her to the floor. She tried to roll, but he held her firm. She tried to rise, but couldn't lift his weight off the floor. "You can get off now."

"Maybe I will keep you here for a while. It might humble you."

"Get off me!" She squirmed, but he leaned down, pressing on her back. She could hardly move now. "I'm humble enough." It was hard to breathe, and his grip on her arm was hurting.

"If I were your attacker, do you think I would get off?"

"No."

"Then you need to try harder."

"How?" Suddenly, his weight was off her, and she could see his legs near her face. She got to her feet, rubbing her wrist. "That hurt."

"Sometimes, if they get you down, there is no way of getting them off. It's better not to let them get that far. And don't compare, because you will never be as good as me. I'm not being arrogant; I'm just stating a fact. Our goal here is not to compete or for you to be better than me."

She knew he was right. "I know that. I want to try flipping you again."

"Are you sure?" He raised an eyebrow, and she nodded. He pointed a finger at her this time. "No complaining."

"I won't." She understood what might happen but couldn't let it get to her. He came up behind her and placed his arm around her neck. She gripped his arm, stepped to the side, and turned her hip towards him. She stooped, but the same thing happened as last time, so she let go. "What am I doing wrong?" she asked, frustrated.

"Here, I will show you." He had her put her arm around his neck again, then flipped her over his shoulder as slow as he could to show her the method.

Once again, her dress flew over her head, but it wasn't as embarrassing as it had been the last time. This time it gave her butterflies at the thought that he saw her bare legs and underwear. The feeling confused her because she shouldn't be having it. She stood quickly, her dress falling around her legs. She looked at him standing before her. The top two buttons of his shirt were undone, and the hair on his chest was exposed, sweat glistening on the hollow of his neck from the exertion. "I think we should stop for the night," she said.

"It is late. When do you work tomorrow?"

"The morning shift."

"I will be by at five." He took his coat and tie from the couch, draped them over his arm, then stopped when he was at the door. "You did well tonight, but you'll have to do better tomorrow. I won't be as easy on you."

"I didn't think this was easy."

"You will tomorrow night." He opened the door and disappeared into the hall.

Chapter Twelve

Eva rolled onto her back, then onto her right side, struggling to fall asleep. All the physical activity had woken her up, and her relaxing candlelight bath had been wasted. Her time with Bauer was interesting. He knew more about fighting than she had realized or given him credit for. From what she understood, he had been in fights as a child and a teen.

She turned the things he told her over in her mind, trying to cement them to memory, but then she thought about the two times she tried to flip him. What was the comment that he made? She was sure he was just trying to get under her skin, and he succeeded. She thought about her butt in his groin, remembering the feel of him beneath his pants and it not being as she had expected. Maybe his comment wasn't just to annoy her? Spending the evening with him and their proximity made her realize how lonely she had been. How she missed the feeling of her skin against someone else's, and how she wanted, for just one night, someone to tell her everything was going to be alright, that they had her. She hungered for it and craved human contact. Was this her baser instinct or something else? *Oh, enough of that. This is what happens when you let your mind wander,* she scolded herself. She rolled onto her left side and closed her eyes, willing herself to fall asleep.

Her alarm rung loudly in her ears, so she reached up and tapped it with her hand, and it fell silent. She pulled herself up, leaning against the headboard, feeling surprisingly sore. She threw the blanket off and made her way to the bathroom. She hurried into her uniform, ate breakfast, then walked across the street to the hospital.

Bauer's comment about being harder on her today had her worried. What exactly did he mean by that? If she was this sore now, she wondered how she would feel tomorrow morning. She also wondered how many times they were going to do this. She knew he would leave for Paris soon but didn't know when exactly that was.

At lunch, she sat with Dr. Möller, like they always did in Berlin. For some reason, things seemed more straightforward then, even though they, in fact, weren't.

"So, how do you find your new apartment?" Klaus asked.

"It's fine. It will be nice when Ingrid gets here."

"I'm sure."

"Klaus, how do you know so much about the SS?"

"It's pretty common knowledge, the way they are, I mean."

"But they can't all be bad. I'm not trying to defend them. It's just I have a hard time believing that every single one of them is bad."

"Let me put it like this. I have not met a good one yet. Even bad people can do nice things once in a while if it is worth their time. It's good that you moved out of that house." He shook his head. "I still can't believe you lived there with him. I don't know what you were thinking."

"I was thinking that he left me with little choice. He made it very clear that I was going to move here, that I couldn't stay in Berlin, and I couldn't tell him no."

"What I don't understand is why he made you come here with him. Is it because he wanted to keep tabs on you or because he has feelings for you?"

"Both, I think."

"Which one is more prevalent, his distrust for you or his feelings for you?"

"I don't know. I think it has changed over time."

"You mean his feelings for you have become stronger than his suspicions?"

"Yes."

"Well, you have more than one reason to stay clear of him then. I can't tell you what to do, but you know what I think you should do." He looked at her intently, deep in thought.

"What?"

"Nothing." He picked up his bowl and stood from the chair. "I'm needed in pre-op. Why don't you come over on Sunday, and we'll have dinner?"

She smiled. "What time?"

He thought for a second. "I think I should be home by six. Sorry about the late time, but I won't be able to get away sooner."

"It's all right. I have no set dinner time."

He left the table, and she watched him walk away. The sun coming through the windows made the white tile walls reflect the light back into the room. For some reason, she disliked this room. It reminded her of a room from a psychiatric hospital you would see in a movie. It was so bland, impersonal, depressing.

She pushed her chair back and collected her dishes. She tried not to think about tonight. She was so conflicted about Bauer coming over for their second round of practice, and she hated how it made her feel. *I need to focus on my anger. That is how I should see him. If I can hit him a second time, that will make me happy.* She smiled at that thought.

Before she was finished for the day, she assisted Dr. Möller with the surgery on a man who had broken his arm and tore some of the flesh from his leg on a barbed-wire fence. "I'll meet you in the recovery room," he told her.

"Alright." She pushed the bed with the man out of the operating room and down the hall to the recovery ward. She placed the bed into an empty spot, then started an IV. She wrote his vitals on the clipboard, hung it from the end of his bed, and then glanced around the room for Dr. Möller, but he wasn't there. She checked her watch. It was almost a quarter to five. She was supposed to be off by four, but the surgery ran later than expected. She paced the floor near the bed for what seemed like forever. *Where could he be?* she thought. She looked around again, thankful to finally see Dr. Möller walking into the room.

"How is the patient?" he asked as he rounded the bed, taking the clipboard from the end.

"He is doing well."

"His blood pressure is a little low. We will have to monitor that."

"Yes, I noticed that too. I'm hoping it will be normal by tomorrow." She checked her watch again. It was now twelve past five.

"Do you have somewhere to be?" he asked, noticing her look at her watch.

She gave a nervous chuckle. "No, only home. It's just I was supposed to be off an hour ago."

"An hour over is not that bad, not in our line of work."

"I know. I'm just exhausted today." That wasn't a lie. She was already worn out from the practice she did with Bauer the night before, and the long day at work did her in. She didn't know how she was going to practice with him tonight. She didn't have the energy for it; she was spent.

"You can go now if you want."

"Are you sure?"

"I know you want to go home, and I'm almost done, anyway."

"Thank you." She did and didn't want to go home. What she wanted was to go home and rest, not go and spar with Bauer. "What do you want me to bring on Sunday?"

"Bring some bread."

"I can do that. I'll see you tomorrow." He gave her a smile as she walked away. She didn't bother to change out of her nurse's uniform and hurried across the street to the apartment.

She ran up the stairs to the second floor and stopped when she got to the top. She looked down the hall but didn't see Bauer. Then she remembered he had a key, the thought still unsettling her. She trudged down the hall, stopping in front of her door. She put her hand on the knob and twisted. As she had expected, it turned with no resistance. He was punctual and didn't like being late, so it didn't surprise her that he was already there. It was half-past five, and she was sure he would be annoyed at the very least.

She opened the door and peered in, searching for him, but he wasn't in the living room. She stepped inside and softly closed the door behind her. She took off her shoes and laid them on the floor next to the door so that she could walk quietly through the apartment. She peeked around the open door to her bedroom, but he wasn't in there either. *Why would he be?* she wondered. She then went to the kitchen and stood in the entryway, looking into the room. Bauer was standing over the sink, drinking a glass of water with his back turned towards her. He was not wearing his hat or jacket, and the sleeves of his white shirt were rolled up past his elbows. He sat the glass in the sink, then turned, halting when he noticed her.

"Ah, there you are." He looked at his watch. "I'm sure I told you five."

"Yes, you did. Sorry. There was a last-minute surgery, and I couldn't leave at four."

He looked at his watch again. "I cannot stay too late. I have to pack. I'm leaving in the morning."

This surprised her. He had said in a few weeks but was leaving much sooner. "Oh, that is quick. I thought you were leaving in a week or so?"

"You look disappointed. Will you miss me when I'm gone?" he said with a hint of a smirk, just visible at the corner of his mouth.

She responded before even thinking about what she was saying. "No." The word stretched longer than necessary as the pitch of her voice dipped low and then went high.

The look he gave her showed that he didn't quite believe her. "Well then, let's get this over with so I can pack." He walked past her into the living room, and without asking her for help, he began moving the furniture like last time. Eva went to the side table with the lamp and pushed it against the wall, and then he moved the couch. He straightened and turned to her, taking her in. "Did you get any pants?"

She looked down at her nurse's uniform. "No, I didn't have time."

"That will have to do. Come and stand in the middle of the room."

She came and stood in front of him. "What are we going to learn this time?"

"Because we don't have a lot of time, and I'm leaving tomorrow, I will just teach you how to get out of someone's grip."

He showed her different techniques but hardly spoke a word to her unless it was necessary. It was starting to annoy her. She didn't know why he was being closed off. She had her ideas but couldn't be sure. He showed her how to momentarily incapacitate someone allowing for an escape. They had been at it for almost half an hour, and she was growing tired. She hadn't recouped from the previous night, then the long day at the hospital, and now this, the continuous exertion was wearing on her. She did the last foot stomp and fist to the groin, then took a step away from Bauer, turning to look at him. She put her hands on her hips, looked down at the floor, and let out a long breath. "I need to take a break."

"Sure." He went to the couch and dropped onto it, wiping the little bit of sweat from his forehead with the back of his hand. She didn't want to sit on the couch with him or be that close. So, she sat on the floor, linking her arms around her knees. He stood up and went into the kitchen, returning after a minute with two glasses of water. He handed her a cup, then returned to the couch and sat back down, taking a drink of his. He drank deeply, then rested the cup on his leg.

Eva watched him, not drinking hers. Only when he had the cup back in his lap did she drink from her glass. She sat it on the floor beside her. "Did you mean it, Wilhelm?"

He leaned back into the couch and took another drink of water, staring at her over the rim, then lowered the glass back to his leg. "Mean what?"

She furrowed her brows. He had to know what she meant. "What you said to me in the cottage, that you loved me?" Part of her still doubted it, but something deep inside told her he did. She felt like there was something more, and she wanted to know.

"Are we really going to talk about that?"

She looked away for a second, focusing on the faded white paint on the wall, then back to him, nodding. "Yes. I need to know."

"Why bring it up again? You made it plain what you thought of me that night. I understood you never wanted to speak of it again and preferred to pretend I never said it. Unless you want us to plan our future, I don't see the point. I'm sure you would rather keep this locked tightly away."

"No, I don't."

He put his glass on the floor beside his feet and leaned forward. "You showed me most vehemently that you wanted no part of my love, so I had expected you to have the decency not to discuss it again."

"Wilhelm, you are the one who changed how things were. I was more than happy for it to stay the way it was, with a mutual dislike for one another. You are the one who came here. I didn't tell you to come; you offered. And you are the reason I am in Dieppe. So, I'm sorry if I haven't asked your forgiveness for wounding your inflated ego."

"I am not the only one here with an inflated ego."

She glared at him. "Now I think I see. You only told me you loved me to entrap me. You wanted to play with my emotions so you could break me."

"That is what you think?"

"Yes. You are a bastard." She got to her feet and walked over to him, kneeling on the floor beside him, sitting on her calves. She wanted to look him straight in the face. "At the time, I was so disgusted when you told me you loved me, and I didn't care why you said it, but now I do."

187

Now he was angry. "You don't care about me. You are only concerned with yourself. I think you wanted to talk about it now because you don't know your own feelings, but of course, you never even considered if it was fair to me." She started to stand and move away, but before she could, he took hold of her upper arms and pulled her to him, clamping her body between his legs, clenching tightly so she couldn't move. Her anger at him flared. For a moment, she thought he was going to kiss her. His face was so close, but he didn't. He stared at her, his eyes burning into hers. She should have realized long ago that one didn't meddle with someone like Bauer. Right now, he was untouchable, the one with all the power. He could bring death to someone with just a look, a wave of his hand, or a single word.

For a long moment, neither of them spoke. The creaks and groans of the expanding radiator heater and the unison of their breathing were the only sounds in the room. Finally, in a low, strained voice, Bauer spoke. "I am aware that you know what it is to love and be loved. To know how happy and comforted it can make you feel. But, I also know that it was one-sided, that you didn't see your feelings returned in the actions of the only one you thought that could ever know the true depth of your heart. Well, now you know how it feels to be me." She didn't break eye contact with him but held his intense gaze. Then, without warning, he leaned in and kissed her. His warm lips pressed firmly to hers, lingering there a while before he finally broke away and pulled back a few inches. She saw something in his hazel eyes that she didn't understand. There was a tenderness in them, but that was only on the surface of whatever dwelled underneath.

"I think you have mistaken me for one of the desperate girls you have bedded in the past."

"No, I misread the look in your eyes." He searched her face before leaning in and kissing her again, but she stayed still, not resisting or kissing him back. He finally broke the kiss, their faces so close that their lips were almost still touching. "Did you not like the kiss?"

She shook her head, and something flared in his eyes. "No, it's not that."

He let go of her arms and leaned back into the couch but didn't release her from his legs. "It's strange because I couldn't marry you even if I wanted to. That is if I even wanted to get married or had time for a wife."

"Then why have you come here? Why do you harass me?"

"You know why, because I cannot stay away."

"But you had said in the cottage that you will not marry while there is a war to fight."

"If ever a woman could change my mind, it is you, Eva Abrams."

"Now I know you are lying."

"If I were, I wouldn't be here now. I have told you the truth, then and now. Marrying a German woman is what needs to happen, but I don't want any of them. What I want I can't have."

"Want, that I don't doubt. You want me as your whore."

He leaned forward and put his hands on each side of her face, forcing her to look at him. "I think we both know that is not true. I have never thought of you in that way, as something to use and discard. Let me tell you what I think of you. I will add that I didn't always think this of you or know you as I do now. To me, you are special. You are caring, a fighter, and braver than I gave you credit. I admire you for all of those reasons and the things that make you who you are. I know I have hurt you, and I will forever be sorry for that. But I care for you like no one else can, even Gerhardt. You are mine, Eva Abrams."

She focused on his face. "You say I am yours, but how can that be?"

"Because I will never love anyone else the way I love you." He let out a long breath and released her face, leaning back again. "The truth is, I have never been in love before you. But I think you," he tapped her forehead with a finger, "have a misguided notion of what love is. You have imagined it in your head to be something it isn't. Love is not always beautiful. It can have many faces and mean different things. It all depends on who the people are in the love affair. Sometimes it can be passionate, possessive, or even destructive. It can lead you down into a darkness that will swallow you up."

She felt her eyes burning with the onset of fresh tears and put her hands on his knees to push herself free, and he released the grip of his legs.

"You confound me, Eva. You despised me because of how I treated you. And I admit that I was not kind to you. But now you don't like that I am nice to you. What the hell do you want? Would you rather I go back to treating you as I had been? I have never met a more frustrating person." His voice was agitated and alarming.

She could sense his anger was simmering just beneath the surface. She cleared her throat and shook her head several times. "No… no, I don't want that. Of course not."

He looked at his watch. "I have to go. I am leaving very early in the morning." He stood from the couch, and she took a few steps back. He walked past her into the kitchen, retrieved his hat and jacket from the table, then returned to the living room and stood by the door as he slipped the gray military jacket over his shoulders. He buttoned it up the front, then pulled his officer's cap low on his head. He looked at her, then touched the brim of his cap and reached for the doorknob.

"Wait," she said, taking a step forward as she held out her hand. "Don't hate me. You don't understand what it is like for me. I don't exactly understand it myself."

"I don't hate you, but I have to go." He opened the door and slipped out into the hall, shutting it softly behind him.

She stared at the closed door. She felt everything and nothing. He told her goodbye, but what kind of goodbye was it? She didn't know, and even more, she didn't know which one she wanted it to be. She no longer felt like she could trust her own heart. She had been so opposed to him. But now, she wasn't sure that she was.

Chapter Thirteen

January 22nd, 1942

Bauer had been gone almost six days, and she had thought of him every single one of them. Even though Ingrid arrived today, she still struggled to feel completely happy. Inside, there was sadness, confusion, annoyance, and a strange sense of fear. She was going through a whole range of emotions she didn't understand. She didn't completely know why she was feeling some of these things. What was she afraid of, and why was she sad? Eventually, she would have to ask herself the question she has been avoiding for a while now. What did she really feel towards Bauer, because it wasn't what she used to feel for him? What did it all mean? What was she going to do about it? How did she even feel about it? She could not ignore the situation or her feelings any longer. Did she want Bauer gone from her life? If they were not going to be together, could she handle him constantly showing up and being around but not fully in or out of her life? Would it be dangerous for her if he was absent? And the biggest question of all. Did she want Bauer in her life? Could it be that she had grown to care for him without even noticing? Did she love him? She didn't think it could be called love, but maybe a deep respect. But if she didn't love him, was it fair to give him hope? He loved her, so it would send the wrong signal if she spent too much time with him. She was certain he would not completely disappear from her life, which only meant one of two things. It could be volatile and dangerous, or it could be pleasant and safe for her. He could very easily start treating her like an enemy of Germany again. Or she could let him love her and use it to her advantage.

"Eva." She jumped at the sound of her name, dropping the fork she was holding onto the plate. "Ingrid is here," Dr. Möller said, standing in the open doorway of the nurse's lounge. He glanced to the fork. "Are you alright?"

"Yea, I'm fine. I will come with you." She took the napkin from her lap and laid it on the table next to the plate, and followed him to the main floor.

Ingrid was waiting in the lobby of the hospital. She was still wearing her coat and hat, her purse hung in the crook of her arm, and her suitcase was on the floor at her feet. Eva smiled widely when she saw her.

"Ingrid," she called from across the room, and hurried to her, pulling her into an embrace.

"Oh my God, it is so good to see you," Ingrid squealed as she squeezed Eva tight, a broad smile on her face.

Eva could hardly breathe. "It is good to see you, too," she strained to say.

Ingrid pulled away and looked Eva up and down. "So, where is this apartment?"

Eva looked at Klaus. "Go. I will have one of the other nurses cover for you."

"I can come back later," she told him.

"There is no need. Go, I'm sure you two have a lot to catch up on."

"Will you come over later?" Eva asked him.

"When my shift is over." He gave a slight smile, then turned and sauntered down the hall back to the patient ward.

Ingrid grabbed Eva's hand and squeezed it tightly. She looked around the hospital. "I can't believe I am in France. I have always wanted to come here. To think of all those hot French men with dark hair and sexy accents."

Eva chuckled. "You haven't changed."

"Can you blame me? Look around. We are in France, the most romantic country in the world." She held her arms out to her sides as she turned in a circle. "We definitely need to go to Paris."

"Ingrid, how will you flirt with the French men if you can't even speak French?"

"You will teach me." She gave Eva a childish smile.

"Um, I can. But it takes a long time to learn a language."

"I know, but it will be faster because I'm in France."

Eva sighed. "Get your stuff. The apartment is just across the street." Ingrid picked up her suitcase and linked arms with Eva. They stepped into the courtyard that the apartment shared with the hospital. Overhead was a thick cover of clouds, and a chilled breeze whistled through bare branches of the trees. "Ingrid, you need to be careful here. Guys aren't going to treat you the way you think they will."

Ingrid's smile faded. "What do you mean?"

"The French, they hate the Germans. It is different for me only because I am American. But I have worked at a German hospital and have been seen with Germans, so they are not too fond of me either. But it still will be worse for you."

"They can't all hate us."

Eva stopped walking and turned Ingrid to face her. "They will look at you only as a German whore. They would even go so far as to rape you if they weren't afraid of the German men and the repercussions."

The look on Ingrid's face changed. It turned from innocent excitement to horrified realization. "That is awful. But the French women seem to like the German men."

"That is reality. And yes, some of them do, but if Germany loses the war, they will pay for it. Probably with their life." Eva took Ingrid's arm and pulled her along. She led Ingrid up to the apartment and unlocked the door, holding it open for her.

"Oh, this is cozy."

Eva looked around the small space. "It's alright." She showed Ingrid to her room and sat on the bed as Ingrid inspected the room, opening and closing the drawers of the small dresser, rubbing her hand along the lumpy white plaster, peering at the view out her window, and checking the size of the armoire.

"Do you like it?" Ingrid asked.

"The apartment?"

"And this part of France. You had never been here before now, right?"

"No, I hadn't. I like it, but I think I prefer La Chapelle."

"Sure, that is where you met your boyfriend."

"He isn't my boyfriend."

"But you two were together?"

"We were, for a time."

"If you like La Chapelle, why did you come here?"

"There is nothing for me there, not anymore. And I didn't choose to come here."

She closed the doors to the armoire and came to sat next to Eva. "What?"

"That Officer from the hospital in Berlin made me come here."

"Him? Well, if the French hate us so much, maybe they will kill him."

Eva gave a forced smile. "Maybe. But if they did that, the German military would kill many French people as retribution. You don't want to make the Germans your enemy. I know first-hand what that is like."

"I suppose you are right."

Eva made them dinner, then helped Ingrid unpack. She didn't wait for Klaus because she knew he wouldn't get off until late. "When do you start work?" Eva asked.

"In two days."

"It will be nice to have you there."

Ingrid looked to Eva as she pulled things from her suitcase. "It will. And I'm so excited we will be living together." Ingrid was folding one of her slips when her face turned pale, and a groan escaped her closed lips. She covered her mouth and jumped to her feet, running out of the room.

"Ingrid?" Eva tossed the dress and the wooden hanger she was holding onto the bed and hurried after her. Ingrid was in the bathroom, kneeling over the toilet, vomiting up her dinner. Eva knelt beside her, putting a hand on her back, rubbing up and down. "Are you sick?"

Ingrid coughed then spat one last time into the toilet before moving away, leaning against the wall. Her face was flushed and clammy, and a few small pieces of hair that had come loose from her bun were sticking to her forehead and cheek. "I don't know what is going on. It has been like this for weeks now. I can hardly keep any of my food down, and I feel sick to my stomach all the time. I thought it was from rotten food at first, but it didn't go away after a few days, so I wondered if I had the stomach flu, but when it went on longer than a week I knew it wasn't that because the stomach flu doesn't last this long."

Eva took a deep breath. "Let's get you off this cold floor." She pulled the cord and flushed the toilet, then helped Ingrid to her feet, leading her back to the bedroom by her elbow. "Lay down, and I will get you some water." Ingrid laid on top of the comforter, tucking her hands under her head. Eva went to the kitchen and filled up a glass with water and started to return to the bedroom but found that she needed a minute. She sat the cup on the counter and put both hands on the sink, bracing herself as she leaned forward. She was pretty sure she knew what was happening to Ingrid, but she needed a little more information. *Stupid girl,* she thought. *How am I going to tell her that she is pregnant?* She straightened, taking the cup from the counter. She walked back into the bedroom and handed it to Ingrid. "Drink this." Ingrid took the cup and took a few large sips of the water. "Ingrid, are you still with that German doctor, the one I saw you with in Russia?"

Ingrid's face turned somber. "No. He broke up with me after we got back. He said I was just a child, too immature for him."

This was worse than she had thought. Ingrid wasn't even with the man anymore, the one whose baby she was carrying. She shook her head in disgust. "A child, huh? Maybe he should not have been having sex with a child then," Eva said with venom.

"Ingrid's eyes filled with tears. "I have never been with anyone like him before."

Eva sat on the bed next to Ingrid, taking her hand. "He didn't deserve you. Ingrid, how long have you been feeling this way?"

She thought for a few seconds. "Only a few weeks, maybe a little longer."

"How long ago was the last time you had sex with him?"

She flushed. "I can't tell you that."

"You need to."

She pursed her lips and blinked at Eva a few times. "Why?"

"I will tell you in a minute. Just answer the question."

"Um, maybe six or seven weeks."

Eva nodded. "And do you remember when your last period was?"

Ingrid leaned away from Eva so she could see her face better. "What?"

"Ingrid, I think you might be pregnant." Ingrid's mouth parted, and she stared at Eva, gaping in confusion. "Yes, Ingrid. I think you are."

Ingrid looked away and down at her stomach, focusing on it as if this was her first time seeing it. "Now that I think about it, I haven't had a period in over two months."

Eva nodded, not surprised that she was right, and held Ingrid's hand tighter. "What are you going to do?"

Ingrid lifted her head to Eva. "Keep it. What else would I do?"

"Nothing. It's that he is not going to raise this baby with you."

"I have my family."

"And what will they say when you tell them you are pregnant, but still unmarried, and that the father doesn't want to be with you?"

Her face fell. "I didn't think about that. They won't be happy. My father will be furious with me. He didn't want to let me leave to be a nurse. He thought it was a bad idea. He will say this proved him right."

"Why don't you wait for a while before you tell them. At least until you get used to the idea of being pregnant."

"Yes, I will wait for a while."

Eva leaned back on the bed, took Ingrid in her arms, and stroked her hair. "I am sorry you have to go through this alone, without the father or your family, but you have me. I will help in any way I can."

"I know you will. I don't know what I would do without you. You are always the responsible, sensible one."

Eva chuckled. "If only that were true. I am often playing with fire, standing on the precipice of some danger or another, or always in some kind of trouble. This time it is being loved by the devil. What's even worse is that I might be in love with the devil."

Ingrid pushed herself up on her elbow. "What do you mean?"

"I don't even know where to begin."

"Try."

Eva nervously smoothed the folds of her dress. "SS Obersturmbannführer Bauer." Eva knew that just his name would be enough for Ingrid to understand.

"No. That evil man?"

"I told you, the devil."

"Wait, he loves you?"

"He has professed it several times. And kissed me twice."

Ingrid sat up, leaning against the headboard. "And you... love him, too."

"See, that is just it. I don't know. It is so confusing. He is so confusing. Everything about this confuses me. But I think I might."

"And you don't want to love him, right?"

"Of course, I don't want to. How could I have fallen in love with him, of all men?"

"Love is not a slave to opinions or people as we are," Ingrid told her. "Just look at me."

"I'm not sure he even means it. Maybe he just wants me for sex."

"Telling someone you love them is not the usual line you tell someone when you want to have sex with them, Eva."

Eva looked away, not wanting to meet her gaze. "No, it's not. But sometimes, love isn't enough. Do you ever feel like you are a piece in someone's twisted game, and you are being played against your will?"

Ingrid was confused. She shook her head. "No. What does that even mean?"

"Nothing."

"Is being loved by him so bad?"

"I don't know. I'm not sure which one is worse, being loved by him or being hated by him. Everyone has a dark side, but his is more prevalent than most people I've met. Even though the way he treats me has changed, it still frightens me when I'm around him."

"I can see why. He looks scary."

"But what is even more terrifying is that he scares me, but I like the fear."

Ingrid angled her head to the side, her eyes locked onto Eva. "What do you mean by that?"

"If I have to explain it to the then you won't understand." Ingrid didn't bother to disagree. "But do you know what?" Ingrid shook her head. "I have never been so surprised by a person. They are never as they seem. And I agree with you about love. It is indiscriminate. We can fight it and tell it no, that we will not love a person, but it doesn't care what the person is like. I don't want love like this, painful and constantly changing. I can't have the man I want, no matter how I feel. I hate those three words, too." She stared off into the distance, looking at the blank wall across from the bed.

"But love can be beautiful, too. And it is unconditional. That means he will love you no matter what."

"Let me tell you something about love, Ingrid. Love is not unconditional. It has its limits. I tried to convince myself that I was only in love with Gerhardt, but that was not true. I can never tell Bauer, though. He can never know."

"Why, why can't you tell him?"

"Because then I would be tied to him, in a way I don't want to be. I am already beholden to him for what he has done for me. I don't want to belong to him, and if I told him that I reciprocated his love, he would think I was his. There would be expectations, an obligation to give myself to him fully, body and soul."

"You haven't slept with him then?"

"I am against having a sexual relationship with him most emphatically." She glanced at her watch, noting the late hour. "It is getting late. We should get ready for bed. Dr. Möller will be here soon, and then we need to get some rest."

The following morning, Eva left before Ingrid was out of bed. She wanted to get the shopping done early and have some time alone to think.

Fog hung low over the town, making it hard to see the streets, so she stayed near the walls of the buildings in case a car veered off the road. She could hear the wails coming from the seagulls as they flew overhead, but she couldn't see them. She took a deep breath, blowing it out as the steam clouded in front of her. The cold air helped bring her out of the grogginess that lingered that morning. She had barely slept a wink last night. All she could think about was Ingrid's pregnancy and her confession to Ingrid about Bauer. It felt good finally admitting it to herself and to someone else. Although she still wasn't sure how she felt about this new revelation.

She crossed the street and waited in line at the bakery, hoping to get some of the fresh bread that was made that morning. She stood behind two older women holding their mesh grocery bags, huddling close, trying to stay warm in the frosty morning air. They both had their heads covered with scarfs and wore long, black trench coats and wool socks with brown boots. Some people had gotten in line behind her and Eva was glad she arrived when she did before the line grew too long. She shifted her weight from one foot to the other and turned her head to admire the misty city streets when the man behind her stepped uncomfortably close. She lifted her foot to take a step closer to the two women in front of her when something hard pushed into her back. The man leaned in close, his mouth near her temple.

"Do not make a sound. Step out of line and walk towards the coast."

Eva was terrified and apprehensive about moving from the line. The people around her were her only protection. She didn't know exactly what the man had at her back, but it felt like a gun. She quickly scanned the area around her, panicked, still unsure of what to do.

"Move!" he said more forcefully this time.

She turned to the left, stepping out of line and started walking, the man following close by her, slightly off to the side and still poking her in the back with the object. After several blocks, he spoke again.

"Turn here."

He pushed her in the direction of another street to their left. They followed it down until they reached the rocky beach. Then he took ahold of her arm and pulled her along, quickening the pace. He brought her to a small shack that was in serious disrepair, pulled open a rickety wood door, and pushed her through. She almost fell on her way in but caught herself by grabbing hold of the back of a broken chair. The man came inside and slammed the door behind him. The air was cold and dank, smelling of musty, wet wood. Eva glanced at the man who brought her there, then at her surroundings. There was a table and two chairs in the center of the room, a makeshift kitchen to her right, and at the back of the single room shack was a mattress on the floor with sheets hanging around it for privacy. But the thing her eyes froze on were the five other people in the room, and to her surprise, she recognized two of them. One was the man she had met in Paris when she was there with Madame Blanc. And the other man was none other than Helmut.

She gaped at him, disbelieving her own eyes. "Helmut... how did you—"

"Escape? It wasn't easy, but I managed to stay alive long enough to be smuggled out of Germany. I can't say the same for the others." He glared up at her from the chair he was in. "You know, Derek is dead because of you. He died, as did the others, all because of your lies and deceit. He even tried to help you, and that is how you repaid him. By giving him and the others over to the Gestapo. You traitorous German whore," he spat.

What he said came as a shock. It was like he had punched her in the gut. "No. I did not. The Gestapo was after me, too. It was Lina who betrayed you," she blurted, without thinking of the possible consequence of her speaking.

He smacked the palm of his hand down hard on the table, and she flinched. "Stop lying. It wasn't Lina. It was you. It was always you."

She was desperate. She needed to convince them of her innocence. "I… I have proof."

He looked at her; his light blue eyes bore into hers. "What proof?"

"The contact, the one in the German high command. They approached me right before I came here. They said it was her all this time, that she was feeding information to the Gestapo. She had infiltrated the resistance so she could keep them informed about our movements and activities." Eva's words were rushed, coming quick and frantic.

"Why would they contact you?"

"Because it so happens that I know them, and they knew I was the one accused of being the traitor."

"But you are a collaborator," the man she had met in Paris barked. "I saw you with a German officer, then another one on the day we were supposed to meet. You keep company with the Germans."

Eva didn't know how to defend herself because it was true. She did keep company with the Germans, and had been romantically involved with one and was dangerously close to being romantically involved with another. "I will admit I was involved with the first one you saw me with, but that is over, and he is on the Russian front. The second one was only with me because he was suspicious. He is also the one who had me arrested on multiple occasions."

"But you went to him for protection in Berlin. You lived with him here, and he killed one of our men and took the other prisoner. And it doesn't appear that he is after you anymore."

She looked away so they could not see her face. "No, he is not. He has developed some sort of attachment to me. I don't know why. But that is the only reason I am still alive. He knows I was with the resistance, but he has kept that from his superiors in Berlin."

"Oh, but that is good," Helmut said, glancing at the others. "You can do for us now what you would not do in Berlin. You have access to one of the people we wanted. You will help us now, because if you don't, you will not see the sunrise."

His threat did not surprise her but still sent shivers down her spine. "No, not anymore," she said in a shaky voice. "I told him I hated him, and now he has returned to Paris." That was not entirely true, because it wasn't recent that she told him, and that was not the reason he had returned to Paris. But she needed them to think it was.

"You still have a better chance than anyone here. You have helped us in the past, so maybe you can convince us of your loyalty and redeem yourself by helping us again. We need you to get as much information from him as possible, using any method necessary. We want him dead, but we want to know what he knows first. He will die by the end of this war, that I promise. You can bring him to us, in a manner of speaking. When we have no more use for him, you will lure him to a place where we can kill him, unless you would rather be the one to do it? But I don't think you have it in you to follow through. So, you bring us SS Obersturmbannführer Bauer, and we will consider letting you live."

She swallowed hard. How could she tell them no? She now realized that she did not want Bauer to die. But how could she possibly keep him alive and herself? They would kill her if she didn't comply. She wanted to help Bauer but didn't know how. If she told him about the resistance, Bauer would have them all killed, and she wasn't sure she wanted that either. She had to stall. But if she didn't tell Bauer about what was happening with the resistance, and he found out she helped them again, he would most certainly have her arrested, and this time he would not stand between her and the fate that awaited. Her mind was running circles around itself, but she had to make a snap decision. She would agree to it, then go back to the apartment and figure out what was to be done. At least there, she would have some time to think. Time to think about what she was going to do.

"Do you believe killing him is really the answer? If you do this, kill him when you are finished, there will be reprisals. And it won't be like killing just any officer. The reprisals for killing him will be in the hundreds."

"We know this," Helmut confessed.

"And you don't care?"

"We do. But in war, there will always be sacrifices," the Frenchman said.

"What if it were your family?"

"They have already killed my family," he snarled.

She looked at him, this time not knowing what to say. She didn't feel like there was anything she could say. "Alright, I will do it, but only if I have your word that you will leave me alone once I give you him?"

The man exchanged a glance with Helmut, who nodded. "Fine, you have our word," he said reluctantly.

"How and when do you want me to do it?" she asked.

"The next time he is in Dieppe. Do you have any idea when he will return?" Helmut asked.

"I don't."

"We will contact our people in Paris and have them watch him. As soon as you learn he is back in Dieppe, let us know. Leave a note under the altar at St. Jacques church, and we will get it. Then you will move forward with your part."

"So, an officer of the mighty German army has fallen in love with you. What is it about you that makes German men weak in the knees? Because I see nothing special about the person standing in front of me. Just a cheap, worthless specimen of a human. Do you spread your legs for all of them?" the man from Paris asked.

What he said struck a nerve that had never been plucked. Her fear of him was gone, and she lunged at him, but the man who brought her caught her wrist, holding it tight. She glared up at him, but he didn't release her. "For starters, it is none of your damn business what I do. And no, I have only slept with one, one time. I have never been with any other."

"Even as worthless and insignificant as you are, they still don't deserve something so pretty. They should stick to fucking their own women."

"You don't decide who they sleep with, and you don't get to choose for the women of your country either."

He stood up, this time more angered by her words than by her attempt to hit him. "You are no better than those other women who let the Germans under their dresses. They do it for what? More food, luxuries like perfume and lipstick that only the Germans can get unless it comes from the black market." He looked down at her legs. "Maybe silk stockings."

"I didn't do it for a price."

"No, I'm sure not all of them do. Do you know how many half German bastards are running around this country?" She shook her head. "Thousands of them. And do you know how insulting and humiliating that is? How that emasculates the French men?"

"I don't think the French women are doing it to be hurtful."

He ignored her response. "They are like bitches in heat. They only go after the German men because they are in control right now. But that will change."

"I think you misunderstand women. I did not base my choice on who was the victor, and I doubt the French women do either. And if you feel emasculated by the French women choosing German men, then maybe you weren't men to begin with."

He struck her hard across the side of the face. Instantly, there was a burning, stinging feeling on her cheek, throbbing into her jaw. Her left eye felt like it might explode from the impact.

"Julien!" Helmut yelled. "Tell her the rest."

He never took his eyes off her. Not even to look at Helmut. "Do you know who he is?"

She reached up and placed her cool palm on her cheek. "Of course I do."

"So you know that he is the head of the Gestapo for France?"

"Yes."

"Well, the best way to get the kind of information we need is for you to become close to him."

"You mean have sex with him?"

He hesitated for a second. "Yes, that is what we mean."

She felt sick with disgust and contempt for what they were asking her to do. "There are other ways to get information. And you should know that he will never turn against Germany."

"None that will be as effective. No one else could do it as easily as you. He will trust you if he's in love as you say. And he will turn against Germany, if you are good enough, even if he doesn't realize that is what he is doing."

She laughed cynically. "Then you do not know him. I am probably the person he trusts the least. You do not need to trust someone to love them. Love is involuntary, but trust is earned, and I certainly haven't earned his."

"This isn't a negotiation. You will do what you have to."

"I will try, but it might fail. I think you overestimate my sway with him. I don't have some hold over him. My influence is limited."

"Then earn his trust. Use your feminine charm, and before you know, he will be putty in your hands."

"He is not that kind of man. But I said I will try."

"Take her back," Helmut said to the man who had brought her. He gave a quick nod, then took hold of Eva's arm. When they were back on the street, she jerked her arm away, walking a few feet ahead of him. Everything that had happened, including what she had just agreed to, in its entirety, was finally starting to register. Her body felt strangely weak, and she thought she might fall over. She didn't even turn around to look at the man when they arrived at the apartment building. She went up the stairs, into the apartment, then to her room. She shut the door and sat on the edge of her bed, staring at nothing as worry knotted her stomach. She felt like her world was about to stop spinning. *What did this mean? What did this mean?* She repeated in her head. *Oh God, I have to sleep with Bauer. But is that such a crazy idea? No, I won't have to. I will be able to get what they need another way. Or can I? Shit, I don't know.* Her mind was in such turmoil. A knock on the door pulled her out of her contemplation.

"Eva?"

"Come in, Ingrid."

The door opened, and Ingrid poked her head in. "Are you alright? You were gone when I got up, and I noticed you had taken the grocery bags but didn't come back with any food."

Eva had completely forgotten about the food. She put her hand on her forehead. "Oh, I forgot. I met up with some people I knew and got distracted. I will go back out later and get some. You can come in. You don't need to stand at the door."

Ingrid came into the room and sat next to her. "I feel so awful. This can't be how the whole pregnancy is."

"No, I don't think so. I'm pretty sure it will only be in the beginning."

"I hope so."

Eva didn't sleep that night, but laid awake, listening to the still, dark apartment. She ran all the scenarios through her mind. Why was she being pushed at Bauer? It seemed like forces from all directions wanted her with him. Since she had been in this time, their paths had constantly been crossed. In the beginning, it was never a good thing, but lately, it had not been all bad. If Gerhardt found out she was sleeping with Bauer, she was sure he would never take her back. But why did it matter what he thought? He was with another woman now. It was no longer his concern what she did. The thought of Bauer coming back to Dieppe terrified her. She made it clear that she did not want to be with him. Would he even want her now? And how was she going to go about accomplishing this? She wasn't exactly an expert at seduction.

No doubt he would see right through it and know she was up to something because why else would she suddenly change how she felt about him? She rolled onto her back and stared at the ceiling. *How had everything gotten so twisted?* She wondered.

Chapter Fourteen

February 15th, 1942

When Ingrid was home, she slept most of the day and still struggled to keep her food down. Eva guessed she was around eleven weeks now, but of course, there was no way to be certain. She had come up with this gestation period based on how long Ingrid said it had been since her last period, which would have made her around eight weeks and twenty-four days. And as far as days went, it had been twenty-eight days since she'd seen Bauer. Eva didn't know when or if he was coming back to Dieppe. Helmut had been waiting outside her apartment a little over a week ago when she came home. They thought Bauer had come back, but she informed them that he hadn't. "I was serious when I said he does not want me. He might not come back at all," she had told him.

She looked down at Ingrid's head on her lap as she rubbed her silky, golden hair. Ingrid so reminded Eva of a child in this moment. Eva shook her head. *A child having a baby,* she thought. Somehow Eva had taken up the role of an older sister, and some days it was more like a mother. When Eva first met Ingrid, she had found her annoying. Later it changed to only thinking she was a silly boy-crazed girl, then mutual respect, and finally fondness. But she now knew that Ingrid had planted a seed in her heart that had grown into a beautiful flower. She gently lifted Ingrid's head from her lap and slid off the couch, laying it on the pillow. She got a pen and a piece of paper from the kitchen drawer and wrote a note, leaving it on the side table near the couch. She needed to get out of the house. She had been stuck there the last two days with Ingrid, caring for her. She put on her coat, hat, and gloves, picked her purse up off the floor, and quietly left. Now and then, she would walk by the building Bauer had worked in when he was in Dieppe, hoping to see him. She should just ask someone about him but never could bring herself to do it. To be honest, she was fine with him not being there.

She again stared across the street at the humble structure, watching men in grey uniforms come and go, but still there was no Bauer, just like all the other times she had stopped by. Two soldiers crossed the street and walked by her, and she turned and stared at their backs. Then the idea struck her. She hurried after them, hoping her question wouldn't seem odd or suspicious. "Excuse me?" she called to them in German.

They both stopped and turned at the same time, eyeing her curiously. "Yes," a thin, short, dark-haired man said. He looked very young to her. Maybe only nineteen or twenty.

"I am sorry to bother you, but do you know if SS Obersturmbannführer Bauer is in?"

"He is not here today," the taller of the two answered. He also was skinny but with sandy blond hair and wire-rimmed glasses that sat upon a hook nose. His uniform looked too big for him as it hung loosely on his thin frame. As if he had taken it from a much larger man.

Eva thought carefully about what she was going to say next. The man had said, "not today." Did that mean he was here in Dieppe and just not in today? Or did he just word it wrong? "So, will he be in tomorrow?"

The men exchanged a glance. "I don't know," the taller of the two said again. "Why do you want to know?"

"We are old friends. Is he back from Paris, then?"

"He has been back a few days now." The one with dark hair stared at her after answering. "What is your name, Fräulein?"

"Eva." She chose to omit her last name. So he had been back for days and hadn't bothered to visit her or even let her know he was in Dieppe. Maybe what she told the resistance was true. That he didn't want her now, even if she didn't realize it at the time. "Thank you." She started to leave but then decided she would risk asking if they knew where he lived. "Sorry to bother you again, but do you know where he is staying?"

"I think the house he was staying in before. The one near the beach."

She was a little surprised but relieved that he was staying there. "Thank you again." She turned and hurried towards the coast. She cupped her hand over her eyes to block the winter sun that hung low on the horizon, making the sky look an unnatural color of orange and the water an odd, dark inky blue. She was almost jogging down the hill towards the cottage now, but when it came into view she halted, gazing down at it. She took a moment to catch her breath and clear her mind, but she couldn't stop the persistent, unwelcomed thoughts. They came fast and chaotic, and her palms grew clammy. The invading thoughts, and knowing she was close to Bauer gave a sensation of him being all around her, thickening the air. The opposing emotions were strong, and she faltered, putting her arms out as she swayed, feeling her equilibrium shift. Just thinking about interacting with him made her nervous like she was going to vomit. What was she even going to say to him? They had not convinced her that she had to sleep with him to get the information they wanted, but at the very least, she had to get on his good side and make him think she really wanted to be his friend.

She took a deep breath and studied herself, then continued down the hill. His car was parked on the street in front of the house, so she assumed he would be home. She stopped when she got to the front door but didn't knock. Her breaths were coming fast, and her heart was pounding like a base drum. She had to continually tell herself that she could do this. She finally lifted her hand and rapped three times on the door. She could see smoke coming from the chimney, and a light was on inside. The door opened, and Bauer was standing in front of her. At first, his expression was neutral, but it soon turned to surprise. He arched an eyebrow and cocked his head to the side in obvious confusion. She had no idea what he was thinking. "Eva. What are you doing here?" She opened her mouth to speak, but her mind went blank, and her lips failed to move. A funny squeak was all that came out. "Well, what do you want?" His voice was now rigid, and had now turned sharp.

This pulled her from her momentary paralysis. "I wanted to know if we could talk?"

He gave her a quick once over but never moved to admit her. "Talk about what?"

"Can we talk about it inside? It's cold out here."

His face softened a little, but he still didn't move out of the doorway. "I don't have time right now to talk."

Eva's face fell. "Oh. Can I come back another day then?" A movement behind Bauer caught her attention. She peered around him and looked down the hall into the kitchen. A woman was standing at the counter with her back to them. She looked a little shorter than Eva and had blond hair pinned in a neat bun. The way she leaned over the sink, she appeared to be doing the dishes. "Oh, shit," she gritted under her breath, too quiet for him to hear. Eva's eyes darted from the woman back to Bauer, and for a brief second, their eyes met. Then he broke the hold and looked away. He still stood with his arm resting on the doorframe, blocking her way. "I'll go now." She turned and started back up towards the road. She didn't really know how to feel at this instant. The sound of the door shutting behind her made her feel rejected somehow, slighted, and by Bauer, of all people. Then she felt someone take hold of her arm. She instinctively turned, trying to pull away.

"Eva. Stop." She did and looked up at his face. "I can't talk today."

"I know, you said that." She did not hold the annoyance back.

His face looked strained. "Yes, I said not today. But I was going to tell you to come by tomorrow around the same time, and we could talk then."

"No, that's fine. We don't need to talk. It's not important anymore."

"You obviously had something you wanted to discuss with me, or you would not have come here. I know you asked around to find out if I was back in Dieppe. And you wouldn't have done that if you didn't feel it was important."

"I don't want to bother you while you have company. When your date goes home, then we can talk." For the life of her, she could not understand why she felt some resentment towards this woman whom she had never met.

Bauer's face, as usual, was unreadable. "She is not my date, just someone I have known for a while who came to visit from Berlin."

Eva looked down at the dirty snow on the street and bit her bottom lip. "Alright, I will be here tomorrow around the same time." He nodded, then went back inside. She hurried away from the house, feeling strange about the whole encounter. When she got back to the apartment Ingrid was making some food, the scent of it wafting through the apartment. "That smells delicious. What is it?"

"Just some potato and carrot soup. My stomach is upset, and I can't tell if it's because I'm hungry or because of the pregnancy. So I thought I would try eating."

"Do you want me to make it so you can sit down?"

"No, it's not too bad at the moment. I'm tired of laying down and sitting."

"I don't blame you." Eva took off her coat, hat, and gloves, hanging them on the coat rack along with her purse. She came and stood next to Ingrid and peered down into the pot of boiling vegetables. "I'll cut some bread and put it on the table. If only we had butter, but I haven't been able to get some for weeks."

"It's so hard to get anything these days."

"I know."

The thought that she could no doubt get some from Bauer if she really wanted, or real coffee, sugar, extra tea, and any of the other hard to get items occurred to her. She didn't care, though; she would not ask him for any of it. She quickly went to the straw basket they kept bread in and pulled out the rest of the loaf. She cut it into two pieces and put it on plates, setting them on the table. Ingrid brought the pot of soup, placed it in the middle of the table, then sat down. She dipped them both some into a bowl then took a bite of her bread.

"Aside from being sick, how do you feel?"

Ingrid looked down at her stomach. "Fat," she said at her small but visible belly. "And tired all the time."

She pulled her brows together. "You are not fat." Eva thought she looked thinner than she was a week ago, and her skin had lost its normal color, replaced by an ashy appearance. "Do you work tomorrow?" Eva asked.

She swallowed the piece of bread. "Yes, the morning shift. You?"

"The morning shift, but I have somewhere I need to be after work, so I won't come home when I'm off."

"Oh, where do you need to be?" Ingrid glanced up from her bowl.

"Just something I need to take care of. Something that's been a long time coming."

"That sounds suspicious. Should I be concerned?"

"No. It's not like that. Just some bad blood that I'm hoping to clear."

"How long will you be gone?"

"I'm not sure. I don't think it will be too late."

"I will probably be asleep when you get home, anyway."

Eva gave a faint smile. "That's good. You need it. How long can you work before they make you quit?"

"I don't know. What am I going to do, Eva? How am I supposed to take care of this baby and me without a job and no husband?"

Eva reached across the table and took Ingrid's hand. "We will find a way, and you can stay here with me."

"You can't support all three of us."

"I can if we are careful with money."

Ingrid shook her head. "I'm afraid I will have to go home."

"No, Ingrid. You don't have to go home unless you want to. Let's not worry about it now. We still have some time to figure it out."

"I don't believe you are thinking clearly, Eva. I don't see how it could work."

"You let me worry about that."

That morning Eva went to work expecting it to be like most other days, but it wasn't, and the day seemed to drag on. Eva knew it was because she was nervous about tonight. She did not know what would happen, which brought on a fear that she could not fight back. One of the fundamental things she worried about was how this was going to affect her life, and not just her remaining time here in the past. She was aware that it could change a lot of things. That was inevitable. And whatever happened tonight would be irrevocable. It would shape her and the rest of her life forever. But would it be for the better or for the worse?

"Eva." She glanced up to see Klaus. I thought I could have you and Ingrid over for dinner this evening. How does that sound?"

"Oh, I already have plans, and Ingrid isn't feeling well. Maybe we could do it this weekend?"

"This weekend works fine for me. Ingrid was not feeling well last week, either. Is she alright? I could take a look at her?"

"I'm sure she will be better soon." Ingrid had told no one else that she was pregnant. And when she was at work, she would wrap her stomach in a cloth to hold in her growing belly. Eva had told her how it might not be good for the baby, but Ingrid insisted she didn't have a choice. That she had to work for as long as possible. Eva could understand her plight.

He gave her a sidelong glance, considering her response. "If she doesn't get better soon, I want you to let me know."

"I will." Eva had no intention of telling him and felt bad about lying. But the truth was, there was nothing he could do for Ingrid. What she was going through were normal symptoms of pregnancy. She needed to tell Ingrid that Dr. Möller was growing suspicious.

When Eva got home from work, she filled the tub with hot water and soaked in it for a long time. Partly because she needed to feel clean after her shift at the hospital and partly because she needed to relax before meeting with Bauer, although nothing could prepare her for that. She focused on the length of her naked body under the steaming water feeling like she needed saving. She wasn't sure what she thought of going all the way with Bauer. How could she give herself to him in that way? Even if she gave her body to him, she was still unconvinced that she could ever truly give herself to him in the way he wanted.

She sat up, splashing the water, causing it to almost spill over the sides of the tub. She pulled the plug and stepped out, drying herself with the towel. Her skin quickly cooled from the chill in the air, covering her body in goosebumps. She shivered and wrapped herself in the towel, tucking the corner under. She went to her bedroom and took a fresh dress from her small larch wood armoire. She put on her underclothes and slipped the dress over her head, doing the three buttons in the front. She tied the belt that came with the dress, then sat at her small vanity. She put on her hose, pinned her hair up, applied a little makeup, and dabbed her wrist with the one perfume she owned. She did not wear it often because sometimes it bothered the patients, but this seemed like an occasion for it. She was going to try and seduce a man, after all. She stood up, going to the living room to get her coat and purse. Ingrid was sitting on the couch, drinking a hot beverage. Eva could see the steam rising from the cup in her hand.

Ingrid took a deep breath. "You are wearing perfume."

Eva smiled. "I am."

"And you are wearing one of your nicer dresses." She eyed Eva suspiciously. "What is it that you are going to do?"

"Just taking care of a few things."

"And that requires one of your nicer dresses and some perfume?"

"It possibly does."

Ingrid gave her an incredulous look. "What are you not telling me?"

Eva turned to Ingrid as she tied the belt of her coat. "Goodnight, Ingrid."

Ingrid put her cup on the side table and pushed herself upright. "Wait, you can't just—."

Eva closed the door while she was still talking. This was not a conversation she wanted to have with her now. She stepped outside and was once again assaulted by the cold winter air. The sun was low in the sky, and the remaining daylight was fading fast. The clear night sky was going to make it extra cold. She followed the empty streets towards the coast, maintaining a brisk pace. She kept her hands in her pockets and her face turned down, trying to stay as warm as possible.

She tried not to think about how cold her face was and instead focused on what she had to do tonight. She could not have any doubts about what might happen. She needed to go into this with total confidence in herself and no objections to her actions. Her hope was that she could wake with no regrets in the morning. But if she was lucky, she wouldn't have to do it at all.

The tan-colored stone cottage came into view with the backdrop of the channel behind. It really was a cozy place, inside and out. It had a very small, white front door in the middle, a window on each side, and one tiny upper window for the bedroom that was on front side of the house. The other upper windows were on the back of the house, overlooking the coast, and the door in the kitchen led out to the beach. It would have been fun living that close to the water in warmer weather. The slant of the roof faced the front of the house, and you could see the wood shingles in their neat rows if you were on the street.

She walked past the black German car, down the three steps, and then paused at the front door, taking a deep breath. She was shaking but didn't know if it was from the cold or her nerves. She could not hesitate much longer, or she might turn around and leave. She knocked on the door with her gloved hand, then dropped it to her side. Her mind went to the woman she saw with him the day before and wondered who she was and what she meant to him. Was he using the women for his personal comforts? Was she using him for hers? She knew that what she was planning on doing would be taking advantage of him in a way, but at the same time, she felt like in return, he would be taking advantage of her. But she didn't want to be used twice. They could use each other for sex, fine, but she didn't want him to do that to her while he had another woman on the side. She would feel used emotionally and physically if he did, even though she hoped to keep emotions out of it. But she knew that was not possible, at least not for her.

The door opened, and Bauer stood in the entryway. He was still wearing his boots, but his hat and jacket were off, and the suspenders of his pants were hanging to his sides. He didn't say anything to her but moved to the side so she could enter, unlike the last time. She stepped inside, sat her purse on the floor, then removed her coat, hat, and gloves. He gestured for her to enter the living room, and she did. She chose to sit on the end of the couch near the fire. She felt like she was frozen down to her bones. Her fingers and toes were numb, and her face hurt. Bauer came around and sat in the chair across from the couch so he could look at her. He moved his hands out to the sides, palms up in a questioning gesture. Now that she was here with him, she didn't know what to do next.

Noticing her silence, he spoke. "I'm guessing there is an actual reason you are here? You said you wanted to talk?"

"Yes, I do." She folded her hands in her lap and looked at the round area rug in the middle of the aged wood floor. For some reason, her eyes rested on a dirty spot that she had not noticed before when living here.

"Well?" he said, losing his patience.

"I wanted to talk about the last night we were together and what we had talked about."

He sighed and covered his eyes with his right hand as if he was suddenly exhausted. "This again. I think we have said all we can about that."

"See, that is where you are wrong. I have some things I would like to say about it. I need to say."

He removed his hand from his face, laying it on the armrest. "I'm listening." The life was completely gone from his voice.

She thought about what order things needed to happen in. First, she needed to assure him she didn't hate him. Then she needed to convince him she felt the same way he did. Getting him to believe her could be tricky, though. But for her, everything was tricky because she wasn't sure what she felt for him. She liked it better when she hated him. That was simpler. "I wanted to start by saying that I don't hate you. Not anymore."

"Well, isn't that a relief." He didn't try to keep the derision from his voice.

She saw that he stiffly turned more to his side in the chair and crossed one leg over the other. She tried to ignore his comment and continued, struggling to be brave.

"I also wanted to say that I am sorry for my part in what happened to you. Please forgive me?"

In this, she was sincere. She had been riddled with guilt since that day. Not just for what she did to him, but for all the people who died and were injured. An expression she had never seen before flashed across his face, but he didn't speak, then his eyes locked on her, looking eerily calm. She couldn't tell what he was feeling. No one knew what was happening behind those hazel eyes.

"You seem annoyed or angry with me, but I don't know what I've done this time to upset you."

"I am just trying to figure out why you are here."

"To clear the air. There is animosity, distrust, malice; there is a lot between us, and I want to fix it."

"And you think an apology for assisting with an attempt on my life is the way to do it?"

This was not going how she had expected. He was so unreceptive. "It's a start," she said. He rubbed his hand over his shiny hair and waited for her to continue. "That night… when you kissed me, I wasn't trying to reject you."

"But you already had. I was careless to let it go so far. We were together, close to one another, and I let the moment get the better of me."

This was precisely the kind of thing she needed him to tell her, to confess what he still felt for her. "I didn't kiss you back and tried to get up because I didn't want to give in to temptation." She took in a deep breath to calm her nerves. Well, this was it. There was no going back now. Her words could not be retracted.

"He uncrossed his leg and sat up straight. He turned his head slightly to the side and looked at her, considering what she said. "Do not tease me, Eva." His face was hard and his eyes threatening.

There was never a time that she did not find him, at least a little scary. Keeping her chin down she tipped her eyes up at him. "I'm not." She creased her forehead, realizing that she actually meant what she said, which surprised her. Maybe they would both learn something tonight.

He leaned forward, resting his elbows on his legs and intertwining his fingers. "Eva, you had told me that I looked at you like a whore, which isn't true. But I could not give you anything more than a physical relationship. Even though I would want more, I can't. I have explained that to you several times. When the time comes for me to marry, it should be a German woman. So as much as I would like," he paused, "want to touch you, to feel your skin, to know what it was like to have you and be with you in that way, it would be unfair to you. You don't want to be known around here as a German mistress because lovers are all we could be."

She felt like he shocked her with a cattle prod. She was stunned. What did this mean now? If she could not get close to him like the resistance wanted, would they kill her? She blinked rapidly a few times, listening to her voice inside. Would it once again be because of him that she lost her way? She honestly didn't know what to say, so she stood up and went to the window, looking out onto the street. She needed to change her tactics. She knew he was still sitting in the chair. He did not follow her to the window. "Is that a rule, marrying a German woman or just expected?" She wasn't considering marrying him, but was that the only way to get close? And would she actually be OK with just sex and nothing more with him? She had never had a relationship like that with a man, so she didn't know.

This time, he stood and came to stand next to her. "Expected, but race and nationality are aligned. And it could affect your citizenship as well."

She turned and looked up at him. "How? What do you mean?"

"I'm an attorney, Eva. I do understand some of the laws of other countries. You have lived out of your country for over two years. And if the man you married is not eligible for citizenship, which I am not, because America is at war with Germany right now, you could lose yours. Women's marital denationalization is common in Europe and is still done on some occasions in America."

Eva was horrified. She was unaware that countries did that in the 1940s. "I didn't know," she said with a slight shake of her head.

His eyes bore into her, and she felt like he was undressing her with them. "I wanted to know what those lips felt like on mine, and now I do. I have to be content with that."

She didn't know why she thought this would work. "I understand. I'm the moon." She wasn't ever going to break through that wall he's put up, so there was no point in staying. She took a step, but he caught her hand, bringing it to his lips and kissing the palm softly. This took her by surprise. She had not expected him to show her any affection. His kiss was tender, and his lips were warm on her cool skin. Emotions flooded her senses, making her a little dizzy. She reached up with her other hand and caressed his face, the most intimate thing she had ever done to Bauer. It felt strange but not uncomfortable or appalling. He leaned down, giving her a tender kiss on the forehead, but not the lips. They were standing so close that she was actually aware of the pressure of his leg against hers. Then he took her in his arms and held her tight to his chest. It was strange because she never thought she would find herself here, in this man's arms. But they were oddly comforting, strong, and protective around her body. If she could get him to make love to her, maybe some emotional door would open, and all of his thoughts and feelings would pour out, and he would freely give them to her. He loosened his hold on her, and she looked up at him. Then, while she had the courage, she stood on her toes to narrow their height a bit and went to kiss him, but he pulled back, tightening his arms around her again, preventing her from moving up any further. Then he let go of and took a step back. "Wilhelm?" she said, confused by his sudden change.

"I think it's best if you leave now. Coming here has only upset and disappointed you." She didn't answer but looked up at him, tears pulling in her eyes. She blinked, squeezing the lids tightly shut for a second before opening them. A few ran down her cheeks and fell to the floor. Bauer slowly lowered himself down on the couch. "It is really cold out tonight," he said. She sniffed and wiped each cheek with the back of her hand. "Eva, why are you crying?"

"It is exceptionally cold out tonight, isn't it?" I should have brought a jacket or sweater to wear under my coat." She knew he was trying to defuse the tension in the room.

"I think it will be better if you don't come here again. Every time we see each other, it only upsets you."

"Seeing you doesn't upset me."

"What am I to think, then?"

"You know what it is that hurts? That fact that you still hate me even now. I know you say that you don't, but sometimes it still feels like you do."

He played with the cuff of his shirt sleeve. "You know that is not true. My God… by this point, you should know it. Since Berlin, I've had no eyes or thoughts for any other girl. When I'm away, nothing occupies my mind more. The one thing I am sure of is the truth that I feel inside about you. More than what I have been taught or what I'm told to believe or have learned from others."

His words were wrecking her brain and her already unsteady emotions. "Please, just stop," she said, choked up. The color had drained from her face. All the powerful emotions conflicting inside and the roller coaster events of the evening were actually making her feel sick.

He looked up at her complexion and obvious discomfort but didn't stop. He felt he needed to get this out. "It isn't enjoyable to have been made a fool of when someone uses your own feelings against you. To take their desires and wants and use them as a weapon against them."

Eva blinked away the tears. "I don't know what you mean."

"Oh, I think you do."

"You are the one who is emotionally closed off. So how could I use your emotions against you?"

"Not now, not like this. If we did what you wanted, where would it lead? If we went all the way tonight, you would regret it in the morning. I have a reputation in this country, and you would have it too, by association. You would be hated after."

She wondered if underneath his words was a veiled threat. "I know about your reputation. In any situation where I was with you would be only heartbreak. But his whole time, this whole damn war has bound me to you. Every time I leave, you pull me back."

"So you are willing to risk your heart, your reputation, with no boundaries and no fear of the consequences?"

"I already have once. But I did it because I knew it was worth it."

Her remark seemed to push the conversation in a different direction. "Yes," he agreed soberly. "I'm sure it was. Are you certain you felt so little for me when we met as you still pretend? The way you acted the last time I was in your apartment and how you act now suggests otherwise."

"I think you forget yourself," she whispered, forcing the words out."

"Oh no, I don't. Do not talk to me about manners and forgetting one's self." He glared at her in the dim firelight.

All the conflicting things inside her suddenly found an outlet. The mixed motives for wanting to see him tonight. The annoying and strange liking of his affection. Her feminine curiosity at this mysterious, interesting, yet confusing specimen of a male who stood before her. All these things suddenly merged into indignation to keep out something more potent. She was as much alarmed at her own feelings and exasperation at him as she was at his towards her. But the situation had to be saved if she was ever going to survive.

"I was wrong to ask you to meet with me. I had wanted your friendship, nothing more."

"You must have your feelings under excellent control. You somehow have managed to turn them around and point them in the direction you want. That is a quality I have as well, except when it comes to you, I can't. You keep secrets and lie to me as well as yourself."

"What secrets?"

"I don't know, you tell me. I don't pretend to be open about my life and who I am, but at least I am truthful about my feelings for you."

Trembling, she turned and walked to the hall. He followed and stood in the living room entryway. "You are right. I should not have come. I had hoped that we could be friends, but I see that can never happen now."

"No, Eva. I don't think we can be just friends."

She pulled on her coat and wrapped her scarf around her neck several times before turning to him. "In a way, we are both trapped here. By coming here, I thought that we could put our differences aside and be a comfort for each other, but you forget nothing and forgive no one. Perhaps I expected too much. What I had said to you recently was spoken out of anger and fear in the heat of the moment. But I agree with you now. After tonight, we shouldn't see each other again."

Eva could not believe she was telling him this, knowing it jeopardized her life. The thought of the resistance coming after her scared her, but he also frightened her. As did his feelings for her, her feelings for him, and what they came so close to doing terrified her more. Was there a way this man didn't intimidate her? She couldn't think of any. She had not seen that part of him yet. She was still shaking from the events of the evening and the chill in the house. He took her hand and kissed it, but she shrank from his touch as if his lips burned her skin. She could tell by the look on his face that he thought he had become repulsive to her. He let go of her hand, crossing his arms over his chest.

"Forget this ever happened. Maybe it would be better if you forgot about me all together. I don't think we have any more to say."

"Yes," he agreed. "There is no more we can say."

Eva did not know why, but she had a feeling of desolation. A complete emptiness weighing on her chest like a ball of lead. She felt contempt for herself and for him. He had a way of always making her feel like this. She thought he had behaved badly, but the truth was, so had she. It would be so easy for her to play the jilted lover. Even though he had upset her with his attack, her defense had more than leveled the score. Even with the situation as it stood, she could, in a single sentence, strike a more painful blow at him than he could her. He was intelligent and clever with his words, but not even with all the ingenuity his hurt might devise could he cause as much pain.

"Goodbye," she said grimly. He did not return her farewell, only closed the door behind her. What a failure she was. She couldn't even seduce a man who claimed to love her.

Chapter Fifteen

February 20th, 1942

It had been five days since the last time she saw Bauer. She hadn't seen anyone from the resistance either. They probably thought she was well on her way to getting information from him. She hoped they would be merciful when they found out the truth. But she knew that was just a pipe dream. Every time she found her self-control waning, he would creep back into her memory. It was like he was in every corner of her mind. She would see him at night when she closed her eyes. She thought about him more often than Gerhardt these days. Just knowing that made her feel angry and a little sad. Even though the thoughts were not the same as her feelings. But she couldn't tell if they were equal, only that they were different. This also upset her because she knew deep down that her feelings for Bauer were changing and becoming stronger. He had somehow taken up residency in her head, penetrated her heart, and she hated him for it. She felt like something dark was playing with her mind. The emotional strings he pulled were different ones than Gerhardt pulled and arguably more intense. His presence made her feel strange, and she was convinced nothing was what it seemed anymore. She had the urge to confess all of this to someone, but didn't know who. Ingrid was busy with her own problems, Klaus would disapprove, and the priest was in Berlin. She wasn't sure how Heidi or Liesel would react if she told them about it. Liesel would almost certainly disapprove, but Heidi she was less certain of.

She looked up from the nurse's desk at the front of the patient ward and peered at the clock on the wall. It was time for dinner. She had told Ingrid that she would meet her in the cafeteria and didn't want to be late. Ingrid was getting ready to start the night shift but was going to come early to eat her dinner with her. Eva wasn't eating because Dr. Möller was taking her out for dinner tonight. She put the patient records in the basket on the desk, hung up her apron, then walked down the sunny hall with the windows toward the cafeteria. She found Ingrid sitting at a table in the corner; her expression glum, and her complexion ashen. When Eva approached the table, Ingrid looked up, giving a forced little smile.

"How are you feeling today?" She didn't want to comment directly on her appearance.

"I'm alright. I have been feeling worse lately. I don't know if that's normal."

"Worse in what way?" Eva sat down in the chair across from her.

"I'm not sure. I can just feel it."

"Ingrid, I think you should talk to Dr. Möller. But if not him, then another doctor."

"Can you help me?"

Eva didn't feel completely comfortable playing doctor with Ingrid. "I can try. But you have to promise me that if I can't help, you will see an actual doctor?"

"I promise."

"Can you tell me what your symptoms are?"

"Well, I feel different in general, but I have also been having cramps. Some in my stomach and some in the lower back area."

"I will do some reading and find out what I can. But Ingrid, you really need to be taking it easy."

Ingrid's face turned serious. "I can't stop working, not this early."

"We might have to figure something out. I don't know a lot about being pregnant, but I do know that you are at a higher risk of losing the baby in the first trimester."

She looked down at her stomach that was pulled in by being tightly wrapped. "I've heard that."

"Then take my advice and stop pushing yourself so hard."

"You know why I have to."

"I can try to make up the difference financially if you need to work fewer days."

"I'll think about it. You never told me if you were able to fix whatever it was you went to do the other day," Ingrid said, changing the subject. "I think it has something to do with that officer from Berlin."

Eva looked at the dings on the metal table to avoid Ingrid's probing gaze. "No. I actually made it worse. Now I have even more problems to fix. Why do you think it has something to do with him?"

"Because of what you said the night you told me I was pregnant. You know you can ask for my help if you need it."

"I know, but this isn't something you can help me with." She had almost forgotten she told Ingrid about him.

Eva watched Ingrid eat in silence. She felt bad for her. She couldn't imagine going through what she was all alone. It was so cruel what the baby's father did, abandoning her like that. But in his defense, he doesn't know she's pregnant. Eva wondered if Ingrid should tell him. Maybe that would change the situation for the better. At the very least, he could help her financially when the baby came.

"Ladies," Dr. Möller said as he entered the cafeteria. "How are you, Ingrid? You look unwell." He stood next to the table, staring down at her, his forehead creased with concern and his hand on his hip, pushing up the lab coat like he always did.

"I am fine, sir," she told him. "Just been feeling a little under the weather. It should pass in a few days."

"Let's hope it does." He looked from Ingrid to Eva. "Ready?"

"Let me grab my coat and purse. I'll meet you in the lobby. Give me a few minutes."

"Alright. Take care, Ingrid." He patted her on the shoulder.

"I will."

When Dr. Möller's footsteps were faint in the hall, Eva spoke. "See, he is already suspicious. You should really tell him. He can help you more than I can. My knowledge of this is limited."

"No. He might tell someone else. It might get back to... him."

"Don't you think maybe he would want to know that he is going to be a father and be a part of his baby's life?"

"No. When he left me, he lost that chance."

"But that is not fair to him. He has a right to know and decide if he wants to be involved as a father. Just because it has ended between the two of you doesn't change the fact that you two made a child together. You shouldn't keep him from it."

"That is easy for you to say because you are not pregnant." She jabbed the food with her fork.

"No, I am not. But I hope that if I ever am, I will tell the father, even if we were no longer together. The father's relationship with the mother and his baby is independent of each other. He can choose to be in their life and not the mother's, except on a limited basis because that would be unavoidable."

"You and I are different in that way," Ingrid said.

"But he could help you, Ingrid."

"I don't want his help."

"I think you are being very foolish then." Eva stood from the table. "I will see you tomorrow." Ingrid nodded. Eva hesitated, feeling she should say more but not knowing what, so she left the cafeteria and went to the nurse's lounge and got her things. When she made her way to the lobby and could see Klaus talking with another doctor while he waited. He turned when he saw her come to stand beside him.

"I can explain it in more detail tomorrow," he told the other doctor.

"That would be good," the man said in rough German. He was not a military doctor or German. He was one of the civilian doctors at the hospital who could speak German.

"What was that about?" Eva asked.

"Just a technique I use when suturing patients."

Eva smiled. He did love his work. "Where to this time?"

"There aren't a lot of restaurants in Dieppe, but still enough to surprise you for a while."

"Is it alright if Ingrid comes with us sometime?" Eva felt sorry for Ingrid, who needed the food more than her.

He gave her a side glance. "Sure, it is."

She slid into the car with Klaus, then it pulled away from the hospital. They weren't in it long before it pulled to the curb in front of a row of narrow brick buildings that lined a narrow winding street. Eva leaned forward so she could see out the window better. A quaint little restaurant that reminded her of the one in Disney's Lady and the Tramp was to their right. The front of the brick building was framed with wood painted a lime green color. Some of the paint had started to peel from the years of sun exposure, and there were two red and white awnings. One over the door and one over the only window. They got out of the car, and she squinted through the window of the restaurant as they walked past on their way to the door. It was packed, mostly with German soldiers.

"Are you sure we are going to get a table?"

"Oh yes, I called ahead.

He pulled open the door and they stepped into the small lobby, and Eva could see that it was actually bigger than she had thought. The building was narrow but deep, extending far in the back. The smell of cigarette smoke and cooked food flooded her nostrils. A man came out of the kitchen and asked in French if they had a reservation. Eva instinctively told him yes.

"Sorry," she told Klaus the second after she spoke.

"It's alright." He gave the waiter his name, and they followed him to a table in the center of the crowded room and then he disappeared amongst the people.

Eva shrugged out of her coat and pulled her scarf from around her neck, hanging them over the back of the chair across from Klaus, then sat down. "You know, you will have to let me pay for myself one of these times."

He smiled. "No, I don't think so."

"You make me feel bad, Klaus, always paying for me when we go out."

"I can afford to. Besides, who else do I have to spend my money on?"

"Yourself."

"I already do that, but it's not the same."

She gave him a berated glance and looked down at the menu. When the waiter came back to take their order Klaus asked for a beer, and she chose a glass of white wine. "So what is going on with Ingrid?" he asked after the server had left.

Eva choked on her wine, coughing, and tapped her chest. "Just a cold, I think." She sat her glass on the table. "Why do you ask?"

"She has looked unwell all week. Colds usually don't last that long."

"If she continues to feel sick, I'll have her come in and get checked. She insists she is alright and doesn't need to see a doctor."

"I'm a little worried that it's something more serious."

"It might be." The waiter brought their plates of food and refilled their cups. The food looked and smelled delicious. Eva's stomach cramped from the aroma of it. She never ate like this at home. She was limited to what she could get with the ration coupons. The main thing she ate was bread, cabbage, potatoes, and carrots at home. Mostly root vegetables were what she could afford. She picked up her fork and took a bite, savoring the flavor as all her taste buds came alive.

"Can I join you?" a voice from behind asked.

Eva jumped, dropping her fork. She didn't need to turn around to see who it was. She knew who it was by the deep, smooth voice. The fork made a loud clink when it hit the glass plate, then fell to the floor with a clutter.

He bent down and picked it up, holding it out to her. She slowly looked at the outstretched hand, then up to him. His face and hair appeared particularly dark in the dim lighting.

"I would get another one," he said as she took it from his hand.

"Of course, you can join us," Dr. Möller said, gesturing to the empty chair between him and Eva. Bauer pulled it out and sat down, lighting up a cigarette. He inhaled deeply, drawing on the cigarette as the tip glowed orange, then he blew out a cloud of smoke. Eva didn't know how she should look at him. Should it be with surprise, anger, annoyance, what? "Do you want to order?" Dr. Möller asked him.

"No, thank you. I have already eaten." He called the waiter over and asked for a brandy, then rested his hand on the table, the cigarette fixed in between his index and middle finger.

She watched the smoke from it go up in little circles, then looked at the side of his face, noticing that he never once looked at her but kept his gaze fixed on Dr. Möller. "How do you like the hospital here? Oberfeldarzt Möller."

"I like it. At the hospital in Berlin, we hardly had a moment to rest. Here it is much slower."

Eva watched as they talked, not taking her eyes off Bauer. He hadn't said a word to her since sitting down, but his presence was all-encompassing. She was annoyed at how intelligently callous he could be. For the life of her, she could not figure out why he was here at their table, especially after their last encounter.

Bauer finished off his brandy with the same hand he was holding the cigarette, then sat the glass on the table with a thud. "If you will excuse me." He stood up and walked to the back of the restaurant towards the bathrooms.

Klaus turned to Eva. "If I might be so bold in saying, but he is only here at our table because of you." Slowly, she looked at Klaus. Her eyes had been fixed on the direction

Bauer had walked. "I had asked you once before if you knew him, and I will ask again. Do you truly know this man?"

His question confused her. "Yes, I think I do."

He shook his head. "No, you don't. Everyone seems to know him except you. SS Obersturmbannführer Bauer is one of the most wicked men in the German army. I asked around about him after the last time we had dinner. You would not believe the stories I heard. And the things some of the soldiers told me that he does to women. I will not repeat them here. He is out of touch with reality. I honestly believe he is a little insane, a devil of a man. People like him wants to watch the world burn."

"I know people say he is crazy, but people are crazy for a reason. Something happened to them in their life to make them that way. You don't just turn crazy or mean without something causing it. It's pain. I think that is what drives people to be that way. Inside they hurt and don't know how else to deal with the pain. So, violence becomes the easiest way for them. But I don't think he is insane. I think he is misunderstood." She could not believe she was actually defending Bauer.

"There is nothing good in him," Klaus insisted.

"What about how he cared for that girl in the hospital? Or the way he looks after his mother? And the things he has done for me. He can't be all bad. There must be some good inside of him, somewhere."

Klaus leaned back in his chair and crossed his arms his chest. "My God, you do love him." She opened her mouth, but he held up his hand to stop her. "Don't even deny it. Like I

245

said before, it doesn't make you a bad person because you love a bad person. It does, however, make you naïve. I had always hoped to see you with a nice man. You are young and can't spend the rest of this war in the hospital or hanging around with me. You should live your life, but not with someone like him."

"I know you will not understand, but can I have some time alone with him after we eat? And I did hear everything you said, but there are still things that need to be resolved between us."

He pulled his head in surprise, blinking at her a few times. "I don't think you should do that."

"Please."

"I'm not worried about what you will do. I'm worried about what he will do. You may think he is your protector, but he isn't. Trust me, I am trying to protect you from him."

"He won't do anything to me." Eva looked up as Bauer was approaching the table. He sat back down and ordered a second brandy, and Dr. Möller had his beer refilled again for the third time, but Eva was still on her first glass of wine.

"How is your hunt for the French rebels going?" Klaus asked.

"They are still out there and evasive, as always. But I will catch them, eventually." He took a sip of his brandy then sat the cup back on the table. "In my entire career, I have never lost anyone. I will turn over every rock and check every crevice until I flush them out. Someone always slips up. It's just a matter of time. Usually, I only need one, and then they rat out the others."

His words made Eva tense. She could only imagine what he would do if he found out she was working with them again, whether it was voluntary or not. "That is terrible," she said, focusing on him, a five-o-clock shadow clear on his face.

Finally, he looked at her. "That is the nature of the game. It is war. The rules that apply in peacetime do not apply now. We will do anything necessary to get results."

"Well, I think war is awful and unnecessary."

"If you want peace, then war is sometimes necessary. But I wouldn't expect you to understand that."

"Why? Because I'm American?"

"No, because you are a woman."

"I don't know which one would be more offensive. If you had said it because of my nationality or the fact that you did say it because of my sex."

"I did not intend it to offend. Women don't plan wars, and women don't fight in them."

"And women don't start them," she added.

"Yes, that too."

"That doesn't mean we don't understand them."

"I'm sure you understand more than he knows," Klaus interjected, eyeing Eva.

"Maybe it would be better if women were allowed to fight," she said.

Bauer smiled, putting out his cigarette in the ashtray. "No, that would be a terrible idea."

She could feel the anger at him rising. "And why is that?"

"Well, there are many reasons, but I will name some of the most obvious ones. Men trying to save the women or keep them out of harm's way, putting themselves in more danger, is one."

"Then maybe they shouldn't try to save them."

He ignored her. "Another is respect and temptation."

This comment confused her. "What does respect have to do with it?"

"I understand what he means," Klaus interjected, staring at Eva with a look she didn't understand. "And I agree with most of what he is saying."

"Well, I don't. So please explain?" She bore her eyes into his.

Bauer turned in his chair towards her. "Women constantly remind men of their baser, animal nature. Rather, that is trying to protect, dominate, or seduce them. This is why some men don't respect women. They hate that females have that kind of control over them. Men love power, control, and strength. To have that stripped away by what we view as the weaker sex is humiliating. It's maddening. Men blame women because we can't quit them. It is the same for all men. We are infatuated with women, and I am no different." He lit another cigarette and took a drag, blowing it out into cloud. "There is a woman who haunts my every thought. It is pathetic, really, because I can't have her. If I were to take her for myself, it would be her undoing. I think me being with her would cause sadness to her family and the people who know her. But she will be mine. I will have her."

Eva gaped at him, her breaths slow and shallow, her skin feeling hot. She could not tear her eyes from him. The silence at the table was heavy.

Klaus cleared his throat. "I think it's time to go home. Are you ready, Eva?" He gazed at her with pleading eyes.

"I think I will stay a while longer if that is alright with you?" She knew he didn't want her to stay here with Bauer, but she had to talk to him. There was all the dancing around things that needed to be said, from both of them, but mostly from her.

"No, that's fine." Klaus stood, dropping some money on the table for the food and drinks. He looked at Bauer. "Be nice to her!"

"Why would I be anything else?"

"You know why. I don't want to see a single tear stain on her cheek tomorrow."

"You won't."

Klaus didn't move, but stared down at him with his grey-blue eyes, then walked around the table to Eva. He kissed her on the cheek. "I will speak with you in the morning." He said it more as a heads-up than a suggestion. He gave Bauer one more warning glance, then walked towards the door.

Eva watched him leave, feeling vulnerable and alone at this moment. She looked at Bauer, folding her hands on the table. "Why are you here?"

"Tonight, we are going to get drunk," he said as an answer.

She looked at her watch. "I have to be home before curfew."

"I'll walk you home myself."

"You want both of us to walk to my apartment while drunk?"

He gave a wicked smile. "Sure, why not? Or we can sleep where ever we fall."

She huffed. "Uh, I don't think so."

He waved the waiter over and had him bring them a bottle of wine, schnapps, and whisky. He sat a small glass in front of Eva and filled it to the brim with schnapps. "Drink up."

She took a sip and wrinkled her face. He had downed his and was already filling the glass again. She took a breath, closed her eyes, and dumped the liquid into her mouth. She swallowed, then coughed. He smiled and poured more into her glass. She threw it back in one gulp and sat the glass on the table. She now felt like she had enough courage to ask him about what he said.

"You will have her?" she asked while giving as brave a face as she could.

He emptied his glass into his mouth, never moving his eyes from her, and she watched as his Adam's apple moved as he swallowed. The way he was looking at her reminded her of an animal who had spotted its prey. His eyes were dark and wild. The eyes of the devil, just like Klaus said, and the tongue of a serpent. How could anyone fall for a man like this? How did she fall for a man like this? Sometimes she wondered why women liked men at all. Hairy bodies, flat chests, lack of curves, or the softness of the female skin. Yet there was something seductive about it because it was so different. They looked different and felt different when you touched them. The rougher skin, their size, and the overall hardness of their bodies. She didn't know why women liked this, but they did.

"Can you play the piano?" he asked, breaking her train of thought.

She raised a brow. This was not the response she had expected. "Umm… a little."

He stood up, took her hand, and pulled her from the chair. She was a little unsteady on her feet from all the alcohol she had consumed. He led her through the crowded room to a small upright piano seated against the wall in the back corner. He sat on the bench, then tapped the spot beside him. "Take a seat," he said. She did, wondering what he was doing. He placed his fingers on the ivory keys and began playing a tune she didn't recognize. He made a few mistakes but didn't stop playing. When he reached the end of the song, he laid his hands in his lap. "Do you think you can play the tune now?"

"I think so." She put her fingers on the keys, and he did the same. He started first, and she tried to predict what the next note would be but played one wrong key after another. Sometimes he would reach across her hands to play a key she was missing, which always made her tense. At one point, their hands brushed, and she felt the spark between them.

She reached for a key, and he laughed, brushing her hand away. "That is my key. You are supposed to be playing the F minor."

His relaxed, playful manner took her by surprise. In all of their interactions, she had never seen this side of him before. She didn't know if it was because of the alcohol, because of her, or both. She watched him play, and he noticed that she had stopped.

He took her hands and placed them back on the keys. "What song would you like to play?" he asked.

"I have one." She started to play My Heart Will Go On from the 1997 movie Titanic. She knew no one would know this song because it hadn't been written yet. He listened for a few seconds, then started playing with her. She could not help but smile as he tried to keep up. He wasn't half bad. He began adding more notes, making it sound richer than it would have if it was only her. As they played, she glanced down, noticing that his legs were slightly apart, and his left knee was resting against hers. Their shoulders were almost touching, and their hands were close on the keys. The song came to an end, and she suddenly felt faint and had a thirst that only water could quench. She noticed that the room had grown quiet as the other people in the restaurant were now watching them play. Claps erupted from behind them, and Eva turned, feeling embarrassed.

She leaned in closer to Wilhelm. "I'm going to the bathroom." He nodded.

She stood up and left the room, following a small hall to the back of the building. There was a men's and women's bathroom with the doors facing each other. She went into the women's and locked the door behind her. She used the bathroom, washed her hands, and got a drink from the sink. She lifted her head from the faucet and looked at her flushed face in the mirror. She thought the alcohol and being so close to Wilhelm must have caused it. She splashed her face with some cool water, hoping to lessen the flush. She returned to the main area, and Bauer was playing a new song. There was a bottle of vodka sitting on top of the piano, his jacket was off, and his sleeves were rolled up. She came and sat next to him again and waited for the song to end.

When he finished, he looked at her. "Play," he said. She thought for a second, then decided to play the song from the movie Oscar. It is a fast-paced and funny song and more challenging than any they had played so far. She tried to play it the best she could from memory but struggled. Wilhelm was having an even harder time. He continued to mess up the notes, making the song sound worse than it already did. He laughed at himself as he struggled, and it was infectious. She started to laugh as well, at him, herself, and the song.

When they stopped playing, he took a drink from the bottle on top of the piano. Eva held out her hand for it, and he raised an eyebrow, then pushed it into her palm. She took a swig, and it made her eyes water. He took the bottle out of her hand and drank from it again before standing up from the bench. He nodded his head for her to follow him. They walked back to their table, and he took his grey military jacket from the chair and pulled it on. He got his cap and gloves, and she retrieved her purse, coat, and scarf. She walked beside him to the door, and he took his coat from the wooden rack just to the left of it. Neither of them said a word, but she knew there was significance to them leaving. She just didn't know what yet.

As they walked in the cold February night, she tucked her head lower in her coat and quickened her pace to keep up with him. It started to rain, and she knew it would later turn to snow, but the rain would freeze on the roads before that. She didn't know where they were going but continued to walk beside him in the drizzling rain, wishing she had an umbrella.

After a while, she realized they were walking west toward the coast. And that is when she knew where they were heading. They were going to the cottage.

Her face was numb, and she could not believe how cold it was. It felt like she was walking in a freezer. They finally reached the cottage, and Wilhelm stopped at the front door. He glanced at her with a knowing look. "Are you ready to go in?" he asked.

"God, yes." A flush spread across her face as soon as she said it. She meant because she was cold. She glanced to the door, knowing everylast boundary between them would crumble if she walked through it. He took a key from the pocket of his black leather trench coat and stuck in into the lock, then pushed the door open, putting an arm around her waist, escorting her inside through the small wooden archway. She had a heightened awareness of his body and felt a hunger from being with him that stirred deep inside. She was aware it was there in both of them at this moment, not just in her. A different type of trepidation began to rise in her now. She and Wilhelm had kissed once before, but this was a massive step for her. She got the impression that tonight she would endure a military-style attack on her body.

Wilhelm let go of her, and apprehension grew inside as she prepared herself. He locked the door behind them, then turned and focused on her. She cast a nervous glance at him and their eyes met, but she couldn't explain what she saw in his. Heat? Thrill? Anticipation? All of those seemed possible and a spark of tension lit between them as she thought about how close they were about to be. Her cheeks heated, and she looked around the room and let out a shuttering sigh, nervous about crossing so many boundaries with him. She turned back to him, this man she was about to give herself to.

"This one time," she said, wondering if it was the truth.

"Yes." He gave her a predatory look, and his gaze darkened. He took a step towards her, a lethal glint in his eyes, and her first instinct was to move away, but she fought it. She was in no position to tell him to go away or fight her way out of her situation. He would never let himself get close to her again if she did.

This is how you survive, she reminded herself, but her heart was racing despite her steel resolve. As much as she wanted to scream and rage at Wilhelm for this situation she found herself in, she didn't want to give him the satisfaction, and it wasn't entirely his fault. Before the resistance pushed her into his arms, she and Wilhelm had always circled each other, even before either of them realized it.

He drew even closer and gently caressed her hand, the pulse of his warm fingers rippling through her. She noticed his gaze dropped to the low neckline of her dress that was visible under her open coat.

"It's nice to see you in something more feminine than that nurse's uniform." As he spoke, he reached out and placed his fingers lightly on her neck, letting them trail softly over her skin.

She tensed at his touch, and her stomach was doing flips. She knew what this man was capable of. She was aware of what lay beneath that handsome exterior. How could she ever forget what he had done to her? And the stories that were told about him. He might look and seem like the hero on the outside, but Wilhelm was a monster inside. She was almost certain of this. And she could not allow herself to ever forget it. But however hard she tried to remind herself of who she believed he was, she could not stop his touch from making her shiver.

He breathed out a small, quiet laugh as his hand drifted lower. He leaned in, holding her closer by the hips, his voice not much more than a whisper, and his warm breath caressed her ear. "Eva," he said, his voice emphatic. "Do you trust me?"

Attempting to suppress a cloud of fear, she glanced around the room, trying to find her confidence. Their eyes met, and Wilhelm gave her a slight smile, his hazel eyes warm upon her.

"I trust you," she told him, even though she wasn't sure she did.

He caressed her arm. "Good," he said, and she was overwhelmed by the level of emotion in his eyes. He slipped his arms around her waist and pulled her body against his. She forced herself not to resist, not wanting to show him her fear or discomfort, so she let him hold her. She let him nuzzle her neck. Remembrance of the other man, not this person before her now, but his true self, images of him years ago flashed before her. Him in her room back in La Chapelle, holding her dress. She tightly shut her eyes, fighting against the memories. He laid gentle kisses on her throat, and her memories of him recoiled at his touch, but her body responded to him differently.

How could he have such an effect on me? She wondered.

He spoke as he kissed her, his lips brushing her skin as they moved. "Are you trying to convince me that you have feelings for me, or yourself that you don't?" He was taunting her now as he moved his kisses lower.

She couldn't stand the tension between them anymore and pushed away, trying to catch her breath. She looked in another direction, eager to distract herself from thoughts of what they were going to do and what he was just doing to her. "I…" she paused, struggling to find words. Partly because she wasn't sure she knew the answer to his questions, and partly because the answer to them both was a resounding yes, because she was trying to seduce him, and she was also trying to convince herself that she didn't have feelings for him.

Wilhelm walked past her into the living room and began stacking wood on the hearth. After a few minutes, there was a fire crackling in it, giving off a lambent, soft, radiant glow that lit the room. She walked in and sat on the couch near it, enjoying its warmth. She glanced over at the little round side table that she used to sit her tea on when she lived in the cottage. She also used to sit The Wizard of Oz there when she would read it.

Where are you, Gerhardt? Don't be lost to me too, like my family and Jon. Before misery could take hold, she pressed her longing for Gerhardt, her family, and her friends firmly away. Everything outside this room needed to be pushed out. This room and Wilhelm, that's all there is tonight. She turned her focus back on the fire and everything surrounding her. Wilhelm was now sitting in the chair he always did, watching her, his hand resting on the cushioned armrest. He appeared relaxed and placated, but she could sense the maelstrom in him just beneath the calm surface. She glanced uneasily away, then forced herself to look back at him again as vulnerability took hold. "Wilhelm, I have heard that you... well, do some pretty crazy things with women."

For a moment he didn't speak, but continued to watch her, his eyes slowly moving over her, taking her in. "Relax," he finally said. "You are safe tonight, and this evening won't be anything like the stories you have heard. I will not force myself on you or harm you if that is what you are afraid of."

So he had heard the stories. She frowned at him. "You can be pretty aggressive when you want to be, which is often."

The side of his lip pulled at some private thought. "I can be," he agreed as he retrieved a bottle and two glasses from a tray on the other side table near the chair. He raised and met her gaze once more. "But I will try not to tonight."

She nodded and took in a deep breath. Wilhelm had lessened some of her anxiety, but as reassuring as he was being, she was still apprehensive about tonight.

He sat one of the cups down on the table by her, his brow furrowed as he took her in. "Eva," he said with understanding. "It's not going to be whatever it is you are imagining. If I did this exactly how I wanted with no consideration for you, then I would have you on your hands and knees as I took whatever I wanted, whenever I wanted, and however I wanted. But that's not what's going to happen tonight."

Her eyes widened at his words and the image it put Into her head. "You don't know what I'm imagining." She squeezed her hands together. Wilhelm gave her a waited look, then bent down, pulling her hands apart, taking them in his as he traced a gentle circle on her palms with his thumbs. "Do you know how scary and confusing all of this is?" she asked. "I don't mean just tonight, but all of it." She frowned at him. "So much about everything that has happened to me in the last three years has felt wrong. I am treated like I know nothing and have little control over my own life. Partly because I am a woman, but also because I am in a land that is not my own. First, you were after me, now the resistance wants to kill me, and I am always looking over my shoulder in fear that they will find me." It dawned on her that she was confiding in Wilhelm. He, too, seemed surprised by her sudden candor, but his focus remained unwavering. The frustration, fear, and anger pulled to the surface as she involuntarily shivered in response to how unforgivingly unfair this time could be.

"Eva," Wilhelm said as he stood, then gently pulled her from the couch, his voice deep and emphatic. "And someday you can kick them so hard in the balls that they are spitting up their nuts. I will give you that satisfaction."

She gave him a surprised look, unexpectedly comforted by his violent sentiment. "The thought of that actually helps."

He gave a low laugh as he reached up to caress her cheek with his index finger. "Good, I meant it." He picked the glass up off the side table and held it out to her. "Drink this; it will relax you."

"What is it?" she asked as she peered down at the brown liquid in her cup, sitting back on the couch.

"Port wine. Have you ever had it before?"

"No."

"It's strong. Not like other wines you've had."

"Good. Because I'm really nervous."

He paused, his eyes flicking up to meet hers. "I don't think you will be for long. But I will take it slow tonight. I don't want to hurt you. I know you have only done this once. It might take time for your body to warm up, this being only your second time. It's better to not go right for it in the beginning."

For a moment, she was confused, then it dawned on her, and her face warmed. "Skilled in deflowering virgins, or barely not virgins, are you?" she asked hotly, embarrassed by his words.

He smiled and sipped his wine. "No, I have actually never been with a virgin. You are the closest thing to a virgin I will have been with."

Feeling apprehensive, she sipped her wine, wrinkling her face at the strong bitter taste. The dry liquid burned as it went down. She opened her eyes and looked at Wilhelm, surprised that he could drink it so easily. He was sipping the wine, his gaze intent on her. She took another small sip as the wine began to relax the tension in her body, but her emotions and suppressed thoughts rose to the surface. Gerhardt's face and his eyes that were so blue she thought she would drown in them lit in her mind along with the memory of his embrace, his kisses, and the one time they made love. *Gerhardt!* she thought. Sadness engulfed her, feeling uncomfortably sharp as it filled her heart with pain. *This should be with you. We were supposed to be together.* She sipped the wine again, desperate to let the all-encompassing feel of the alcohol push back the grief. *He is not yours, Eva; you have to let him go.* She told herself. She took in a long shuttering breath as the wine's effect sank in deeper, calming her. She realized that she had never removed her shoes, coat, or scarf, only her gloves. She sat down her glass and stood up, taking off her coat and draping it over the back of the couch. Then she slipped her shoes off, pushing them to the side with her foot. She took another sip of her wine, then set the glass back down on the side table and considered Wilhelm. The casual way he was sitting, hips pushed forward, leaning casually on one elbow, his glass loose in his hand.

"Have you been with many women?" she asked, remembering him mentioning he had been with other women, then again maybe she didn't want to know.

He sipped the rest of his wine slowly, sitting the cup on the table beside him. She was surprised that he seemed a little guarded by her question. "A few."

It stung a little to hear this, which was ridiculous because he was not hers either. Eva mentally chastised herself. It was clear that he was experienced. "What constitutes a few?"

His brow tightened. "Well, I've never been with another German for what it's worth."

Now, this surprised her but didn't answer her question. She tried to shrug off the ridiculous hurt that was strong enough to cut through the haze of the wine. "That's surprising," she said.

He gave a malicious smile. "I don't mess with the German ideology of purity regarding Arian female virginity. That can be a touchy subject."

She was uncomfortable with thoughts of who he had actually been with. "So, whores?"

Wilhelm leveled his gaze on her, unamused, throwing an incredulous look. "No, Eva, I don't want women I have to pay for."

She was now even more confused, but then her thoughts horrified her. "Please tell me you've never been with a prisoner?"

"Eva, I'm disappointed you would even suggest that."

She furrowed her brows at him. "If you haven't been with whores, Germans, or prisoners, then who?" She knew she was being intrusive, but this entire situation was kind of intrusive.

Wilhelm let out a long sigh. "Is this really important that you to know?"

Yes, but it shouldn't be, she thought. *And I don't think I can be with you if you've been abusive to women in the past.* That thought made her uncomfortable.

"Yes," she told him. "I need to know."

He reached for the wine bottle and poured some more into his glass, then set it back on the table. He tipped it, watching how the light from the fire played on the liquid. "There were some new secretaries in Austria. They were Norwegian girls who needed jobs to help support their families, so they came to work for the Germans. We would get new ones every year, and they were far away from their home and lonely. Let's just say that they have a different moral viewpoint of their women than we do, regarding…" He gestured towards her, then himself, with his glass. "There were several instances throughout my time there where one or more of the girls and I fell into mutual attraction, so we pursued that attraction. What I got from these women was just a temporary release." He took a sip from his glass then rested it on his leg. "Also, several female SS personnel, all Austrians, though." Her mouth was slightly ajar as she stared at him. He laughed. "Don't ask questions you don't want answering, Eva."

She narrowed her eyes. "You have a strange love life, which sounds complicated and a bit hollow."

He sighed and gave her a slow once over. "Yes, I do."

"SS?" She couldn't quite wrap her mind around it. "But aren't they mean, with their guns, clubs, and low moral compass?"

He gave a curt laugh. "I guess I like dangerous women." He pointed to her with his glass. "Obviously. And Eva, female SS members do not have guns. None of the women in the German military carry guns."

"What kind of soldier doesn't carry a gun?" she asked wryly.

"They aren't soldiers."

"Of course not," she said sarcastically. "Well, I guess it's good you like dangerous women since you might be risking your life tonight. Because I can beat you up now."

He smirked, remembering the fluke punch. "I'm ready for you this time." There was a mischievous gleam in his eyes. "And your coordination is off since you've had that wine." He flashed her a sultry smile and stood up, pouring more wine into her glass.

She looked Wilhelm over as he poured the wine, really noticing him, and it roused her, causing butterflies in her stomach. She imagined his body under his pants and shirt, taking in his smooth muscular movements, his warm hazel eyes, remembering that she saw him naked. She realized he had never seen her naked before, that he didn't know what she looked like, but she knew what his naked body looked like. Her face turned a scarlet red, but she was sure he couldn't see it with only the light of the fire. She took a sip and slid her tongue over her lips. The wine no longer bothered her like it did at first. She opened her eyes and smiled at Wilhelm as she watched him take her in, the burning firewood crackling softly in the background. *He is being so patient,* she realized. Keeping his desire pressed firmly inside. But she also knew that she couldn't stall forever.

She stood with bated breath and set her wine down. "Would you unbutton these?" she asked him as she turned her back to him, her heart beating fast in her chest. Wilhelm's eyes darkened, and the tension in the room became palpable. She watched breathlessly as he set down his glass and rose in one smooth motion, coming up behind her. He gently caressed the sides of her arms, and she drew in a shuttering breath, his touch intensifying the already existing tension between them. She could feel the warmth of his body radiating all along her back, her breath hitching in response to it. She was surprised and embarrassed that she loved the smell of him. She closed her eyes, leaned back against his chest, and breathed him in, turning to nuzzle her cheek against his warm neck as his own breathing increased. Wilhelm slid his hand between them, moving back a fraction as his fingers made quick work of her buttons. Then he tugged her dress down, and it dropped on the floor, puddling around her feet, revealing her silky, once white camisole top and bottom. Wilhelm's arms slid around her, his hard body pressing against hers, his desire no longer being held back as she could feel his erection poking into her back. She looked at him again over her shoulder, breathing erratically as she was swept up in sudden anticipation and the entrancing feel of his body searing into hers. Her desire was now more powerful than any aversion to him.

Wilhelm's breath was warm against her ear, his deep voice an inviting whisper. "Take off the bottom."

She turned and sat on the couch, aware of how unsteady she was from nerves, desire, the wine, and her draw to him. She took hold of the camisole skirt and pushed it down around her ankles. Dressed now in only her thin silk white camisole top, panties, and silk stocking. She met Wilhelm's fiery gaze, then laid back on the couch, basking in the feel of his eyes on her, wanting him to look. He brushed her leg for a brief moment, and she lowered her eyes just as he removed something from a leather bag by the chair. It was a small tin box that he opened, taking out something rolled like a rubber band held together in the middle with a piece of brown paper.

"Is that… a condom?" she asked, a little embarrassed. Wilhelm nodded, took off the paper, and unrolled it, laying it on the table. She flushed over the need for a condom because of what was about to occur. She had never had a condom inside her before and was unsure what it would feel like and whether or not that feeling differed from the feel of bare skin. Gerhardt hadn't worn a condom, but then again, when they made love, it really wasn't planned. She was a little surprised that she hadn't gotten pregnant and considered herself extremely lucky that she hadn't.

Wilhelm's expression grew serious as his gaze slid over her, his desire radiating out towards her. "That fabric is thin. I can see through it." He looked at her, the lust in his eyes growing more insistent.

She looked down, her nipples clearly visible through the thin, white fabric. "Of course, you would notice that." She teased and bit her bottom lip.

"The wine has relaxed you, I see."

"It has," she said, nodding her head slowly up and down.

"Good," he said. "Because I'm going to take that off of you." She swallowed, the tension picking up in the room. She moved from the couch to the floor, pulling the blanket along with her. She laid it beside her and reached up, taking her glass of wine from the table. She took a sip and then another, hoping it would help calm her nerves even more.

"Where did you get the tattoo on your arm?" Wilhelm enquired to the small bird on her left wrist, his focus intent as he looked at it.

"Egypt, years ago," she explained. "When I visited with a group of friends as a teenager. I have another one too." Without thinking first, she pulled up her camisole to show him the tiny Eye of Horus and could sense Wilhelm's focus scattering for a moment as he stared at the small tattoo on her naked abdomen near her pelvic bone, his gaze growing liquid before he raised his eyes to meet hers.

"You were in Egypt?" he asked, a little hoarse.

She nodded as she glanced down at her glass, the wine such a lovely reddish-brown color. "I had alcohol for the first time there too, which is funny because they don't drink alcohol, and I was underage," she confessed to him with a mischievous smile. "I drank too much one night in Cairo with another girl, then we wandered the streets until morning."

Astonishment was clear on his face. He leaned forward, his face pulled into an expression of puzzlement. "Did you just say you drank alcohol in Cairo and stayed out all night?"

"Uh-hum." She grinned at him and took another sip.

Wilhelm took a deep breath, pondering this. "Well, the odds of your survival probably just got a whole lot better. If you managed to keep yourself alive through that, then you can take care of yourself better than I thought."

"Why do you say that?" she asked.

"Because that can be a dangerous city even during the day for someone who isn't from there, even for a man."

"Well, I drank quite a lot and quickly found that alcohol makes me feel…," she gave him a slow smile, "relaxed." Eva was aware that she was already slightly drunk and couldn't control its effects on her.

Wilhelm's eyes took on a suggestive gleam. "Would you like me to loosen you up more?"

Her heart quickened, a hard pounding in her chest. "Yes, I believe I would."

Wilhelm seemed amused at her brazen actions. He stood, took the glass from her hand, set it on the table, then pulled off his shirt in one smooth motion and pitched it into the chair. He then removed his undershirt and tossed it on top of the shirt. His partial nudity was a shock, and a hard spike of desire flashed through her. She swallowed as her eyes wandered over his handsome frame. She had seen him without his shirt after he was injured and then again when she watched him fight. But she wasn't fond of him then when he was at the hospital, plus he had wounds and bandages all over him, so it was hard for her to see his body in a positive or attractive way. She couldn't see the beauty of him then that she could now. And when she watched him fight, she was not up close like now. It was hard to notice his lack of a shirt then because she was too confused about what was happening, uncomfortable with the whole situation and shocked by the violence of the fight.

His chest was muscular, with some dark brown hair on his upper chest that went between his pecks and a line that trailed down his stomach, disappearing into his pants. She remembered seeing the hair on his chest from before. Embarrassed, she quickly looked back to his face and found that his smile had turned feral. Wilhelm removed the pistol strapped to his side, his wallet, and a small knife, setting them on the table. He then sat and removed his boots.

"Are you sure you won't need them?" she challenged, nodding to the gun and knife on the table, attempting a fierce look while trying to lighten the tension in the room a little.

"As dangerous as you are, I highly doubt it," he jested and shot her a grin. "Lie down," he said in a deep command. She complied, and he kneeled on the floor, softly rubbing his hands over her. They flowed over her body, moving in a caressing wave, sending delicious shivers through her. Some spots were relaxed and others shockingly pleasurable where his hands touched, pushing down on her bare skin. Her breathing deepened as a shiver radiated down through her core.

His eyes took on a carnal look, then he leaned over. Her chest shook from having him so close, and she could almost taste his mouth. She parted her lips as he hovered, feeling him about to take his bite, and she craved it. She craved him. He pressed his mouth to hers, soft, but possessive, dragging her bottom lip out with his teeth. She sucked in a breath, the excitement rushing through her. Then, he moved down and caught her nipple through her camisole, and she let out a cry.

"It's a lot more enjoyable with your clothes off." He lifted his eyes to her.

She stared at him for a long, tension-fraught moment. Her words were low when she spoke. "Then take them off."

For a moment, neither of them moved. The logs crackling and popping in the fireplace were the only sound. Then Wilhelm was next to her in one smooth movement. He focused on her with searing intensity, his hands sliding up her camisole, then it was off in two tugs, and the rest of her clothes in one smooth motion. He had the fervent intensity of a pro. There was no hesitation, no awkwardness, Wilhelm was not shy.

He leaned down, and his mouth claimed hers, then he lowered himself onto her, his muscular body pressing sensually against hers, hard and warm, exciting her. She could sense him straining against his careful control. He managed to get his feelings in check and pulled back from her, almost like he did when she tried to kiss him. His touch was softer now, his raging passion a little more contained. He waited for her, letting the intensity build as he kissed her ardently. His passion was an inferno whose flames leaped towards her and then pulled back, like the cadence of a dance, keeping with the tempo. Teasing her by withdrawing, giving heated glimpses of his full passion. Slowly, she caught on, and they began to find each other's rhythm, faltering less and less, exploring each other's bodies as they did. She liked the feel of his hard thigh muscle beneath her hands, the jutting of his hip bones that were visible under his pants. She reveled in the power she seemed to have over him at this moment.

His hands were firm on her, and her skin sparked with increasing longing for him. These things surprised her, cutting through the haze of her own self-control. She dropped her hands to her sides and he grazed his fingertips over her outstretched palms, sending tingling waves of heat through her entire body. How could such a small act have that kind of effect? He put his mouth on her bare nipple now, shocking her. His tongue moved over it as his teeth grazed her skin. The sensuous glimpses of his half-naked body moving against her were intoxicating.

Suddenly his weight was gone, and he was sitting up next to her, eyes fixed down on her. "Lie on your stomach," he hoarsely instructed.

Enamored by him, she eagerly complied. Wilhelm traced his fingers over her back, leaving a tingling sensation in their wake. More and more, she was sinking into the pleasure he was giving her.

"Move your legs apart," he told her, his voice deep with desire.

She did as he said, and he slowly moved his hand down her body, sending shivers through her as he put his hand at her apex. Enjoyable tension built, then it coalesced in one spot between her legs, and as he moved his fingers again and again on and in her, the intensity building, then a sudden explosion of shuttering ecstasy overcame her. Her neck craned to the side and her back arched as she cried out, a throbbing heat enveloping her, wave after wave of it taking its time receding.

She squeezed her eyes shut and let out a long, shuttering breath. Only then did he move back beside her. He rolled her onto her back, his half-clothed body sliding on top of hers. His own hard desire pressed where she could still feel the pleasure he had just given her. She still had her eyes closed, wanting to revel in this feeling for as long as she could and bask in the incredible sensation he had given her. She wasn't sure how, but she could still feel it, only she couldn't distinguish if the feeling was still coming from her body or her mind. She turned her hips to try to hold on to the edges of that feeling, pressing herself against him as she did. He rolled half off her again, and she heard a slight click and could feel him unfastening his pants. She opened her eyes and then turned quickly away when he removed his underwear, the room spinning, her heart thudding in her chest. The sensation he

271

gave her still racing through her. Wilhelm gently slid back over her, nothing between them now, just skin pressed against skin. She could easily feel the entire length of his body pressing enticingly against hers. He propped himself up on one elbow, placing his palm on her stomach, then slid his hand lower, putting it between her thighs. She let out a ragged breath, her hands tightening on him. She caught a glimpse of his erection and nervous surprise mixed with sudden want. It was so intimate, the sight of him. It was thick and hard, sticking straight out. Her breathing deepened in response. A man's body aroused; she had only seen this once before in this way, and it was in darkness. There had barely been enough light in the room to see much of anything. She had seen patients erect, but that could hardly be considered intimate.

Wilhelm's body pressed against hers as he kissed her on the mouth, then the neck, long and sensuously. A hunger took hold as their passion intensified, and she pulled at him to move on top of her completely. He obliged and shifted all the way on her, the full pressure of his weight pressing into her body now. Then, a jolt of stretching pain caused her to tense for an instant as it rippled through her. She gasped at the sensation she had not felt in so long, her opening tight around him, and it surprised her that it hurt a second time. Wilhelm paused, now deep inside her, one hand grasping her hip, his mouth almost touching hers, his hot breath on her lips. He was breathing hard as he waited for her, all firm control, as the sting of his entry receded. He brought his mouth back to hers and kissed her deeply, sending a different kind of ripple through her. He waited for her grip on him to loosen, then he moved in her, slowly at first.

She gasped at the fullness of him. It wasn't overwhelming like it was the first time, but the pleasure intensified, balancing out the pain. Her mind and body were now open to receive him, and she welcomed every touch, every movement, every sensation. She arched her hips towards him as he moved downward, the awareness of him running through her. Wilhelm's movements were smooth and in enticing rhythm with the motion of his mouth and tongue. He loosened, then tightened his grip on her, teasing her body. She slowly fell into sync with him, moving her body with his as waves of pleasure pulsed through her. She pressed her hips forward again to meet him and felt his smile on her mouth. This time was not an explosive rush or as ecstatic as before when he used his fingers. The slight sting at the edges of the skin that was around him was holding her back, but a more mellow, sultry pleasure coursed through her, dampening her pain.

She let out a sigh of pleasure and contentment and glided her fingers down his muscular back, feeling the goosebumps they were making. Wilhelm's control began to fracture as he picked up the intensity of his rhythm, his touch becoming increasingly impassioned with a growing hunger as his thrusts into her built. He savored her, holding her upper thigh with his hand, digging his fingers into her flesh as he kissed her breast, using his body to persuade her body to reach the intensity he felt. Once she reached the height of his sensation, she felt a passion she had never experienced before, not even with Gerhardt. This feeling she had never known existed. It was a feeling she never thought she would have with him. A feeling she never thought possible with him.

She wrapped her legs tight around him and placed her mouth on the front of his neck near the Adam's apple. She pressed her hips hard against him as he came down, scratching his back sensually with her nails. That is when he lost all control. He thrust hard in her, again and again, his breathing hot and ragged as he gripped at her fiercely.

"Christ, fuck you feel good," he growled.

He drove a gasp from her lungs with one final thrust that flooded her with warmth as he let out a groan that came from deep in his throat. He gripped her, his jaw pressing into her shoulder, his breath hot, every muscle in his body rock hard as he gave one, final, quivering shake. His eyes met hers, and they were alert but unguarded. The wild yearning in them stunned her, and she almost shrank back from the intensity of it. After a long moment, Wilhelm's breathing evened out, and the raw, ardent intensity of his gaze dimmed. They lay like this for a moment, her stunned from what they had just done and him in nirvana. He pulled out in one smooth motion as she clung to him, still in a haze from the heat of their desire and the intensity of the moment.

"No, don't go," she pleaded.

Wilhelm gave a low laugh as he moved off her onto his back, now staring at the ceiling, one hand resting on his muscular stomach. His breathing was still deep and ragged. She sensed a distance forming between them and clung to him, hanging onto his arm. But he was suddenly lost in thought, elusive. She was still affected by the force of their combined passion, overcome by a pleasurable heated daze, but still alert enough to realize that he had been incredibly considerate in how he had handled her tonight. There was only a slight throbbing ache where he had been, mingled with the hot lingering pleasure. He turned on his side and met her eyes.

"I think I'm still swimming in the intensity of what just happened," she told him. "I have not known passion like that."

One finger traced lightly along the curves of her side. "It's only a reflection of what I feel," he said, his voice throaty. "I have wanted you so much, Eva." He moved a strand of hair from her forehead. "You are so beautiful." He looked at her body with deep appreciation, as if she was Aphrodite lying before him. His gaze lifted to hers, and the affection in his eyes struck a chord deep inside her heart. He traced little circles on her thighs. "Have I managed to subdue you then?" he teased, sending a shiver through her as he now rubbed his finger over her palm.

She coughed out a laugh, and even through their passionate thrall, she managed a look of searing defiance. "No."

Wilhelm chuckled low. "I didn't think so."

He lightly touched the tip of her nose with his finger, smiling wickedly, before his eyes grew serious. His smile faded, and that ardent fire flashed in his eyes one last time before being drowned with conflict. Wilhelm eased onto his back again and stared at the ceiling once more, his expression unreadable.

She was too relaxed from the sensations coursing through her to feel the sting of his withdrawal. The pull of him, the wild pleasure of being with him, and the nefarious way they were together blended and swept her into a deep sleep.

Chapter Sixteen

When her eyes fluttered open, the aurora of the morning sun was bathing the small living room in light. Eva stared up at the plaster ceiling and wooden beams as rays streamed across it, and the events of the evening came rushing back into her foggy mind, as did the many feverish dreams she had.

She heard a noise and lifted her head, looking around the room. Wilhelm was up, and she could tell he had showered even in the early morning light. She could smell the scent of soap mixed with the other scents in the room. He was already in a fresh pair of pressed pants as he retrieved his starched shirt from the chair, pulling it over his shoulders, buttoning it, and tucking it onto his pants. She turned onto her side, a little confused by the location she had slept, and met Wilhelm's deep gaze. As he pulled the suspenders over the crisp white shirt his eyes quickly moved from her face to her chest, and she saw a spark in them that reminded her of last night. She looked down at herself and was completely jarred out of her groggy, sleepy state, realizing that she was still fully naked as humiliation set in. She jerked the blanket that was arbitrarily wrapped around her legs up over her breasts, tucking it tightly under her arms.

This is wrong, she thought, questioning the wisdom of sleeping with Wilhelm Bauer, even if it was necessary. *This should not have happened.* Her pulse sped up as her emotions intensified, causing her stomach to churn. Wilhelm was professional and constrained, face tensing deep in thought as he grabbed his jacket and shrugged it on. He put some papers in a small leather satchel, eyes flicking toward her now and then, his expression unreadable, as usual. Loneliness crept in, breaking through her weak resolve, making her feel empty inside. She lay still, her messy hair and nakedness startling to her. She noticed the contrast of her state this morning to his orderly demeanor and cold efficiency.

This was a mistake. What have I done? He now has control over me he didn't have before. And to make it worse, I enjoyed it, she thought, remorse blindsiding her. She ran her fingers through her tangled hair in an attempt to make herself more presentable. *This should have been something I only did with Gerhardt. Instead, I gave myself to a man who might care for me but won't devote himself to me.* The thoughts whirled in her head. She knew that this was not done on a whim but to save her life. Even with this knowledge, she could not escape the fierce tide of grief and emotion as it captured her in its undercurrent. There will be no more tender encounters with Gerhardt, no more lazy summer evenings spent together discovering one another, no him cradling her in his arms after they make love. That was gone forever. She curled up into a ball, the cold nipping at her naked body as the fire died down, and closed her eyes, trying to not cry. She wanted her family again. She wanted to tell them she loved them and that she was sorry for ever leaving. That everything had turned to shit and she was in a terrible mess. That they were right to worry about her, and she didn't know what to do. She was lost because she was being faced with impossible choices. She wanted to talk to her dad again like she used to. She wanted her mom to comfort her and her brother to look after her as he always did. The thoughts pressed in on her as a tightness formed in her chest.

She didn't know what Bauer was doing because she couldn't hear him anymore. The room was completely silent, but she knew he was watching her. She could feel his gaze and mentally prepared herself, recalling how insensitive Wilhelm had been in the past. How he snapped at her in La Chapelle, mercilessly watched as she was tortured in Berlin, totally desensitized by the action, and told her when he was in the hospital that she was weak and that she needed to toughen up. She just might lash at him with uncontrollable anger if he said anything like that now, even if he was right.

"Eva," his voice was kinder than usual when he spoke. She opened her eyes, blinking away tears, to find him standing over her next to the couch, holding his hand out.

"No," she said to him in a quiet voice. "I don't have any clothes on." Guilt flooded through her again for her actions last night. She closed her eyes, squeezing them tightly shut, trying to block everything out, including him. *What have I done?* a voice screamed inside.

She heard him move around her. "Eva." She opened her eyes to find him kneeling beside her, his gaze focused on her. "I can only guess that this capricious manner is because of the baptism by fire you've been put through. But I'm not going to leave you to fend for yourself, alone and vulnerable. I will safeguard you in any way I can."

She wanted to scream at him. He didn't know how close to death they both were. "There is no place that is safe for me as long as I am in Europe, only constant danger. There are people who despise me, who want to kill me and watch me suffer." The thoughts consumed her. The knowledge that she would have to fight to survive, but that her odds of survival were bleak. She was so afraid, and the anguish she felt at the thought of dying was suffocating. She started to tremble. She didn't know why all these feelings were coming to the surface now and in front of him.

Wilhelm took her hand, holding it tight in his large, warm one. "I will catch them before they get to you."

This pulled her back from the sinking feeling inside. She looked up at him, her eyes and meeting his gaze. He spoke as if it was an indisputable fact. His words couldn't extinguish her crippling fear, but the certainty in his voice sustained something deep inside her. She stiffly wiped away her tears and picked up his shirt from last night that he draped over her legs. She pulled her hand from his and attempted to put the shirt on under the blanket, struggling to keep it around her as she moved. She noticed he didn't look away and gave him a look of censure. She managed to get it on, and he pulled her to her feet, sweeping his eyes over her body as he did, and his candor surprised her, and she was astonished that he would be so audacious. She shot him a warning glance as she pulled the shirt tighter around herself, desire flashing in Wilhelm's eyes. He came to stand behind her, wrapping his arms around her waist, his breath warm against her cheek. He began to nuzzle her neck, moving one hand from her waist to gently move her hair aside so he could kiss the back and side of her neck. She gave a shiver. The touch of his hand was soothing. She closed her eyes and intentionally leaned into him; her breathing slowed, and the fear that had petrified her seemed to lessen. Finally, feeling a little calmer, she looked up at him.

"If I did not need to get to work right now, I'd take that shirt off you, pull you upstairs into the bedroom, and rapture your body again."

He traced his lips over her jaw as she gaped at him. His honest, unrestrained lust was so shocking that it made her cough out a disbelieving laugh unintentionally. She could tell by his playful manner that he was attempting to comfort her, but the lust was not part of the playing. She realized that attempting to be close to Wilhelm was like trying to close ranks with a feral animal. It was an unnerving sort of comfort, but still a comfort. She would love nothing more than for someone to console her and tell her everything was going to be alright, but she didn't need that right now, and she knew it. Wilhelm might be cold and heartless most of the time, but in truth, that is what she needed. Someone hard that would give some tough love, and this dangerous, ruthless man was offering her that. She marveled at him, and an unexpected feeling of gratitude overcame her. She turned to face him, rose up on the tip of her toes, and pressed her lips to his, feeling the soft warmth of his mouth. She lingered, the kiss lasting longer than she had expected. Then slowly pulled back, noticing a yearning flare in his eyes as she lowered herself back down, flattening her feet on the floor.

"If you kiss me like that again..." he said seriously, his voice low and rough, "I will take you right here on the floor again; the hell with work."

She teasingly slid her hand through his hair, taking some in her closed fingers, and pulled as she rubbed a finger over his skin just above the collar of his shirt. She could feel the desire rising inside, and it scared her. She suddenly realized that she wasn't sure she wanted to let him do that to her again or that she should. She dropped her hand to her side and stepped a few inches back from him. He was studying her intently with those predator eyes of his.

"You should go," she said.

For a moment, he didn't move, then finally broke their gaze and retrieved the leather satchel, gave her one more intense look before going to the hall, taking his black leather coat, hat and gloves from the hook and then walking out the door. She heard it close but didn't move from where she was standing to look out the window. The car engine roared to life, then tires crunched on frozen snow. She finally turned her head to the window, just in time to see the back of the car before it was out of view. She dropped onto the couch, trying to register everything that had happened up to this moment. A wave of anxiety rushed over her. Her chest felt tight, her breaths were coming in quick, panicked bursts, and a surge of nausea pushed its way up her throat as her body rocked back and forth. The logical part of her brain nudged at the edge of panic, trying to persuade calmness. She drew in several shaky breaths as the ringing in her ears eased. "Think, just focus," she whispered, but it seemed almost impossible to believe that this had happened. Once her breathing was under control, she looked around the room, the blanket still wadded on the floor, the dying fire crackling, and his shirt still on her. She stood, pulled off the shirt, grabbed the blanket off the floor, and wrapped it around her as she retrieved her clothes. Once dressed, she draped the shirt over the chair and added some wood to the fire. She sat down on the floor in front of the fireplace and tucked her legs beneath her dress as she tried to warm herself and contemplate what to do next, but her mind would not stay focused on that. The memory of Wilhelm's fiery touch, the way he took her with such a burning heat, and the feel of him inside her dominated her thoughts. It was all so fresh in her memory, almost as if he was still here. Every sensation, the chemistry between them, the passion coursing through her body. It all felt so natural to her, which was alarming. It was new and exciting but terrifying at the same time. Being with him wasn't something she should do. She should not have enjoyed what they did last night, the things he did to her, or his company.

She tapped her cheeks with her palms. "No, Eva. Do not think about him or what you did with him." Feeling a little calmer and more alert, she looked over at the side table where he had the satchel, an idea coming to her. She stood up and went over to it, but nothing was on it. She searched the rest of the living room, but nothing work related was there. She turned towards the hall, then walked across the living room into the entryway and stopped. She peered up for a brief second into the dim light of the stairwell, then she ascended the steps. She felt like she was being watched but knew it was only her being paranoid. The first place she checked was his bedroom. She looked through the drawers, the armoire, beneath the mattress, under the bed, and the pillows but found nothing, only his few personal effects. He had left nothing in his room from work. She sat on the edge of the bed, feeling disappointed. There weren't even any personal things in his room that she wanted to snoop in. Clothes, that was all that was here. She got up and went to search the bathroom, but like in his room, the only things there were his toiletries. She spent the next half hour searching the rest of the house, but nothing turned up that would be of any use to the resistance.

Giving up, she returned to the living room and sat back on the couch, watching the fire die as it gave off its last remaining heat. When it was only embers, she scooped what was left into the metal bucket beside the fireplace and took it out back, dumping it in the snow. She put the bucket back by the fireplace and collected her things. She glanced into the room one last time as flashes of the night before unbiddenly made their way into her mind. It gave her a shiver, and she knew she would never look at this room, or this cottage, the same way again.

She worked the afternoon shift today, so she walked briskly towards home, keeping to the major streets but constantly looking over her shoulder. She felt like she had turned into a nervous wreck, but she had good reasons to be. Since that night she trekked through the woods to Belgium, her life had been a series of mishaps, near-death encounters, and dangerous liaisons.

Eva was relieved when she walked through the door to the apartment, closed it behind her, and locked it. Ingrid was asleep on the couch, covered with the small blanket they kept draped over the back, and a dirty plate and cup were sitting on the floor beside it. Eva tiptoed across the room, trying not to wake her, but the old wooden floor squeaked under her weight.

Ingrid took in a sharp breath, leaned up on her elbow, and squinted across the room. "Eva, where have you been? I waited up for you most of the night, but you never came home."

Eva came and sat at the end of the couch near her feet. "I'm sorry. I didn't mean to stay out so late."

Ingrid pulled herself up, leaning against the armrest. She looked at Eva for a protracted minute, then finally spoke. "I don't understand. You were out with Dr. Möller all night? I thought you were just going to dinner?"

Eva gave a surprised laugh. She had forgotten all about dinner with Dr. Möller. It would make sense, though, that Ingrid would think he was who she was with. But now she had another problem. How was she going to tell Ingrid it wasn't

Klaus she was out with all night? And would Ingrid understand?

"Yes, I went to dinner with Dr. Möller, but I wasn't with him all night."

"Where were you, then?"

"Ummm..." Eva figured she might as well tell her. Why try to hide it from her? She was her roommate and closest friend right now. "SS Obersturmbannführer Bauer." Eva winced as she said his name out loud.

Ingrid's expression turned sour. "You stayed out all night with him?"

"Yes, but I hadn't planned to. Dr. Möller and I ran into him at the restaurant, and when Dr. Möller went home, we stayed and had some drinks."

"But the restaurant isn't opened all night."

"I know. We later went back to his cottage and had more drinks there and I fell asleep on the floor." That was not a lie. She had slept on the floor, only next to him after making love. She would omit that information and hope that Ingrid didn't ask questions, especially the kind she would have to confess to or lie about.

"The two of you drank yourselves into a stupor?" she asked, a little perplexed.

"Not exactly a stupor, but enough to make me drowsy."

"Eva, what is going on between the two of you?" her eyebrows etched up in worry.

"To be honest, I don't know what my feelings are, or what we are doing."

"You had told me you thought you might love him. How long have you thought this? Is that why you saved his life?"

"No. I saved him for… well, let's just say it was for a very different reason. I guess I have noticed my feelings changing for him after we came to France together. I don't know if the feelings were there before, and I only noticed them now, or if they started developing here."

"This man is in the Gestapo, so what are you going to do?"

"I don't know what I am going to do. I feel like I don't know anything anymore." She anxiously looked away, focusing on the wall. "He is in the Gestapo, and that makes it so much harder. I have known him since the invasion of France. For the longest time, we hated one another, but when I saved his life, it altered things. That event is what started the change in him. I think he felt like he couldn't hate me after that."

"What do you think changed it for you?"

Eva had to think hard about that. She looked back to Ingrid. "I don't know. Maybe it was saving his life that started the change in me, too. I don't know if I want to be with him. But even more than that, I don't know if I should."

Ingrid took Eva's hand and enclosed it in both of hers. "I am a German, and I love my people and am loyal to my country. But I don't think every German is a good person, and I don't believe in every cause that Germany fights for. I tell you this because you are my friend, and I know I can trust you, even if you are fraternizing with a man in the Gestapo. The truth is, Eva, he is too cruel for you, even if through and through he is not a bad person. You need someone who has a heart like yours."

Eva gave her a warm smile. "I understand what you are saying. But I'm not sure I can ever break this bond. Do you work today?"

"No."

"Good. I work the afternoon shift and get off at eight. Let's go do something fun. I think we should go to the cinema, and we can get a piece of pie or cake while we're out too."

Ingrid's eyes lit up, but then her face fell. "I don't have enough ration coupons for that."

"But I do. I have been saving some."

"Why?"

"In case we wanted a treat." The excitement this elicited from Ingrid pleased her. It made Eva happy to see Ingrid smile again. She had been melancholy since she found out about the pregnancy.

"I won't go anywhere. I will be here when you get back."

"Alright." Eva pulled her hands free of Ingrid's. "I have to get ready for work now, but I'll see you tonight."

She went to her room and closed the door, needing a few minutes alone. She took a deep breath and leaned against the door. Her nerves were shot, and a wave of emotions flooded her as the undercurrent threatened to pull her down. But she was determined to not cry. She could not crumble from the pressure of it. She pushed away from the door, walked to her closet, and got a clean uniform. She went to the bathroom, took a quick shower, thinking how she was washing away all traces of him, then pinned her hair up in a bun, and applied a small amount of makeup. Ingrid was waiting to use the bathroom when she came out.

"I'll try to be on time," Eva told her as she walked past her to the coat rack.

"I know, but I'll understand if you are late."

Eva walked through the doors of the hospital feeling calmer and less internally tumultuous than she had since the events of last night. Not that she hated what she did, but she felt like she should hate what she did. She smiled when she saw Dr. Möller coming down the long hall in her direction. His white lab coat fluttered around his legs as he walked, looking down at a clipboard. Her smile faded when she realized he would undoubtedly ask her about last night. She pulled her shoulders back, stood up a little straighter, and sucked in a determined breath.

"Klaus," she called.

He looked up when he heard her voice, but he didn't smile. He tucked the clipboard under his arm and stopped when he reached her, studying her face.

"So, what happened after I left?"

"We played the piano and had some drinks."

She noticed the skeptical look in his eyes. "What did he want?"

"Just to talk. I'm alright, Klaus. Really."

"Talk? That isn't all he wanted."

"There is nothing more to say. That's what we did."

"And he took you home?"

Eva opened her mouth, but the words wouldn't form on her tongue. Finally, she found her voice. "I… went home alone."

"During curfew?"

Damn his intrusive questions. She broke eye contact. "No."

"You could not have gone home before curfew? It was already late when I left the restaurant."

"I didn't."

He took off his round-framed glasses and rested his hand on his hip underneath his lab coat. "He took in a deep breath, then let it out. "I cannot say that I am surprised, just disappointed."

That stabbed at her heart. "Please, don't be disappointed in me. I don't know why I didn't say no, but I understand I should have."

"This will only lead to heartache, Eva. Men like him will not ever be husband material. It isn't in their nature. He will never settle down and be a family man and father like you deserve. And no matter what happens with this war, you cannot stay in Germany. You need to go home to your family. That is where you belong."

Her eyes glistened with tears. "I want to go home, but it won't be like I remember. How will I ever be the same after all of this?"

"It will be hard and take work, but it can be done. You have to stop what you are doing with him, before it turns into something serious."

She nodded. "I know."

He put an arm around her shoulders. "Come on, let's get scrubbed in. We have patients waiting."

Eva did the rounds with Klaus, but there were no operations today, and she was thankful for that. Her concentration was all over the place, and her thoughts were scattered. At the end of the day, she finished with her last patient and took the dirty sheets and gowns to the laundry room, then went to find Klaus to tell him bye. She walked through the double doors that led to his small office that was situated on the main floor in the southern corner of the hospital but halted in her tracks when she saw Wilhelm sitting in the chair at the desk across from him, her heart skipping a beat. The two men were talking, but Eva couldn't hear what they were saying. She watched the interaction between them and could tell it was all business, but obvious discomfort was visible on Klaus's strained face. She really wanted to hear what they were talking about, but she didn't dare get any closer for fear that Wilhelm would see her.

She began backing away as she kept her eyes on them. She wanted to leave without them noticing her, but then Klaus and Wilhelm both stood, and she froze. If she moved now, one of them would notice her for sure. She looked around, but for what she didn't quite know. Turning her gaze back into the room, she saw Klaus had seen her. For a second, Wilhelm did not notice that Klaus's attention was not on their conversation, but once he did, he turned to follow his line of sight. Wilhelm's eyes fall upon her, and he paused. Both men stared at her, then Klaus waved for her to come in. Her pulse quickened to a rapid thumping in her chest, and she walked at a deliberate, slow pace towards them.

"Have a seat, Eva. The Obersturmbannführer was just leaving." Eva moved to the chair beside Wilhelm, not taking her eyes from him.

He stood. "Miss Abrams," he said in a professional, impersonal tone, reaching for his officer cap on the desk. "I will be in the lobby. I would like a word with you when you are done here."

Come on, Eva, do something, she hissed, trying to get her mind and body to work in sync, but all she could manage was a nod. Wilhelm, accepting her response, turned on his heels and left the room, his boots clicking on the tile in the hall. She took a seat and looked at Klaus. "Why were you talking to him?"

"I assure you, it was all business. Nothing to concern yourself with." He gave her a heartfelt smile.

"Business?"

"Yes, military business, actually. Don't forget that I'm an army doctor, Eva."

"I haven't. So you can't talk to me about it then?"

"No, I can't." He glanced at his open office door then back to her. Are you are going home, then?"

"I was but wanted to stop and see you before I left to tell you bye. That is when I saw him in your office. Ingrid and I are going to the cinema tonight."

"I am happy to hear that. How is she doing?"

"Fine." Eva smiled through the lie.

Klaus motioned toward the door. "Do you know why he wants to talk to you?"

Her stomach did a flip. "I don't. But I better go soon, or he will start getting impatient."

"Yes, it's better to not get on his bad side."

Eva stood from the chair. "We should do dinner at your apartment soon. I will cook."

He smiled warmly. "We should. We can come up with a date tomorrow." She started for the door. "Eva." She stopped, turning to look back at him. "Bring Ingrid with you."

"I will."

She left his office and walked towards the lobby, feeling more uncomfortable the closer she got. She saw Wilhelm standing by the window, looking out over the courtyard. His back was turned to her, so she took this opportunity to observe him. He was in his full uniform with his black leather trench coat over it. He had his cap back on and was wearing his gloves, and it looked like he had just walked in from the outside.

She came closer to him. "Wilhelm."

He slowly turned his head to look at her. He took her in for a moment before speaking. "Get your coat. We're going for a walk."

She creased her brows. "Why?"

"Just get your coat."

She frowned, uncomfortable at being kept in the dark. She went to the nurse's lounge and retrieved her things then came back to the lobby. "I'm ready. I can't be gone long, though. Ingrid is waiting for me. We are supposed to do something together when I get home."

"I won't take up much of your time."

They walked out together, through the hospital grounds and then onto the sidewalk. She was waiting for him to say something, but he seemed content just being in her company.

"What did you want to talk about?" she finally asked, breaking the silence.

"On Saturday, there is a gathering for the officers, a party of sorts. I would like you to come with me."

She noticed he didn't ask her to come but told her he wanted her to come. "What time?"

"It's in the evening."

"I work Saturday night."

"That's not a problem."

"How is that not a problem?"

"I'll inform the hospital that you need it off."

"But I don't."

"You do if I tell them you do."

And this was the Wilhelm Bauer that Eva remembered, asserting his authority. "Alright. Is it formal?"

"Not exactly formal, but you should dress in something nicer than your usual casual dress."

"I will see what I have."

He suddenly stopped walking. "This is where I leave you. I will pick you up at six on Saturday." He took her hand and pulled the glove down, then planted a soft kiss on the back of it. He let go of her hand and stepped onto the street, walked to the other side, then went in the opposite direction.

She stood in the cold February air, trying to understand what he was playing at. Finally, she turned and walked back to the apartment. When she opened the door, she didn't immediately see Ingrid. She didn't remove her outerwear and walked through the living room. "Ingrid."

"In here," she heard Ingrid call from the bathroom. Eva went around the corner and saw the bathroom door was open, and the light was on. Ingrid was leaning over the sink doing something with her hair.

"Are you ready?"

"Yes. Just give me a couple more minutes. I can't get these last few pieces of hair to stay up." She was trying to pin curls she had made with the curling iron on top of her head.

"Here, let me help." Eva swatted Ingrid's hands away, took the piece of hair, retrieved a pin from the side of the sink, and pinned it in place. She took the other two pieces of hair that were hanging on the side of Ingrid's head and pinned them up, too. "There. It looks good."

Ingrid turned her head from side to side, checking out her hair in the mirror. "It does look good."

"Ready then?"

Ingrid looked Eva up and down. "You aren't going like that, are you? In your uniform?"

"Oh, um, I was planning on it."

"No! You are not going like that. Now go change."

"Fine." Eva went to her room and pulled the first dress from the armoire that her hand touched and changed into it. It was a plain brown dress, but the material was thick and would keep her warm. She met Ingrid back in the living room. "I changed. Now let's go."

"Ingrid looked at her dress and frowned. "Well, I guess that is better than your nurse's uniform."

When they got to the cinema, Eva suggested a French movie to watch instead of a German one. She figured it would not be woven with propaganda. After the movie, they walked to the closest café as Ingrid linked her arm through Eva's, a smile frozen on her face.

"I loved that movie. I didn't understand a lot of what was said, but you translated. The French are so romantic. Can you imagine having a love like that?"

"Yes, I can."

Ingrid's face fell. "Sorry, I didn't think."

"There is no need for an apology. I did like the movie. It was nice to see a show that wasn't about the war for a change."

They took a seat by the window, and both ordered a slice of cherry pie. When the waiter sat the plate with pie in front of each of them, Eva's mouth watered. She had not had pie since she had been in this time. It was so hard to get stuff like this now. Many things were, like coffee, tea, wine, meat, sugar, chocolate, any kind of dessert, and those were just to name a few. Eva took the first bite, and she could swear it was the best thing she had ever tasted.

Ingrid put the fork in her mouth, and her eyes grew wide before they rolled up and her eyes closed. She pulled the fork out and opened her eyes, then covered her mouth with her hand, watching Eva as she chewed.

"Oh my God, this is amazing," Ingrid said after swallowing. "I don't know if it is really that good or just the pregnancy talking."

Eva laughed. "Probably both, because I agree. This pie is amazing. So, I wanted to ask. Have you thought more about what I said, about you telling the father?"

Ingrid pushed her fork through the pie, cutting another piece. "I have, actually. I might tell him. But not yet."

"That's fine. When you feel ready, that is when you should tell him. I'm glad you are considering giving him a chance to be a part of its life."

"He is lucky I am considering it. But I'm not going to let him think I will have him back because of this. And he will not take the baby."

"I agree. You should make that very clear." Eva scraped the leftover jelly from the plate, not wanting to let any of the pie go to waste. "Are you ready?" She looked at Ingrid's plate. Like her own, it was scraped clean. Ingrid nodded, and Eva got her purse from the seat, and they left the restaurant.

They walked arm and arm again back to the apartment, but Eva was on high alert the entire time. She was sure they were being followed by someone. It wasn't that she saw someone lurking in the shadows or turning down the same streets, but she had that undeniable feeling in the pit of her stomach that they weren't alone. She held tighter to Ingrid's arm and constantly looked around, surveying their surroundings. People passed them on the sidewalk, and Eva would eye them, but never once did anyone touch them, follow, or even speak to them. When they were back in the apartment, she locked the door and sighed with relief.

"That was so much fun," Ingrid said. Her face had a glow to it that it hadn't had in weeks.

Eva watched her remove her coat and shoes, happy she did this for her. Ingrid had enjoyed the evening while Eva had used it as a distraction. "I'm going to go to bed," Eva told her.

"Alright. I'll see you in the morning." Ingrid smiled up at her from the couch where she was now sitting. Her curls bounced with the movement of her head.

Eva returned the smile and went to her room, closing the door. She took off her dress, tossed it over the footboard of the bed, and crawled under the blankets. She was too tired to even remove the makeup she put on. She rested her head on the pillow, closing her eyes tight. She lay awake thinking about Saturday but finally lost the fight with exhaustion and fell asleep.

The evening of Saturday arrived quicker than Eva would have liked. She paced the living room floor, already wearing her coat and shoes, waiting for Wilhelm or his orderly to get there. She had told Ingrid that she was going out that night with him, and of course, Ingrid thought it was a terrible decision, but there was nothing to be done about it. Eva went to the kitchen to get a drink, her mouth feeling unusually dry. She pulled a glass from the cupboard and put it under the faucet, and twisted the handle, watching the water bubble as it filled the cup. A knock came from the door, and she froze. She turned off the water and peered at the door. The knock came again, and she set the cup on the counter next to the sink and walked across the living room. She hesitated for a second, then took hold of the knob and turned it. She cracked the door open and peeked around it. To her surprise, it wasn't Wilhelm at the door but his orderly.

The man smiled at her. "I am here to pick you up, Miss Abrams. Obersturmbannführer Bauer sends his apologies that he could not be here himself. But he wanted me to tell you that he will be there later this evening. Something came up that he could not put off."

Eva wondered what that could be. It must be something important for him to stand her up after inviting her. "It is no problem. Did he say what time he might arrive?"

"He did not. But I'm sure he won't leave you alone any longer than he has to."

Eva gave him an uncertain smile, stepped into the hall, pulled the door shut behind her, and followed him out to the waiting car that was parked in front of the building. He opened the back door for her, and she slid in, the cold leather chilling her legs through her dress and stockings. She watched him get into the driver's seat and start the car. Every so often, he would glance at her through the rearview mirror, his light blue eyes reflecting back at her. She looked away and pulled her dress further down, wanting to be there already.

The car pulled in front of the casino, and he put it in park. The building sat right on the beach, and it was arguably the nicest building in Dieppe, but Eva had never been here before. She had only seen it from a distance.

The orderly came around and opened the door for her, and she stepped out of the car and looked over the property. It was an upscale place where the wealthy would go, so it was no surprise that this was where the German military chose to hold a gathering for its officers.

"Thank you," she said.

"You are welcome."

He went around to the driver's door and got in, and she watched him pull away. She looked back at the building and wondered if she was supposed to just go in. She gathered up her courage and walked through the doors into the main lobby. People were milling around the room; some officers, some civilians, and others employees. A young man that worked there walked past her, and she turned and followed him. "Excuse me?"

He stopped and turned to her, giving her a bright smile when he saw her. "Yes."

"Can you tell me where the…," she paused, realizing how it was going to look if she asked where the German officers were meeting. But in truth, it was exactly how it was going to look. "Where the gathering for the German officers is?" she continued.

"Yes. It is straight through there." He pointed to a double set of doors on the far side of the room.

"Thank you," she told him and walked across the foyer to the set of doors. She pulled the heavy door open and walked into a spacious open room with tables placed on one side. It looked like it could be a ballroom. She did not know where she was supposed to sit so she stayed where she was. She glanced around at all the faces in the room but didn't recognize anyone. She found herself wishing that Klaus was here, but she doubted he would be, because it was probably only for the military officers in the Gestapo and the SS, but even if it wasn't, Klaus would not be here, it was not his sort of thing. He hated crowds.

She found an empty table and sat down, putting her clutch on the white linen tablecloth. There were quite a few people already there. Men in uniforms with women companions in fancy dresses. She looked down at her own dress, feeling inadequate in the plain, plum-colored satin dress she was wearing. She waited, looking for Bauer as the room grew more crowded, but he wasn't there. She was frustrated that she had to come on her own. In her peripheral, she caught sight of someone coming toward her table. She looked up, hoping it was Wilhelm, it was a man she didn't recognize in an officer's uniform approaching. He was tall and thin, with sandy blond hair and grey-blue eyes. He had the sort of face that made Eva uncomfortable and strangely fearful, somewhere in the pit of her stomach. Maybe it was because of the nasty scar that ran along the entire right side of his face.

The man stopped at her table and peered down at her. "Now, how come I see a pretty girl sitting all alone?"

"I'm not. I'm actually here with someone."

He looked around the room. "Where? I don't see anyone with you. Everybody I see is already with someone."

"He will be here soon." This man had no idea how much she wanted this to be true. He gave her a feeling she couldn't remember ever sensing around anyone. Wilhelm was scary and intimidating, but this man felt evil down to his core.

He pulled out the chair to the right of her and sat down. She noticed the SS runes on his collar like Bauer and wondered what branch of the SS he was in. She looked at his rank but was unsure what all the German rank symbols meant.

"And who are you waiting for?"

She didn't hesitate to answer. "SS Obersturmbannführer Bauer."

"Ahh, I had no idea he was coming tonight, especially with someone. He never brings anyone to these things. As a matter of fact, he usually doesn't come to these things."

"I guess that isn't true because he invited me."

"Well, it is certainly a first that I know of. I can only think of one person he would even consider bringing. But I will sit here and keep you company until he arrives. Are you sure he is coming?"

She was suddenly alarmed. "Why would he not come?"

"Because his work is the most important thing to him, and that will always come first. I'm afraid you might be waiting a very long time."

She peered at this man, his hollow, soulless eyes staring at her, and she wondered who he was talking about when he said there was only one person Wilhelm would have taken. She shivered and peered towards the doors, willing Wilhelm to hurry and get there. The sound of the band playing echoed through the room, and the surrounding lights dimmed. People took to the floor in pairs and started to dance. She watched them and tried to not look at him. He made her so uncomfortable she could hardly stay in her seat.

He stood up and took her by the arm, pulling her from her chair. "What are you doing?" she asked in an alarmed voice.

"Going to dance."

"No. I'm waiting for—"

"And he isn't here now, so you are free to dance with me."

She looked around, desperate for a way to get away from him. She froze when he pressed her to him and put his hand tight against her lower back. She had stopped breathing, and her lungs were tight in her chest. He started twirling them around the floor, very much in control of the situation and of her. He looked down at her with an expression she knew well, and it sent chills through her. She was certain that this man only looked at women as something to possess. For the fact that they had just met, and he was already looking at her this way, left her with no doubt.

"After this dance, I am going back to the table to wait."

"I don't think so. Why waste the night away over there waiting for him?"

His hand slid lower, moving from her back onto the top of her butt. Her blood ran cold, and she felt dirty like he was tainting her with just his touch. She reached back and pulled at his hand, trying to move it back up to her back. He gave her a sly smile and gripped onto her tighter so she couldn't move his hand. She placed both her hands on his chest and pushed, finally separating them. She glared at him, disgust evident on her face.

"You are coming on too strong. Is this how you treat all the girls you meet?"

"Yes, and most don't mind." He smiled at her like she should feel honored, that to have him touch her was the best thing that could happen to her.

"Well, I am not most girls." She turned and stalked back to the table, retrieving her purse. She turned around, almost bumping into him. "I am leaving. Tell Obersturmbannführer Bauer that I went home?" She took a step to the side and walked past him. To her surprise, he didn't try to stop her, but she could hear his footsteps close behind, but didn't stop or turn around. She got her coat from the rack in the lobby, found her gloves and scarf on a table next to it, and put them on. Then she hurried out into the chilly night air but didn't get far. Someone took hold of her arm and pushed her up against the side of the building.

"Never have I not had a girl I wanted. What makes you think you will be the first?" He grabbed her face, putting his hand under her chin, and squeezed tight, forcing her head up so she would have to look at him. He peered down at her with a darkness in his eyes as the muscles in his square jaw tensed, then relaxed, then tensed again as he pressed his teeth together. He stared at her for what felt like an eternity, then he leaned in and pressed his lips to hers as he groped her right breast.

She tried to push away, feeling the hard, cold brick behind her that kept her in place. She remembered the things Wilhelm had taught her and that he said go for the balls if she couldn't do anything else. She didn't have room to lift her leg and knee him, so she let go of his hands and reached down, taking his balls in her right hand and squeezing as hard as she could. He made a muffled sound while his lips were pressed to hers, then he pulled back, covering himself with one hand and placing the other on the wall for support. She slapped him hard across the face, then bolted.

"You bitch!" he yelled as she ran from him.

Her heart was pounding painful in her chest, feeling like it might burst. Her throat was on fire and dry to where it was hard for her to swallow. Her eyes were watering, and her nose was running, making it hard for her to see. When her legs could no longer move, she stopped and leaned against the corner of a building, trying to catch her breath. This whole thing made her want to cry, but she wouldn't let herself. She lifted her hand and wiped at her mouth roughly, but it wasn't enough, so she reached down and took a handful of snow and rubbed it on her lips, feeling the cold of it as it melted and ran down her chin. She rubbed until her lips were numb, then dropped her hand to her side, letting the snow fall to the ground. She heard a car coming down the road and turned her head in its direction. She immediately noticed that it didn't have its headlights on. Eva pushed away from the wall and stared at it, watching as it came closer. Something about it unsettled her. She turned down the alley a few feet away and walked at a fast pace. The squeak of the breaks echoed off the building, then the sound of a door opening and closing. The hard soles of shoes clicked on the cobblestone not far behind her, then stopped.

"Eva."

The man's voice echoed down the alley, causing her to stop. She turned and looked at the shadowy figure standing at the entry to the alley. She could not ignore him. She understood this day would come when the resistance would

305

seek her out to learn what information she had gotten from Wilhelm. She let out a long breath and walked back down the alley towards the man. Helmut eyed her the whole time, then took her by the arm when she reached him, making sure she got into the back of the car. He slid in beside her and closed the door.

"Drive," he said to the man in the front. He turned to Eva. "We will talk in the car while we drive, then we will drop you off near your apartment. It is safer this way."

Eva saw that the man driving the car was the French resistance fighter from Paris. Helmut had called him Julien when the man had slapped her. She noticed he would continuously glance at her through the rearview mirror. She turned to look at Helmut, wondering why he chose to talk to her tonight of all nights.

"I haven't learned anything yet. I searched the house he is staying in, but I didn't find anything. I don't think he keeps sensitive documents there. Why would he?"

"You never know. I have heard of information being collected from officers' houses and apartments."

"Maybe, but that is the most ineffective way. Having someone on the inside like we did in Berlin is the best way."

"Yes, but that is a luxury we don't have right now. Maybe you can get him to talk. Get him drunk. Maybe he will slip and say something he wouldn't while sober."

"I have seen him tipsy, and he didn't talk. He is always mum when it comes to his work. I was supposed to meet him tonight at a gathering for German officers, but he never showed."

"You have seen him tipsy but not drunk. Next time, make sure he is drunk."

"I can try."

"Have you become... closer to him?"

She didn't quite know what to say to this, but she assumed he didn't know that she had because he was asking. "No. Because I looked in his apartment and found nothing, I don't think there is any point in sleeping with him. I believe getting him drunk would be a better option." She felt that what she did with Wilhelm was private and too intimate to be discussing with him. And in truth, she didn't do it for them. She didn't do it because she felt she had to, but because she wanted to. She didn't know it at the time, but she did now.

"We know why he didn't show up at the thing tonight."

Her eyes grew wide. "Why?"

"Something is amiss. They are looking for someone, but we don't know who. One of us, no doubt, but we don't know which one. The local police are out in force tonight as well." He held out an envelope for her. "Take this, and tomorrow at 8:15, you will meet someone at the corner of Rue Lachambre and Impasse de Jérusalem. They will be waiting there for you. All you have to do is hand the envelope to them and then turn and leave. It is vital that they get what is in this envelope."

"What is in it?"

"It doesn't matter. Just be there by 8:15."

"I work the morning shift, so I can do that." She took the envelope from him and unclasped her purse, putting it inside."

"Good. We will see you again in a week. We don't know what day or time. Just be aware of it. And Eva, don't forget that you are on borrowed time until you bring us everything."

She tensed. "I remember. I'm trying to get it for you."

"What would be the most helpful right now is if you could find out what he knows about the resistance. If he has learned any of our names, or if he knows where we meet. And another thing. We need any food or medicine you can get us."

"That might be difficult. The only food I have is what I can get with my ration card. And this hospital is much smaller than the one in Berlin. If I take medicine, they will notice. And it will seem strange if it starts disappearing not long after I arrived."

"The medicine won't be a problem. There is a doctor in the hospital that is one of us."

She didn't try to hide the shock on her face. "Who?"

"He is French. Dr. Lavigne."

"I know him."

"I would be surprised if you didn't. Talk to him tomorrow, and he will hook you up with some medicine."

"How will I get it to you? How will I get it out of the hospital?"

"You will have to carry it out in a bag. Bring something larger than your purse, and once he gives you the medicine, bring it back to your apartment. We will get in touch with you about where to drop it off."

She shook her head. "No. I can't keep it at my apartment. I have a roommate. She will notice."

"No, she won't, not if you are careful."

"I will try, but if this goes badly, I'm not doing it again."

"You will do it again if we ask. You seem to think that you have a choice."

She remembered what the German officer had told her earlier. Lightning flashed in her eyes. "I am really getting tired of being told that."

He gave her a confused expression. "Just get it done."

The car pulled to the curb, and Eva looked up, realizing that they were already at her apartment. Helmut gestured for her to get out. She opened the door and stepped onto the sidewalk, slamming the door hard. She watched the car pull away, then went up to the apartment, hoping that Ingrid would be asleep. She quietly slipped in, taking off her shoes and coat, then tiptoed to her room but stopped when she heard a noise coming from Ingrid's room.

"Eva, is that you?"

She stopped, cursing under her breath. "Yes."

Ingrid opened her bedroom door and stepped out into the hall. "How was it?"

"Not like I expected."

"How so? He didn't do anything to you, did he?"

"No. As a matter of fact, he didn't even show up, so I left."

"He didn't come to the party he invited you to. Well, that is not something a gentleman would do."

"I guess he got stuck working and couldn't leave."

"A man like him would do that." She placed her hand over her stomach. "I'm kind of hungry. Do you want to eat snacks with me while we drink tea?"

Eva smiled. "I would love that."

Eva showered and put on her pajamas, then they made a pot of tea and got the stale cookies that Eva had traded cheese for. They took it to Ingrid's room and got under the blanket, leaning back on the headboard.

"How are you feeling? Are you still having cramps?"

"I am, but it seems to have gotten a little better." Ingrid held up her teacup, and Eva clinked hers against it. "You know what we need now?" Ingrid said.

"What?"

"Some handsome men to rub our feet."

Eva laughed, choking on her cookie. "That is what got you into this predicament in the first place. The last thing you need is a man."

"I know. But men are just so irresistible."

"No, Ingrid! No more men for you right now."

Ingrid finished her tea and cookies and set her cup on the side table, then turned on her side to look at Eva. "You don't find men irresistible?"

"No. Not most of them. Men are nothing but trouble."

Ingrid playfully slapped her arm, sloshing her tea out of the cup onto the saucer. "I know you are yearning for someone."

"I am not." She dumped the tea from the saucer back into her cup.

"Sometimes I feel lonely. But you have someone?"

Eva sat her cup on the floor, then laid down and looked at Ingrid. "What do you mean? I don't have anybody."

"There was that one man you loved, and there is another man that is smitten with you. You have two men who love you, and I don't even have one. I think the greatest thing would be to have someone's love."

"Oh, Ingrid. It isn't all you make it out to be. Sometimes love can be the cause of all your problems."

"Not always." Ingrid closed her eyes, and Eva knew she was tired.

"I'm going to my room. Go to sleep now."

"Good night," her words slurred as she looked at Eva with heavy eyelids.

Eva went to her room and climbed under the covers. What an exhausting day this was!

Chapter Seventeen

The summer sun warmed Eva's face as she squinted against its brightness. She looked over the vast red earth, and it was all so familiar to her. Her eyes fell upon her Bryce Canyon National Park hoodie that her parents had bought for her. This was the trip her family had taken after she graduated high school. They took her and her brother to all the major national parks in Utah. The first park they visited was Arches, then south to Canyonlands, southwest to Bryce Canyon, and finally, they ended at Zion National Park. She looked up from her hoodie and could see her parents and brother just up ahead, a little farther on the trail. She jogged after them, but no matter how fast she ran, she could never catch up. She stopped, cupping her hand over her eyes so she could see them better. Her mom turned to look back up the trail at her, smiling, then beckoned for Eva to follow.

"Come home," she said.

Her voice was gentle and loving. She gave Eva one more warm smile, then turned her back to her again and continued down the hill. Eva tried to reach out to her mother, but something was restricting her arms. She tried again, and her body jerked, waking her from the dream. She blinked a few times against the darkness; the tip of her nose was cold from the chilly February air, but her body felt unusually warm. As she came out of her groggy state, she became more aware of her surroundings, and it registered that someone was pressed against her back and an arm firmly around her. Instinctually, her first reaction was alarm, but she tried to keep crazy thoughts from running wild in her head, such as, what if this was the man from last night? She reached down and touched the hand that was on her ribs, and she knew it wasn't Ingrid, not that she really thought it was. The hand was large, and she could tell it belonged to a man. She rolled the best she could to her left, making her body press harder against the person behind her. She pulled her arm out from under the arm that was around her and reached up, feeling for a face. She placed her hand on a cheek, and the prickly whiskers from an unshaven face poked her palm. She knew this had to be Wilhelm. She moved her hand over eyes and then a nose. Suddenly, a hand grabbed hers, moving it away.

He brought her hand to his lips and kissed it. "Go back to sleep," he said in a quiet, groggy voice.

She racked her brain trying to figure out how he got in, but then she remembered he rented the apartment for her and had a key. How was she going to explain this to Ingrid in the morning? Would he even still be here in the morning?

313

She lay awake, completely aware of his body, hard against hers, the heat of it warming her as his breath came gently in her hair. Her butt was in his groin, and her back was pressed against his chest as he spooned her. His arm around her was bare, as were his legs, but she could feel the material of her nightgown against the fabric of his undershirt. It was also the same on the lower half of him, and she knew he was wearing underwear.

She rubbed her fingers up the length of his arm, feeling the hair on it moving with her hand. She didn't understand why there was such a want to touch him, to feel his skin under her hand. She scooted her body further back, pressing herself harder against him. It was hard for her to resist the urge not to, and she was pleased that he was holding her.

He made a small grunt. "Eva. It is late, and we should both get some sleep."

She felt his lips moving against her hair as he spoke. "I know," she said. "When did you come in?"

"A few hours ago." His voice was barely above a whisper.

"You know men aren't allowed in the apartment."

"I'm sure they will make an exception for me."

She smiled at his confidence. She didn't speak again so that he could go back to sleep. But she, on the other hand, laid awake for a while, enjoying the simple pleasure of him, liking the human contact between them. She had missed the closeness, connection, and affection of her family the whole time she had been here. But this was different, more intense, and deeply satisfying somehow. It was exactly what she craved, what she needed. She laced her fingers through his and closed her eyes, ignoring the problem that loomed large, because Wilhelm and the life she never knew she wanted beckoned.

She could feel movement on the bed, then the other side of the mattress went up from weight being lifted off it. She stirred, struggling to come out of her groggy state. She opened her eyes, blinking a few times as they focused on her closet door. Light came in around her curtains, making the room appear a greyish color in the early morning hour. The sun was barely up, and the wintry morning air nipped at her nose and fingertips. She was acutely aware of the loss of heat now that Wilhelm was no longer in bed. She turned her head and looked to her left. Wilhelm was buttoning up his shirt and stopped to look at her.

"Good morning," he said in a rough voice.

She sat up, pulling herself back so she could lean against the headboard. "You never came to the party last night."

He looked away from her as he did his tie. "I did, but only towards the end. You weren't there, so I had a few drinks and left. I don't blame you for leaving. And I am sorry that I couldn't pick you up myself or be there with you. It was unavoidable."

"She looked at the window, then back to him. "You are leaving early."

He sighed. "I have to. What kept me last night requires my attention again this morning. I had thought about staying at work all night, but I needed at least a few hours of sleep, and I wanted to see you even if you were asleep."

She could not help but smile a little at this. "I'm glad you came. It's not how I thought I would spend the evening with you, but it was still nice."

He sat on the edge of the bed and pulled on his boots, then stood and shrugged on his black leather coat, tying the belt. He came around the bed and sat on the edge beside her.

"Do you want to spend tonight with me at the cottage?"

She looked at his greenish, hazel eyes with circles under them from a long night, and the dark stubbles of his facial hair. She reached up and rubbed her fingers over it, the wiry hairs scratching at her fingertips. "You need a shave," she told him teasingly.

His eyes darkened. Not in an angry way but from another emotion that was stirring in him. "Is that a yes?"

She gave a slight smile and nodded, then laid her hand flat on his cheek. "I like this. It looks good on you."

He closed his eyes for a few seconds, then opened them and moved her hand from his face, lying it in her lap. He tucked a piece of hair behind her ear, then leaned in and kissed her softly on the forehead. "I'll see you tonight."

Eva then remembered the envelope in her purse that she had to give to someone at 8:15. "What time?" she asked.

He thought about it. "I'll try to be home by nine, but you should come before curfew."

"I will."

He stood up and walked out of her room. She could hear his boots creaking on the wooden floor and hoped that it wouldn't wake Ingrid. As soon as she heard the front door close, she jumped out of bed and went into the living room, picking her purse off the floor and feeling inside for the envelope. She relaxed when she felt it and pulled it out to ensure that it had not been tampered with. She looked at both sides, and it appeared to be just as it was when it was given to her. She put it back in her purse and closed the flap over it. Ingrid was still asleep, but Eva knew she would be up soon because she also had the morning shift.

She decided to make breakfast for both of them. She opened the cupboard to see what food they had left. There was a jar of oats, but they didn't have any butter or sugar. She closed it and looked over at the kitchen table and on the counters. There was a bit of stale bread left and a couple of apples. She opened the fridge and stooped to peer inside. There were five eggs, half a jar of milk, and some cheese. She took it all out, deciding to make scrambled eggs and serve them with cheese and bread.

Ingrid came out of her room when she smelled the food. "What are you making? It smells good."

"Just some eggs."

Ingrid yawned and sat at the tiny kitchen table. "Don't you work the morning shift today, too?"

"Yes. But I wanted to tell you that I won't be home after work."

Ingrid focused on her. "Oh my God, you are going to do it with him tonight."

Eva turned to look at her. "What? No."

"Really? Then tell me, what will you be doing all night if it's not with him?"

Eva turned away from her and stirred the eggs. "I will be with him, but I didn't say we were going to do that."

"You are going to spend the whole night with him and not have sex?"

She turned off the burner and dipped the egg onto two different plates. Cut an apple and divided it, tore off some bread and sliced some cheese, then sat a plate in front of Ingrid and took the chair across from her. Ingrid looked at her pointedly as she waited for an answer.

"You know, you can sleep in the same bed with someone and not have sex with them."

"I don't know that I could."

"You are right. I don't know if you could. But I know I can because he was here last night, with me, in my bed, and nothing happened."

Ingrid's mouth dropped. "How did I not know this?"

"He left early before you were awake. He came in last night while I was sleeping."

"How did he get in?" She poked a piece of bread into her mouth.

"He has a key. He is the one who got us the apartment."

"Oh, that makes so much sense. He got you this apartment, so he could keep an eye on you and have access to you."

How could she deny this? "Probably. I woke up last night with him in bed, spooning me. But we did nothing but sleep."

Ingrid chuckled. "I can't believe the two of you were in the other room together last night, and I knew nothing of it. So, have you and he ever…?" Eva's face flushed, and she looked at her plate. Ingrid's eyes grew wide. "You did. When?" Her voice was high-pitched as she spoke.

"A few days ago. When I was out all night."

"I knew it. But how could you sleep with someone like him?"

"It is complicated, Ingrid. Like I told you before, I think it's become too intimate between us for either of us to leave. I can't back away from this or him."

"Have you tried?"

"In a way. It seems that this entire war, I have been thrown in his path. And no matter how much I try, I can't stay away from him. I know it sounds ridiculous, but there is a magnetic pull between us, and I am fighting against it, but it's pointless."

"Like destiny?"

"I don't know. Maybe he is my punishment, and I'm in hell. At this point, I'm tired of fighting it. I would rather just give in. Besides, if I am in hell, which is what this war is, and he is the devil, at least he knows how to show me some serious pleasure and enjoyment. He brings me a little piece of heaven in this hell I'm living in."

"Wow. That is… I'm not even sure what to say. So, he is… great in bed, then?"

Eva laughed awkwardly. "Well, I've only been with one other man, so it's hard to compare."

"Sure, but how do the two of them compare?"

"Eva felt the warmth in her cheeks. "Ummm, it's… I don't really know how to compare them. It's like comparing apples and onions, or maybe more fitting to say, comparing a tiger to

"It's exhausting. I understand now why they compare people and love to drugs. I always thought it was stupid and cliché. But damn, it could not be more accurate. You are on such a high when you are with them, but once they leave, you crash and are left drained, emotionally and physically." Eva was surprised when she saw Ingrid's eyes tear up.

"I would give anything to have what you have. I want that love that only comes once in a lifetime. You have that, Eva."

Eva placed her hand over Ingrid's. "No, that's not what I said. I still love Gerhardt."

"Then you are exceptionally lucky because you have known love twice. I have never been with a man who has felt like that about me. And I have never been in love like that or felt that way towards another person."

"You will. You just haven't met him yet."

"What man would want me now? No man is going to want to raise another man's baby."

"That's not true. There are plenty of good men out there who will not care that this baby isn't theirs." Eva looked at the clock on the kitchen wall. "We better hurry, or we're going to be late."

Ingrid glanced at the clock, too. "Oh, I didn't realize that was the time."

Eva ate her food and put the plate in the sink. She would have to wash it later. She changed into her uniform and walked with Ingrid across the street to the hospital.

"I'll see you later. I need to ask Dr. Möller something." She didn't want to tell her she was actually going to find Dr. Lavigne.

"Alright.

Eva went to the recovery ward, hoping to find Dr. Lavigne there. She stopped in the doorway to scan the room. There were two nurses in the room attending to patients but no doctors. She climbed the stairs to the top floor where his office was. The door was closed, and she hoped that meant he was inside. She tapped her knuckles on the door and waited. Heavy, fast-moving footsteps on wooden floorboards came from the other side. The door opened wide, and Dr. Lavigne paused, looking at her, a little perplexed.

"Yes?"

Eva wondered if he was expecting someone else and if he knew who she was. She took a step closer to him and leaned in. "I'm here on behalf of Helmut."

He narrowed his eyes at her, then stuck his head out of his office and checked the hall, then pulled back. "Come in." He moved to the side for her to enter. She walked in, and he closed the door, then went to the window and peered down at the courtyard. "Helmut didn't say he was sending someone new. You work here?"

"I do. My name is Eva. Helmut thought it would be easier for me to get the medicine from you and out of the hospital than anyone else."

He eyed her suspiciously. "Possible." He went to a glass cabinet behind his desk and took a key from his white coat, then unlocked it. He pulled out several cardboard boxes, some gauze wrapped in brown paper, and a few other things, then locked the cabinet back. He peered into the cabinet for a few seconds before finally facing her, then held the items out.

"There is some morphine, chloroform, bandages, forceps, scissors, a few syringes, and some sulfonamides. I could not get my hands on any penicillin. That is reserved only for the German officers, not French people. Sorry I could not get more right now. There are eight bottles of morphine there, though."

She took the things from him and looked at the items in her hands. "I know they will be happy with whatever they can get." He nodded, and she went to the door to leave. "It will probably be me who collects it from you next time."

"If there is a next time."

She turned to him and creased her brows. "Why wouldn't there be a next time?"

"You understand it's not easy to get this stuff? And it will only get harder. I will stop doing this if I feel the Germans are suspicious. I don't like the Germans, but I won't lose my life for some rebels who might not even be making a difference in this war."

"I do understand, and I don't blame you. But people must make sacrifices for things to change, and that is what you and I are doing. It is what they are doing."

"But at what cost? When is the outcome not worth the sacrifice?"

"I don't know. I often wonder that myself."

He nodded to the medical supplies she was holding. "Don't get caught with that on your way out, or it will be over for both of us."

"I will do my best and hope it's good enough." She cracked the door open and looked into the hall. It was empty, so she slipped out, shutting the door behind her. She quickly went downstairs to the nurse's lounge, put the supplies in the cloth grocery bag she had brought, and hid it under her coat. She smoothed her apron, feeling a little better now that she wasn't walking around with stolen medicine. She found Ingrid with a patient and tapped her on the shoulder. Ingrid looked up at her from the man she was feeding.

"Did you find Dr. Möller?"

"No, but I can look for him again later. Which patient have you not done yet?"

Ingrid gestured with her head to the patient beside them. "He still needs the bandage on his arm changed."

Eva went to the tray between the beds and picked up the scissors and gauze. She sat on the bed next to the man and gave him a warm smile. "How are you feeling this morning?" He was a middle-aged French man who had burned his arm while working in his blacksmith shop.

"It is better today."

She cut away the gauze and inspected his burn. It was turning a pinkish color, and most of the blisters had gone down. "It is looking much better. You should be able to go home soon. Maybe even tomorrow."

She wrapped his arm in the fresh gauze and stood from the bed. Abruptly, there was a loud sound like glass shattering, and from the corner of her eye, she saw something white moving very quickly from the upper floor of the hospital towards the ground of the courtyard. Before it impacted the grass, a screeching cry echoed off the building and then a sickening thud. Eva ran to the window, along with Ingrid and two other nurses. On the ground was the bloody, contorted body of Dr. Lavigne. Eva was frozen in place, staring at the body of the man she had been talking to not more than twenty minutes ago.

A scream from one of the other nurses pulled her out of her trance. She took in a deep breath, not realizing at the time she had been holding it, then turned and bolted from the room and ran outside as fast as she could. When she reached the courtyard, she saw that people were already around the body in a circle. She came up next to one doctor and looked down at the body and the pull of blood that surrounded his head. She lifted her head to look up at the top floor and saw that the window was broken out of the doctor's office. She looked back down at him again. Why would he kill himself? Then a thought hit her. What if he hadn't killed himself? What if he was pushed from the window and didn't jump out by choice? She looked at the top floor and then at the body again, noticing how far he was lying from the window. She glanced around, seeing that the crowd had tripled.

An authoritative voice cut through the silence, echoing off the brick walls of the courtyard. "Everyone needs to go back inside. Now!"

Dr. Möller came towards her and the rest of the people standing over the body. He wasn't talking to her directly, but she knew he also meant her. The crowd thinned as the people walked back towards the hospital. Eva lingered, gazing at Dr. Möller. She could not hide the horror on her face, and she didn't try. She looked at him, pleading with her eyes for some kind of answer as to what had happened.

He gently wrapped his hand around hers. "I will let you know. Wait for me in my office."

She nodded, then turned and made her way back towards the hospital. Before going to his office, she searched for Ingrid. She found her looking down into the atrium from the windows of the long hall. Eva placed a hand on her shoulder. "Maybe we shouldn't look anymore."

Ingrid turned her head towards her, eyes brimming with tears. "What do you think happened?"

"I don't know. But I don't think he felt any pain. I believe it was quick. Let's come away from the window." She put her hands on Ingrid's shoulders and began leading her away. She took Ingrid to the nurse's lounge and sat her in a chair. "Dr. Möller asked to see me in his office, so I'm going to leave you here."

"Is he going to tell you what happened?"

"I don't know."

"Will you tell me if he does?"

"I will." Eva wasn't sure that was true. She didn't know what he would tell her but was afraid of what she didn't know. She left Ingrid and went to Dr. Möller's office, finding that he was already there.

"Close the door behind you," he said as she entered the room. She did as he asked, then took a seat beside him on the small brown leather couch positioned in the corner of the room. He let out a breath and looked at her with a grim expression. "It is believed that he was pushed. Why someone would want to do that to him, though, I don't know."

Deep in her heart, she already knew he had been murdered. Her fear spiked, realizing she could be next. If whoever killed him was willing to push a doctor from his office in the middle of the day, then they would have no qualms about killing her. He looked at her, and when their eyes met, his face grew even more distressed than before, and she knew that he knew.

"Eva, do you know something about this?"

She nervously shook her head. "No. How could I know anything about it?"

He turned his head, still staring at her. His expression was scrutinizing. He didn't believe her, and that was clear. He waited a few seconds before speaking again. "I know that there are things going on with you that I don't understand, and I don't know that I want to understand all of them or even know what they are. But at this moment, I feel compelled to understand. I see you there in front of me, looking like an animal that has been cornered and knows this is the end for it."

"Is it that obvious?"

"Yes. And I am not the only one who will notice it."

"I don't know who killed him or why." She was telling the truth. She couldn't figure out why the resistance would kill the person who was supplying them with medicine. It did seem suspicious that he was murdered right after he gave her the supplies they needed. Maybe they thought he was going to betray them or somehow knew that he was having doubts. Although that didn't seem likely to her. But if they didn't kill him, then who did?

"That might be so, but you still know more than you are telling me."

She started shaking her head. "I can't tell you. For so many reasons. It would be dangerous for you to know."

He gave a slow nod in understanding. "If that is the kind of thing it is, then simply knowing you has already put me in danger. I am guilty by association. That is how they will look at it, and nothing I say will change their minds."

Eva's eyes watered with tears at the guilt she felt for him. How could she have been so selfish to put him in this situation? "I am so sorry!" she said in a shaky voice.

He took her hand. "Just tell me what it is that has potentially doomed us both."

She thought carefully about what to say and what to leave out. She told him about Dr. Lavigne giving her the medicine and that it was for French in hiding who needed help. She also mentioned that he was having doubts and threatened to quit, and maybe that had something to do with why he was killed.

"And you think these people killed him because of that?"

"I don't know. It doesn't make sense that they would kill him over that."

"It sounds like these people are desperate, and desperate people do crazy things. You can't continue doing things for these people."

"I don't have a choice. They have me by the throat, and they know it."

"We always have a choice. That we don't is just something we tell ourselves. If they really have you by the throat, then it sounds like you have nothing to lose by cutting your ties with them. In that moment of fear, it's either you or them."

She swallowed down hot tears. "I do. It is more complicated than it seems on the surface."

"What do you have to lose?"

"Besides my own life?"

"Yes."

"Someone else's life."

"Who's life, Ingrid's?"

A new fear entered Eva. She wasn't even thinking about Ingrid. "I guess there could possibly be more than one life lost because of me."

"Eva, who are you talking about?"

"I can't talk about this anymore. Is it alright if I return to my duties?"

"If that's what you want, but you can't ignore this for long. I won't tell anyone what you told me, but you and I both know that this is far from being over."

"I understand."

"Why don't you come by my apartment tonight, and we can try to figure this out together?"

She thought about the envelope in her purse and meeting Wilhelm tonight. Right now, she wanted nothing more than to collapse into his arms. If anyone could protect her from the resistance, it was him.

"Not tonight. I am too tired to deal with it now."

"Tomorrow, then."

Eva left his office and returned to the patient's ward. Ingrid was waiting by the window that overlooked the courtyard. Eva came to stand next to her, but Ingrid didn't look away from the glass.

"They moved the body."

Eva looked at the blood that still stained the walkway. "I know."

"What did Dr. Möller say?"

"He said they didn't know what happened but they are looking into it. I imagine the police will be here soon." Ingrid nodded. "Let's get back to it. The patients need us. Staring at the spot where he died will not change what happened."

"Would you please stay at the apartment with me tonight?"

Eva wanted so much for Wilhelm to comfort her and make her feel safe, but who would make Ingrid feel safe if not her? How could she say no, making Ingrid face tonight alone?

"Of course, I will. I'll leave a note at his cottage telling him I can't make it tonight."

"Thank you," Ingrid said in a shaky voice.

The rest of the day dragged on, and Eva continually checked her watch and the clock on the wall. The time seemed to creep along, every second feeling like an hour. She had to be at the corner of Rue Lachambre and Impasse de Jérusalem by 8:15 and could not be late. When the clock turned six, Eva rushed out of the patient ward, put on her coat and scarf, then grabbed the bag with medicine from her locker along with her purse, hat, and gloves. She hurried outside and walked to the corner of Rue Lachambre and Impasse de Jérusalem. She went into a café and sat by the window. A waitress came to her table, and she ordered a tea, knowing that the coffee they a bunny. The only thing they really have in common is that they are both German and male."

"Oh, come on, Eva, you have to tell me something. At least a little about what it was like being with them."

Eva squinted her eyes at Ingrid. "Alright, just the basics." She took a bit of eggs and let out a breath as she thought. "Gerhardt was gentle, sweet, caring, and considerate."

"And what about the other one?"

"Oh boy, how do I describe that man? He is, well, he is intense."

"No, not him as a person, as a lover."

"I meant as a lover. But I would describe him as passionate, hot-blooded, confident, and sensual. He doesn't hold back, he knows what he wants, and he takes it. And I do mean in bed too. I'm not sure I have words to accurately describe what it was like being with him. For me, it was intense with both men but also very different. With Wilhelm, though, it was like being pushed to the limit. You are so close to the edge that the adrenaline almost takes you. But the high from it, from him, makes you want more. It's when you do something because it's dangerous. You know it's stupid and that you are being foolish, but that's what makes it so exciting. The more dangerous it is, the more thrilling, the more you want it. It was like my body was made for him. When he slid it in, he owned me. Nothing compares to having someone dominate you like that, even if it's just in that moment."

For a while, Ingrid just stared at Eva, not speaking. "I have never felt that way before. It sounds incredible."

served wasn't real coffee. The waitress brought out a cup on a saucer and set it in front of Eva. She took the handle of the cup and sipped on the hot beverage, savoring its warmth. The chill went to her bones, and the heat from the tea couldn't reach it. She ordered a second cup, all the while watching out the window for anyone that looked suspicious. The sun had long been down, and she knew the café would close soon. Most of the places closed at five, but the few shops that stayed open later usually closed around seven.

She finished her second cup of tea and retrieved her purse and the bag off the floor, then went outside and headed across the street to the alley. She paced from one foot to the other, trying to stay warm. She was so cold it was making her feel ill. She knew that cold weather didn't cause you to get sick and that it was an old wife's tale, but she could swear she felt a cold or flu was coming on. She sniffed and crossed her arms over her chest, glancing both ways down the sidewalk. It was dark and empty, with only a few street lamps illuminating it. She pulled the sleeve of her coat back and checked her watch. It was finally eleven past eight, and she hoped they would be here soon. A few minutes later, a woman wearing a trench coat and beret pulled low over her long, dark curls walked toward Eva. Her hands were in her pockets, and she eyed Eva with suspicion as she approached. She stopped a few feet away, then inspected her.

"You have something for me?"

"I do."

Eva pulled the envelope from her purse and held it out to the woman. Slowly, she pulled her right hand from her pocket

331

and took the envelope from Eva. She tucked it into her coat and started to leave.

"Wait." Eva picked up the bag with medicine and held it out to her. "Take this too."

"What is that?"

"It's the medicine Helmut is expecting."

"No. My job was to collect the envelope. That was all."

"He is waiting for this as well."

"I have heard nothing of it."

"Please," Eva pleaded as she held to bag out to her. Cautiously, the woman reached for it when a voice rang from across the street, echoing off the buildings.

"Stop! Police," the man's voice called again.

What looked like over half a dozen men in blue police officer uniforms were running across the street towards them. Eva didn't hesitate. She dropped the bag of medicine at the woman's feet and bolted. She ran in the opposite direction and didn't turn to see if the woman had done the same. She could hear footsteps behind her and a man shouting that there were two of them. She knew the police had split up and were now chasing her and the other woman. Eva turned down street after street, sliding in the snow on some corners as she did, but she never slowed. She could still hear the clicks of the police officer's shoes echoing off the buildings somewhere close. She dared a glance behind her and didn't see him, which gave her hope. Up ahead was a car parked on the side of the street. She stopped when she got to it and tried the handle. To her surprise, the door opened. She climbed into the back seat, pulling the door closed as quietly as possible. Then she crawled on the floor and made herself as small as she could. The footsteps became louder until the clicking sound of hard-soled boots passed by the car. They did not stop but continued further down the street until they died away. Even so, Eva waited a few more minutes before she got up. She pulled herself onto the seat when gunfire sounded in the distance. She flinched and dropped back to the floor. There was more gunfire, and she knew they must have caught up to the woman. She squeezed her eyes shut and put her hands over her ears, not wanting to hear it, see it, or think about what was happening.

Chapter Eighteen

She didn't know how long she had waited before leaving the car, but it felt late. She checked her watch and gasped when she saw the time. "Shit." She broke into a sprint. It was way past curfew, and Wilhelm, she hadn't even left him a note, but she couldn't go to the cottage now, not at this hour. She went straight back to the apartment and hurried up the stairs to her floor. She pushed the front door open but stopped in her tracks when she saw Wilhelm's orderly sitting on one end of her couch and Ingrid on the other end.

"There you are," she said as soon as Eva came through the door. She got off the couch and hurried over to Eva. "Where have you been?" she said in a whisper, nervously glancing at the man on the couch.

"I lost track of time. I'll explain later. What is he doing here?"

"I don't know. He only said he had a message for you from his superior."

Eva nodded. She came over to the couch and sat at the other end from the man. "What can I do for you?" she asked him.

He gave her a polite but forced smile as he held her gaze. "SS Obersturmbannführer Bauer sends his apologies that he cannot meet you tonight. He will be working through the night until morning. He wanted me to tell you that he plans to take the rest of the day off and will see you sometime tomorrow."

Eva smiled back. "Tell him it is not a problem and that I will see him tomorrow."

"Very good." The man stood and nodded his head stiffly to her and then to Ingrid. He turned on his heels and left the apartment without another word.

"Well, that is fortuitous," Eva said.

"Why is it fortuitous?"

"Because. I was going to leave him a note at his apartment explaining why I wouldn't be coming tonight, but then I lost track of time and completely forgot."

"And you were out past curfew. What were you doing?"

"Wondering the streets."

Ingrid's mouth opened and she pulled her eyebrows together. "Wondering the streets. Are you mad? What in God's name made you decide to do that?"

"I don't know. But I don't feel well and want to go to bed."

"Are you alright?"

"It's just a cold, I think."

Eva took a quick, hot shower, then crawled into bed. The sheets and blanket felt icy against her skin. She curled into a ball and tucked the blanket around her chin, shaking beneath it. She closed her eyes and tried to fall asleep.

Eva woke to the feeling of cold air coming under the blanket around her back, then the bed went down from the weight of another person. They scooted close to her and let out a long breath, and she realized then that it was Ingrid.

"Hi, Ingrid," she said in a weak, raspy voice.

"Sorry if I woke you. I couldn't sleep. I can't get the image of Dr. Lavigne out of my head. The way his body was positioned and the blood. It hardly even looked like him. And then I thought about you, and that night I found you on the roof, standing on the ledge. What would ever make you want to do something like that?"

"Because at the time, I had decided life wasn't worth living anymore."

"But I don't understand why?"

"It doesn't matter now. I no longer think that."

Ingrid put her arm over Eva and took her hand, then raised her head from the pillow. "You are burning up." She placed her hand on Eva's forehead. "My goodness, why didn't you say something?"

"Because I will be better by tomorrow. All I need right now is some sleep."

"I'm not so sure you will be better in the morning. I know you're off tomorrow, but I work the morning shift. You should come by the hospital if you aren't feeling any better."

"If I get worse, then I will."

She drifted into a fitful sleep, dreaming of home, Gerhardt, the woman in the alley, hiding in the car, and Wilhelm. All the dreams seemed so real, but the ones about Wilhelm were the strangest and most vivid of them. They were standing in a snowy field, roughly thirty feet apart, facing one another. The wind whipped his brown hair around his face. The curled tips grazed his cheeks softly, and his lips and the end of his nose were pink from the cold. She stared at him, waiting for him to speak, confused as to why he was there. A smile broke at the corner of his mouth, but his eyes glistened with fresh tears that spilled over and rolled down his cheeks as he blinked. They caught the light of the sun as they fell on the fresh snow. Eva's face fell, and she held her hand out to him.

"You came," he said, still smiling. It looked sorrowful to her as if, in spite of his sadness, seeing her was enough.

"I didn't go anywhere."

"When you left, I thought I would never see you again."

"I haven't left. I didn't go anywhere, Wilhelm; I'm right here."

"I knew your heart would always be his, but I told myself that you loved me more. I didn't want to let you go, but it was the only way."

"Only way for what?" Suddenly, her body jerked, and she was being pulled fast backward away from him. He continued to stand in the same spot, staring at her with tear-filled eyes. She was the only one moving. "No…" She held out both of her hands, grasping for him. Then there was nothing but darkness. She could feel the mattress beneath her and realized that her arms were held above her, moving through the air wildly. She stopped swinging them but held them up for a few seconds before dropping them to her sides. Slowly, she opened her eyes and surveyed her surroundings. She looked at the ceiling, her closet, over to her dresser, and then at her bedroom door. That was where her eyes paused. In the doorway was Wilhelm, standing on the threshold of her bedroom, leaning against the doorframe with his arms crossed over his chest. He watched her with an unreadable expression and didn't attempt to move any closer or move from the doorway.

She watched him watching her, wondering how long he had been there. For a minute, she struggled to find words but finally settled on a simple greeting. "Hi." Eva was surprised by the hoarseness of her voice when she heard it. She gave a little cough and pulled herself up, leaning against the headboard. Her whole body hurt, and just that action took a lot of her energy.

"Hello."

She cleared the phlegm, hurting her raw throat. "How long have you been standing there?"

"A while. I thought the sound of the front door closing and my shoes on the floor would have woken you. When I got to your room, I said your name, but not even that woke you up. You were having quite the dream."

Her face flushed, but she could tell it was already red from a fever caused by the cold she was now certain she had. "I woke up swinging my arms, but I don't remember what I was dreaming." There was no way she was going to tell him she remembered the dream and that it was about him. "What time did you get off?"

"Around an hour ago."

She only noticed now that he was not wearing his uniform but was in civilian clothes. She looked at the light coming through the window. It did not look or feel like early morning light. "What time is it?"

He checked his watch. "A little after eleven. I didn't expect to find you in bed at this hour."

"I wasn't planning to, but I started feeling unwell last night. I hope that doesn't spoil any plans you have made."

"Not at all. I haven't made plans, but I have a few now."

This made Eva nervous. She didn't feel well enough to get out of bed, much less do anything. She coughed into the sleeve of her nightgown, grimacing. "What plans?"

He went to her dresser and opened the top drawer, pulling out a nightgown and tossing it onto the foot of the bed. He closed the drawer, then opened the second drawer, taking out a pair of underwear, stockings, a camisole, socks, and a bra, tossing them onto the bed as well. She watched in confusion and a little embarrassed as he went to her wardrobe and unhung one of her dresses. He laid it on the bed with the other pieces of clothing, then went to the bathroom, returning with her toiletry bag. He pulled her small leather bag out from under her bed and sat it beside the other items.

"Wilhelm, what are you doing?"

"I'm taking you to the cottage for a while."

She nervously scratched her neck. "Why?"

He didn't answer, only gave her a side glance as he put her things into the bag. He zipped it up, then came to stand beside her. He pulled the blankets off, and she wanted to protest but decided against it. She gave an involuntary shiver against the cold, already feeling like she was freezing.

He took hold of her hand. "Come on, get up and change."

She reluctantly let him help her from the bed, but instantly felt dizzy and lightheaded. She grabbed hold of his arm and waited for a second to feel a little more stable. He didn't say anything to her surprise but stood there, allowing her to use him for support.

"Sorry."

"There is nothing to be sorry for."

She let go of his arm, and he released her hand. She went to her wardrobe and pulled out a dress, then got a pair of socks from her dresser. She went into the bathroom and changed, although it took more effort than usual. She used the toilet, got a drink from the sink, and used Ingrid's hairbrush to make herself look halfway presentable. Her legs felt shaky beneath her, but she hid this from Wilhelm. She smoothed over the front of her dress and took a deep breath, then opened the bathroom door and stepped out. Wilhelm was waiting for her on the edge of the bed.

"You look terrible." Her eyes grew wide. He stood up and closed the distance between them. He took a piece of her hair, rubbing it between his thumb and middle finger. "I mean, you look ill."

"I didn't realize it was that obvious."

"It is." He let go of her hair and went back to the bed, taking the leather bag from the end. "Get your coat and let's go."

She followed him into the living room. "I need to leave a note for Ingrid. She will worry if she gets home and I'm not here." He gave a nod. She wrote Ingrid a note and left it on the kitchen table, knowing she would see it there. They went into the hall, and he took her hand when they got to the stairs. She did not pull it away or protest. Honestly, she felt like she could use the support. She was lightheaded, and her legs were weak and shaky. She hadn't been sick in so long, and had forgotten how bad it could make you feel.

He opened the car door for her, then closed it after she was in. He put her bag in the trunk, then climbed into the driver's seat. She looked over at him. "No orderly today?"

"I gave him the day off."

"How thoughtful," she said before having a coughing fit. By the end of it, her throat was on fire, her chest hurt, and her eyes were watering. From the corner of her eye, she could see that he was watching her. He waited a few seconds, then started the car and pulled away from the curb. She laid her head on the hard, cold window and closed her eyes. She felt like death warmed up.

She was aware of every bump in the road they hit, the feeling of the car turning, but only opened her eyes when it came to a stop and the engine went silent. He got out of the car, went to the trunk, retrieved her bag, then opened her door.

"Come on. Let's get you inside the warm house."

That sounded so nice right now. She took his outstretched hand, and he helped her from the car. He didn't let go as they descended the few steps to the front door, only releasing her hand to reach into his pocket for the key once they were at the door. He unlocked it, and she stepped into the warm entryway. She remembered the last time she was here and what had transpired between them. He shut the door and helped her out of her coat, then took her scarf and gloves, putting them in the small coat closet. He picked her bag off the floor and gestured towards the stairs, wanting her to go up. She did as he directed, and he put his hand on the small of her back as he followed. He sat the bag on the bed in the room he was staying in, unzipped it, and retrieved her nightgown and toiletry bag. He took her hand and led her to the bathroom, shutting the door behind them. By this point, she had stopped trying to figure out what he was doing.

"OK, I give up. What are we doing in here?"

"Just take off your clothes."

Her cheeks flushed. "What?"

He said, slower this time. "Take off your clothes." He reached over the tub, put the stopper in it, and then turned on the water.

She finally understood. He was running her a bath. She started unbuttoning the front of her dress when she noticed that he, too, was taking off his clothes. She had not expected him to get in with her, and she didn't know what to think about that. He finished removing his clothes before her and turned, seeing that she was still in her underwear and socks, watching him. He came over to her without a word, putting his hands on her hips and pushing her underwear down to her ankles.

"Step out of them," he told her.

She did as he told her, then she pulled off her socks, dropping them on the floor next to her underwear and dress. He led her to the tub and turned off the faucet. He stepped into the water first and again held his hand out to her. She placed hers in his and brought her leg over the side of the tub, putting her foot into the hot water. It sent a strange sensation up her entire body. Once she was in, he lowered himself into the water and held onto her as she sat between his legs. He pulled gently on her shoulders so she would lean back against him. His legs were bent on each side of her, the dark hair on them bunching in the spots that were wet. She allowed herself to relax, leaning her full weight into him, feeling his hard chest, and his penis that was pressing on her lower back just above her butt. He reached his arms around her, retrieving a sponge from the side of the tub. He put it in the water, letting it expand, then lifted it up and began so very gently rubbing it over her body, starting with her chest. He moved it over her stomach, legs, arms, and then between her legs.

"Does this help?"

The warm water, his tender sentiment, and just being so near to him made her feel relaxed and a little better. But she still felt like a train had hit her, and she was tired, struggling to stay awake. The warm water and the caressing he was doing with the sponge weren't helping.

"It does. But you didn't have to spend your day off with me."

He dipped the sponge in the water again then rubbed it over her arm. "Who else would I spend it with?"

"Friends. The men you serve with, perhaps."

"I would rather be here with you like this, in the tub."

She reached for the sponge, but he moved it away. "No. Today, I take care of you." He wrung out the sponge, laid it on the side of the tub, then wrapped his arms around her. She laid her head on his shoulder, and he rested his head against the tile wall. The water soothed her aching body, and it was so easy to melt into him. A year ago, she would never have imagined herself in this position, not even in her wildest dreams. Sitting naked in a tub with him and enjoying the sensorial experience. Not just letting him touch her, but wanting him to. He could be so sweet, so tender if he wanted to. But that was a rare occurrence. That was not the side of him most people got to see or had the opportunity to. Unlike Gerhardt, who was a gentleman on the inside and out, Wilhelm was harsh and callous. Emotionally hardened and insensitive most of the time to others' feelings and needs. Not that he didn't see them, he just didn't care. Why he seemed to care about hers still eluded Eva, for the most part. Something else that was also different from Gerhardt was that Wilhelm sugarcoated nothing, not even for her. He was not afraid to step on her toes, and he gave as good as he got.

Eva had closed her eyes, wanting to just lay here and forget the world and how awful she felt. She could feel the back of Wilhelm's fingers softly rubbing her cheek. She opened her eyes, realizing that she must have fallen asleep. The water had cooled considerably, and her body felt it keenly. She took in a deep breath and turned her head to look up at him.

He gave her a little smile. "Sorry to wake you, but the water is getting cold. Let's get out and dry off, then you can go to bed."

"I think I should eat something first. I certainly won't get better if I don't eat."

"I have some leftover potato soup and day-old bread if that sounds good to you?"

"It sounds fine."

They both got out of the tub, and she used his towel to dry off, then slid her nightgown over her head, not bothering to put on her underwear. She followed him down to the kitchen and sat at the little table. She watched him retrieve the soup from the fridge, put it into a pot, and light the burner beneath it. He then sat the bread in front of her and a cup of water. He went back to the stove and stirred the soup a few times. After a couple of minutes, he poured it into a bowl, put the spoon in it, and sat it on the table next to the bread. He placed the pot in the sink, then disappeared into the living room. She could hear him building a fire. The thought of lounging in front of it was so appealing.

She took a bite of her soup, hardly tasting it because of her stuffy nose, but something in it burned her raw throat. It already hurt to swallow, but she didn't want to not eat the soup. He took the time to heat it up for her, and she knew she needed food. She tore off a piece of bread and dipped it in her soup, then put it in her mouth, but it still didn't help with the flavor. She added some salt, hoping it would help her taste it a little better. He came back into the kitchen just as she was finishing the food.

"Do you want to go upstairs to the bed or stay by the fire?"

"I think by the fire." She stood and picked up the bowl, but he took it from her, laying it in the sink next to the pot.

"I can do those later, or the maid will take care of it tomorrow." She nodded and he took her hand and led her to the living room. "Lay down." She laid on the couch, and he covered her up with the blanket that hung over the back.

"You don't have to stay in here with me."

"I can sit and read."

What are you going to read?"

"Gruppe Bosemüller."

"I have never heard of that book."

"It was written in 1930 by Werner Beumelburg."

"I don't know who that is."

He grinned. "You wouldn't. And you wouldn't like the book."

"Why?"

"Because it is about the glories of war and in what way frontline battles should be fought."

"You are right. I wouldn't like that. But you can read it to me, it will put me to sleep."

He let out a breath and feigned annoyance. "Oh, I suppose."

He took the pillow from the chair and put it on the floor by the couch, then sat down and leaned against it near her head. He opened the book to chapter four and began to read the German words. They rolled off his tongue as easily as breathing for him, and she envied his perfect accent. But, of course, his accent in English was far from perfect, and his French was second to hers.

She closed her eyes and listened to the pleasant sound of his rich, deep voice that flowed in a smooth tempo as he read. It was soothing to her and strangely comforting. She tuned out the words, knowing they would be nothing more than German propaganda, and only focused on the sound of his voice. In the background of his reading was the crackling sound of the fire, the warmth of it radiating on her face. Her body had stopped shaking, and she felt warm all over. He hadn't noticed her shivering, and she was glad of it. He was already doing so much for her.

She felt an arm come under her back and another under her legs, then she was being lifted from the couch. Not fast, but slow and steady. She opened her eyes and was looking at Wilhelm's chest. She knew she was in his arms and that he was carrying her up the stairs, but she didn't mind. It was a caring gesture and a very man thing to do. He laid her on the bed and pulled the covers over her, then straightened and started to leave. She reached out and caught his hand.

"You're not going to stay in here?"

"It's a small bed."

"I can scoot over."

He squatted down so that he was at her level. "I take up most of the bed when it's just me. I don't know how we are both going to fit in it. I'll sleep in the other room."

She didn't like this, but she wasn't going to convince him. She wished that everything with him wasn't so damn hard. Her feelings were always tied into knots when it came to him.

"OK. Will you go to work tomorrow?"

"I have to." He leaned in and kissed her on the cheek, then left her alone in the dark room.

This is not how she thought the day would end when he came to get her. She wanted him to stay with her. For some reason, when he told her she would spend the evening at the cottage with him, she assumed that meant in the same bed. She didn't know why she thought that or why she was so emotional. She knew there were only twin beds in the cottage, but she had forgotten.

When Eva woke, it was quiet, only the sound of the shutter on the back of the house rattling in the wind. She sat up and stretched. Her body felt stiff and sore, her head throbbed, and the pressure in her sinuses made her face hurt. She almost felt worse than she had yesterday. She really wanted to stay another night at the cottage, even if it wasn't in the same bed as Wilhelm. Just being there with him made her feel better. Not physically, but inside there was this warmth when she was around him. He cared for her, well, more than that, he loved her. She knew she should not revel in that fact, but how could she not? War was awful, dangerous, and painful. She was always taking care of people, it was nice to have someone look after her occasionally. To care for her and bear some of the burdens of life, to give her a shoulder to lean on and arms to comfort and hold her in their protective embrace. But then she realized that if he was that for her, she was probably that for him, at least for some of it. She was trying to protect him, but in a different way than he was her. She knew without question that she brought him some sort of comfort as well.

She threw the blankets off and put her feet on the cold wood floor. She started to go to the bathroom to retrieve her socks and clothes from last night but stopped when she saw them lying on the floor next to her bag. She picked the socks off the floor and slipped them on then patted downstairs. As she had expected, the house was empty, but to her surprise, there was a fire going in the fireplace. It wasn't a big fire, and she could tell it had been burning for some time. She took two pieces of wood from the basket next to it and put them on the small flames. She then went into the kitchen to look for food and saw a piece of paper on the table and picked it up.

Eva,
As you know, I had to go to work today. I honestly don't know when I will be home, but you can stay as long as you like. If you are not there when I get back, I will try to come and see you at your apartment. I informed the hospital that you are sick and will not be working today or tomorrow. Also, I had some fresh fruit brought over this morning for you. It is on the counter.

Wilhelm

It was true that she didn't feel like going to work, but she wished he hadn't done that. People at the hospital might start asking questions. She looked over at the counter and couldn't believe what she was seeing. The last time she had fresh fruit was when she was in America. She didn't feel like eating much, so she put some of the bread from the table on a plate and then went to the basket with fruit. There were bananas, oranges, and some grapes. She wondered how on earth he got oranges and bananas? The only way to get them that she was aware of was on the black market. One thing she wished had been in the basket were strawberries, but she knew most of them came from America, and they certainly weren't sending any over to the Germans.

She ate two bananas, a handful of grapes, and three oranges. She didn't remember them ever tasting so sweet or so delicious. She savored every bite and wanted to eat more but didn't dare. She didn't want to throw it back up and waste the fruit. She could only imagine how much all of this must have cost him, and she would not waste any of it.

She went back upstairs and sat on the bed, trying to figure out what to do. Did she stay at the cottage and ask to spend another night, or did she go home and hope that he would have time to come and see her? After some contemplation, she decided it was probably better if she went home. She quickly changed into the clean dress that he so thoughtfully packed for her, then took her toiletry bag to the bathroom, brushed her teeth, and washed her face. She brushed her hair and pinned it up. She was starting to feel cold and shaky like she had yesterday. When she got home, she was going to go back to

bed. She put her things in her bag, went downstairs, checked
the fire, and then put on her coat, hat, and gloves. Picking up
her bag to leave, she realized she did not have a key to lock
the door. She would have to leave it unlocked.

The cold air stung her face as she walked the streets back
to her apartment. She felt terrible and hoped that her sickness
didn't turn into pneumonia. The screeching of tires on the road
made her jump. She looked up to see two men climbing out of
a car only a few feet from her. She broke into a sprint,
dropping her bag to the sidewalk so she could run faster. They
were right behind her, and it didn't take long for them to catch
her. They each took hold of one of her arms, and she screamed
as loud as she could with her hoarse voice. They pulled her
back down the sidewalk to the car as she fought against them.
One of the men got in the back, then the other one pushed her
into the backseat, then got in, pinning her between them. She
looked at them, recognizing both men from the resistance
group.

"Why did you run?" the first man that got in asked her.

"You have to ask that?"

"Yes. Why did you run?"

"I don't know. Maybe because I don't want to be pushed
from a window."

The men exchanged a glance, then spoke. "You need to
talk to Helmut. We are taking you to him now."

Her hands were shaking, and she felt she might vomit up
the fruit. She couldn't tell if it was because she was scared,
that she ran, or because she was sick. Probably all of them.

"You need to put your head between your legs."

"If I do that, I will throw up. Don't you have something to wrap around my eyes?"

He frowned, then pulled a handkerchief from his jacket pocket and tied it around her eyes. They hadn't driven for very long when the car stopped, and she heard the engine turn off. The car door opened, and they pulled her from the seat and led her into a building. Then someone removed the handkerchief from her eyes. This was a different place than where they had met the first time.

Helmut was in front of her, holding the handkerchief in his hand. "What the hell happened? They captured Natalie, and Dr. Lavigne is dead."

"He was pushed through the window right after I got the medicine. I thought you had him killed."

"Why would I do that?"

"He was having doubts. He said that might be his last supply of medicine. I thought you knew that, and so you had him killed."

"No. I had no idea. We did not have him killed."

"Then who did?"

"Most likely your boyfriend."

Eva was taken aback. She knew exactly who they were talking about. "He wasn't there."

"He didn't have to be. He probably had some of his men watching the doctor. Or it could have been those fucking traitorous French police."

Eva's mind was spinning. How could Wilhelm have known of Dr. Lavigne, and why would he have him killed? She sat in a chair, feeling like she would fall over if she didn't.

"Look, I don't know what happened. I am stuck in the middle of all of this. I don't want to be here. I understand your struggle and your reason for wanting to fight the Germans. I am on your side. But I don't want to work for you, and I don't want to work for them. All I want is to go home. To get as far away as I can from this hell that I have been living in for the last three years."

He didn't acknowledge what she said and turned from her to look at the other people in the room. "If they knew about Dr. Lavigne, then they will soon find us. We need to move it tonight."

"I don't think we can pull it off that soon," a man said that Eva had never seen before.

"We're going to have to," Helmut insisted. "Take her home." The man took Eva by the arm and led her to the door. "One more thing," Helmut called from behind her. "I expect some kind of information the next time we meet."

She looked at him but decided to not say anything. What could she say? No, that she couldn't or wouldn't get it for him? That would earn her a beating or death. And he wouldn't be satisfied with the truth, either. That Wilhelm tells her nothing because he trusts her even less than they do. She turned away from Helmut and walked with the man who had her arm, along with two other men, to the car. They put the handkerchief back over her eyes once they were in the car. They drove her back to her apartment and stopped a few blocks away. They removed the handkerchief and let her out on the sidewalk, then closed the door and drove away. She watched as the car disappeared out of view, steam from the tailpipe dissipating into the air, but she didn't move, even when it was gone. She looked down, realizing that she had left her bag on some unknown street and would probably never see it again.

She trudged up the road to her apartment building. With a lot of effort, she climbed the stairs to her floor, took the key from her purse, then unlocked the door. Once she was inside, she took off her shoes, hung up her coat, and dropped her purse on the floor. She looked around the living room and, on the table, she could see a piece of paper and wondered if it was the note she left Ingrid. She walked over and picked it up, but it was not the note she had left. Ingrid left her a message saying that she had gone out with some of the other nurses. Eva laid the note back down and went to her room. She pulled back the blanket and crawled into bed, not caring that she was still in her street clothes. It didn't take long for her to drift off into a deep sleep.

A series of loud explosions jolted Eva awake. The apartment building shook, and the glass in the kitchen rattled. Then something fell, crashing to the floor. She bolted up in bed and looked around. The room was dark but now silent. She hurried out of bed and went into the kitchen, turning on the light. A pot had fallen from its hook, which was what made the crashing sound. Sirens blared outside so she went to the window, pulling back the curtain. There was smoke rising from somewhere near the shore, but whatever was burning was out of view.

She put on her shoes and coat and made her way to the street. She headed in the direction of the explosion, along with other people. She could see a lot of commotion when she neared the beach. The German military was not letting people come any closer, but from where she was standing, she could tell that more than one thing was on fire. An artillery battery on the hill was on fire, and she saw a bunker on the beach, and a few anti-tank guns were also burning. She stared at the flames and the thick, black smoke that filled the air realizing that this was what Helmut was talking about. This was going to be bad. The Germans were going to be pissed, Wilhelm was going to be pissed, and that meant the people of Dieppe would be the ones who were going to pay the price, not the resistance.

She couldn't help but be angry at Helmut and the rest of the opposition. Did this actually help the allies? The answer to that was a resounding no. All they did was stir up a hornet's nest, and now innocent people would die because of it. They were not the saviors of France; they couldn't defeat the Germans alone. That wouldn't happen until the invasion of Normandy, which was still two years away. In a matter of days, there would be bodies in the streets or swinging from ropes, as an example to the people of Dieppe. And all she could do was carry on as if nothing had happened. This was going to send the people of Dieppe reeling from the coming retaliations and decimate their hopes of living peacefully with the Germans. All the resistance accomplished with their defiance was a new level of misery, increased hate, and a further deepening of the tension between the two groups of people who occupied the city.

Eva pulled her coat tighter around her and walked away. There was nothing she could do now. She still felt terrible, and the cold night air was cutting through her like a knife. She also knew that Wilhelm would not be coming to see her tonight. Not after this. It will be his priority.

Over the last day and night, the chaos in the city was all-consuming. They rounded five people up every hour as long as the culprits remained free. The people of the city were notified that it would continue until those responsible were captured or turned themselves in. So far, a hundred and sixty people had been killed, either lined up against walls throughout the city and shot, or hung in the center on town from gallows the Germans build for this purpose. They wanted the people they killed to be on display, as a reminder of what happens when you fight against Germany, or betray them. She was seriously considering turning over every single one of them. Why did they deserve to live when innocent people in the city were dying because of their senseless actions?

Wilhelm never came to see her, and every time she went to the building he operated from while in Dieppe, she was turned away. He would not see her. She knew he was busy with what was happening and that it wasn't personal, but it was still upsetting. And she wanted to stand in front of him and see if she had enough courage to confess, even if that meant condemning herself. At least people would stop dying, but she couldn't do that if he wouldn't see her.

She sat with Dr. Möller and Ingrid in his office and picked at her food, not feeling much like eating. Her cold was better, but her nose was still running, and her sore throat persisted.

"I can't believe they are doing this," Ingrid said. "It is so awful. I can't even walk the streets for fear I will see people being shot. And how do we know that one of us isn't on that list?"

"It's a scare tactic. That's the most effective way to get people to do what you want. And don't worry about that. We aren't," Dr. Möller assured her.

"Do you think they will turn themselves in?"

"No," Eva answered before Klaus had a chance to.

"How do you know?" she looked from Dr. Möller to Eva.

"Would you turn yourself in?" Ingrid quickly adverted her eyes to the plate in front of her.

"It will eventually stop," Dr. Möller said somberly.

"But how many will have died by then?" Eva knew he wouldn't answer that.

"Do you think you could talk to SS Obersturmbannführer Bauer about it?" Ingrid asked.

"To do what?" Dr. Möller questioned. "He will not stop killing these people until the ones he's after are in custody."

"No. He won't even see me. I've tried." Eva could feel Ingrid and Klaus's gaze on her.

"He can't be bothered right now," Klaus added. "Like it or not, he has a job to do, and that is what he is doing. It may be cruel, but this is war."

Eva stood up. "I can't sit here anymore. I'm going to go on a walk." She packed up her food, collected her things, and left the hospital. She aimlessly wandered the city, needing to clear her head. Eva's eyes were now wide open to the harsh realization that she had a fragile hold on Wilhelm. That her influence on him was not far-reaching like she hoped, but had its limits. She couldn't stay at home waiting for him to call or come by, it would drive her crazy. The cruel realization was that he probably wasn't going to, and there was no point in hoping that he would.

Feeling helpless and not knowing what else to do, she decided to once again go to where Wilhelm worked. As she got near the middle of town, the number of people on the streets grew. Once at the center, she had to push her way through a crowd. She did not know what was going on until she reached the front. She stopped suddenly, drawing in a sharp breath, then took a step back, bumping into an elderly man behind her. In front of her were seven of the resistance fighters that she saw the night before, hanging from ropes, including Helmut. Their heads were turned in an unnatural way to the side, and on the front of the bodies were wooden signs with French written on them. The resistance fighters of Dieppe were all hanging there, except for one and the resistance fighter from Paris. He, too, was not amongst them.

She stared at the bodies, covering her mouth to muffle the sobs as tears poured freely from her eyes, spilling down her cheeks as she looked at them. She could not tear her eyes away from Helmut, his dead, unblinking eyes looking back at her. She turned and pushed through the crowd and ran until she

358

was away from the bodies. She leaned over, placing her hands on her knees, dry heaving and coughing. When she could breathe again, she stood up, putting one hand on the corner of a building for support. How was she not up there with them, swinging from a rope? She had to see Wilhelm, especially now. She calmed herself the best she could, then returned to where the crowd was gathered around the bodies. This time she did not stop or look at them but kept her head down so she wouldn't see them even by accident. She went into the building and up to the low-ranking soldier at the desk.

"I need to see SS Obersturmbannführer Bauer." She looked right into his eyes, resolute. She was not going to back down.

"Umm… he is—"

"I don't care." She pointed to the phone. "Call upstairs and find out if he can see me."

He hesitated for a second, then picked up the phone and turned the dial three times. "Hello, there is a…" he looked at Eva.

"Eva Abrams," she told him.

"Eva Abrams here to see SS Obersturmbannführer Bauer." He nodded a few times. "Alright." He hung up the phone. "They said he can spare a few minutes. He will escort you there." He pointed to another soldier that had come to stand next to her.

"This way," the man said.

She followed him down the hall that ended in an area that had been made into a sitting room. "Wait here," he instructed, then turned around and left. There were four chairs in the sitting area, but only one door. It wasn't closed all the way, and she could hear shouting on the other side. The voice yelling was unmistakably Wilhelm's. She tiptoed to the door and peered through the opening. Six men were standing in the office on the other side of the desk from Wilhelm, all at attention. Wilhelm was standing on the other side, leaning over the desk, the palms of his hands resting on the top.

"That information was learned almost a day in advance, and you still fucked it up." Wilhelm did not try to hide his rage. "I should have you hung out there with those pieces of shit. If you cannot do your job, then you need to be reassigned. And if there is ever a screwup like this again, you will be dismissed and sent to prison. Now get out of my sight before I really lose my temper. I have to write a letter to Berlin explaining why we still lost fifteen of our men and had to kill a hundred and sixty French people, even though we knew where the resistance was hiding." There was fury in his eyes and barely controlled anger that boiled just beneath the surface.

"Yes, Obersturmbannführer," one man said, and then they all did a hail Hitler solute.

The men turned to leave, and she hurried to the chair closest to the door and plopped in it, breathing heavily. The door opened all the way, and the man coming out paused for just a second when caught sight of her but then walked by in silence as the other men followed. She did not attempt to enter the office. This was not the moment to get on Wilhelm's nerves.

"Eva."

She noticed the clipped tone in his voice. The way he said her name sent chills up her spine. She stood and slowly stepped into the office doorway but did not enter. She looked at him, standing with his hands on his hips, his white shirt unbuttoned at the top, the muscles in his neck tight.

"Well, don't just stand there. Come in, and shut the door," he snapped.

She flinched, then hurried and closed the door behind her and walked to the desk, taking a seat. She didn't know what to say. She started to speak but was tongue-tied.

He seemed to calm a little at the sight of her and sat in his chair. He rubbed his temples with one hand. "I didn't have time to come and see you. I'm sure you know why."

"I do," she finally managed. "Why, Wilhelm? Why did you kill all of those people?" She couldn't keep the sadness and pain out of her trembling voice.

"I don't have to explain my reasons to you. But I will give you a basic answer. Because it was necessary."

"Could you have not shown some compassion?"

"It is not my job to be compassionate. With you, I choose to be."

She was feeling so many things right now. She was hurt, scared, angry, sad, and the list went on as the full range of her emotions engulfed her. "Why am I still here, Wilhelm?"

He scoffed. "Don't be stupid, Eva."

His words stung. "I'm not being stupid." She pointed to the window. "They are out there, hanging, and I am in here, alive."

"Yes. And you know why that is." He moved his hand from his temples and leaned forward, linked his fingers together, and rested his hands on the desk. "I chose to not have you arrested and hung today with the others." He pulled his fingers apart and leaned back in the chair, rubbing his hand through his dark, wavy hair. "I have work now that needs my immediate attention. Make sure you close the door when you leave."

How could he dismiss her so easily? "So that's it? You have no more to say to me?"

"Not, I don't, not right now." His eyes were fixed on her. "If you want, I can come by your apartment when I am done, although I don't know when that will be."

"Sure."

She didn't try to hide the frustration in her voice. Nothing about any of this made sense. Why was he being so cold towards her? She knew he was under a lot of stress from the pressures of work and that many lives had been lost from his orders in the last few days. But it was like he had completely shut his emotions down and his feelings for her with them. And how did he find the resistance, anyway?

She quickly stood from the chair and walked to the door. She opened it and stepped into the hall, slamming it behind her. She stared at the four chairs lined up against the wall of the small lobby, feeling dejected. She wanted him to come to her apartment, and at the same time, she didn't. Right now, she was so angry at him and confused by his actions and treatment of her that she could slap him.

When she got home, she tossed her purse on the floor, roughly pulled off her coat and scarf and hung them up, then went to her room and shut the door.

Soon, there was a knock. "Eva, are you alright?"

"I'm fine. I just want to be alone right now."

"OK. If you need anything, I will just be in my room."

"Thank you."

Eva laid on her bed and pulled her knees to her chest, wrapping her arms around them. She didn't know why, but the night she spent with Gerhardt in Paris came into her thoughts. Watching Madama Butterfly, the feeling of joy at seeing the American flag, him giving her the necklace, and holding his hand out to her in a symbolic gesture. All the memories of that night flooded in, bringing tears to her eyes. She could feel them run down her face and fall onto her nose and then the bed. *Where are you now, Gerhardt? Are you well? Do you ever think of me? I love you so much my heart hurts. It aches for you.* She put her hand on her chest and clenched it, squeezing part of the dress in her fist. She swore that she could feel literal pain in her heart radiating through her body. She squeezed her eyes tightly shut and cried, getting the part of the pillow her head was on wet.

She felt a hand on her shoulder gently shaking her. "Eva. SS Obersturmbannführer Bauer is here to see you. He is waiting in the living room." Eva sat up and wiped the still wet tears from the side of her nose.

"I don't think I want to see him right now. Would you please tell him I'm sorry and that I will talk to him later?"

"I can, but I don't think he will accept that."

"Why?"

"I told him you were sleeping, but he insisted I wake you up."

Eva sighed. No was not in that man's vocabulary. "It's fine. I'll go talk to him." She slid off the bed and peeked into the living room. Wilhelm was sitting on the couch with his legs crossed and his cap beside him. Eva quietly walked around the couch and stood in front of him. He looked up at her but made no attempt to move. She crossed her arms over her chest, her face fixed in a somber expression.

"Get your coat and shoes on."

"Why?"

"Because we both need a distraction."

She gave him a sidelong glance. "What distraction?"

"Get your coat and shoes on, and I will show you."

She hesitated. "I'm actually kind of tired."

"We won't be gone for more than a few hours. Then I will bring you home if that's what you want, and you can sleep."

She let out a long breath through her nose and unfolded her arms. She went to the door and slipped on her shoes, then took her coat from the rack and put it on. She picked her purse up off the floor and then turned to him. "I'm ready." He stood, placing his cap back on his head.

The ride was quiet as neither of them spoke to one another. Eva would occasionally glance at him, but he never looked her way. He was always staring out the window when she would chance a peek. The car pulled in front of the only cinema in Dieppe and turned off the engine. Wilhelm got out while his orderly came around and opened Eva's door for her. She stepped out and looked at Wilhelm questioningly.

"A movie?"

"I thought it would be nice to think about something other than what happened today."

"True, but I'm not sure this is going to cut it."

"Let's go in and find out."

He went to the ticket counter, paid for two tickets, and then handed one to her. They went into theater number two, and Eva read the name of the movie above the door. Caprices was the name on the sign.

"What is the movie about?"

"It's a comedy."

She wasn't sure she wanted to see this. They found two seats and sat down. He removed his hat and gloves and laid them on the seat next to him. There weren't many people in the theater tonight, so they pretty much had their pick of seats. The room darkened, and the screen lit up, then music echoed through the room.

As the movie played, people would laugh at the funny scenes. Eva didn't feel much like laughing but appreciated the light content of the film. Wilhelm reached over and took her hand, bringing it to his lap, which took her a little by surprise. She looked over at him, but he was staring straight ahead, watching the screen. She didn't try to take her hand away but had mixed feelings about it. She was still angry at him and frightened by what had transpired over the last two days. Actually, she was a little frightened of him right now. She was sitting beside this man that was capable of terrible things.

He held her hand through the entire movie, only letting go when 'the end' displayed across the screen. He let go and stood up, retrieving his gloves and hat from the seat, putting them both back on. Still, he didn't say anything to her. She followed him to the car that was waiting out front. He opened the door for her, and she thanked him. Just like the drive there, the drive back was equally as quiet. She wanted to say something but didn't know what. So instead, she watched the building go by, wishing the last two days had never happened. The only positive thing about it was that she didn't have to hide from the resistance anymore, try to protect Wilhelm from them, or worry every day that they might kill her. But that also meant she didn't have to be with him anymore. Did she want that? She didn't know. She didn't know what she wanted because she didn't understand her own feelings. She had no idea what this meant for her future. Maybe she could find a way home now. Maybe.

The car pulled in front of her apartment, and the orderly got out and came to her door, opening it for her. "Good night, Eva," Wilhelm said, looking across at her.

She stared at his face and into his eyes and could tell that he still had his wall firmly up and his emotions carefully locked away, out of her reach.

"Good night."

She got out of the car and gave him one more glance before walking away. To her surprise, the apartment was dark when she came in. "Ingrid," she called, but Ingrid didn't answer. Eva could see some light coming from under the bathroom door and lightly tapped on it. "I'm back." She opened her mouth to tell Ingrid that she was going to shower once she was out and then go to bed early when she heard a moan come from the other side of the door. She tapped on it again. "Ingrid!" There was another moan, followed by a long cry. Eva turned the handle of the door, and it opened. Ingrid was sitting on the bathroom floor, leaning against the wall. Her legs were spread, and her dress and the floor around her were covered in blood. Eva ran to Ingrid's side and dropped to her knees. "Ingrid, what happened?"

Ingrid took a bloodied hand and gripped it hard around Eva's lower arm. "It hurts so bad, Eva."

She rubbed Ingrid's arm. "It's alright. I'm going to take a look." Eva lifted the heavily blood-soaked dress and peered under. Ingrid wasn't wearing any underwear, so it was easy for Eva to see. A tiny baby head was hanging out of Ingrid; its little face was purple. "Ingrid, what happened?"

"I don't know," she said through tears. "I was in the kitchen eating when I felt water running down my legs, leaving a puddle on the floor. Then this terrible pain started, so I hurried to the bathroom. As I got into the bathroom, blood started running down my legs, so I sat on the floor. I could feel the baby coming out, but then it stopped, and I was too afraid to do anything else. I didn't want to hurt it."

"Ingrid,' Eva said softly. "The baby is dead. It's too little to survive outside of the womb."

Ingrid gave a high-pitched cry. "What... no, no." She frantically tried to pull her dress up. "That isn't true. Please... Eva!" Jagged sobs escaped her mouth as she pleaded.

"It is. I am so sorry." Ingrid's cries came in fits, and she pulled up her dress and looked between her legs. "No," she screamed and tried to stand, pushing up off the toilet.

"No, Ingrid. You can't stand up." Eva pulled her back to the floor. "We have to get the baby out of you, or you will bleed to death. She took the towels off the hooks and laid them under Ingrid. "I'm going to pull the baby out now, OK?" Ingrid nodded her head. Eva took hold of the tiny head and pulled. A shoulder and one arm popped out, then came the other shoulder and upper body. The rest was easy. She quickly wrapped it in a towel so Ingrid wouldn't see. "I have to get a knife from the kitchen to cut the umbilical cord. Do not unwrap the towel."

Ingrid shook her head. "I won't."

Eva ran to the kitchen, grabbed a knife from the drawer, and hurried back to the bathroom. She cut the umbilical cord then hid it in the towel too. "I'm going to phone Dr. Möller and have him come over in an ambulance." Again, Ingrid nodded. Eva carried the baby in the towel to the living room and gently laid it on the couch. She picked up the phone and called Dr. Möller, telling him what had happened. He said he was on his way, so she hung up and returned to Ingrid. "Dr. Möller is coming, but I have to get the amniotic sac out while we wait."

"Is that going to hurt?"

"I don't know, but I don't think it will." Eva took hold of the umbilical cord that still hung out of Ingrid and pulled. Gently at first, but then a little harder. Finally, it moved, and the sac came out. She wrapped it in a towel as well and laid it on the floor. "They will clean you up at the hospital." She sat on the floor next to Ingrid and put her arms around her. Ingrid leaned into her and wept, and all Eva could do was stroke her hair and try to comfort her the best she could.

Chapter Nineteen

April 1ˢᵗ, 1942

Nothing had felt the same since that day. Many people had lost their lives, Ingrid lost her baby, and she and Wilhelm's relationship had changed. There was no longer a reason for her to be with him, and so she didn't know where to go from there. But it didn't matter anyway because he had gone back to Berlin on March third and she hadn't seen him since. She didn't know if he was still there or if he had returned to Paris, where the Gestapo HQ was for France. It had been almost a month, and every minute of it, she had felt empty. She questioned his reasons for not returning and wondered if he was upset with her or just too busy to make time for her. She had this overwhelming feeling of loneliness. She no longer had anyone, not Gerhardt, not Fabian or Sabina, not the resistance, not even Wilhelm. She often wondered what the hell she was doing here. She didn't belong in this time, with these people, or in this country.

Eva took a piece of paper and sat at the kitchen table, deciding to write Jon. She didn't know if it would get to him, but she had to try. She kept it short, only telling him she was alright and where she was. She folded up the paper and put it in an envelope, licked the glue, then sealed it. She would drop it off later today.

Ingrid came through the front door in a rush, shutting it hard behind her. "Eva. A car with Nazi flags flying from the hood just pulled in front of the apartment."

Eva laid the envelope down on the table and stiffened. "That doesn't mean it's him or that whoever is in it is here for me."

"I think it is, though. Why else would they be here if not for you? There is a man in the back who looks like him."

"Well, if it's him, then there will be a knock on the door." As if she had conjured someone up, a loud tapping echoed loudly from the door. Ingrid jumped and turned to look at the door. Eva took in a breath. "I'll get it." She slowly stood from the chair when the knock came again, louder this time. She went to the door and opened it a crack. She stared into Wilhelm's hazel eyes, frozen in that position like he had cast a spell on her.

"Do I get to come in?" he asked, a hint of irritation in his voice.

"Yes, of course." She moved to the side and opened the door wider for him. He stepped in, and she shut the door. "I didn't know you were back in town."

"I just got back only yesterday, but I have to leave for Paris tomorrow."

She nodded. "I see. Well, I'm glad you stopped by to say hi before you left."

He gave her an amused look. "I'm not here to say hi."

Those words filled her with unease. "Oh. Why are you here, then?" She was determined to keep a wall between them."

"I will be in Paris a week or so before going to Lorient."

She creased her brows. "Lorient?"

"Yes, for a couple of days. I thought I would ask if you wanted to accompany me to Paris? I would drop you off in Dieppe on my way to Lorient."

Eva looked at him like he had just confessed to her he was an alien. She cleared her throat. "I would have to check with the hospital. I'm not sure they will give me the time off on such short notice."

"You know, I could take care of that for you in a matter of seconds. So don't make up excuses and just tell me if you want to go."

Eva looked at Ingrid, who gave her a brief encouraging nod. She turned back at Wilhelm. "Yes, I will go with you."

He betrayed no emotion as he spoke. "We leave at eight tomorrow. Make sure you are ready. I will come up and help you carry your bags down to the car. I will see you then." He quietly left, saying nothing more.

Once he was gone, she returned to the kitchen chair and sat down. What had just happened? She looked at Ingrid, who was standing near the couch watching her. "Ingrid, if you don't want me to leave, I won't go."

Ingrid came and sat next to Eva. "No, I want you to go. I can tell you have been unhappy since he left."

Eva shook her head. "It's not just that."

"Yes, but it is part of it."

"It is." She felt a small amount of shame in admitting it, but what was the point of lying? She had already surrendered to him physically. She shouldn't have to lie to herself or others anymore about whatever was going on between her and Wilhelm. Although she would probably forever tell lies about what was between them, at least to herself. But she was addicted to the love he gave her. There was no other way to put it. And the truth was, she didn't want to stop seeing him. She was a gluten for punishment because she didn't know if she could give him up.

"I'm going to go to Klaus's and say bye. I don't want to leave without seeing him."

"Yes, you should."

Eva leaned over and put an arm around Ingrid. "I know I will only be gone for a few weeks, but I'll miss you."

"I'll miss you. But don't think of me; just focus on you and him."

Eva pulled back a fraction. "What do you mean by that?"

"Come on. He asked you to go to Paris with him for weeks. I don't know if you are serious about him, but he is certainly serious about you."

Eva let her arms fall to her lap and leaned back in her chair. "I know."

"And you don't know if you want him to be?"

"No, I don't. I'm so conflicted about all of it. I want him to, but I feel like I shouldn't."

"Because he's a Nazi?"

"That, and the fact that he is Gestapo, which means he does or has to do awful things. How could I love someone like that or be with them?"

"I understand why you feel conflicted."

"It feels so good when I'm with him, but it also feels so wrong at the same time. My mind is constantly telling me to leave when we are together, but then it reminds itself that it doesn't want to. It's always in conflict, and then the argument starts again. The truth is, I don't want to fight it anymore. My strength and will to deny him fades quickly when I'm around him. And if he does something kind or loving, it's all over, and I'm right back where I started. I need him, his constant strength that I lack. I need his touch, his comfort, and why I don't fully understand. Like I said, I know I shouldn't love or want to be with him. I should try to be strong like he is, but I don't know how he does it or how sometimes he switches off his emotions. Every time I give in to him, it might be a mistake, but as strange as it sounds, what he gives me I'm happy with, I take it willingly. There is this feeling when he holds me; when he touches me, there is no way to really explain it. I'm in love with him. It's different from Gerhardt. I fell so hard this time I probably have bruises from it. Trust me, it was not graceful or elegant. But it's also frustrating because I don't understand him most of the time. He is so tender one moment and cruel and elusive the next. He's full of many complexities; anger, hurt, loyalty, and love, and they are all cloaked deep within him."

"So do what you said, and stop trying to fight it. Just let go."

Eva met Ingrid's eyes. "I didn't want to love him, you know."

Ingrid put her hand over Eva's. "I do know."

"See, if you don't love someone, they can only hurt the body, not the heart. But I have given him the power to hurt both. He could cost me so much, and yet there are times I would gladly take the pleasure and joy he offers along with any pain and tell myself it's worth it. When am I going to learn? I'm afraid I never will because the feelings I have for him, I know, have blinded me to who he really is. Besides, I'm basically a prisoner here. I don't think he will ever let me leave. But it's not only his fault. I stay here of my own accord, too. There is something about him that makes me want to keep coming back for more. I don't know; maybe I'm crazy."

Ingrid looks at her, puzzled. "Are you saying you haven't done everything that could have been done so you can go home?"

"Yes. I could have done so much more. In the beginning, I tried hard, but then I met Gerhardt and didn't want to leave. Then there was SS Obersturmbannführer Bauer, always standing in my way. First, because he hated me, and now because he loves me. But I have also stopped trying. One, because I don't know what else to do, and two, because I have

375

found myself in love with him as well. I am literally trapped here by my heart. It all makes me so mad." She checked her watch. "I better go so I can get back in time to pack."

Ingrid moved her hand. "I don't think you will ever be free, Eva."

Her face etched with confusion. "Free?"

"Yes. Free of him. From what you told me about him and the strange dynamics between the two of you, then you are done for."

"I will never stop fighting to be free, even from him."

"Would it be a terrible thing if you weren't?"

"I don't know the answer to that, but I think it would be better. It might not be what I want, but it is certainly what I need."

Eva traveled the half-mile to Klaus's house. She stood in front of the cherry oak door and hesitated. She would have to tell him where she was going and who she was going with. And, of course, he would say to her not to go. She pushed the button to the right of the door, and it buzzed. Heavy footsteps came from the other side. The door opened wide, and Klaus stood before her in pajamas.

"Eva. What are you doing here?"

"Can I come in?"

"Yes, please. Come in." She stepped in, and he took her coat, hanging it on the rack next to the door.

"I can't stay long, but I wanted to see you."

"Come in here and have a seat." She followed him into the small sitting room and sat on the dark, gray striped couch. A fire was burning in the fireplace, and she saw a cup of what looked like rum sitting on the table beside the chair next to the fire. "Is Ingrid alright?"

"She is fine. But I wanted to come and see you tonight before I leave in the morning."

"Oh, and where are you going?"

She realized she could just tell him she was going to Paris without telling him she was going with Wilhelm. He didn't even know that Wilhelm was back in Dieppe. And if Wilhelm dropped her off on his way to Lorient, Klaus would never know she was there with him because she would return alone. And if Wilhelm came back to Dieppe after a few days in Lorient, then it would look like he had just returned from Berlin. Yes, she would let Klaus think that. She would inform Ingrid not to tell him otherwise.

"I am going to Paris for a week or two. I need a break. I got a pass, and I am leaving in the morning."

He smiled. "I am glad you are getting away for a while. I think we could all use a break after what happened a few weeks ago."

"Yes, I think you are right. I know it is only for a few weeks, but I couldn't leave without saying bye to you." He stood up, and she did the same. He wrapped his large, fatherly arms around her in a comforting embrace. "You are a good girl, Eva. I'm sorry you have had to suffer this world we men have created."

"I was really barely more than a child when I came here. I can see that now. But I didn't get the chance to mature or experience the world around me as I should have. I didn't get to choose the last three years of my life. My time here has changed who I was, and I would forget a lot if I could, and some of it I wouldn't change for the world." She moved her head from his chest and smiled up at him. "You are part of what I would keep the same. You help make it bearable."

He cleared his throat and let go of her, and she swore she could see a glisten in his eyes. "You should get home before curfew."

He walked with her to the front door. "I'll see you in a few weeks," she said as she retrieved her coat.

"Be safe."

"I will."

Eva had packed that night and went to bed early. She did not want to be tired in the morning. She told Ingrid she did not tell Klaus that she was going with Wilhelm to Paris, and Ingrid promised she would not say a word to him.

When Eva woke the next morning, she changed into a black skirt and a white ruffle shirt, curled the tips of her hair, and applied a little makeup. She rarely wore any at the hospital. She carried the few bags to the living room and sat them by the door. She was nervous, her palms were sweaty, and her heart raced, but she didn't know why. In the last few months, she had seen quite a lot of him, so she shouldn't be nervous about it now. He had only been gone a few weeks to Berlin. She forced herself to stop pacing and went to the couch, and sat down. Ingrid brought her a cup of tea, then sat beside her.

She looked at Eva over the rim of her cup as she sipped her tea. "Your face is very pink."

Eva looked at her, horrified. "What?"

"Yes. It looks like you put on too much rouge."

Eva sat down her cup of tea and ran to the bathroom, putting her face close to the mirror. Just as Ingrid had said, her cheeks were very flushed. "No," she moaned. She went back to the living room and got her compact with powder, then went back into the bathroom. She hadn't put on blush, but Ingrid didn't know that. She took the puff, dipped it in the powder, and patted her cheeks. When she was satisfied that no one could see the pink under the makeup, she returned to the living room and stuck the compact back in her purse.

"Is that better?"

Ingrid leaned in closer to her. "Yes."

Eva picked up her cup of tea when a knock came from the front door. She jumped, almost spilling the tea on her lap. She set the cup back on the table, got up, and quickly went to the door. She peeked through the view hole and saw Wilhelm waiting just on the other side. She opened the door, and he gave her a half-smile.

"Are you ready?"

"I am."

"Good." He walked past her into the apartment without being invited. "Are these all of your bags?"

"Yes. Just those two." He picked both suitcases up and waited for her to get her purse from the couch. She put on her coat and scarf and gave Ingrid a hug.

"Bye, Eva. Remember, don't overthink it," she whispered in Eva's ear as they embraced.

"I'll try not to." She kissed Ingrid on the cheek, then followed Wilhelm down the stairs and out to the car. He put her bags in the trunk, then opened the door for her. "Thank you." She got in, and he went to the other side, sliding in next to her.

The car pulled away from the curb, and they were both quiet for the first ten minutes, but once they were on the main road heading north out of Dieppe, he spoke. "You will be on your own a lot of the time. But I thought we could go to La Chapelle if you wanted."

She turned in her seat to make it easier to look at him. "No one knows I am going to Paris with you except Ingrid. I would like it if it stayed that way, especially if we go to La Chapelle." At first, he didn't say anything, and she saw an emotion flash in his eyes for only a fraction of a second. Pain, or maybe anger, at her not wanting to be seen with him casually in La Chapelle.

"I have some business I could conduct in La Chapelle. You might tell the town's people that you came with me because it was the only opportunity you had to visit."

"I think they might believe that. At least most of them." He remained silent, but she would not let this car ride be like the last one they had together. "Why were you yelling at those men?"

He looked over at her. "They cost a lot of people their lives."

"You were furious at them, but I can see why you would be upset about that."

"And that was only a fraction of how mad I was."

"You looked pretty angry to me."

"No, it was very well contained. When I was talking to those men I never let out the rage I was feeling. If I had, they all would have been shot."

She was glad she had never seen that side of him. "I want you to know that the reason I didn't tell anyone in Dieppe except Ingrid and prefer that no one in La Chapelle know we came together is not for the reason you might think."

"Oh, and what do I think?"

"That I don't want to be seen with you in public. And if that is what you think, then you are right, but not for the reasons you have imagined. They hate Germans there, and they already know about Gerhardt and me. I don't want them thinking I am with another German or even think I like another German."

He raised an eyebrow. "And do you like another German?"

She honestly wasn't sure how to answer that. She gave him a side-long glance. "Maybe I do."

"And is that so wrong?" he asked obvious displeasure on his face at her discomfort.

"It could be. So how are the accommodations in Paris and La Chapelle set up?" Feeling more uncomfortable with how the conversation was going.

"I was planning on you staying with me, but now I'm thinking you don't want to."

"I didn't say that, but how would that work?"

"I have a small apartment in Paris because that is where I spend most of my time when I'm not in Berlin. If you want, you can stay there with me, or I can put you up in a hotel."

"No, I'll stay with you. Will, I have my own room or…."

"It is small, and there is only one bedroom. Is that going to be a problem?"

"Um…well, that depends. What did you think would happen while we're there together?"

"Eating, sleeping, showering…" he trailed off. A suggestive look in his eyes.

"Eating, sleeping, and showering? OK." She turned to the window. She could feel the flush on her face but didn't want him to see it.

It was only a two-and-a-half-hour drive from Dieppe to Paris, and the time flew by quickly. The car pulled in front of a long, off-white building with the typical blue French roof. Wilhelm's orderly opened the door for her, and she met Wilhelm behind the car. When he opened the trunk, she reached for her luggage.

"I'll get it."

He took the bags from the trunk before she had a chance to, and the orderly reached in for the other two that must have been Wilhelm's. He carried them inside the building and up the flight of stairs to the third floor, which was the top floor. He set the bags on the tile on each side of him and reached for a key in his pocket. He unlocked the door and opened it, sitting her bags just inside the door. He took the two from his orderly, who then gave him a quick salute and walked back down the hall. Wilhelm gestured with his hand for her to enter first. She took a step over the threshold into a small apartment that was like a modern-day studio apartment. It was an open floor plan with the bathroom the only separate part of the apartment. She sat her purse on a small table near the front door, walked to the middle of the living room, and turned in a circle to take it in. It was clean, tidy, and elegant but simple in its own way. She knew that he, of course, was not the one who cleaned it. He was standing at the door, watching her.

"Do you eat in the kitchen, or do you go out and eat when you are here?"

"I keep a small amount of food here, but I usually eat with the men. There is a restaurant just a few blocks away that caters to German officers. If you were to go in there, Germans are just about all you would find, except for the occasional French woman that some of them bring."

"Alright. Well, that might be a little awkward."

"Of course. We can get whatever food you need. But if you want, you can come to the restaurant with me sometimes."

Eva didn't want to feel like she was on display the way she was sure the German men viewed the French women. "I'll think about it." She clasped her hands together. "What now?"

"I have to go to work, but I suppose you can do whatever you want. Within reason," he said, stressing the words. It was partly playful but partly serious.

"I wouldn't do anything that wasn't within reason." He narrowed his eyes at her. "What day are we going to La Chapelle?"

He thought for a second. "I have a lot of work to do here that will take up the next few days, but I shouldn't think it will take longer than three or four days."

Like at the cottage in Dieppe, Wilhelm was gone most of the time, and she once again found herself alone. He had given her some extra ration cards to buy food so she didn't have to use hers, and she stocked the kitchen with things she could use to make several different meals. During the day, she revisited the sites of the city but avoided any place she had gone with Gerhardt. It was too painful to remember, and she didn't want to be unhappy. The weather was still cold, but she preferred to be out in the city than sitting alone in the apartment. So far, it was not an auspicious start to the trip. The two nights they had been there, she was already in bed when Wilhelm came home. He never once tried to touch her or make a move of any kind. He would crawl in beside her and fall asleep. She wondered why that was and wanted to ask him about it but didn't know if she should. Why did she even care? She came here because… well, she didn't really understand why she came. She shouldn't care. She should be glad and relieved that he was leaving her alone. But why did he ask her to come if he was going to ignore her most of the time? She honestly didn't know. It made little sense to her. Maybe he thought she would get mixed up with what he thought were undesirable people if he left her alone for too long, or perhaps he thought she would try to run. He did look at her sometimes like a roaming cow that often wandered off the pasture.

The next day had been much the same, but that night Wilhelm told her he was going to take her to dinner at the restaurant. "I don't know. I already have food here that I can make."

"No. You are going to have to do better than that. Tonight, you are going with me. I know I have left you alone a lot, but I have more time this evening than I have had in a while."

"I know you will not let me say no, so of course, I would love to go," she said with a hint of sarcasm.

He didn't dignify her with an answer but instead went to the door, took her coat from the rack, and held it out to her. She pulled it from his hand and put it on, slipped her feet in her shoes, and retrieved her purse from the hall table, then crossed her arms and gave him an indignant look. In return, he gave her a triumphant grin.

The hotel was only three blocks from the apartment, so they walked. They left their coats at the front and headed into the large room filled with tables and chairs. She peered at other tables in the room and noticed that the people at them were watching her and Wilhelm as they walked through the restaurant. All eyes were on them, making her feel uncomfortable. This was precisely why she didn't want to come here.

Once they were seated, conversations started again, and the restaurant became noisy with talk and laughter. She leaned over the table and spoke in a quiet voice. "Do they think I'm a prostitute?"

He glanced around the room. "It's possible."

The nervousness she was feeling turned to anger, and her eyes grew wide. "You took me here knowing that this might happen."

"Just because they might think you are doesn't make you one. Besides, they won't remember you by morning, so I wouldn't worry about it."

She leaned back in her chair. "I cannot believe you."

"Why does that bother you so much? Have you seen the way the French people look at me?"

"That's because you invaded their country, but I am not what these German men think I am."

"If it bothers you that much, we can leave after we eat."

She was already here, so she might as well eat something. "Alright. But I want to leave right after."

"If that is what you want."

His voice was level and calm, but she knew he was annoyed and would no doubt never bring her here again. "I'm going to go to the restroom. If the waiter or waitress comes before I'm back, you can order me whatever you order." He gave a nod, and she got up, scanning the room for the bathrooms. In the corner of the room was a hallway. It was the only place she could see where there would be a bathroom. As she suspected, they were down the hall. She went into the ladies, used the toilet, then washed her hands and brushed through her hair with her fingers. She took more time than she needed, not wanting to go back out into the restaurant to be gawked at, but at some point, she was going to have to. Finally, after staring at herself in the mirror for no other reason than to take up time, she left the bathroom. She started back towards the table when she saw a man sitting with Wilhelm. But it wasn't just any man; it was the man from the dance who tried to force himself on her. She had never told Wilhelm or anyone else about what happened that night. It was scary and humiliating, and she didn't want anyone else to know. It never crossed her mind that he would be here, but then she tried not to think of him at all after that incident outside the casino.

She stood staring at him, then realized half of the room was looking at her as she stood like a statue in the open. Wilhelm turned his head and saw her frozen in the middle of the room. He gave her a confused look, then waved for her to join them. Slowly, she walked towards the table and was happy that he was sitting in the chair next to Wilhelm's. She would not have to sit directly beside him. She sat in the chair on the other side of Wilhelm, not in the one across from him like she had been.

"Why were you standing there?"

"Oh, um, I don't know." She couldn't look at the man or think of an explanation.

"Eva, this is Oberleutnant Jurgen Pflüger." She gave a nod, then looked away again.

"We have met before, Jurgen said."

Eva's head jerked towards him. She could not believe he had mentioned to Wilhelm of their meeting. Wilhelm looked surprised. "Really? Where?"

"At the dance in Dieppe."

Wilhelm looked at Eva. "That's funny; she never mentioned it."

Jurgen eyed Eva. "I'm sure she just forgot. Isn't that right?"

She swallowed hard and nodded. "Yes." The word sounded forced.

Wilhelm watched her for a second, then turned back to Jurgen. "So, how long are you in Paris for?"

"Only until tomorrow."

"Well, it's good that we bumped into you before you left."

Wilhelm had ordered for her while she was in the bathroom. They brought out the food, and Eva ate in silence while the two men talked. Her hands were sweaty, and her heart was racing. She had difficulty eating her food but kept spooning it into her mouth anyway so she didn't have to talk. She was happy that Wilhelm was a buffer between them. Even though she ate continuously, she was the last to finish her food. Wilhelm and Jurgen ordered a couple of beers once their plates were taken away. She continued to watch them as they drank and talked, noticing that Jurgen kept letting his gaze drift to her.

"Do you want another beer?" Jurgen asked Wilhelm.

He tipped his cup, looking at the small about of beer at the very bottom. "Sure. I need to go empty this one first. Order me one."

"I will."

Wilhelm got up from the table, and Eva panicked, also standing. "I'm just going to the bathroom. We aren't leaving yet." For a moment, she looked between the two men, then finally sat back in her chair. Wilhelm glanced down at her, then disappeared out of view, and Jurgen put his arms on the table and leaned forward, bringing himself closer to her.

"You know, there was this girl in Belgium when I was stationed there. Dark curly hair, olive skin, nice figure, a pretty thing. I tried to be nice to her, but she treated me like I was nothing. And then I learned she was a Jew and a Bolshevik. She, someone so unclean, a subhuman would think that she was above me, better than me even. So, do you know what I did?" Eva shook her head, tense in her chair, wanting more than anything in this moment to not be here. "I grabbed her by the hair and dragged her up the stairs, kicking and screaming. I took off my belt, and I beat her until she stopped moving. While she lay on the bloodied on the floor, I tore off her dress and had my way with her." He smiled, a sadistic glint in his eyes. "And while I had my way with her, I whispered in her ear all the things I was going to do to her next and the things I was going to do to her family once I was done with her. And why did I do this, I'm sure you are wondering? Because she deserved it. I didn't know if she was dead when I left the room. She wasn't moving when I was done, and I left her there on the floor like a dead dog. What was one less Jew, one less Bolshevik?" Before Eva had time to react, he reached across the table and grabbed hold of her wrist, his fingers squeezing tight around it like a vice, digging into the skin. "So, do you think that I'm going to let some American slut tell me I can't have my way with her too, an enemy to Germany?"

Suddenly, he let go of her hand and leaned back in his chair, a very different kind of smile now on his face. It was like his entire face transformed, as well as his demeanor. As soon as Wilhelm sat down in his chair, Eva understood the reason for the sudden change. She stood up, rushed from the table, and hurried to the bathroom. Not waiting to see if he spoke to her. She went into a stall and closed the door, sitting on the floor as she hugged her knees to her chest. Her whole body was shaking as she cried and tapped the back of her head against the wall. There was no way she was going to leave this bathroom while that man was at their table. She rested her face on her knees and tried to clear her mind, but the fog was heavy.

She had no idea how long she had been in the bathroom when someone knocked on the stall door.

"Excuse me, is there someone in there?" a woman asked in French.

Eva lifted her head and took some toilet paper, wiping her eyes and nose. "Yes."

"Is your name Eva?"

She sniffed and wiped her nose again. "It is?"

"SS Obersturmbannführer Bauer has asked if I would come in and get you. He wants you to come out. He says it is time to leave."

"Can you please tell him that I will be right out?"

"Yes, I will tell him. Are you alright?"

"I'm fine. Thank you."

"You are welcome. I will go tell him."

Eva heard the woman leave the bathroom and knew she had to make herself presentable before she came out. She stood up, opened the stall door, and went to the sink. She looked at herself in the mirror and was petrified. Her face was puffy, her mascara was now smeared under her eyes, and her skin had patchy red spots on it. There were also streaks in her face powder from the tears, and she didn't have her purse with her to fix any of it. She went back to the stall and got some more toilet paper, wetting it in the sink. She rubbed the mascara from under her eyes the best she could, then took her fingers and rubbed at her cheeks, trying to fix the makeup. Once she had decided she couldn't make her face look any better, she smoothed her clothes and peeked out the bathroom door. She found their table and saw that only Wilhelm was sitting at it now. She felt an overwhelming sense of relief. She came out of the bathroom but was unsure how she was going to explain to him why she had left the table suddenly, why she had stayed in the bathroom for so long, and why she now looked like she had been crying. She sat down in the chair next to Wilhelm and tried to not make eye contact with him.

He leaned down a little and looked at her. "Where did you go?"

"The bathroom. My mascara was flaking off in my eye, making it water. Then the other eye started watering, and now most of it has been rubbed off." His eyes were still fixed on her, and she felt the weight of them. "Are we leaving now?"

"Yes."

He stood up, and she followed him to the front of the restaurant and retrieved her coat. On the walk back to the apartment, she was quiet but felt like she needed to ask him about Oberleutnant Jurgen Pflüger, so she waited until they were inside and sitting on the couch.

"How long have you known Oberleutnant Jurgen Pflüger?"

"A while."

"And what kind of person is he?"

His eyes narrowed. "That is a very specific question."

"I'm just curious."

"He is one of the biggest assholes in the Nazi party."

"Really. How do you know that?"

"It's easy for me to identify someone like him. It takes one to know one."

She nearly snorted. "You are nothing like him."

"I have never pretended that I was a good person." He watched her for a minute. "I thought we would go to La Chapelle tomorrow. We should get some sleep so we can get an early start in the morning."

Eva knew he changed the topic on purpose. "I would like that."

They each took turns showering then went to bed, and Eva was painfully aware that he was taking great care not to touch her. What was even more confusing and frustrating were her feelings on the matter. Part of her didn't want him to touch her, but another part of her wanted to be angry at him because he wasn't. Had he changed his mind about her? Was what he had with her just a one-time thing? She could not help but feel a little rejected.

Chapter Twenty

The drive from Paris to La Chapelle seemed to take forever. But they finally arrived just before eight and pulled in front of Madame Blanc's Château. Eva was nervous and excited but mostly nervous. The orderly opened the door for her, then went to the back of the car to retrieve their bags. She walked up the steps and stopped in front of the familiar, large oak door, and pulled the rope that rang the bell. After a few minutes, the hinges creaked, and the heavy door opened. Adele stood in front of Eva, mouth agape.

"Eva. What are you doing here?"

"I had an opportunity to come back to La Chapelle, so I took it."

Adele looked past Eva and saw Wilhelm standing next to the car, arms crossed over his chest, leaning against the side as he watched them. "Is this the opportunity that you had?"

Eva turned and looked in his direction. "It is. This was the only way I could come back. He was coming here for work, and I asked if I could come with him. He asked why, and I told him I wanted to visit some old friends. He agreed, and so, here I am."

"I am sorry that coming with him was the only way you had to return, but we are happy to see you again." Ingrid opened her arms for Eva to give her a hug, and she happily embraced her.

Wilhelm came up the steps and stood beside Eva, his orderly following behind. "Good day, Mademoiselle." He touched his index and middle finger to the tip of his cap. "I hope you were informed of my arrival."

"I was, but they didn't tell me she was with you."

"I wanted to surprise you," Eva told her.

"Is that the German officer we are expecting?" Madame Blanc's voice echoed from behind Adele.

"It is, Madame. Please, come in." She looked at Eva. "Madame Blanc is in the sitting room. She will be so excited to see you."

"I'm excited to see her again, too."

Adele stopped at the threshold of the living room. "Look who has come back to visit." Eva stepped into the entryway and smiled at Renée.

"Oh, my dear." She sat her teacup on the coffee table and stood up. "It has been so long. I had no idea you were coming." She came to stand in front of Eva, put her pudgy hands on her shoulders, and kissed each cheek.

"It was sort of last minute, and I wanted to surprise you."

"How long will you stay for?"

"A few days, at least."

Madame Blanc's smile faded when she saw Wilhelm step into view. "I did not know it was you they were talking about when they said a German officer would be coming to stay."

"I am sorry to disappoint."

"Well, at least you brought her with you." She glanced back at Eva.

He gave no indication of what he thought of her remark. "Yes, I brought her. If it is not too much trouble, I would like the same room you had me in last time."

"Of course. Eva, what room do you want to stay in?"

"I don't care. You can put me in whatever room is most convenient for you."

"I can make the room on the main floor for her?" Adele asked Madame Blanc.

"Yes, that would be most convenient. Why don't you do that."

Eva couldn't help but feel that they were making sure she was as far from Wilhelm as possible. She took her bags from the orderly and gave Wilhelm a quick glance before following Adele down the hall to the back room. It was the one Gerhard had stayed in the last time they were here. She didn't know if this would be better than staying in her old room connected to Gerhard's old room, which was now Wilhelm's, or if staying in the last room Gerhardt did would be worse. Only time would tell.

"If you want to wait here, I will go get a set of sheets."

"If his room needs making up, you can just leave the sheets with me. I can make my own bed."

"I don't mind doing it."

"If you're sure?" Eva said.

"I am."

Eva sat on the bare mattress and waited for Adele to return. She didn't see Wilhelm or his orderly in the hall and figured he must have gone upstairs. Soon, Adele returned with the set of sheets, and Eva stood to help her make the bed.

"It's been a while since you've been here. What have you been doing?"

"Well, as you know, I was in Berlin for some time. But then I went to the Russian front and worked at some hospitals there. We moved around a lot because it was dangerous to stay in one place for too long."

"I guess I'm a little surprised that you went there."

"Why?"

"It is dangerous there, but mostly I'm surprised because you were helping the Germans, prolonging the war."

"I wasn't prolonging the war. I was helping men who were dying."

"Yes, men who will now go back to fight, killing more men from the allied countries."

"I would help anyone. It's just that I happen to live in an area occupied by the Germans."

"That doesn't mean you should help them. In no way should they be allowed the upper hand."

Eva straightened and let go of the sheet. "I am not helping them win the war. We cannot stand on the sidelines and be useless while a war is going on around us."

"But the Germans are not the ones you should help keep alive."

Eva walked around the bed and came to stand in front of Adele. "They are not the only ones I have been helping." She leaned even closer and lowered her voice to a whisper. "In Berlin, I helped the small resistance cell there. But they turned against me because they thought I was a collaborator, so they tried to have me killed. Do you know who helped me?" She pointed to the hall. "Him, the head of the Gestapo in France, helped me. And not because I gave him information. Then, I assisted the resistance here in France. And do you know what they tried to do?" Adele averted her eyes. "Yes, Adele. They, too, tried to kill me and almost succeeded. And he saved me yet again. I am not saying he is a good person, but I am alive because of him. I understand now that I am the only person I can trust. The reality is that I have been the only one I can rely on since I've found myself stuck in this war. In the beginning, I had to fear the Germans, but lately, it has been the resistance. And very easily, it could change back to the Germans. So, my loyalties lie with myself, and I will do whatever I need to in order to survive this fucking war."

"I didn't know."

"Of course, you didn't. How could you?"

"That doesn't mean you should choose them. Why is it that you always seem to prefer German men? Aren't American men good enough for you? Maybe a British man? Or heaven forbid you fall for a man from France. But of all the German men that surround us, you had to pick him."

"If you don't want to trust him, I get it. But he saved my life, so I do. At least to a certain extent. And it's not that I seek them out or even necessarily choose them. You can't command love. It doesn't ask you who you want to be with. It isn't concerned with time or place, or rather or not the person is good or bad, or if they are of the same nationality as you. It doesn't seem to care. And yes, it is true; I do love Gerhardt. But that man," she again pointed towards the hall, "SS Obersturmbannführer Bauer, I do not love him." She knew that wasn't true but had to lie to Adele.

"I'm sorry if I misunderstood. But you spend a lot of time with the enemy."

"Out of necessity." She walked back around the bed and snatched the sheet she had dropped, then they made the rest of the bed in silence.

"I will leave you to it. There are fresh towels in the bathroom upstairs for you."

"Thank you." When Adele was gone, she sat on the bed and considered what to do next. Finally, she stood up and opened her suitcase, retrieving her toiletry bag and her nightgown. As she walked toward the stairs, she could hear voices in the sitting room. She peered in and saw Adele and Madame Blanc having tea. "Hello."

They looked up. "Eva. Why don't you join us?" Madame Blanc said.

"I will. Thank you." She sat in the empty chair beside Adele and poured herself a cup of chamomile tea. "How has life in La Chapelle been?"

"Quiet, now that most of the Germans have left. Of course, there are still a few here, but it is not as it was. Adele has told me that you went to the Russian front."

"I did, but I am living in Dieppe now."

"Dieppe, really?"

"Yes. It has been interesting."

"I'm sure it has been. And you came here with that horrid man. Isn't he the one who arrested you?"

"Yes," Eva chuckled to herself at the irony of it. "But it was all a misunderstanding." She glanced at Adele, then took a sip of her tea.

"I would hope so."

Eva was feeling tired and wanted to shower and go to bed early. Strangely, she hadn't seen Wilhelm again since they arrived at Madame Blanc's. She finished her tea and set the cup and saucer on the coffee table. "Thank you for the tea. I think I will turn in for the night."

"What are your plans for tomorrow?" Madame Blanc asked.

"I'm not sure yet. I thought I might visit Sabina's grave and maybe spend a little time in the town. I'm sure I'll have time to visit with you some more tomorrow."

Madame Blanc smiled. "That would be nice. Goodnight, dear."

"I will. Goodnight."

She left the sitting room and slipped upstairs. She waited at the top for a second and could hear Madame Blanc and Adele's voices echoing from down below. Once she was confident they weren't coming up the stairs, she went to Wilhelm's door and listened. She glanced towards the stairs one more time, then lightly knocked on the door. She could hear the floorboards creaking on the other side, then the door opened. Wilhelm looked at her curiously.

"I wanted to know what the plans were for tomorrow?"

"I have work, so you can spend some time with Madame Blanc."

"Alright. Are we doing anything together or…."

"Do you want to do anything with me?"

"Of course."

"But what could we do in La Chapelle that the locals wouldn't notice?"

"I suppose we could do something in the evening after everyone is asleep."

He considered this. "Maybe. I will find you tomorrow after I'm done if it's not too late."

She nodded. "Goodnight."

"Goodnight, Eva," he whispered.

The night was restless, and the morning was bright, and she could no longer sleep, so she got up early. While she was eating breakfast, a thought entered her mind. She felt a need to write Gerhardt a note, and she knew exactly where she wanted to leave it. She would put it in the hole of the tree in the meadow. It held a special place in her heart. It was a place where memories were made and shared. Memories that she would cherish forever. She took a piece of paper and a pen from the upstairs office and wrote while she finished her breakfast. When she was done, she folded the paper up and stuck it in the pocket of her dress. She put her coat and shoes on, told Adele she was going to walk to town, then left the house.

She looked at the fields as she walked, noticing that a few of the trees had already started to bud. In some ways, it was like she had never left, but it would never feel the same again. Not with Sabina and Fabien gone forever from this place. There was a slight chill in the air that nipped at her nose and the top of her ears, but she didn't mind. She wanted to walk. She needed this walk.

She could see the edge of the town but turned off just before she got there on the small dirt path that led through the trees and ended in the meadow. Here in the trees, it felt like the world stood still, and she loved it. The gentle breeze blowing through the branches calmed her, so she closed her eyes and listened. When she reached the meadow, she stopped, gazing out over it. The wind made ripples on top of the pond. It was so quiet, so peaceful. In the middle of the meadow stood the lone tree that Gerhardt had told her about so long ago. She stepped out into the long grass, wading through it until she reached the tree. Under its long, overhanging branches was the enormous trunk of the white oak, and in the middle, the hole, barely bigger than her fist. She took the piece of paper from her pocket and held it in her hands, then brought it to her mouth and pressed her lips to it, and put it deep in the hole.

"I hope this finds you one day, Gerhardt." She stared at the hole for one long moment, then turned and made her way back through the meadow, down the trail, and out to the main road.

The village looked the same to her, and she wondered if all the shops were still owned and run by the same families. Some people watched her, some only glanced up as she walked past, and others paid her no mind. Just on the other side of town was the small cemetery they buried Fabien and Sabina in. Eva wished she had flowers to put on their graves, but it was still early in the year, and they hadn't bloomed yet. She stopped at the rock wall surrounding the cemetery and looked at the rows of old tombstones. The clouds that moved overhead cast leopard spots on the ground, shading some of the stones while others were still in the sun. She walked through the narrow opening, glancing at the names on the stones as she made her way to the back. She found two newer ones side by side. She squatted down in front of them and traced her fingers over the words.

"Hello, little one. I think the flowers will bloom soon. If I can come again in the summer, I will bring some and put them on your grave. I'll make sure to pick all your favorites. I am living in France again, in Dieppe. I live with a friend of mine. Her name is Ingrid. I think you would like her." She looked at Fabien's grave. "I hope that wherever you are, you have found peace. I cannot tell you how sorry I am for what has happened. It's all because of me, and I would undo everything if I could.

None of it was fair or right. But I want you to know that I am surviving. It's not easy, and every day is a struggle, but I'm not giving up. I will not let your deaths be in vain." She sat down in front of the tombstones, staying for over an hour. She told them about all that was happening in her life, how she missed her family, Gerhardt, and her feelings and confusion about Wilhelm. But a lot of the time, she just sat there, enjoying the quiet serenity.

She stood up and stretched her stiff legs. "I hope I can come back soon. I love you." She left the cemetery and made her way back to the house. As she walked, she found herself hoping that she could spend the evening with Wilhelm. If he didn't come to her, she would just have to go to him.

When she was back at the house, she went inside and found Madame Blanc. "What would you like to do today?"

"The rent has to be collected from the tenants of my nearby properties. It's been weeks and needs to be done today."

"That's alright. I can come with you and help. I have nothing else to do right now."

"Oh, that would be so nice." She checked her watch. "We better get going, then. It always takes a while. Adele will stay here and work on dinner. Do you mind driving?"

Eva had only driven a car once the entire time she had been here. Fabien's truck. And she knew that all the vehicles had a standard transmission, but she could really only drive an automatic. She had struggled with the truck, trying to shift it into different gears. She had stopped to see what she was doing wrong, but then couldn't get it moving again and finally gave up, leaving it on the side of the road and hitching a ride into Paris.

"Umm, I haven't driven in so long. I think it would be better if you drove."

"Nonsense."

"The truth is, I never finished learning how to drive."

Madame Blanc frowned. "That is unfortunate. You should really learn."

"I know, and I will."

"You might need to someday. It could save your life."

Eva thought her last sentence was a little strange. "I promise I'll learn."

Renée patted her hand. "Good."

Eva followed her to the car and got into the passenger seat. She felt bad making an old woman drive, but there was no way she was driving them anywhere. She wondered if Wilhelm would be willing to teach her. She would have to ask him about it.

They divided up the properties so that it would go faster. It surprised Eva at how poor some of the families that rented from Madame Blanc were. And also how rundown some of the houses were. They were in disrepair, with leaking roofs, broken windows, and cracked foundations. Some of the houses didn't even have wood covering the dirt, and the tenants lived on dirt floors. Some did not have running water, and others only had an outhouse instead of an inside bathroom. She had no idea it was this bad. She wondered why it was this way. She suspected that Madame Blanc could not find someone to fix them or that maybe she couldn't afford to pay anyone. Eva thought if she had some experience, she would offer her help, but she knew nothing about working on houses.

Finally, they finished collecting the rent and returned home. Adele had dinner ready for them, and Eva was glad. She had not eaten since that morning and was starving. She wondered if Wilhelm was going to eat with them but suspected that he wouldn't. After dinner, Eva would wait until Adele and Madame Blanc went to bed, then go to Wilhelm's room.

She laid her fork on the plate. "I think I will turn in for the night."

"So early. I thought you might have a nightcap with me?"

She glanced at the clock that sat on the mantel as it clicked away the seconds. "I suppose I can stay for one."

"Oh, good. I will ring for Adele. Let's go into the sitting room."

Eva took her usual spot on the couch, and Madame Blanc rang the little silver bell that sat on the end table.

"Yes, Madame?" Adele said when she appeared in the doorway.

"Bring in two glasses and the bottle of brandy."

"Right away."

"Do you like brandy?" Madame Blanc asked.

"I like OK. It's a little strong, though."

Madame Blanc gave a playful smile. "I know."

Adele returned with two glasses and a crystal bottle with a matching crystal stopper in the top and sat them on the coffee table. She poured each glass half full and handed one to Eva and the other to Madame Blanc. "Thank you, Adele." Adele left the room, and Madame Blanc held up her glass. "Here's to the end of this war."

"I second that." Eva held up her glass, then took a sip. It burned as it went down, but it made her feel warm from the inside out. By the time Eva finished, each of them had refilled their glasses three times, and she felt lightheaded. She sat the cup on the table and stood up, truly noticing the effects of the alcohol now. It made her tipsy, and she felt braver and more confident about going to Wilhelm's room. "I'll see you in the morning."

"Goodnight, dear."

She showered quickly, then quietly went to Wilhelm's door but didn't hear any noises coming from the other side. She went downstairs to her room and lay in bed, waiting until the house was quiet. Once she was sure that Adele and Madame Blanc were asleep, she tiptoed down the hall and back up the stairs. Gently, she knocked on the door and waited, listening. She heard footsteps on the other side, then the door cracked open. Wilhelm looked at her, squinting his eyes. It looked like he had been asleep.

"Eva, what is it?"

"I thought we were going to do something?"

He looked at his watch. "It's late."

"I know. I could just come into your room."

"The bed is too small. Besides, we don't want anyone to hear us talking."

"You never came and got me."

"I was busy all day. I'm sorry. If you want, I can take part of tomorrow off, and we can do something. Go to bed, and I promise we will spend time together."

She didn't completely believe him. She was disappointed and once again felt rejected. "Alright, but I will hold you to it."

"I will finish around noon," he assured her. "Meet me outside of town by the crossroads. Don't go all the way to the roadblock, or the guards will ask what you are doing."

"I'll be there." She turned around and could hear his door click shut. She returned to her own room and crawled into bed. She lay awake thinking how his words seemed like hollow lies, but that could be because she felt hurt. Her eyes grew heavy, and the alcohol helped her drift to sleep.

She sat in the high brush on the side of the road, picking blades of grass and running them through her fingers as she waited. She thought about last night and how she felt when he turned her away. If she wasn't in love with him, why did she feel this way, and why was she so disappointed last night? Is her heart lying to her, or is she lying to her heart? It was enough to make her go crazy. Every time she thought about him, she wanted him; she needed his touch. And if she wasn't in love with him, why would that happen? Why would she miss him so much when he wasn't around? She wouldn't feel this familiar ache in her heart if she didn't. There was no way this was just an infatuation. When she imagined being with someone, it was no longer Gerhardt. It was about Wilhelm.

His arms are around her as a lover, and she always surrendered to him in her dreams.

While she was lost in thought, something reflecting in the sun drew her attention. She looked up the road in the direction of town as a black car came towards her. She stood up and brushed off the back of her dress. The car pulled to the side of the road beside her.

Wilhelm leaned over and opened the passenger door. "Get in."

She did as he said. "Where are we going?"

"Where do you want to go?"

That question should not have stumped her, but it did. She didn't want to go anywhere in La Chapelle that she went with Gerhardt, anywhere that was special to them. But she also didn't want to be seen with Wilhelm. She remembered yesterday thinking that maybe he would teach her to drive a stick. She turned in her seat and looked at him.

"Are there a lot of little roads like this one around La Chapelle?"

He narrowed his eyes at her. "Yes. Why?" He was suspicious of her question.

She smiled at him. "Because I want you to teach me to drive."

His eyebrows came together in confusion. "You don't know how to drive?"

"Not really, no. My mom and dad used to sit me on their lap and let me steer when I was little, so I can do that, but I have never really learned to shift or how to work the clutch."

He put his right hand on the top of the steering wheel and leaned back, considering her request. "Alright. I suppose there's no harm in it." He put the car in gear and turned it off. He opened the door and stepped out.

She enthusiastically opened her door and hopped out, going around to the driver's side. She sat in the seat and closed the door, put both hands on the steering wheel, then looked at him.

"Alright, with your left foot, push the peddle on the far left all the way to the floor." She remembered that was the clutch from Fabien's truck. She pushed it down. "Good. Now the car is already in first gear, so start it." She reached up and turned the key in the dash, and the engine roared to life. "Now, as you slowly let up on the clutch, push down on the throttle. She did as he said, and the engine sputtered, then stalled. "You didn't give it enough gas. If it sounds like the engine is going to die, push harder on the throttle, but not too hard." She pushed the clutch in again, started the engine, and tried again. The car lurched forward, moving ten or twelve feet before again stalling.

"OK, what am I doing wrong?" This was what kept happening with Fabien's truck. She had no idea how she managed to take off the first time, but she could never repeat it.

"You keep letting up on the gas. You need to consistently push on the peddle. The motor will sound like it's racing, and that is when you shift. Switch, and I'll show you." She got out and went to the passenger side and got in. He slid into the driver's side, pushed the clutch to the floor, and started the engine. "Now, watch what I do." She leaned over to watch his feet. He slowly let up on the clutch as he pushed on the gas. The car rolled forward slowly at first, but as he pushed on the throttle, the car accelerated, and the engine raced. He pushed in on the clutch again as he let up on the throttle and pulled the shifter down, and the engine stopped racing, but as the car moved faster, it started to race again, so he repeated the process. "Do you see what it is I'm doing?"

"I do."

"Once you get the car moving, it's usually easier. Do you want to try it again?"

"I do. I won't learn if I don't keep trying."

He stopped the car, put it in neutral, and then pulled the emergency brake. She went around to the driver's side and got back in behind the wheel. Remembering everything he did and what he had told her to do, she attempted to make the car move without stalling it this time. The first two times she tried, the car jerked forward and died. But the third time, she got it to roll forward without killing the engine.

"Don't let up on the gas," he told her. "Push it a little harder." She did, and the engine raced. "Now let up on the gas while you push in the clutch, then pull the shifter down into second gear. She pushed in the clutch and let up on the gas, and took the shifter, pulling it down, but it didn't go into second gear. Instead, it made a horrible grinding sound. He put his hand over the top of hers and moved the shifter all the way to the left and then down. "Release the clutch," he said, a sense of urgency in his voice. She moved her foot off the clutch, the car making a slight jerk. "Hurry, push back on the gas." She did, and the car moved faster. "There, you are getting the hang of it. Now shift up to third. I'll help you." She put her hand on the shifter again, and he put his over top of hers just like before and moved it to the middle, then straight up. She released the clutch and pushed on the gas.

She could not help but smile that she was driving a standard. "I want to try shifting to forth. But on my own this time."

He gestured with his hand. "Go ahead." She took her foot off the gas, pushed in on the clutch, and pulled the shifter straight down. It ground at first, but after a second, she found fourth gear. "Alright, chauffeur, where to?" he asked facetiously.

She smiled and thought of where she could go that would be private. She wanted to find somewhere they could be alone, just the two of them, and away from prying eyes. She felt like he had been avoiding her lately. Anytime she thought about her and him, she always ran into the same internal struggle. She couldn't deny any longer that she wanted to be with him, but she still grappled with whether or not she should. She knew the answer, but more and more, it was becoming harder to fight what she wanted and easier to ignore what she should do. But deep in her gut was the sneaking suspicion that the closer she drew to him, the more he pulled away from her, and she didn't understand why. The sinking feeling that twisted in the pit of her stomach caused some apprehension.

She saw a dirt road up ahead, but she didn't know where it led. She was certain that she had never been down it before and saw that it led into the trees. She pushed on the brake, and the car slowed, engine sputtering.

"You need to shift into a lower gear," Wilhelm told her.

She quickly pushed in the clutch and put her hand on the shifter but hesitated, unsure where the gears were or which one to shift into. Before she had time to react, Wilhelm brushed her hand off the shifter and moved it smoothly into a lower gear. She released the clutch and looked at him. His expression was unreadable, and for some reason, she worried he thought she was stupid or a slow learner. She looked back to the road and tried to focus on driving and not him. She saw a spot where she could pull off and tried to remember what needed to be done when she got there.

"Where is second gear?"

"All the way to the left, then down." She shifted into second gear without much grinding, then pulled off the road at a small dirt clearing near the trees. She held the brake and the clutch simultaneously and looked at him for further instructions. He put the shifter in the first gear position. "Turn off the engine, then let off the break." She did, and the engine fell silent. He looked at her expectantly, waiting for her to say why they were there.

"I thought we would go for a walk."

He didn't immediately answer, then finally responded. "I like walks." He opened his door and stepped out, and she did the same.

Eva moved through the brush and weeds, feeling them rub at her bare ankles. The crunching from their shoes was the only sound as they made their way deeper into the forest.

Neither of them spoke, but she could feel his eyes on her back as he hung a few feet behind. She knew he wondered why they were there. She hadn't planned what they would do today. This was a last-minute decision.

She needed to break the tension that hung in the air. "How long will we stay here in La Chapelle?"

"Another day or two."

"And then you will go back to Paris and me to Dieppe?"

He looked out into the trees. "Yes."

She nodded, disappointment filling her. She felt defeated and still uncertain of her future. She had told herself that he would never break her, and yet he had. Not in the way she meant then or how he thought he would, but in a more permanent way. He had thoroughly broken down her walls and destroyed her defenses to where they could never be repaired. He always could cause her pain, but now he had in his power the capability to enact immeasurable suffering with just his words if he so chose. No amount of asking would make him come back to Dieppe with her because she knew his duty always came first.

"Do you want to sit for a minute?" she asked.

"Sure."

She sat on a fallen log, covered in moss and lichen, and he rested beside her. She looked out through the trees, focusing on the rays of light that cut through their canopy. "It's so pretty and quiet like nothing else exists but this. Protected and safe from the world as if the war can't touch us here." The breeze lifted the ends of her hair and carried the scents of the forest with it. The birds' singing echoed all around them, and the sun warmed her bare arms. She closed her eyes and inhaled, never wanting to leave this serene place.

"It is beautiful and peaceful, I will admit."

She opened her eyes and looked at him. He was watching her, his expression was soft but guarded. His eyes looked greener than brown in the sun, a trick of the light. A gust blew through the trees, and a piece of his neatly combed hair fell to the side of his face. She reached up to brush it aside, and he cupped his hand over hers and held it, lingering for a few seconds before moving it from his cheek, and laying it in her lap.

"We should go."

"Why?" she asked in a whisper.

"Because I have things that need to be finished before tomorrow."

"But that isn't the only reason. Do you not want to be here with me?"

He pulled his eyebrows together and stared at her. "Oh, Eva. There is nothing I would rather do right now than spend the afternoon in the woods alone with you. But there are some things that need my attention." He paused for a second, looking to the ground, searching for the right words to say. "Perhaps it is better if we are not alone."

His statement confused her. "I don't understand. Why would it be better?"

"I have thought about that night we spent together every day since. If I close my eyes, I can feel you, smell the scent of your hair, and in the dark, you whisper that you love me. And the way it makes me feel... I want to hold on to it, savor it, and then I open my eyes, and reality is there, waiting to disappoint. You told me you could never love me because I am a monster. And you know what? You are right. I am. So it is better that we are not together. You made it clear that what we shared that one night would be the only time it would happen, and you were smart in doing so."

She stared at him, confused. "So you no longer want me?"

"I would love to put you at ease and tell you that I don't, but it would be a lie. I always want you, and that is a problem. I'm sorry if that is not what you wanted to hear."

How did she respond to this? Should now be when she tells him that she loves him too, or did she let him continue thinking that she didn't? "Wilhelm, you should know that I don't think of you as I once did. I thought that was obvious. Do you think I would have willingly let you do those things to my body if I still despised you? I would not have been intimate with you if I did." That wasn't exactly admitting her love for him, but it wasn't a denial, either.

"No, I imagine not. But it changes nothing. I will not leave you alone in this war to fend for yourself, that much I have promised you. But there will be nothing else. As I have told you before, I am expected to marry a German woman. And you don't want to stay here. You have made that obvious. You need to be with someone who will make you happy and won't cause stares and resentment from your countrymen. And who will not take you from your family."

"I didn't know we ever talked about being together. But who I choose to be with is no concern of anyone else, whether they are my countrymen or not. I decide who, when and where I will be with someone."

He stood up. "It's time to leave."

She rose from the mossy log. "What? No."

"Eva, please don't make this difficult?"

"I'm not; you are." She put her hand on her forehead, flustered. "I hated you for so long, and that was easy. But this is so much harder. I'm unsure what to be with you. Your friend, your lover? You just as a distant protector, that's not what I want. I have been fine on my own. I don't need you in the background, lurking in the darkness. It will be a constant reminder that you are close but always out of reach, never attainable. I would rather not have you in my life at all."

"But you are not fine on your own," he snapped. "You have no idea how many times you've been on death's doorstep. And every time I've pulled you back, sometimes completely unaware. And you are neither of those things. You are not my lover, and we can never be friends."

His works cut her like a knife, wounding deep. She stayed, thinking the pain was worth it, but now she could see that it wasn't. She pushed past him and started back towards the road. When she heard his footsteps close behind, she turned her head and called over her shoulder. "I'm walking back, alone."

He matched her pace and came up beside her. "It is over eleven kilometers back to town."

"I don't even know how far that is, but it doesn't matter. I'm going to walk."

416

Anger burned in his eyes. "If I have to carry you back to the car and put you in, that's what I'll do."

She stopped walking and looked up at him. "Can I not have some time to myself?"

"Yes, you can have all the time you want to yourself once we are back at the house."

"I don't want to sit in the house."

"Then you can go on a walk there."

"Why not let me walk now, then?"

"Because it is too far."

She wanted to walk, but she wanted to do it even more now because she was angry at him. "It's a good thing you don't get to make those choices for me." She turned and headed down the narrow path again at a brisk pace. He walked past, then stopped, turning to face her, blocking her way. "You will either get in the car of your own accord, or I will put you in it. I will not ask again."

She hesitated, not sure what to do. She knew he was serious, but did she continue to defy him? Why did he always get his way? The fact that he did was something that always angered her. "You wouldn't dare."

He narrowed his eyes. "I would. Just try me."

"Move," she pleaded. Hot tears from the anger burned in her eyes as she tried to keep a level head. She lifted her chin a little higher, trying to appear braver. He continued to stare her down but made no attempt to move out of her way. "You confuse me, Wilhelm. You say you love me and that you want me, but you reject and discard me like an old shoe that you no longer have use for."

His expression and demeanor were capricious. "I don't treat you like an old shoe at all. You are so far off the mark. You are like a delicate jewel. One that is beautiful and rare but prone to cracking if handled too often or too roughly. You have to be put behind a glass to be admired at a distance but not worn or touched."

This was not what she expected him to say. "Is that all I can hope for?" He didn't answer, but his expression said it all. She walked around him, and he didn't try to stop her this time. She went to the car and got into the back, wanting the distance between them. She leaned against the seat as he came around to the driver's side. He got in and slammed the door, causing the car to shake. He stared at her in the review mirror before starting the car and pulling onto the road.

Chapter Twenty-one

They had barely spoken a word to one another during their last few days in La Chapelle. She, at the time, appreciated the distance but strangely, by the end, found herself missing his company. Wilhelm had informed her that he would take her back to Dieppe and return to Paris alone. She did not wonder as to the reason why; she knew why.

Once they returned from La Chapelle, Wilhelm had gone back and forth between Paris and Dieppe several times but never came to see her.

Eva picked at the food on her plate, tearing off a piece of bread and sticking it in her mouth. "Alright, what is it?" Ingrid asked. "Since you returned from Paris, you have been acting strange. You're distant and hardly speak to anyone."

"I'm sorry."

"You don't need to be sorry, but I would like to know what happened while you were there."

"Nothing. I guess that is part of the problem."

"You went to Paris and La Chapelle with him, and nothing happened between you two?"

"No, except that he told me I am like a delicate jewel that needs to be protected behind glass and not held or touched."

Ingrid stared at her with a blank expression. "I don't understand. What does that mean?"

"I'm not sure exactly. I think he was basically saying he would be in my life but only at a distance. And it will be that way for the rest of the war."

"Why?"

"I don't know." It was the truth. She didn't know all his reasons, but she suspected a few. Eva looked at the clock. "It's time for me to go home. I'll see you later."

"Alright." Ingrid gave her a forced smile.

Eva cleaned up her dishes and walked the short distance to the apartment. She put the key in the lock and turned it, but the bolt did not move. *That's weird,* she thought. She turned the key the other way, and the door locked. She stared at it, puzzled. She swore that she had locked the door when she left for work. She turned the key the other way again and unlocked the door. She twisted the doorknob and pushed the door open, peering inside the mostly dark living room. She couldn't see anything and didn't hear any noises coming from the apartment. She relaxed and stepped inside, flipping on the light. She hung her purse on the coat rack and turned, jumping as she drew in a breath. Wilhelm was sitting on the couch with his legs crossed and hands resting on his knees. On the coffee table was a bouquet of flowers lying next to his officer's cap.

She was fixed where she stood for a second, looking between him and the flowers.

"Are you expecting to talk from across the room?" he asked.

She shook her head. "No." She came over to the couch and sat at the end, farthest from him. She gestured to the flowers. "What are those for?"

"To mend heartache, although I know that flowers are inadequate. I got you orchids. I remembered they are your favorite."

She looked at the assortment of orchids and the array of colors they made. There were purple, pink, yellow, red and spotted white, all wrapped together in brown paper like a rainbow. The arrangement was stunning. She looked at him and gave a faint smile.

"Thank you. But you are right; they are inadequate." She picked up the bouquet and sniffed the flowers. "I thought I was only to be admired from a distance?"

"I guess I am someone who can't resist the pretty thing in front of them, tempting them. I touch when I'm supposed to only look. And if I'm not careful, I will steal it. Slip it into my pocket while trying not to break it."

She looked at him. "I don't break so easily."

"We will see. The flowers aren't the only thing. I'm here to take you back to Paris with me."

She noted that he didn't ask if she wanted to go but was telling her he was taking her. She was uncertain what this shift meant. "Alright. When?"

"Tonight."

Her stomach did a flip. "But I work tomorrow."

"It's been taken care of. Go pack; I'll wait."

She stood up stiffly, glancing at him before turning and going to her room. She closed the door and looked around the perimeter, trying to process what was happening. Finally, she went to her dresser and quickly packed enough clothes for a few weeks, then her toiletries and some makeup. She wrote a note to Ingrid and left it on the coffee table on their way out, explaining where she was.

She lay awake in Wilhelm's bed that night, looking at him as he slept. She was in his Paris apartment and in his bed, and just like the time before, he never made a move or so much as touched her. She knew he had reservations about being with her, some of which she understood and some she didn't. If only she could pull the thoughts from his head. He was expected to marry a German woman as a party member and because of his rank and position, but she recognized that he didn't want to. She didn't question if he wanted to be with her anymore. She knew he did. But like him, she had no idea how this was supposed to work. She didn't even know what this was. She had grown to like it, though, more than like, but she still didn't know what the hell she was doing. She was conscious of her mind and feelings now, enough to know that she would do whatever he wanted, whatever made him happy. It was love. That she was certain of, because there was nothing else it could be.

She reached over and gently touched his cheek. He was lying on his back with his head turned away from her. The dim light of the moon was making his skin and hair look particularly dark. Her touch hadn't woken him, and she was glad. She knew she was invading his space, but it was so hard not to. He was sleeping in his underwear and undershirt, and a couple of buttons at the top of the shirt were undone. She moved her hand from his face and traced her fingertips over the top of his pec muscles, the chest hair tickling her fingers. Then she moved her fingers along the defined muscles of his arm and down to his hand. She lifted his hand and brought it beneath the covers, putting it under her night shirt and pressing it firmly between her legs. She wanted him to touch her. It was hard spending this much time with him and being so close but not being intimate. The memory of the night they spent together was fresh in her mind. Everything he did felt right, and he made love to her with such care and attention. He brought out something inside of her she didn't even know was there, and he did it so skillfully. It was easy for him to bring her to orgasm and a high she had not known before. But he didn't touch after that, he wouldn't. She doubted it had anything to do with lack of desire, but he was holding back, and she didn't understand why.

Her mouth opened, and she drew in a breath at the feel of his fingers and the pressure of his hand against her. She didn't know if what she was doing was right because he was asleep, so it wasn't exactly consensual.

His eyes opened, and he turned his head on the pillow to look at her. It only took seconds for him to realize what was happening. He didn't immediately try to remove his hand but locked eyes with her. She couldn't tell what was happening in his head, but the want in her eyes was unmistakable. He leaned up on one elbow and slowly pulled his hand away, then sat up in bed.

"Well, that is one way to get my attention," he said in a husky voice then looked at his watch. It was seventeen minutes past one in the morning. "I think I should sleep on the couch from now on."

She sat up in bed, too. "What? No. I'm sorry. I know I shouldn't have done that. I took advantage while you were asleep, and that was wrong."

He coughed out a laugh. "Took advantage of me? Hardly. But I will not do that with you. Not tonight or any night."

It was like she had been in a desert for days, and he had a well full of cold water but wouldn't give her any. He could quench her thirst but taunted her and denied her instead. It probably would be better if he slept on the couch, but she didn't want him to.

"Why?" she asked in a small voice. "You don't want me anymore?"

"Because if I didn't, it would be me taking advantage. I always want you, and I don't mean just your body."

"No, it wouldn't be taking advantage. Not if I wanted you to, and I do."

"It still would." He threw the blanket off to get out of bed, but she caught his arm.

"If that one night was enough for you, I get it, but it wasn't for me."

He turned towards her and cupped her chin in his hand, then leaned in and kissed her deeply. His lips pressed so hard against hers she thought they might bruise. He pulled away and looked at her ardently. "What we did was reckless, but I couldn't stop. You are making it hard for me not to do it again, and I am trying to be good. Being near you is like playing with gasoline, and you are handing me a match. Don't misunderstand me. I like the rush, but look what happens after. Have you ever seen a forest once a fire has consumed it? In that, I am barely succeeding, but I can't give you up completely, which is why you are here now in my bed, and why you will be here again. I don't think there will be a you and me by the end of this war, but if I can have you even in the smallest way now, I will." The edge of his tone softened slightly. "I need to keep some semblance of distance from you."

She scowled in frustration, all of her emotions straining towards him, desperate for release. Without another word, he slid off the bed, picked up his pillow, took the blanket from the end of the bed, and walked to the couch.

She didn't move but stared into the darkness. She could still feel the lingering of his lips on hers and reached up to touch them with her fingers. She didn't know what to do. She felt like crying and wanted to scream out of frustration. She laid her head roughly back on her pillow and closed her eyes but knew that sleep would not come anytime soon.

Over the next couple of days, he had done just as he said. Every night he slept on the couch, and her in the bed. She wanted him; she craved him, even if it was just to have him next to her in bed again. She had asked him to come back, promising that she would keep to her side and not touch him, that all they would do was sleep, but he told her no. He was firm in his resolve. He said it would be too much of a temptation if he returned to the bed for both of them. He said they could enjoy each other's company in different ways. If he truly did want her like she did him, then why did he deny himself as well as her? She was never completely clear about his reasons.

That morning, after he left for work, she went to a café and sat alone. She had a cup of coffee, real coffee, and a small tray of cookies. It was odd not being at work or having anything that needed her attention. It made her feel lazy, and she didn't like it. She cleaned the apartment whenever it needed it, but that wasn't often, with only the two of them there. She bit into the cookie and savored its sweetness while watching people walk by on the sidewalk. She ate the four cookies on the plate and finished her small cup of coffee. She felt a little tired and thought she might go back to the apartment and take a nap. She had not slept well after that night. Knowing he was so close, the tension that always seemed to hang in the air, and the worry she had about everything surrounding the situation, kept her up at night.

She trudged back to the apartment, admiring the beauty of Paris and the fine weather they were having. It was a single-story apartment, so she didn't have to climb any stairs, which made her happy. She unlocked the door and went in, putting the extra key in the bowl that sat on the narrow hall table. She went to the couch to lie down and rest her eyes for a bit. The blanket Wilhelm used was folded up and lying on top of his pillow. She smiled, picked up the blanket, unfolded it, and laid down. Her head sunk into the pillow, and she pulled the blanket up around her neck. She drew in a deep breath. The pillow and the blanket both smelled like him. She closed her eyes and fell into a dreamless sleep.

A tapping from the front door jolted her awake. She pushed herself up on one elbow and rubbed at her eyes with the back of her hand. The knocking came a second time, and she realized someone was at the door. She threw the blanket off and went to the door. There was no peephole, so she could not see who it was. She pulled the door open but then paused. Standing before her was a tall, slender woman with long blond curls that cascaded around her shoulders, contrasting with the blue satin dress she wore. One side of her hair was pinned up, and her lips were painted a deep red. The woman looked at Eva, surprise clear on her face too. Obviously, she didn't expect her to be there.

"Who are you?" she asked in a suspicious tone.

"Eva Abrams."

The woman looked past her into the apartment. "Is Wilhelm home?"

"No. He is at work. Do you want me to tell him you came by?"

She gave a furtive smile. "No matter. I will see him at the party in Berlin."

Eva's thin, forced smile faded. "What party?"

"The one in Berlin on the 19th. All the high-ranking officers are expected to be there."

Eva did not know what party she was talking about. "So he is attending?"

"He is." She looked across the street quickly, then back to Eva. "I have to run. Nice meeting you." She turned and gracefully glided down the sidewalk in her elegant heels as her hips swayed.

Eva stood in the doorway, gaping at her. Who was that? The woman never gave her name. She was going to talk to Wilhelm about it. Why would he not tell her he was going to Berlin next week?

She found things to keep herself busy while waiting for him to come home. Even though it was Saturday, she knew he would work late. He almost always worked on Saturday and often on Sunday, too. She was in the kitchen figuring out what to make for dinner when she heard the front door squeak open. She sat the potatoes she was washing on the counter and hurried into the living room, wiping the water from her hands on a dishtowel.

He paused, looking at her, eyeing her with confusion and suspicion. "What is it?"

She cleared her throat. "Nothing. I was just getting ready to make dinner." She stood patiently waiting for him to remove his jacket, cap, and shoes before she asked him about the party and Berlin. Once he was seated on the couch, she sat down beside him. "Someone came by to see you today."

"Oh, who?"

"A woman." She noticed that he stiffened.

He didn't look at her. "What did she want?"

"She wanted to see you, but when I told her you weren't home, she said it didn't matter because she would see you at the party on the 19th in Berlin."

He rubbed his palm on his knee. "I didn't tell you about it because I wasn't planning on going."

"She said you were going because it was expected of you, as it is all the high-ranking officers."

"It is, but I still wasn't going to go," he said, annoyance seeping through.

"Why wouldn't you go if they expect you to?"

"For one thing, you are here, but also, I don't want to go. Those kinds of things don't interest me."

"I could go with you."

He finally looked at her. "Is that what you want?"

"Well, I'm here to spend time with you, so if you go to Berlin, I will go with you."

He sighed. "I really should. My superiors will not be pleased if I don't. It's all a show of unity and support."

"Then it's settled. We will both go." She gave him an encouraging smile. "What day will we leave?"

"The 19th is a Sunday, so we will leave on Saturday. It's about an eleven-hour drive, giving us the rest of the day and the first half of Sunday to rest. You should know that it is a formal event, so wear something nice."

Wilhelm worked for most of that week, and Eva found herself alone, but that wasn't unusual. He would leave early in the morning, some days before the sun was even up, and not return until late in the evening. She wondered if it was deliberate but knew he would not admit to it even if it was. She was excited but also nervous about going back to Berlin. She hadn't seen Heidi and Liesel in so long. She would write them letters, but that was the only correspondence they really had.

As the days went by, Eva found herself thinking more about the woman who came to his apartment. He had been reluctant to talk about her, telling her she was just someone he knew from Berlin. That she was a friend and nothing more. Eva didn't quite believe that but didn't want to press him for more information. She didn't want to anger him. In truth, it wasn't any of her business, and she didn't want to appear jealous or desperate for his attention. After that night he rejected her, she had forced herself to seem more or less indifferent to him, what he did and who he associated with.

She had already packed her things to prepare for the trip tomorrow morning. And that night, she tossed and turned, struggling to fall asleep. Finally, around midnight, she drifted off, only to be woken an hour later by the wind that whistled outside the window. Eva leaned up on her arms, trying to bring her eyes into focus. She glanced at the alarm on the nightstand. It was after one in the morning, and Wilhelm still wasn't home. Turning over she set up and rubbed the sleep from her eyes, slowly feeling the fogginess dissipate. She looked around, the moonlight streaming in from the window, falling across the white duvet. She plopped back down on the pillow and stared at the wall. For a few days now, she had considered going back to Dieppe when they returned from Berlin. It was too hard doing this close yet separate thing with him. It would be easier if she were in a different city. The distance would be good for her and probably for him, too.

She lay there for a while longer when finally, the front door opened, and Wilhelm came into the apartment but didn't turn on the light. He knew she would be sleeping and didn't want to wake her. She listened to his boots on the wood floor, the rustling of his jacket, the rattling of keys. There were a few other sounds she couldn't identify while lying with her eyes closed, pretending to be asleep, then the bathroom door clicked shut. She rolled onto her back and sat up. She didn't know why she was having such a hard time falling asleep. She laid back down and listened to the water running, then it stopped, and he get out. After about five or six minutes, he came out of the bathroom and lay down on the couch. She stared at the dark sofa, trying to make out the shape of him on it, blinking slowly before her eyes finally didn't open.

The clinking of dishes woke her. She opened her eyes and looked at Wilhelm still in only his underwear and undershirt, taking dishes from the cabinet. She sat up and cleared her throat, and he turned to look at her.

"What time is it?"

"Just after seven."

"What are you doing?"

"Making eggs."

A smile broke at the corner of her mouth. "You cook now?"

"I think I can figure out how to make eggs. It can't be that hard."

"What kind of eggs are you going to make?"

He thought for a minute. "Fried."

"Ok. I will go change and not interfere."

He narrowed his eyes at her. "You don't think I can make eggs?"

She smirked. "I didn't say that."

She slid off the bed and went to her bag, retrieving a clean dress. She gave him a side glance as she walked past on her way to the bathroom. She changed and freshened up, wondering how he was doing with the breakfast. She brushed her hair and applied a bit of makeup. She looked in the mirror at her tired eyes and the few zits popping up on her face. She leaned closer to the mirror and inspected them, knowing they were there because it was close to that time of the month.

For a reason unknown to her, the thought that Gerhardt might be at the party came to her mind. She considered this, and her heart beat faster. What would he think if he saw her there with Wilhelm? Would he be angry with her or hurt at her obvious betrayal? She didn't believe she could stand to hurt him in that way. Even though he was back with his fiancée, her being with Wilhelm was not even comparable. It was so much worse.

She took a deep breath and tried to clear her head. She came out of the bathroom and went to the kitchen. Wilhelm was already eating, but there was a plate on the other side of the table with her food. She sat in the chair and looked down at the eggs. They were slightly burned, and the yoke was hard in the middle. The sight of it warmed her. She didn't care that the eggs were overdone and dry. He tried for her, and that was

J.L. Robison

all that mattered. She looked at him, giving him an affectionate smile.

"Thank you!" She seemed to have caught him off guard.

"Sorry, they are burned. I was trying to find the cheese and forgot them for a minute."

"It's alright," she said, continuing to smile at him. She forced herself to eat all the food on her plate. When they were done, she insisted on cleaning up while he changed, and he let her. He was fast and walked into the kitchen dressed as she was finishing the dishes.

He came to stand beside her. "Are you about ready?"

"Yes. My stuff is already packed. This is the last plate."

"I will put the things in the car. My orderly is already here."

She looked at him. "How do you know?"

"Because I told him to be here at eight."

"Right." This did not surprise her.

The drive seemed long, and she hated the silence between them. She didn't think he was ignoring her on purpose, but he was occupied with papers. She thought about their first long car ride together and how she had wanted to ride up front. Now she didn't think she would, even if he told her to.

She would glance over at him from time to time. He had an expression of focused concentration on his face, the look she remembered from before. The way he had always appeared to her in the past. It was a look that would frighten and intimidate people. The look he would have when his guard was up, while he was working, and when dealing with people that weren't her. He used to give her that look too, but

433

not anymore. Confirming what she was just thinking, he lifted his head from the papers in his lap over at her, and his expression softened.

"We should be there soon," he assured her.

She gave a slight smile. "I'm fine."

"I know I haven't been much company, but I hadn't planned on going to Berlin, so this could have waited. But now it has to be done, so it's not waiting for me when I get back."

"I do understand. Don't worry about me." He gave her another apologetic look, then turned back to the papers. She laid her head on the window, deciding to take a nap. There wasn't much else to do. She felt a gentle tap on her leg and lifted her head.

"If you want, you can lay your head on me?"

She hesitated for a moment. "Alright." She scooted closer to lay her head on his shoulder, but he lifted the papers from his lap.

"I have to move my arms. It would be better if you laid your head on my lap."

She had never had her head on his lap before. This was uncharted territory. She scooted back to the door so she would have room to lie down in the seat. She slowly lowered her head on his legs, pulled her legs up on the seat, and closed her eyes. His legs were hard and warm under her head, but she didn't mind. She had her face turned away from him on purpose, knowing how awkward it would be for her if she were to lie the other way.

As time passed, she was aware of his slight movements and the motion of the car, but none completely brought her out of sleep. After a while, she opened her eyes and looked up at the ceiling of the car. She rolled her head to the left and felt her cheek pressing against his stomach and the belt of his pants. She looked up at him, and he was looking out the window. There weren't any papers in his hand, and she wondered how long ago he had finished.

He looked down at her. "Good morning." His eyes were soft and his expression relaxed.

She blinked a few times. "Hi." She had rolled onto her back at some point while she was sleeping. "How long have I been asleep?" She was also aware that his left hand was resting on the thigh of her right leg.

"A while. We are almost there."

She pushed herself up and slid to her side of the seat, rubbing her hair with her palm, trying to fix it after sleeping. She gave him a side glance. "Hopefully, that wasn't too terrible."

"Why would it be?"

"I just didn't want to inconvenience you or make it awkward."

"You didn't," he assured her.

She turned away, blushing slightly as the memory of their last night in bed together resurfaced. Looking back, she couldn't believe she had done that. What must he think of her?

"How much longer?"

"Maybe twenty minutes."

"Good. Where will I stay?"

He looked as if he had not considered this. "I guess you will stay with me."

"I don't have to. I know that Heidi and Liesel would love to have me stay with them."

He eyed her, not smiling. "If that is what you want."

"I think I do. Besides, how would we explain any of this to your mother? I'm guessing you haven't told her the things that have happened between us since the last time I saw her?"

"No, I have not. Maybe it is for the best if you stay with them."

The car pulled in front of her old apartment. "I will pick you up tomorrow before the party. It starts at six, so I will be here at five-thirty."

"Alright. I'll see you tomorrow." He gave a reluctant smile as his orderly sat her bag on the sidewalk beside her.

She smiled back and closed the door, then watched the shiny black car pull away. It made her feel alone and sad. She was going to have to promise herself to never fall for another German ever again.

Chapter Twenty-Two

April 19th, 1942

When Wilhelm's car picked her up promptly at five-thirty, he was not in it. The driver informed her that he would meet her there but had been held up at work. This was all sounding so familiar to her. Wilhelm inviting her to a party that she would end up going to alone.

The car traveled for some time before turning onto the gravel drive that led to the vast grounds of the grand Baroque-style palace just outside Potsdam. She knew it was there but never went to see it when she lived here. She wondered about the party and what kind of event it was that required such a grand place.

The car stopped in front of the double, curled stairs that led up to the main entrance. The red brick structure stood counter to the fading blue sky that was littered with white and grey clouds. She stepped out of the car, and the gravel crunched beneath her heels. She walked up the steps, and the shawl she wore slid down to her bent elbows as she held up the hem of her dress. She had gotten a new dress just for this event because Wilhelm had told her it was formal. She had gone by herself and picked out a blue lace gown with lilac flowers embroidered into the skirt.

Once inside the building, she realized it was the most ostentatious place she had ever seen. She turned slowly in a circle to take it all in. The grand hall showcased majestic paintings, crystal chandeliers, statues, and fountains. The marble walls around her were entrusted with shells, semi-precious stones, and fossils. Her mouth was open in awe as she looked at the room. She had the most amazing sensation come over her, as if she was royalty, attending a grand ball with the gentry of its time.

Her hand smoothed down the fabric, over the curve of her bosom, and then over the hymns as she prepared to enter the main area.

She wandered through the packed room, taking it all in. There were small groups of people conversing amongst themselves, while others made the rounds through the crowd as they mingled. Occasionally, men would come and talk with her, but she was quick to dismiss them. She had no desire to be pursued by anyone. She grew concerned as more time passed, and she still hadn't seen any sign of Wilhelm. She moved out of the main hall to look for him, and the music grew quieter. There was still no sight of him, and she tried to keep any panic at bay, but she was almost running through the rooms now, the crowds growing smaller as she drew further away from the main hall. She hurried down a wide, dimly lit passageway and then into a large drawing room. Small groups of soldiers converged around tables, a few bearing the markings of high-ranking officers, their conversations quiet in the room. In the crowd were a few soldiers wearing the SS runes, like Wilhelm. She looked around, breathing heavily, her senses intensified and wary. Eva's eyes rested on each one of them, frantic to locate Wilhelm.

"Excuse me," she said to a blond-haired officer who wore the three silver pips and two silver stripes on the black collar patch of his jacket, indicating he was a captain. He turned to her, regarding her curiously, as he took her in.

She tried to pull on the little courage she had. "Do you know if SS Obersturmbannführer Bauer has arrived?"

His eyes flickered over her dress, then back up to her face as he cleared his throat. "I have not seen him."

Eva excused herself as cordially as she could and walked away from the officers. She returned to the main hall, ate some finger food from the table to keep herself busy, and scanned the crowd, looking for Wilhelm. She was worried that he would not come again. While she ate, she was aware of someone who came to stand close beside her, but she didn't look to see who it was.

"I didn't know you would be here," a smooth, feminine voice said.

Eva turned her head to the left and looked at the person. Standing next to her was the same woman who came to Wilhelm's apartment, in her elegant onyx gown, with a white, satin shawl over her shoulders. Her hair was neatly pulled back into a French twist held in place with a jeweled pin. There was no surprise that she was here.

"Yes, he invited me."

"I'm sure he did." The woman looked her over in a scrutinizing way. "You were working in Berlin, right?"

"Yes, last year. But I work in Dieppe now." Eva wondered how the woman knew she had worked in Berlin.

"So close to Paris." She eyed Eva with conjecture. "I feel a need to ask. What are you doing with Wilhelm?" Her words were intrusive.

"I don't know what you mean. I'm not doing anything with Wilhelm." She thought about how he had rejected her.

"I know that isn't true, and so do you. To be honest, I'm surprised he has had time for you at all."

"Why would he not?" Eva tried to seem indifferent and keep any inflection out of her voice.

"He is very busy. Even too busy most of the time for those important to him."

Eva sat her plate on the table behind her. "And who are those that are important to him?"

"His mother, the people he has known for a long time who are significant in his life."

"I don't think you have to know someone for a long time for them to be important to you."

"Well, what I know is that he had a life before you and continues to have a life after you." She looked at Eva's face, and a smile touched the edge of her lips. "Yes, he has told me."

Eva swallowed hard. "What has he told you?" She hoped the woman could not hear the concern in her voice.

"Just that you were a distraction for a while." She moved from Eva's side to stand in front of her and raked her eyes over her, posturing with a hand on the curve of her side and a hip pushed out. "I can see why he found you diverting." She took a step closer, putting her face nearer to Eva's. She could smell the women's perfume. "You are not good enough for him." Her teeth were clenched through her fake smile. "You are not fit to clean the mud from his boots. An American, not sympathetic to our cause, and no doubt mingle with the dark-skinned people who live in your country. I have heard you have so many of them there."

Eva moved to walk past her, but the woman grabbed her hand roughly, holding on with furious desperation as she stared into Eva's eyes. Eva gave a small cry and tried to pull away, but the woman's nails were digging into her palm.

"I know you are in love with another man."

Eva stopped struggling and returned her stare with equal venom. "And he told you that too, did he?" The memory of Gerhardt stirred in her thoughts.

"I think you are playing a dangerous game," was all she said. The woman turned her head and gazed into the crowd. "I have noticed for some time that you have had an admirer. Oberleutnant Jurgen Pflüger has been watching you from across the room since you arrived. Now he is a man you should focus your attention on." She waved him over but never loosened her grip on Eva's hand. Eva looked at the man as he made his way towards them and tried to pull her hand

441

Lose, but he was upon them before she had time to free herself. "I will leave you two alone," the woman told them with sickening sweetness. She let go of Eva and disappeared into the crowd.

"We meet again," he said, a cruel smile on his face. "Aren't you supposed to be on the Russian front, working at some smelly hospital?"

She went still, her breathing tight. "You need to leave me alone," she ordered.

"I just hate it when people are rude and don't say please."

Her anger reared, overtaking her fear temporarily. Forcing herself to stand a little taller, she met his gaze squarely. "Please!"

He let out a throaty laugh, turning his gaze back on her. "You have no allies here," he said threateningly.

She glared at him, her courage faltering. "Leave me alone," she said in a menacing voice, which was contrary to how she felt. He reached out, putting his hand on her waist. Anxious, her gaze darted toward the door at the back of the room.

He glanced that way too. "Do you think you could make it all the way to the door before I stopped you? Even if you made it out of the room, where would you go?" he asked with malignant politeness. "It appears you are all alone. You don't know anyone at the party except Wilhelm, but I don't see him here at your side. While Wilhelm and I were in officer training together, I quickly noticed that he was intelligent but lacked when it came to empathy. He truly believes in what he is fighting for, but that is it. His real drive and feelings are only for his duty; his true motivations lie there. He prides himself on being mentally and emotionally strong. And I must confess that I agree with those assumptions. Being in love is a weakness, one that he would never afford himself. Why do you think his men follow him? Why do you think he can inspire such loyalty? He is impressive, a leader amongst men. Which is why he would never lower himself or the image he holds in such high regard for someone like you." A gleam of savage satisfaction lit in his eyes as he read her expression. His gaze scanned over the low cut of her dress and the cleavage that spilled out from the top. "You look like a whore. Maybe that is the real reason you came here dressed like that." He glanced down at Eva's shaking hands. "No one here," he moved his hand to span the room, "will care what I do to you. Are you even aware of what this party is for?" An expression of triumph on his face.

She had to force her words out. "No."

"The Fuhrer's birthday party," he laughed with cruel smugness.

Eva's head snapped up to him, shock registering on her face. "Hitler's birthday party?"

"Yes, did he not tell you?" She shook her head. "Well, shame on him. Klara and Wilhelm are together, I believe. That is why she is here. He is only coming for her. I know she has had her sights set on him for some time. His mother fully approves of Klara, and a union between them if it comes to that someday." His look turned carnal as he watched her breast rise and fall with her breathing. "They are good together. She is exactly the kind of woman who can handle a man like him. She can match his vigor and drive. And she has the same love and devotion to Germany and the party as he does," he continued. "I think he realizes that now. Lately, he has had little time for meaningless physical pursuits."

His hand slid lower on her waist. Eva's eyes scanned the room. No one was even looking in their direction, and her gaze dropped down to her shoes. She was wearing a new pair of silk pumps that matched her dress. They were pretty but hardly suited for running. She considered if she should take them off and decided the answer was yes. Slowly, trying not to attract his attention to what she was doing, she slipped her feet from her shoes and stood on the balls of her feet so he wouldn't notice the loss in height. Her heart pounded in her chest, a low thumping in her ears, and the rush of adrenaline was dizzying. She gave one quick glance behind her, then lowered the stocking soles of her feet down, contacting the cool floorboards.

Noticing her silence and mistaking it for defiance, his eyes darkened. "I know it has to hurt that he is choosing her over you, that she is better suited for him." He flexed his fingers on her waist as his demeanor became more aggressive. "She will fight for what is hers. She will tear you to pieces over him if she needs to." He lifted a finger to swiftly trace the side of her neck. "Thwart that and she'll slit this pretty little throat of yours without a moment's hesitation." Before Eva had time to even react, his hand moved to her throat. She flinched, frozen in place. She tried to swallow as his hot hand pressed against her skin, fingers digging in, and her feet felt glued in place to the floor. His lip curled in a snarl, exposing his white teeth. "She would never let you destroy his life. To have him become a traitor to his country. She would rather see him dead."

A cheer erupted in the room, and Eva was able to turn her head slightly to see what the commotion was. Hitler was standing at the far end of the room, obviously having just arrived or only now appearing amongst the crowd. Jurgen's hand loosened a fraction on her, and she seized his momentary loss of focus. She balled her hand into a fist and hit his hand hard, knocking his arm down. Then she punched him in the gut with as much force as she could muster. He doubled over and muttered something under his breath. Panic coursing through her, she turned and ran, not looking back to see if he had recovered. Her feet slid on the floor in her stockings, but she didn't slow. Her heart was racing to the point of pain.

"You fucking bitch," he snarled.

His words sent a fresh wave of fear through her. She slid into a wall, trying to turn a corner, knocking a picture to the floor at her feet. She was desperate to get away, and fueled by the fear of what he would do to her if he caught her, she turned down one hall after another. She pushed her way through the crowds of people, collecting glances of censure. She bumped into people, some fairly hard, knocking drinks or food from their hands. She would have to feel bad about it later. Right now, she had more important things to worry about.

"Come here!" Came a cry from behind her.

How was he so close? She pulled the skirt of her dress up to her knees and picked up her speed, wishing she had not worn stockings.

"I'm going to make sure you go to prison. And you won't come out unless it's under a sheet," he yelled from behind, his voice sounding more distant this time.

She found herself at the back of the palace, and just in front of her were the doors that led outside. She ran right at them without slowing and pushed one open with the momentum of her body, feeling the cool air wash over her as the door slammed against the wall. She was able to gain some distance between them by sliding around corners and using those precious few seconds to her advantage. Now that she had traction in the gravel, she pushed her legs harder, the little rocks digging into the soles of her feet, but she hardly noticed. She needed to lose him and find a place to hide until he gave up looking for her. She could no longer hear him shouting and knew that he must still be inside or went the opposite direction than her. The only sounds she could hear was her own breathing, loud in her ears, and the crunching under her feet. Her sides ached, and her throat was on fire as she ran the length of the building, watching the dim lighting on the ground in front of her that came through the palace windows streaming across drive. She changed her direction and dropped down a flight of stairs that was set beside a long, rectangular reflecting pool. Her feet pounded the concrete steps until they finally gave way to grass. Once she felt the soft, cool blades under her feet, through her now torn stockings, she stopped.

She leaned over and put her hands on her knees, trying to catch her breath. She listened to see if she could hear anything, the sound of footsteps or voices, but she couldn't hear any sound except her own labored breathing. She held her breath for a second to listen again but heard nothing. The pain in her throat and sides lessened, but she felt like she was going to vomit as nausea swept through her. She always felt this way when she pushed her body too hard. She knew she had to get away from here, away from all of them.

She straightened up and stumbled forward. The glow from the moon offered the only light around her. Her bare arms and the upper part of her back and chest were fully exposed to the night air, making her cool and causing goosebumps to form. She crossed her arms and moved her hands up and down them, trying to rub away the chill. She looked at her surroundings, which were the rear gardens of the palace. She had no idea how big they were but was going to keep moving in the opposite direction, away from the palace until she ran out of grass. The wind caught her hair, blowing it around her face, and she pulled a piece away that stuck to her lipstick. She continued to walk but still couldn't see the edges of the garden and realized it was larger than she thought. All around her were flowers and bushes, some laid out in curves, some shaped like an S, and on both sides were trees. So many so that she felt like she was in an oddly manicured forest. She knew she had to find a way out of the gardens. She could not go back through the building. That would only serve to lead her back to him.

She continued forward, hoping soon she would reach the end. The garden had an eerie feel, and she shuttered. She stopped walking and looked around, the vastness overwhelming her. She had the sudden sensation of being trapped in a labyrinth.

Frustrated and afraid, she went to the edge of the tree line and sat down. She considered what would happen if he found her and if she could use the skills Wilhelm taught her to fight him off. She did not know if he was good at fighting, but she knew he was bigger and a great deal stronger than her and thoroughly pissed. She prayed because that was the only thing she could think of.

"Please, God, don't let him find me?"

She looked at the inky shapes around her, regretting her choice to come back to Germany. The feeling of dread and trepidation rushed through her, and she didn't want to be alone, and it was Gerhardt she found herself wishing were here.

"Why did you leave me?" she whispered in the dark. The longing she felt for him was powerful as it took hold. It was never subtle but always profound and intensely painful. She angrily wiped back the tears. She didn't want to cry. She wanted to be brave and to feel safe. She knew that if Gerhardt were here, he would wrap her in his warm arms and take her far away from this awful place and that horrible man.

Several yards away, she heard movement in the gravel, and the feeling in her stomach twisted into an uneasy knot. She realized that she was not alone and wondered if whoever it was could see her. She got to her feet and frantically searched the trees and tall hedges. She no longer heard the sound, but they were still there, she could feel it. She wondered if this was the same feeling a prey animal had when it was being watched by the predator who was going to kill it. The danger was real, and her whole body was covered in cold sweat. She wondered how she could have been so stupid to go to this dark, empty place alone. So far away from the party that no one would ever hear her screams.

The crunching in the gravel returned as a shadowy figure stepped into the light just on the other side of the trees from her. She knew who it was, and the fear almost consumed her.

"Oh God, help me!" she whispered under her breath.

The reality was so much worse than she could have imagined. In her mind, she saw it all. Everything that was going to happen to her in the next few minutes.

He watched her, the whites of his eyes reflecting the moon's light, giving them an unnatural appearance. He looked around like he was checking to see if they were alone. She took a deep breath and prepared to flee. Her only hope now was to make it back to the palace before he caught her.

His head snapped back to her, and she froze, his gaze boring into her. A grin formed on his lips, and she had a stark remembrance of the last time they were together, alone, in the dark.

"Do not come any closer," she warned, struggling to keep her voice from shaking.

"Why? Who is going to stop me?" He scanned the gardens. "I don't see Wilhelm around anywhere, or anyone else for that matter." His voice was pleasant and velvety as he toyed with her.

"If he cannot find me at the party, he will come looking for me."

"Oh, I doubt that. I don't even think he is here." He started making his way across the walkway, drawing closer.

She immediately took a step back, seeing that he was coming towards her, her hands fisted as she licked her dry lips. She walked backward between two trees, continuing to move away from him. She looked down, eyeing the gun on his side. She wanted to try to grab it but would not have time to unholster it before he stopped her. *If you use his gun, you might kill him, and then they will kill you*, she cautioned herself. She hit something hard and realized she had backed into one of the trees. In a fraction of a second, he was in front of her, and she had no time to react. The evil intent was clear in his eyes. She flinched when he lifted his hand and rubbed her cheek with the knuckle of his index finger.

"Wilhelm would be upset if he knew what you were doing." Her anger at him pulsed through her. She had to say something, anything, to try and deter him.

"Maybe, maybe not," he said as he moved his hand to the side of her neck. "Your supposed devotion to Wilhelm Bauer is pathetic. I have heard that you've already been with another German." He sneered at her. "Wilhelm wasn't there to help you last time and he won't be here now." His eyes narrowed as they dropped to the tight, plunging neckline of her blue dress. "Wilhelm is finished with you, I suspect. This is what he does. He beds pretty girls, then moves on once he has had them."

The dread rose in her throat, and she tried to step away from the tree. But he was faster than her and stepped to the side, grabbing her arm, his other hand going to her neck like before as he pushed her back against the tree.

"I almost had you last time," he whispered, his breath warm on her ear.

"Is this what you do to all the girls?" she asked, breathless. The hard bark of the tree poked into her back, hurting her spine.

"No, only the ones who don't have the right to say no. After that night, I followed many of your comings and goings, but most of the times I saw you, he was with you. I had not expected Wilhelm to be so intensely relentless in his... infatuation with you." His face grew serious, and his eyes scanned over her several times. "Frankly, I don't think he ever really wanted you."

She tried to cry out, but only a strangled sound escaped her lips as he tightened his grip on her throat, and pressed his body against hers, pushing her harder against the tree as the look in his eyes darkened.

"I will report you," she barely squeaked out. She wanted to sound threatening, but she was sure she was failing at it. "I'll tell your superior officer and make sure everyone at that ball knows what you did if you don't let go of me."

He smirked and tightened his grip to where she could hardly take in a breath. "You think they will care or believe you? Besides, when I'm done, any thought of struggling will have been beaten out of you. And any pathetic attempt to accuse me will only end in sealing your own fate. Besides, if Wilhelm found out he wouldn't want you anymore. You would be tainted in his eyes."

"You asshole!"

The words were barely loud enough to hear. She reached to his side, trying to find his gun, but he quickly released her throat and covered his weapon with his hand. She was not just going to lie down and wait to die. She would fight until she got away or he killed her, but she would not go down without trying, giving him as much hell as she could. She hesitated to fight harder for the gun, knowing all too well what would happen if she shot him, especially if it killed him. And there was the real possibility that he would shoot her.

As she hesitated, thinking of what to do next, he seized the opportunity. In half a second, his fist was in the air, then it struck her hard on the jaw, and before she had time to fully register what had happened, he swung again, this time hitting her in the stomach. She cried out as an excruciating pain traveled from her stomach and shot up her back, the air rushing from her lungs in fits.

"How does it feel, you slut?"

He grabbed her by the shoulders and shoved her down, the back of her head hitting the dirt with a forceful smack. She could feel herself going under as a wave of darkness crashed over her, his voice and her own now drowned out by a loud ringing in her ears. She tried to sit up, but with remarkable speed, he was on top of her, his weight pressing down on her, pinning her to the ground. She blinked, trying to focus her vision, and looked into the hollow, blue eyes that stared down at her. They were blazing with excitement, hate, and lust. He put his bent arm on her neck to hold her and help in silencing her.

She struggled to breathe as the weight of his whole body pushed against hers, crushing her beneath him. She was trapped and wondered when that moment would come that you knew you were beaten, and wondered if she should give up trying to escape, deciding that maybe that time might be now.

"I've been waiting to do this, and now that I have you I'm going to relish every minute of it. Breaking your body will give me a satisfaction I can't even express," he said with such disdain.

Her vision once again began to fade, this time from oxygen deprivation. He moved his free hand up and pulled at the top of her dress, exposing one of her breasts. He smiled and rubbed the nipple with his thumb before moving his hand to pull the skirt of her dress up. "Do you know how to suck cock? Because when I shove mine down your throat, you will take it and love it."

She took some of his hair in her right hand and pulled it as hard as she could, but she was close to the point of losing consciousness. She tried to scream, but only a squeaky, breathy sound came out. She doubled up her fist and hit him on the side of the head with her knuckles. It wasn't hard, but it was enough.

Wicked anger clouded his face, and he moved his arm from her neck long enough to hit her in the head again. Before his hand contacted her face, she let out a blood-curdling scream, then there was a searing pain on the left side of her face. He put his arm back over her throat and pulled her dress up to her waist, then slid his fingers under the elastic of her underwear so he could remove them.

Abruptly, and unexpectedly, his weight was gone, and she sucked a sharp breath back into her lungs, then another, holding her throat as the breaths came in jagged heaves, and her vision slowly returned. With all her strength, she pushed herself up into a sitting position.

Wilhelm was only a few feet from her, his face savage with rage, looking like he wanted to tear Jurgen limb from limb. He held Jurgen by the hair, dragging him across the gravel, his legs flailing as he pulled at Wilhelm's hand.

Wilhelm took the gun from Jurgen's holster and swiftly tossed it into the trees. With only the dim light of the moon, she did not see where it went. Wilhelm took Jurgen with both hands and slammed his own head against Jurgen's face, then put a hand on his forehead and shoved his head back, smacking it hard against the nearby tree. It sounded like a bat hitting a baseball.

"You made a grave miscalculation when you touched her. You should have stayed in your place, but you tried to take something that belonged to me because you underestimated me, and you will regret having done that. Do you know what happens to someone when they take something that is mine?" Wilhelm hissed.

He then reared up his fist and slammed it down across Jurgen's face with such force that a cracking sound came from his skull, knocking the wind out of him as his body whipped to the side. Wilhelm released him, and Jurgen fell to the ground like a sack of flour. Wilhelm bent on one knee beside

Jurgen and lifted his upper body by the collar of his shirt, and there was the rasp of material ripping, sounding strangely loud in the quiet night. Wilhelm brutally pounded his fist against Jurgen's face again and again as he futilely wailed, Jurgen's suffering evident. Jurgen's face was covered in blood, running down onto his jacket and smeared over his once white teeth.

The sight of what was happening frightened and surprised her more than she expected it to. She was speechless and could not seem to find her voice to call out and tell Wilhelm to stop. She turned over and crawled on her hands and knees farther away from the two men. She then sat back down and watched the mayhem unfold before her eyes.

Wilhelm stopped hitting him and rose, his fists still clenched at his sides as he hovered over the bloodied body at his feet, leering down at him. His breaths were coming hard and fast as he focused on Jurgen.

Even in the dim light, she could see the savage look on Wilhelm's face. The dangerous gleam in his eyes that told her something had switched inside him. Right now, he was not thinking of her and had no concern for his own welfare. His fists were covered with Jurgen's blood and his own, but he didn't seem to even notice. Pain to him was just an illusion, a sensation that his mind could shut down if it needed to. His focus was single-minded, his intentions clear. He was going to hurt this man and cause him as much pain as possible before killing him in the most brutal way.

Jurgen coughed, and blood sprayed from his mouth, then he spit up more blood before trying to get to his hands and knees, making painful groaning sounds as he did. He finally struggled to his knees and, with a lot of effort, hung onto the tree and pulled himself up on his feet. Wilhelm tightened his fist, and Jurgen held his hands in front of him to shield another blow and pleaded, showing he was willing to surrender.

Eva sucked in a breath, praying it was over. She had seen and experienced enough violence for one day, for one lifetime. To her utter shock, Wilhelm swung his left fist, making another cracking sound as it contacted Jurgen's jawbone.

"You can't tap out," Wilhelm snarled. "I have just started."

Jurgen fell to the ground again, then an agonizing sound came from deep within him, and Eva actually felt sorry for him. She let out a gasp of horror as blood poured from Jurgen's mouth onto the grass. A tooth fell out into the puddle of blood by his head. Wilhelm lifted his foot and kicked Jurgen in the ribs with the toe of his boot, not caring that he was already down. Jurgen pleaded and cried for clemency, but it fell on deaf ears.

She covered her mouth to suppress a cry, tears welling in her eyes. She feared Wilhelm would not stop. There was something so fierce and violent in his face, and his actions were the most brutal thing she had ever seen. She was afraid he might actually kill Jurgen.

Jurgen tried to crawl away from Wilhelm on shaky hands and knees, but Wilhelm closed the distance and beat him even more viciously. Jurgen's weakness and cries for him to stop seemed to only enrage Wilhelm more instead of cooling his temper or invoking any kind of sympathy.

He kicked Jurgen in the throat, and a gurgling sound escaped his lips. She looked away when there was another sickening sound of a breaking bone as Wilhelm methodically tore his opponent apart.

She didn't know what bone he broke this time, nor did she care to find out. What she saw Wilhelm doing now was nothing like what he had done in the ring. This was something she had never seen before, a side of him she didn't even know existed. It was a threatening, uncontrollable, murderous rage. Jurgen had angered Wilhelm and his vengeance was swift.

She could hear footsteps on the gravel coming towards them. They weren't walking but running in her, Wilhelm, and Jurgen's direction.

When the approaching footsteps got closer, an authoritative voice yelled, "Obersturmbannführer Bauer, stop!" Wilhelm halted mid-swing, his gaze still locked firm on Jurgen. He stayed like that for a few seconds before carefully raising his hard eyes to meet them.

Eva stared at the high-ranking officer she didn't recognize. He was standing next to another officer, and six soldiers accompanied them. All the men had a stunned expression on their faces as they observed the scene in front of them. Eva wondered who had summoned them. Maybe the sounds of the man's agony could be heard all the way to the palace.

His breaths still coming hard, Wilhelm was unflinching at their words. He didn't even seem deterred by their presence. He narrowed his eyes at them, and the soldiers who had been standing in front drew back a few feet, recoiling at his icy stare. Only the older, high-ranking officer did not seem to falter.

"You cannot kill another officer," he said, speaking deliberately slow, each word drenched with his anger.

Wilhelm looked away from them and down at Jurgen, then back to the men. His mouth curled up into a cruel smile, a wicked glint in his eyes.

"He is an officer and a loyal German, and a member of the party," the older officer growled.

Wilhelm was still unaffected as he remained by Jurgen, calm and callous, his fists clenching tighter as he flexed the muscles in his hands.

"I will do everything in my power to see that you are punished most severely," he threatened.

She looked between them and noticed that the man did not move any closer to Wilhelm, nor did any of the other soldiers.

Wilhelm let out a laugh of derision.

"I will also have you arrested," the man added, not backing down.

Wilhelm eyed him unconvinced, then glanced back at Jurgen, who was now comatose on the ground, lying in a pool of his own blood.

Everyone waited, and Eva held her breath as Wilhelm considered, time seeming to stop, then he took a few steps back from the dying man.

The soldiers looked relieved, apparently no one wanted to be the one to try to arrest Wilhelm Bauer.

"Take him to the hospital," the older man instructed the soldiers, motioning towards Jurgen. But never once did he take his eyes off Wilhelm.

The soldiers gave Wilhelm a wide berth as they came to recover Jurgen. Four of them lifted his limp, bloodied body and carried it across the garden, then up the stairs.

Eva hung onto a tree and drug herself up, her legs shaking beneath her. The older officer's eyes briefly met Eva's as he shot a glance at her, his expression full of confusion, then turned back to Wilhelm. "Wilhelm, follow me inside. We need to talk," he said in a steely tone, eyeing her again. "Alone." The man stared Wilhelm down, showing that he didn't have a choice but to accompany him back to the building, then turned and walked down the path towards the palace.

Wilhelm flashed a gaze at her, his face unreadable, but a reflection of violent anger still burned in his hazel eyes. He didn't say a word to her but turned and sauntered in the direction of the palace.

She watched his back as he disappeared into the night. Now that she was alone, she sobbed, racking, shuttering breaths. She looked down at herself, horrified, as she realized her breast was still hanging out of her dress. She pulled the dress up over it, hiding her partial nudity and shame. Then she turned towards the palace, not wanting to show her face, not wanting anyone to know what transpired in the garden.

Once she was inside, she could hear their voices echoing in the hall and followed the sound. They went into a room, and Wilhelm slammed the door loudly behind him, rattling a vase on a table. She was happy that they did not return to the main hall where all the other people were. Eva sat on the floor of an adjacent hall, leaning against the wall. The hall was close enough to the door that she could hear the loud voices on the other side.

"…and you are really willing to waste your whole career, for her?" the older man's severe voice pressed. "For a foreign girl who you shouldn't be with anyway? Who probably doesn't even like you?"

"That is for me to decide. And foreign or not, she was not his to have."

"Was? Are you indicating that he is dead?"

"When I stopped, he was still alive. But I hope he dies a slow, painful death that takes weeks." The venom in his voice cut through the air.

"What is she to you, anyway?"

"A friend."

"Is that all? It seems like it is much more than that. Does she feel the same about you?" There was silence. "So, you did this for someone who doesn't even feel the same as you. If she has told you anything that contradicts that, then she has played you. All she wants is the help you have in your power to offer her. You are not someone who can be easily deceived, that I am sure of. You are an exemplary officer, one of the best I have seen. You are capable of getting even the most resilient people to break and spill their secrets. The ones that are as tough as nails, and somehow you still get them to crack. But for some reason you decided to believe this girl and think she is worth jeopardizing your reputation for."

He had endangered his own life to help her. Her stomach turned sour, and she could taste vomit in her mouth now. She had not realized how much he risked for her. This was all going to blowback on him, not her. She had a sinking feeling inside because she did this to him.

"She isn't worth it. You could have any of the eligible women in Berlin, and you chase after a foreigner. You should have let him have her. He would be doing you a favor."

"I would choose my words more carefully if I were you!" Wilhelm cautioned. His voice was deep and aggressive.

She didn't hear anything for a while and suspected the hostility was rising in the air between them. She wondered if Wilhelm scared the man he was talking to.

"The girl is a traitor to her country and a threat to ours. And you are blind if you can't see that. Are you trying to be a revolutionary? I know you don't want to get married, and I thought you didn't even want to date, but to make such an open display of defiance of our views for a girl who has probably long dishonored herself. And who is from a country with people who cavort with those of color. How do you know she isn't one herself?"

"Are we done here?" Wilhelm's tone was icy and detached.

"We are not," he growled firmly. "Not until you assure me you will not try to kill Oberleutnant Pflüger or harm him a second time."

"On the condition that he never lays a finger on her ever again, and if he does he will die at my hands," Wilhelm answered calmly, not a hint of insincerity in his voice.

There was silence in the room, and Eva wished she knew what was happening.

"I don't think she is worth all of this, and I hope you figure that out soon," she heard the older man say finally.

Footsteps approached the door, then it flew open, and Wilhelm walked past her, making his way back down the hall in the direction they had come from. She figured he hadn't seen her there. Then, the footsteps came back in the direction of the room, and Wilhelm stepped into the hall, just a few inches away from her. He had seen her in the corner of his eye as he walked by then turned back, not expecting her to be there.

She felt paralyzed, completely vulnerable and unready to confront him. Her heart beat a steady, rhythmic thump in her chest as she looked up, dry blood still covering him. It was on his face, in his hair, on his hands, and on his clothes.

Something flashed in his eyes as he registered her, and his face changed. The hardness in his expression softened, replaced by a look of intense concern. A look of anguish, of solace, and it shocked her. So much had happened tonight, and the intensity of his gaze disarmed her. She stared into the warm hazel eyes looking down at her, but that was all she could manage.

He came to her side, lowered himself to the floor beside her, and leaned against the wall. He didn't speak or move to touch her but sat there at her side in silence. She leaned into him, took hold of his arm that rested on his bent knee, and brought her head to lay it on his bicep, her whole body shaking as she clung to his steady arm. He let her hold him, being what she needed at this moment. It was something so vastly different from what she needed in the garden.

"I feel dirty, violated, and I will never be clean again," she told him in a quiet, shaky voice.

He took her right hand and rubbed it between his, slowly, methodically, then her left hand as if brushing dirt from them.

"Is that better?"

She nodded, still trying to control her shaking body. He removed his jacket and draped it over her, then wrapped his arm firmly around her while holding her head to him as she silently wept. They sat this way for a long time, and when her tears finally slowed, he stood and stretched his hand out to her, his gaze impassioned.

"Come with me."

She was a little calmer now and more aware of her surroundings and the gravity of the situation. She stared into his intense eyes, the blood still covering him, the wounds on his hands, the violent display that had just taken place. For a moment, she considered taking his hand as a part of her wanted to surrender and take comfort in the security of him like she had just done a minute ago, but she faltered now. Both of their emotions ran hot, and she knew his was just as raw as her own and barely contained beneath the surface.

She crossed her arms tight around her chest, battling against the urge to give in to him. She feared him in a way she never had before, and she didn't want him to know. She could still remember Jurgen's weight on top of her, his hand on the bare skin of her breast. She felt unworthy of Wilhelm's kindness and love. She continued to sit on the floor but kept her eyes locked with his. He didn't move his outstretched hand, but she also didn't take it.

A different emotion flashed through Wilhelm's eyes as his expression turned to bewilderment. He observed her body language. Then, the emotion in his eyes changed, and his confused look faded, his demeanor more austere now. He dropped his hand to his side, and she got to her feet without his help. Eva ran her trembling hands over the torn lace of her dress, feeling an odd need to fix it, to mend what had been broken. When she had finished with the dress, she reached up and touched her face where Jurgen hit it. The memory of what had happened filled her with dread. It would haunt her dreams for a long time.

Wilhelm's eyes watched her, growing darker and more impassioned with every second. Shaken, bruised, and in a tattered gown that had undoubtedly been beautiful only hours ago. "I should not have stopped. I want to kill him," he said aloud, but more to himself than her.

She met his gaze once more but quickly looked away, not wanting him to see the emotions in her eyes. Wilhelm saved her from a monster and stepped into a messy and complicated situation to save her from a truly nightmarish fate, and not just this time. If it wasn't for him, she wouldn't even be alive right now to experience this horrible night that he saved her from. She didn't know what the next few minutes would be like. She didn't want to be alone, but she didn't want to be alone with him either. She knew that he would never do to her what he did to Jurgen, but the memory of it was still too fresh. Liesel was working, and Heidi had gone to visit her family, but being at the apartment alone would probably be better than being alone with him right now. She didn't speak and was painfully aware of the silence that stretched between them.

Wilhelm's jaw tensed, and he looked just over the top of her head as if trying to reign in some strong emotion, and then his eyes met hers, and once again, he offered his hand to her. She looked into his eyes, and it caused her to pause, unnerved by his piercing gaze and the memory of his out-of-control violence towards Jurgen, who would have raped her without Wilhelm's intervention. Or she could have possibly been dead without Wilhelm's help.

"You do not need to be afraid," he tried to assure her in the softest, most unthreatening voice he could muster right now. She reached out and took his hand, and he promptly pulled it through his bent elbow, looping her arm through his.

Chapter Twenty-Three

Eva struggled to keep up with the long strides of Wilhelm's legs. She wanted to tell him she didn't want the people at the party to see her this way, but the main hall was the only way to the front. The music grew louder, and she tensed, knowing they were close. Voices echoed down towards them, and for a second, she considered turning back. The overwhelming urge to hide herself was growing. Everything about this night was surreal like it was all a bad dream. But she knew that it would no longer seem like a dream as soon as she was alone in her bed.

He pulled her into the room and people looked in their direction. All eyes turned towards them, lingering on her and the state of her appearance. It was obvious they wondered why she looked the way she did. Her dress and stockings were torn, she was barefoot with dirt in her hair, on her feet, and on her dress.

Eva felt like the room was closing in on her, and she could hardly breathe. She glanced up at Wilhelm and noticed tension in his clenched jaw and a fire still burned in his eyes. It was dimmer than it had been, but it was still there, just beneath the surface. Several officers in the room approached them to speak to Wilhelm, but he didn't stop. He looked down at her, his gaze hard, sending a shiver through her, which was impossible to suppress.

He motioned to his orderly, who was waiting by the front entryway. He walked at a fast pace in their direction. "Is the car ready?" Wilhelm asked in an aggressive tone, but not towards his orderly personally.

"It is." The orderly's gaze darted to her, but his face remained straight, not giving away any thoughts. "I will go pull it around now." He promptly turned and went outside, and Eva and Wilhelm followed.

"It won't take long for the car to be here," he told her, obviously ignoring her shudder at his gaze. His emotions were better controlled now, firmly held at bay by his steely willpower.

Minutes later, the car pulled around the front, and when it came to a stop, Wilhelm opened the back door for her, and she slid in, then he got into the back with her. The car pulled away and headed into the night. The tension between them was heavy in the air and made her uneasy. She looked at this man in the back with her, no longer recognizing him. His draw was nothing like Gerhardt's alluring, infectious personality.

Gerhardt's charm seemed to come naturally, and being with him was as easy as breathing. Wilhelm, on the other hand, was nothing like that. There was not a captivating draw to him but more like a force of nature that she had to guard herself against, or it would swallow her up in its maelstrom. It was fascinating to watch, but it could be deadly if you got too close.

She felt uneasy, so she turned away from him and closed her eyes, but all she could see was the violence he had enacted. The blood, the agony, the sound of the breaking bones. Her eyes flew open, and she realized that it must be similar to what happened to the man who stole his sister's medicine. She remembered his mother saying he had come home with blood on him. There was no doubt now that he killed the man who ultimately robbed his sister of her life. Then a more terrifying thought took her. What would he have done to her if there was no attachment between them and if he had never fallen in love with her? She saw what it was like to be on the wrong side of Wilhelm's emotions, to be on his bad side. She was lucky she was not, that she had somehow found herself on this side. But she had not always been on this side. The hair on her head stood on end at the memory of their past encounters.

She turned to look at him, and he watched her from the other side of the seat. His arms were crossed, and his expression was weary and tired, but in his eyes, there was conflict. His stare almost felt confrontational, and she wondered if he was upset with her or himself for what had happened. She was sure he never could have imagined he would have done that for her in the past, given their complicated history with each other. This most certainly hurt his reputation with the party and his standing with the Gestapo.

She tried to imagine what would happen to him over the next few days. There would be ridicule, that was certain, and there could be a punishment. He had to know there would be consequences, but still, he chose to protect her, anyway. She thought it was obvious that her love for Gerhardt was still strong, but Wilhelm overlooked that for her. He could have left her to her fate, but he didn't. None of this, though, silenced the echo in her head that he was a dangerous man capable of horrific violence. And that somewhere in him was the capability to inflict extreme pain and brutality on others and not even care. To look at another human and want them dead and feel nothing as you kill them.

Suddenly, she had an all-consuming urge to not be in his presence. "Where are we going?"

He didn't immediately answer and was silent for a few seconds. "My apartment."

She shook her head. "No, I don't want to. I want to go to Liesel and Heidi's."

Concern, frustration, and anger flared in him. "You should not be alone right now. You might have a concussion."

"I need to be alone. Please," she pleaded. Her hand was resting on her leg, and she could not stop it from shaking. He reached over to take it, but she quickly pulled away. She felt ashamed, tainted, and, in a way, defiled. She could not have him noticing this, but she also didn't want a man, any man, to touch her right now. The thought made her feel sick to her stomach. Then she thought about what Jurgen said, about Wilhelm not wanting her anymore after he touched her. That still remained to be seen.

He eyed her, and she could see he was considering whether or not he should do as she asked. Finally, he turned to his orderly. "Take her where she wants to go," he said and gave him the address of her old apartment. The driver acknowledged the change in orders and drove to her old apartment. He pulled in front and put the car in neutral but didn't turn off the engine.

Eva got out of the car, and Wilhelm got out with her. "I'm not sure what is going to happen, but I will have to report to my commander. I might not be able to see you at all tomorrow."

"I am sorry it has come to this. I never wanted to get you into trouble."

He gave her a smile. "It's nothing I can't handle. Don't worry about me." He leaned in and gave her a soft kiss on the cheek, and she stiffened, but either he didn't notice or didn't acknowledge it. He pulled back, and his expression was unreadable. He watched her go into the apartment building, then got back into the car and left.

She closed the apartment door behind her and locked it. She was out of her dress before she was even in the bathroom. She turned the shower as hot as she could stand and stepped into the tub, the water cascading over her head. She washed the dirt from her hair and off her body, then she lathered her body with soap again and scrubbed with her nails, trying to erase the feeling of Jurgen from her, but no matter how hard or how long she scrubbed, the feeling wouldn't go away. She felt like there was blood and dirt on her that would not come off, so she lathered up again and again. She lowered herself the floor of the tub under the showerhead and rubbed until her skin was raw and hurt, hot tears mixing with the water. She pulled her legs to her chest, wrapped her arms around them, and stayed that way until the water grew cold.

Finally, she rose to her feet and turned the knob, shivering from the water and the events of the evening. She could not seem to make herself move out of the tub. The tears flowed freely, and inside, she was crumbling. She stood and lifted one leg out of the tub, almost falling. She had no strength left in her body and hardly had the energy to dry off and dress herself. She slid a nightgown over her head, went to her old room, and closed the door. She curled up in the bed, hugging the blankets. Another wave of emotions hit her, and she felt sick. She closed her eyes, but all she could see was Jurgens's face above hers and Wilhelm's unbridled rage. The whole night she was in and out of sleep, and the events of the evening played in her mind regardless of whether she was conscious or not.

The dawn had broken and Eva squeezed her eyes closed against the bright sun coming through the window. She hurt all over but was only now noticing it. With everything that happened last night, she had not registered the pain. The adrenaline that coursed through her also masked it. She rolled onto her back and moaned. She brought her hand to her neck, then to her face. The left side felt puffy, and her eye was partially closed. Her entire face throbbed and stung, and her bottom lip had a split in it that was sealed shut with dry blood.

Slowly, she sat up and assessed the rest of her body. There didn't seem to be anywhere that didn't have a bruise, and her thoughts went to Jurgen. If she was in this much pain, she could only imagine what he must be feeling right now. Her thoughts then went to Wilhelm, and she wondered what had happened to him. Had they already punished him? And what was his punishment if they did?

She wanted to know but could not face him now, and it might make it worse for him if she showed up, and she didn't want that.

She slid to the edge of the bed and barely had the energy to do that. She put her feet on the floor and stood, only realizing now that there were cuts on the soles of her feet.

"Ow."

She sat back down because it hurt to stand. How was she going to do anything? After a few minutes, she stood again and went to the bathroom. She bandaged her feet and finally looked at her face in the mirror. It looked worse than it had yesterday, and there was no way she was going to let Wilhelm see her like this. She walked out of the bathroom and went into the kitchen.

When Liesel saw her, she gasped and stood from her chair. "Oh, my God. What happened?"

"It is a very long story. But in short, I was attacked in the gardens of the palace last night."

Liesel came around the table to embrace her, but Eva backed away and held up her hands. "Please, I am in so much pain that I would scream out if anyone touched me." Liesel did as she asked and returned to her chair. Eva joined her, ate a small breakfast, and had a cup of tea. Her stomach still felt unsettled.

"What now? Are you still leaving for France today like you had planned?"

"No. I think I will stay in Berlin for another day or two." She wasn't sure if Wilhelm was returning to France today as well. And didn't want to risk seeing him. "I'm going to visit an old friend today, and then I will decide what to do."

"Alright. I'm going to sleep for a while." Liesel eyed Eva, not understanding what transpired, and it worried her.

After they finished breakfast and Liesel was in bed, Eva left the house. She wore a pair of sunglasses to try and hide her face, but the only thing it covered was her black, swollen eye. She got stares from people on the street and the occasional glance from someone on the tram, but no one said anything to her.

The tram arrived at the stop near the church, and Eva got off and walked the single block there. She pulled open the first heavy, large wooden door, then went through the second door into the chapel that smelled of burned candle wax. It was empty and quiet as she made her way to the confessional booth at the front, but she saw it was empty when she got there. She went to the long hall at the side, walking the distance to the priest's office at the end. The door was closed, so she lifted her hand and gently tapped her knuckles on it. She heard footsteps on the other side, then the door opened.

Father Becker stood in front of her, surprise settling on his face. "Eva. I did not expect to see you here." His eyes fixed on her face. "Come in." He moved out of the doorway so she could enter his office. Eva went to her regular chair and sat down, and he went around the desk and took his seat. He waited for her to speak first.

She removed her glasses and laid them on her lap. She tried to give him a smile, but it hurt her face, so she relaxed the muscles. "A lot has happened since the last time we spoke. There are things that transpired, and I don't know how to process them. I cannot make sense of any of it."

"Tell me about these things, and I will see if I can help."

"That man I hate or thought I hated. I am now bound to him. I am indebted to him. I owe him my life and my respect as well as my gratitude." She moved her hand over her face. "This is the result of something that happened last night. The thing that he saved me from. If he had not found me when he did, I would probably be dead. He has Told me he loves me. He has saved me from a horrific fate and risked his own reputation to do so. But everything with him is so complicated and difficult to the extreme. I care for him, but somewhere inside, I still hold some resentment towards him. And after what I saw him do last night, I am afraid to be around him."

"Are you in a relationship with him?"

This was a question she was not prepared to answer. She considered how much time they spent together, how she would stay at his apartment for days, sometimes more than a week, and the fact that they had lived together for a while in Dieppe. Then there was the not-so-small thing of them being intimate.

"I don't know what you would call it, but I guess that is as good a description as any."

"Relationships can be a good and bad thing, often at the same time. They may give us joy and pleasure in the other person's company, but they can also be extremely painful. This is a vulnerability that comes with romantic attachments."

"So why do people enter into them, then?"

"Because they make our lives richer. They can increase our joy and sense of belonging. And they offer us the chance for a family."

"And if the person doesn't offer us those things? If they are bad for us, no matter how much we might enjoy being with them? When people are in the throes of love, they don't always make the wisest decisions. I don't know how it is even possible, but I love him and despise him."

"I think sometimes we feel or believe we don't like someone because we don't want to love them but are unable to free ourselves from the feelings we have for them. Or maybe the love is not reciprocated."

"But as you know, I am in love with someone else."

"Yes, the man who chose to be with another woman." He raised an eyebrow at her. Implying that it only proves his point.

"And if his love is the only love I want?"

"Maybe we should appreciate the love we have instead of the love we desire. If you ignore the love that is given, you

475

might find yourself without either. Some people are just not meant to be together. No matter how much they want it to be so."

She could not discount the truth of what he said. "So what now?"

"Have you thanked him for what he did?"

She felt a twinge of guilt. "I have not."

"Why?"

"A lot happened very quickly last night. I was in pain and distraught, and it slipped my mind."

"When you leave here, you should thank him."

"I don't even know where he is. What he did to help me… well, I think it got him into trouble."

"Then you should find out where he is."

"Yes." She stared at the bookshelf behind him. "I should." She stood, and he did the same. "Thank you for your advice."

"You have a lot to consider. Just make sure you don't let the negative emotions you are feeling get in your way of doing what is right."

"I will try."

She left the church and sat on a park bench across the street, her sunglasses back on. She knew she should try to find out what happened to Wilhelm, but the thought of it made her nervous. She stood, walked to the tram stop, and took it to the Reich Security Office, the Nazi headquarters for the Gestapo. As she walked the long length of the tan, five-story building, it made her feel ill at ease. Her stomach twisted, and her heart raced. She was beginning to have second thoughts, but she had to do this. She needed to do this. She could not hide the concern for him she felt inside. She went up the steps and through the arched entryway. She stopped in her tracks when she saw the same woman who tried to have her escorted out the last time she was there, sitting behind the desk. This was not going to work in her favor. Instead of going to the front desk, she decided to wait and see if she could spot another officer. Perhaps they would tell her where he was and what was happening to him.

She loitered by a window at the front, watching the people come and go. Finally, to her relief, an officer with a briefcase came into the building, walking at a fast pace.

She hurried after him. "Excuse me, sir. Sir…."

He stopped and looked at her. "Yes?" His face was placid, but in his eyes, she could see impatience.

"I am so sorry to bother you. I am here to see SS Obersturmbannführer Bauer. Do you know if he is in?"

His eyebrows creased, and his lips settled into a straight line. He eyed her for a second before speaking. "He is currently unavailable. I'm sorry." He turned from her and resumed his fast-paced walk with long strides.

She chased after him again. "Will he be free anytime today?"

He stopped again, and this time his face was strained. "I'm afraid not. I don't think he will have time to see you at all."

"Why?"

"I cannot discuss these matters with you. I am afraid you have wasted your time." He walked away from her, but this time she did not follow.

The anxiety was making her hands shake. What was happening to him? And why was the man so apprehensive to talk about it? She feared the worse. What if they were going to have him shot? She frantically looked around the room, wondering what else she could do and who she might talk to. She felt helpless and feared for him. She was desperate to learn of his fate but didn't know how to do that. She walked to the doors and pushed her way outside, taking a deep breath. She paced, one hand on her hip and the other on her forehead. She stopped, realizing she had possibly one way of finding out. She walked to the nearest restaurant and went inside to the wall that had small rooms with payphones. She stepped inside one and closed the door. She took a coin from her purse and inserted it into the machine, then turned the dial for the operator.

"I would like to speak to Oberst Heinrich Schmitt at the Reich Security Main Office," she said when a woman's voice came on the other end of the receiver.

"Who is calling?" the operator asked.

"Eva Abrams. He knows me."

"I will put you through." Eva heard a clicking sound on the other end, then ringing. It rang over and over, but no one picked up. The operator came back on the line. "Do you want me to try again?"

Eva let out a breath. "No. Thank you." She hung the phone up and let her hand rest on it. She had hit yet another dead end.

Eva stayed in Berlin for three more days, trying to find out what had happened to Wilhelm. But she was no closer to knowing than she had been the first day. She still could not get in touch with Oberst Heinrich Schmitt, which also had her worried. In the four days she had been here, her bruises faded from the angry, reddish color they had been to a bluish-purple that was slowly beginning to look green. And the swelling of her face had gone down some. She did not want Ingrid or Klaus to see her like this, but she could not stay in Berlin until it had disappeared entirely.

She boarded the train that would take her back to Dieppe, feeling defeated. She took a seat next to an elderly man and sat her purse on her lap and her bag between her feet. She was too hyped to sleep but couldn't get her brain to focus on any one thought. She tapped her foot on the floor and looked around the train car. She had tried everything she could think of to get information about Wilhelm, but every time hit a wall. Maybe he returned to Paris and had been too busy to contact her? As soon as she thought about it, she dismissed it, knowing it wasn't the reason.

The train ride felt like an eternity. It made a stop in just about every town along the way, and her papers had been checked twice. When it pulled into the Dieppe station, she felt a sense of relief. She picked her bag off the floor and stood, making her way through the car, and stepped out onto the platform. She wondered how she was going to explain this to Ingrid and Klaus. They would, of course, ask questions. How could they not? She would if the situation were reversed.

There was no public transportation in Dieppe, like in Paris or Berlin, but it didn't bother her. She walked into town, as a light fog hung over the city, blurring out the buildings. She didn't feel like going to the apartment just yet. She knew Ingrid would probably be home, and there would be questions. She walked up and down the cobbled streets until she was at the city's edge. Before her, at the foothill, was the vast expanse of the channel. The water looked pearlescent and swirled with choppy waves, rocking the boats that dotted its surface.

She sat down in the tall grass, putting her bag beside her. She bent her legs and rested her arms across her knees, watching the ebb and flow of the tide. The air smelled of fish, saltwater, and baking bread from somewhere in the distance. She wanted to cry but felt strangely numb inside. Though if she talked about what happened or saw Wilhelm right now, her sand wall that held back the tide of turmoil would crumble, and the chaos and confusion would rush in, leaving her in a disarray of distress and sorrow.

She forced herself to her feet and picked up her bag. She had to face them sometime. She turned and started walking back towards Dieppe. She glanced at the houses in the distance that littered the hills, looking down over the town. As she walked through the streets, she saw a woman sweeping her porch, another woman beating a hanging rug with a broom, and an old man smoking his pipe in a shop doorway. Both women glanced in her direction, but the man watched her with unbroken concentration. She was sure she stood out, especially now.

Once in the apartment, she put her bag and purse on the floor, went to the couch, and sat down. Her whole body still ached, and she was utterly spent.

"Eva?" she heard Ingrid call from her bedroom. Ingrid came into the living room as she put pins in her hair. "I didn't know you were coming home today. "How was Par..." Ingrid stopped mid-sentence, her hands moving from her hair. "Oh my God." She rushed to Eva's side and dropped onto the couch next to her. She reached up and touched Eva's cheek gently, with only the tips of her fingers. "What happened to you?"

She wasn't sure how to answer. "Someone attacked me in Berlin." She was surprised she could say it so calmly.

Ingrid's face turned to a look of intense confusion. "Who attacked you?"

"A man at a party."

"I don't understand. Why would he do that?"

Eva turned and looked at her. She saw the moment when what had happened registered in Ingrid's eyes.

Ingrid lifted her hand to her mouth. "No! So you were...?" she trailed off.

"Almost."

"How did you get away?"

Eva's eyes burned as she tried to hold back the dam of tears. "Wilhelm Bauer. He found us."

"He helped you?"

"Yes. In a way."

"In a way? What does that mean?" she asked gently.

"He found the man on top of me and pulled him off."

"So, that's a good thing."

Eva shook her head, and the tears flowed now. "No, it's not. He beat him in such a cruel way. He was like a feral animal who got free. He was going to kill him until two other officers and some soldiers stopped him." She looked at Ingrid. "I have known him for years now and spent a lot of time with him, but you never really know what is happening inside somebody. You never truly know who they are. You have the misconception that because you love them, you know them, but really you never do. I saw a side of him I had never seen before, a side that scared me. The rage in his eyes, the brutality, and violence he inflicted on that man without feeling anything other than the hate. I believe he had completely switched off all emotions but that one. He was so consumed by bloodlust, rage, and a thirst for murder."

"Maybe he never wanted you to see that part of him? He changed into that person for you because that is who you needed him to be at that moment. He is enamored with you. You have to ask yourself, would he have done that for anyone else?"

Eva wiped her nose with the back of her hand. "That still doesn't make it right." Ingrid put her arm around Eva's shoulder and rubbed her. "Even after seeing him like that, I cannot hate him. He is who I crave, although it will take some time for me to feel comfortable being alone with him again. But how I feel makes me hate myself. I mean no offense by saying this, but he is German, and it is a country that has started two world wars and has done unspeakable things. He stands for everything I should be against. And he is in the Gestapo, the worst of them. Yet, the only time I feel safe, or whole, is when I'm with him." Eva squeezed her eyes shut, feeling the tears run down her cheeks.

"It's alright." Ingrid took Eva in her arms and held her. "What of the man who did this to you?"

"I know he is in the hospital, but I'm not sure he will survive. He haunts me every time I close my eyes. There are these dreams where I am in the dark alone, and he is coming after me. He always catches me and whispers things to me I can't get out of my head, and Wilhelm never comes. Sometimes, the dream starts where I am with Wilhelm, and I think the dream will be sweet, but then he comes and beats Wilhelm to death, and there is nothing I can do to stop it."

"I am sorry. For everything. Where is Wilhelm now?"

Eva pulled away from Ingrid so she could look at her. "I don't know. He risked everything for me, and now I don't know where he is or what is happening to him. One officer that came to the garden was of a higher rank than Wilhelm, and he said Wilhelm would get into trouble for this. I overheard them talking in an office, and he was not happy with him. Wilhelm took me to my old apartment that night, and I have not seen him since. I tried to find out while I was in Berlin, but no one would tell me anything."

"With his rank and position, I can't think it would be too bad. At least not death."

"I'm not so sure."

"You will see him again, Eva."

"I'm going to go to bed. I feel like I haven't slept in weeks." Eva stood up, wincing a little from the pain.

"Have you seen a doctor?"

"No."

"You should. Maybe you could see Dr. Möller tomorrow."

"No. I don't want him to know anything about this. He didn't actually rape me. He just tried."

"Can I help you with anything?"

"Thank you, but no. I'm just going to go to bed." She went to her room, and for a while, she lay awake, listening to the thunder in the distance, then it began to rain. It was a light, rhythmic patter on the slate roof, and it lulled her to sleep.

Chapter Twenty-Four

May 27th, 1942

The sky was beginning to brighten outside, and on the grass and trees, the heavy dew left during the night sparkled in the early morning sun. It was just after six, and Eva had been up for over twenty minutes, still in her nightgown. She stood barefoot on the kitchen floor, cooking breakfast. Ingrid was still asleep, but the smell of the food would wake her soon.

Eva had five eggs scrambling on one pan and shredded potatoes in another. If she was back home, she would be cooking bacon with it too, but most people couldn't get bacon now. Instead, she was finishing it off with toast covered with jam. It had been a while since they could even get butter.

Ingrid walked into the kitchen. "That smells amazing."

"Thank you. Have a seat. It's almost done." Ingrid sat at the table, and Eva dipped out some of the eggs and potatoes onto her plate, then she put a piece of toast on the side. She fixed herself a plate and sat at the table across from her. "It's been nice weather. We should go to the beach soon."

"Yes, I need some sun." Ingrid looked at her pasty arms.

They would talk about the weather, what they hoped to do this summer, and work, but never Wilhelm or what happened in Berlin. And together, they came up with a story for Klaus. He seemed to, at least in part, believe it. It had been almost five weeks now, and Eva had not seen or heard from him. There had been no news whatsoever. She told herself stories of what happened, but she really didn't believe any of them. She tried her best to not think about it, but it was hard. She couldn't help that her thoughts always went to him. She missed him and couldn't see the end to the pain that gripped her like a vice. At first, the thought of him and being with him terrified her, but those feelings towards him were normal after what happened. Anyone would have been afraid of him after what he did. But later, the fear subsided, and she only felt a twinge of it if she thought about that night. However, she was still struggling to rid herself of the other feelings. Her body still felt tainted and dirty, and no amount of scrubbing or time passed seemed to take it away.

Her emotions, as of late, had confused her. Inside there was this conflict, two opposing feelings. One, she felt unclean and never wanted to be touched or looked at by a man ever again, and the other was that she craved him now more than ever. She wanted to feel his lips against hers, to have his touch wipe away the memory of Jurgen's, who was the last man who touched her. But it hurt her every time she thought of Wilhelm and how much she needed him. In a way, she still hated that she loved him because she didn't want to but couldn't stop. She hated that she wanted him; she hated that she thought of him; she hated that he wasn't around, and she wanted to be angry at him for all of it. But really, how could she blame him? It wasn't just his fault.

"Do you work today?" Ingrid asked her.

"I go in at nine."

"I work the afternoon shift. I guess I'll see you there later."

Eva looked at her watch. "I should get ready. You can clean up or leave it, and I'll do it when I get home."

"You cooked. I'll do the dishes."

Eva gave her an appreciative smile, then went to her room and changed into her uniform.

When she got to the hospital, she saw that the number of patients had increased from the night before and wondered why. She found one of the nurses from the night shift. "Why are there so many more patients this morning than last night?"

"There was an incident at a bar last night." The look on her face was grim. "Some of the men got out of control and attacked some of the women there who weren't prostitutes. That started a fight amongst the men, and it turned into a full brawl."

"That is terrible. Are the women alright?"

"A couple of them are here. One is in a terrible condition."

Eva swallowed hard. "Where?"

"She is in the next room." Eva followed her to a room with the door open. "In here," the nurse nodded with her head.

Eva looked into the room at the young woman lying on the bed.

"I have to get back."

"Sure."

The other nurse left, and Eva continued looking at the woman. Eva slowly approached the bed. Her face was swollen and bruised, worse than hers had been. But visible wounds weren't just on her face; they were all over her body. Eva pulled back the sheet and lifted her gown, then took in a sharp breath. She dropped the gown and had to look away.

"You poor girl," Eva whispered.

She wondered if this was what her body would have looked like after Jurgen was done with her if Wilhelm had not intervened. The sight of her was too real for Eva. She hurried out of the room and down the hall, stopping and leaning against the wall as she tried to slow her breathing. She took several deep breaths, then went to help with the other patients. Several of the rooms had the German soldiers, three or four to a room. As Eva checked their bandages, she wondered if one or more of them was responsible for raping the girl in the other room. She had a hard time making eye contact with them or even looking at their faces. She did not want to remember what they looked like. Jurgen was already branded in her memory. She did not need them there too.

She finished as quickly as she could, then went to find Dr. Möller. He was talking with another doctor, so she waited a few feet away for him to finish.

He noticed her and said bye to the other doctor, then came over to her. "Eva. Do you want to go out to eat lunch today?"

"I would like that."

"Good. Let me put the lab coat in my office."

"I'll meet you by the front door." He patted her on the shoulder.

She watched him walk down the hall for a second, then went to the nurse's quarters and got her purse and waited for him by the front door. She stood at the window and watched the little red squirrels run across the courtyard. They would flick their tails, then run up a tree. They were not like the large grey squirrels she was used to seeing in America. Just one more thing that wasn't like home.

"Ready?"

She turned around, and Dr. Möller was standing behind her, his military jacket and cap on. He always looked strange to her this way. She was used to seeing him in a lab coat and no cap.

"Yes."

They walked together to a café that was only ten minutes away. It was a warm day, and the sun felt good on her face. Eva was glad she seemed to be handling Wilhelm's absence a little bit better. She was determined to not bend or break. She was keeping it together and needed it to stay that way.

They sat at a table outside and ordered their food.

"Any plans for this beautiful weather we have had?"

"Not really. Ingrid and I might go swimming at the beach sometime this week. What about you?"

"I have some leave coming up soon and thought I would go back to Germany for a week."

"You should. What will you do while you are there?"

"Just relax and hear my own language spoken for a while. My brain hurts from all this damn French."

Eva chuckled. "I can understand that. It's probably a crash course in French for you."

"My French has gotten rusty over the years."

"I would say you are improving." She looked at his tired face. "It's been a long time since you've taken time for yourself."

"It has."

Klaus had noticed over the weeks that Wilhelm had not been around and asked her about it. She told him they needed him in Paris and he didn't have time to come to Dieppe. It sounded believable enough, but that story would not hold up forever. She tried to act normally whenever she was in front of Dr. Möller. She could not let him know completely how she really felt inside when it came to Wilhelm. And she wanted to forget what happened too and try to move on. But if people continued to ask her about it or how she was doing, it would only prolong the memory and the pain. She wanted to feel that, in the end, she was the one who won, who came out on top, not Jurgen. After all, he was the one who wound up in the hospital, fighting for his life, not her.

They walked back to the hospital after they ate, and Eva went to her locker, put her purse away, and then headed to check on the patients.

"Eva," Dr. Möller called, motioning to her at the end of the hall.

She walked down the corridor and noticed his face when she neared. "What is it?"

"Follow me to my office."

"Klaus… what is it? Is something wrong?"

He didn't answer, but led her to his office, opened the door, and waited for her to enter. She glanced up at him as she walked past, confused about what was happening. Worry and apprehension filled her. She went to his desk, and Klaus walked beside her. She started to sit down in a chair, but he took her arm and pointed to the window that overlooked the center courtyard. A German officer stood with his back to them, holding his cap under his arm as he looked down below. She stared at the back of him, then he turned, and her knees almost gave out from underneath her. She grabbed hold of the back of the chair for support. Wilhelm's hazel eyes stared back at her, and she was speechless. His dark hair was combed in a deep side part, his uniform was freshly pressed, and his boots were immaculately polished, but his normal olive-toned skin had an ashy hue to it, and his complexion was lighter than usual. Around his eyes were faint dark shadows, but other than that, he appeared to be okay.

Klaus hesitated next to Eva for a second, with a watchful eye on Wilhelm before he spoke. "I'll leave you two alone. I'll be just outside."

His footsteps creaked on the floorboards behind her. Then the door clicked shut. She never turned her gaze from Wilhelm. Tears burned in her eyes, and she pulled in a shaky breath. She was overcome with relief that he was alive and grateful for what he did for her. She wanted to find some way to express it.

"I don't know what happened to you, but I am sorry I played a part in it. I would hate it if what happened hurt your reputation or standing with others." She swept her eyes over

491

him, wanting to run to him, but held back. She didn't know what was appropriate right now. She had lost so much sleep over him, and now he was here in front of her.

He brought his hand to his face and rubbed his eyes, and sighed before meeting her gaze, his expression hard. "I don't care what anyone thinks of me." He motioned between them. "And I don't care what they think of this, whatever it is. It's none of their business."

There was tension between them, and it felt familiar to her. And by the intense way he was looking at her, she knew he felt it too. It wasn't anger; it was a different kind of tension. One that rose from the remembrance of their kisses, the affectionate pull between them, and the intensity of a passion they held for one another.

She felt uncomfortable and stepped back from him a fraction. She was a little ashamed of her feeling at this moment. Ashamed by her attraction to him and his power. Even stronger was the betrayal of her feelings towards Wilhelm because part of her heart still belonged to another.

"I have to be back at work now. I wanted to let you know that I was alive. Come to the cottage tonight around nine, and we can talk more then. I'm sorry our meeting now has to be so brief," he said, breaking the momentary spell between them.

It was odd how dismissive he was. Something about his demeanor was strained, and she sensed that something significant had happened to him. She gripped the chair tight with her right hand.

"Then you should go."

Wilhelm made no move to leave and considered her closely. His demeanor softened a little, and he gave her a curt nod before putting on his cap. "I'll see you later." His words sounded like a promise.

"I'll come." He walked across the room, gave her one last glance, then opened the door and was gone. He never came more than four or five feet from her and never tried to hug, kiss, or touch her. Shortly after Wilhelm left, Klaus came into the room and closed the door.

He looked at her expectantly. "What did he want?"

"Just to say hi, and to let me know he was back in town for a while."

"It seems odd that he came here to do that. He could have waited until you were off and came by your apartment."

"I guess it was more convenient for him to come now." She knew the real reason, but that was between her and Wilhelm. "I'm going to go stock the medicine cabinet now." Klaus nodded, and she left for the storage room.

She could hardly focus for the rest of her shift. Anticipation for tonight had her nerves shot. She wanted to hear what he had to say, where he had been, and what had happened to him.

When her shift was over, she got her purse and practically ran from the hospital. She went to the apartment and changed out of her uniform, ate, then paced the living room. She had almost three more hours to wait, and the time was creeping along. She couldn't stay in the apartment any longer. She got her purse and left, walking the streets before finally making her way to the beach. The cottage wasn't far, so she would wait here until it was time.

She tossed rocks into the waves, the nervousness she already felt increasing as the minutes ticked by.

Finally, her watch read nine, and she made her way across the rocky beach towards the cottage. The sun had just finished setting on the horizon, and the temperature was cooling in the late May evening.

She climbed the hill, taking the small path that led to the back of the cottage. When she got to the top and came around to the front, she was surprised to see that his car was already parked in front. Her breath hitched in her throat, and her heart pounded hard against her ribs. She walked to the front door and paused, then knocked. She rubbed her thumb over her sweaty fingers and tried to calm her breathing. The door opened, and Wilhelm looked at her. He was still in his uniform pants, but his jacket was off, and his hair was no longer neatly combed like it had been when she saw him at the hospital. He had obviously been rubbing his fingers through it.

He moved to the side for her, and she walked through the little entryway, and he closed the door. He motioned for her to go into the living room. She went to the couch and sat down, but to her surprise, he did not sit in the chair he usually did, but instead came and sat beside her, closer than she would have expected. She had to fight the urge to move away, not from disgust but from a spite of warring emotions. She waited for him to speak, but he didn't, so she broke the silence between them.

"What happened to you?" She could not keep the concern from her voice.

Wilhelm moved closer and gently took her hands in his, and she let him. He shook his head as he looked at her. "Whatever horrible thing you think happened to me didn't."

She furrowed her brows. "They didn't punish you?"

"They did, but it is hardly worth blinking an eye at. They are paying me lieutenant wages for three months, and my leave has been cut in half."

"That's it?" She was skeptical.

He broke eye contact. "The reason you had not heard from me for so long is that I spent four weeks in prison."

So that wasn't all that happened to him. Her eyes widened, and she stared at his face in horror. "Oh, Wilhelm." Her eyes burned with tears that threatened to spill over.

"And this is why I didn't tell you. I didn't want you to try to come and see me, and I knew what your reaction would be. It wasn't that bad. I had my own cell, three meals a day, and I still did what work I could from there. I am too valuable for them to kill over beating up a lower ranking piece of shit. And with my experience and position, they weren't going to make the punishment too severe. Reduced pay, halved leave, and a month in prison is nothing."

"But none of that would have happened if it wasn't for me."

"Eva," he said, hesitation in his voice, his face serious.

She looked at him, and the inescapable urge to vent built, and she could no longer contain it. After telling Ingrid some of what happened, she had not spoken a word of it to anyone and suppressed it from her memory the best she could. But it was always there, festering, and unresolved. "I can't get him out of my head. He terrorizes me even in my sleep," she said, her voice cracking.

A flash of pain passed over Wilhelm's expression. "I know," he finally said, an edge to his voice. "But he is rather incapacitated at the moment." A wicked gleam lit in his eyes at the memory of what he did to Jurgen. "He can't hurt you anymore. He can't get out of bed or even take a piss on his own."

She looked away, overcome with emotions, as she wrestled with crippling grief. Tears flowed down her cheeks as she was swept up in a yearning for him so powerful that it threatened to undo her.

She tightened her grip on him as his fingers remained firm around hers. She cried as the tapping of rain hit the window beside them. Wilhelm reached up to touch her cheek, and she leaned her head against his palm. His hazel eyes were fixed on hers, and she could see they were filled with a compassion she hadn't expected. His outward expression of support felt like a lifeline, and she clung to it. He moved his hand from her face back to her hand as he slightly let down his guard, the gate to his emotional wall opening. He pulled her to him, took her in his arms, and held her protectively against his warm body. A reflexive shudder ran through her as he tightened his embrace. Her emotions were running hot, and he must be aware of them.

Wilhelm sucked in a hard breath, his whole body tensing as his grip around her loosened. His sudden reaction alarmed her, and she struggled against his strong arms, freeing herself after several long seconds. She looked at him as her emotions surged uncontrollably through her, breathing erratically. Wilhelm set his ardent gaze on her. For a long moment, neither of them spoke. She could see the confusion in her own eyes mirrored back in his. She wondered why he tensed. Had she done something wrong? There was a change in him, and his guard was back up. What she needed the most now, he would not give her. After the five long weeks since the attack, she knew he was the only person who could help her forget. Maybe he thought she was tainted as well, and he didn't want her anymore. His sudden withdrawal brought fresh tears to her eyes, and she tried to blink them away. In his eyes, she saw his firm resolve crack as he watched her cry, knowing her tears now were because of him.

She reached up and placed her hand on his cheek. Wilhelm stilled and remained withdrawn, but he didn't stop her. She moved her hand down his neck to his shirt and undid the first button, but by the time she got to the second one, she knew he would stop her before she got any farther. She tried with the button again, but her fingers faltered, so she let her hands drop to her lap. She closed her eyes so he couldn't see them glisten. She felt his hands on her waist as he pulled her onto his lap and brought her head to his chest. He brushed the hair away that had fallen on her face when he moved her and kissed her eyelids, then her wet cheeks.

"I don't think that is really what you want," he whispered.

She looked up at him but didn't say anything. She wanted to show him it was exactly what she wanted. She leaned up and pressed her lips to his. She wanted him to kiss her like he had that night he took her on the floor. It was raw and explosive, and she yearned for that now. He did not return her kiss, but she moved her lips on his, tasting him. She could smell his cologne and feel the softness of his full lips. She pulled away and searched his face, hoping to see the same desire in it she was feeling. But she couldn't read anything. It was a blank canvas staring back at her.

"Do you want me?"

"Oh hell," he said. "Eva, I always want you."

He leaned in and placed his lips on her neck. The sudden hardening of his mouth against her throat brought a helpless response from her, so quiet it was barely audible. She felt faint, as he brought his lips to hers and kissed her with raw, naked hunger until she couldn't breathe.

He moved his hand to her back, and she had the sensation of falling as he laid her on the couch. Then he was on her. She laced her fingers in his hair and pulled his head down to hers. She wanted him to kiss her again. She wanted it to be intense, and she wanted him not to stop. The feel of him sent a warm rush through her, and it was like coming home. She pulled his shirt out from his pants and put her hands under it, rubbing them up the length of his muscular back. She knew every part of his body, but it still felt strange.

She opened herself up to him, letting him touch her freely, and he did. She wondered if he had done this to her many times in his imagination because he seemed to know her body so well. He knew how to touch her and where to touch her. She had thought before that he was disarming, and she wasn't wrong. With any man other than Wilhelm, the intimacy and sensuality would have been repugnant to her. But being with him now was her choice, and she had the right to command her own feelings, and she was. Jurgen tried to take what she was willingly giving Wilhelm now.

He traced his lips over her jaw, and her heart thumped hard and slow in her chest. He slid his hand behind her head and pulled her in, bringing his lips decisively to hers, and she let out a moan. He then paused for a second, their faces close as he looked into her eyes, a question in them, and she understood. She reached for the hem of her dress and pulled it up, then took his hand and slid it down the side of her leg, moving it in between her thighs. She was going to let him know that she was wet and ready for him. That there was no apprehension in her. She wanted him as much as she figured he wanted her.

He moved his hand from her legs and pulled her dress up further, tearing it at the seam as he dragged it over her head and tossed it to the floor. Then he put his hand on the couch to support his body. It was large and wide next to hers. She could see his forearm flexing under the sleeve of his white shirt. With slow deliberation, he lifted his other hand and touched the side of her neck, his warm fingers gliding down her side. He was less in control now, and she saw a fiery recklessness in his eyes. She pushed his suspenders off his shoulder and finished unbuttoning his shirt, sliding it down his strong arms. He finished taking it off and tossed it on the floor beside her torn dress. She undid his pants, and they were thrown on the floor next. He took off her bra, slip, and underwear but left her stockings and garter on. She pulled his underwear down, sliding her hands over his butt and onto the thick, muscular thighs of his legs.

He reached down, and she could feel pressure between her legs, her body tensing, all her senses heightened. Then came a dull pain that quickly faded as he pushed into her. She held her breath as pleasure moved through her whole body in that single movement. Her body pressed against his, his hand resting on her leg. She looked up at him and took a breath, holding it, then he lifted his hips and brought them down with a force that pressed her into the couch.

She had been waiting for it. Her breath escaped her lips in a soft moan. He kissed her deeply, unapologetically, but he attempted to be considerate, though his touch and thrust were rough and growing more frantic. She didn't mind, wondering what it would feel like if he let himself go, no longer holding back with carefully placed restraints.

She had one hand on his back and one on his leg, leaning her body into him. He put his hand on her jaw and opened her mouth, his breaths coming deep and ragged. Something urgent and searing flashed through her as he ran his tongue expertly on her upper lip while still holding her mouth open. When he brought his mouth back to hers. She bit his bottom lip, pulling it with her teeth. He made a low growl and thrusted harder. So, this was Wilhelm then, when he gave up some of his precious control. This was the man underneath the careful exterior. Passionate, intense, and a primitive fury that was powerful and forceful. She was utterly out of her depth, and she didn't care. At this moment, all she wanted was to taste him, feel him, and to let him ravage her in the most savage way possible.

A flash of Jurgen touching her breast lit in her mind, making her flinch, but he didn't seem to notice. She took his hand that was on her jaw and brought it to her left breast, placing his large, hot palm over it. He didn't resist but moved slower, not wanting to orgasm just yet, wanting to prolong this as long as he could. He put more of his body on her, the weight of it pressing her farther into the cushions of the couch. He moved his hand from her breast and brought his lips to her nipple, taking her into his mouth as the stubbles on his face brushed against the soft skin. Then he kissed all around it and trailed his tongue down to her stomach, then to her other breast. He bit the nipple, tugging, then rubbed his lips softly against her, teasing, stimulating, and it was electrifying. But then he pulled back, leaving her raw and wanting.

"Don't stop," she said, breathless.

While still looking at her, he brushed his fingertips against her ever so gently, and every part of her body burned and tingled with a heat that seared through her. He put both hands on the couch, one on each side of her, to hold himself up. The muscles flexed in his arms. She rubbed her left hand up his bicep, feeling the hard muscle pulled tight under the skin from the tension of his weight.

He moved now, with such speed and force that she couldn't help but cry out. His thrusts were hard against her and unrelenting. Her legs and body began to shake, and she grabbed onto his shoulder, digging her nails into it, trying to not scream. He came down hard one last time, splitting her open, and groaned against her neck. She could feel the sweat on his body as he lay on her and the heat radiating from him.

Chapter Twenty-Five

He slumbered beside her on the floor, their legs intertwined as she rested her head on his chest. They had been that way for a few hours, but she was wide awake and couldn't fall asleep. She thought of what they did and smiled. She felt like she couldn't get enough of him. Her body was tired and sore, but she didn't care. She didn't want to sleep. She wanted the pain, the aching that came from the pleasure he gave her. She wanted him in her, his weight on top of her. She wanted to hold him there forever.

Her fingers uncurled, stretching towards him, softly running them down his arm, across his stomach, and to his navel, stopping just as her fingers reached his pubic hair. She wanted to move it down farther and touch him, but she didn't want to wake him. She moved her hand back to his chest and closed her eyes, enjoying his warmth. She would get cold lying naked on the floor if it wasn't for his body heat.

The movement of her head being placed gently on the floor woke her. She opened her eyes and looked up at him, completely naked, standing over her. She admired his handsome form, his powerful, lean body that was wrapped in defined muscles. She smiled up at him, and he tilted his head to the side, looking at her pensively.

"Do you know what I missed most when I was in prison?" She shook her head. "Your pretty smile."

For some reason, this embarrassed her, and she hid her face in her arm.

"I need to get ready for work. You can join me upstairs in the tub if you want."

Her cheeks flushed a dark pink, and she moved her head to look up at him. "How am I supposed to say no to you right now?"

His expression grew carnal. "You could stay here on the floor, but I suspect you want to clean up as well."

She looked down at herself and remembered that she had not cleaned herself off after they made love. Between her legs felt sticky, and it all came rushing back. "You are right. I do want to clean up."

She followed him up the stairs into the bathroom, and he turned the knob, filling the tub with water. She remembered the last time they took a bath together and had expected him to touch her, but he didn't. And she wondered if he would this time. He climbed into the tub first, then she stepped in, sitting between his legs and leaning back against him like before. He took the sponge from the edge, dipped it into the water, and rubbed it over her stomach. He went lower and cleaned the cum from her legs and between them.

She moved her head to the side to look at him, and his whiskers scratched her cheek. "You need a shave." She reached up and rubbed it, feeling the stiff hair under her fingers. "I could shave you," she suggested. He leaned away, looking down at the her with a raised eyebrow. "I shaved you in the hospital, remember?"

"I do."

She grinned and pushed herself up, stepping out of the tub. She went to the medicine cabinet and got his razer, the brush, and the stuff to make the shaving cream. She mixed some in the bowl and brought it back to the tub. She sat it on the edge, then stepped back into the water, facing him this time. She bent her legs and scooted up towards him. She rubbed the white cream on his face, accidentally getting it on his lips.

"Sorry," she laughed and wiped it away.

He glared at her, and she couldn't hold back the smile that pulled at her lips. She took the blade and moved it down on his cheek, a scratching sound coming from it. She moved his head back and forth as she went, and he watched her carefully. When she finished, she inspected her work and then laid the blade on the tub's edge.

"I think I did a good job."

He rubbed his face with his hand and gave her an approving nod. "Not bad." He reached up, put both hands on her hips, and pulled her closer to him, pressing his lips gently but firm against hers, then broke the kiss. "Stand up," he told her. She looked at him questioningly, and he narrowed his eyes at her. "Are you disobeying an order?" he asked in a severe tone, but she knew he was teasing.

"No, sir." She leaned in close to his ear, her voice lowered to a whisper. "I would do anything you want." She pushed herself away from him and stood.

He stared up at her face, then his gaze dropped, and his expression turned carnal. He bent his legs up and had her step back. She did, and he put both of his legs between hers.

He motioned with his index finger. "Come down here."

She lowered herself to her knees in the tub, now straddling him. He rubbed his hands up her thighs, over her hips, and to the curves of her waist. His penis was erect, and he guided her down onto it. She rested her hands on his shoulders and closed her eyes, sucking in a breath as she felt him. He leaned up, bringing his head level with her chest. He pulled down on her hips, and she lowered herself more, then he pulled up on her.

"Like that," he said as he looked up at her, the haze of lust thick in his eyes.

She lifted herself up, then down, and repeated the motion using only her legs. She picked up the pace, and he made a grunt, closed his eyes, and pressed his forehead into her stomach as he gripped her hips tight, his fingers digging into the soft flesh. His breathing increased and became more ragged, as did hers. Then, he let out a throaty groan and flexed his hands on her, so hard it hurt a little. He held her down on him, not letting her rise as tense waves rippled through his body. She rested her head on top of his and breathed hard into his hair.

Finally, she leaned back and looked at him. His face was relaxed, and he looked up at her with a fervent gaze. She could see the affection he had for her in his intense stare, and she had to look away.

He planted a soft kiss on her stomach and gently pushed her back, moving her off him. "I'll get out now. You can stay in and clean yourself up."

He stood and stepped out of the tub, pulled the towel from the hook, and wrapped it around his bottom half. She sat back in the water and watched him. He winked at her, then walked out of the bathroom, closing the door behind him. She scooted down and leaned back, feeling languid. She rested her head against the wall and closed her eyes.

The sound of the bathroom door opening jolted her, and she realized she had fallen asleep. Wilhelm was looking at her from the doorway.

"I'm leaving now, but come back tonight around the same time. There is something I want to talk to you about."

A smile cracked at the corner of her mouth. "OK."

He closed the door, and she heard his boots on the stairs, then the front door closing. The water had gone cold, and the skin on her hands and feet looked like prunes. She got out and pulled the plug, then went to the main floor in a towel to retrieve her clothes. She picked up her dress, then drew in a surprised breath as she stared at the large rip. She had completely forgotten he tore it in his haste to take it off.

"Crap."

The tear was along the side, and she might be able to hide it until she got home. She went back upstairs and dressed, hanging the towel on the wall. She pulled the torn seam closed the best she could, got her purse, and left.

She could hardly contain a smile as she walked home, but it quickly faded. She remembered that he spent a month in prison because of her and was being punished in other ways too. She knew he must be playing it down for her sake. He didn't want her to worry about him, but she did. She couldn't comprehend how quickly things between them had progressed, and it left her reeling. She knew it would happen eventually, but she wasn't prepared for the magnitude of his impact on her. The depth of his emotions and the ferocity of his love. He made her feel safe, and when she was with him, she felt fiercely alive. But in the back of her mind, she could not ignore the nagging feeling that she was using him. For comfort, for protection, to feel loved and wanted. She allowed herself to be with him for all these reasons, and he was happy to give her all of them because he loved her, but was her love for him equal to his love for her?

She pushed the thought from her mind. Now was not the time to question her motives. What was done was done, and there was no going back. In the pit of her stomach, she knew Wilhelm would never let her go. She was what he wanted, and now he had her. Why would he ever give that up?

She went into the apartment and dropped her purse by the door. "Eva, where have you been?" Ingrid came towards her, worry etched on her face. "I was up all night, thinking you would come home."

Eva covered her face with her hand. "I am so sorry. Wilhelm came to the hospital yesterday. He is back in town, and I spent the night with him."

"Why didn't you let me know?"

"Because I didn't know I was going to spend the night with him. I wasn't planning on it."

"Next time, just let me know."

"Again, I'm sorry. I will actually spend tonight with him, too."

A smile broke at the corner of her mouth. "Oh, really?"

Eva sighed. "Look, I can't hide it from you that I am sleeping with him. It is so obvious that is what's happening. But please, don't make a big deal out of it."

Ingrid lifted her hands in front of her. "I'm not."

"I don't even know exactly what it is we have. I believe it when he says he loves me, but I realize there is still a lot about him I don't know."

"What do you want?"

Eva looked at her. "What do you mean?"

"I mean, do you want to be with him?"

"If I didn't, I wouldn't be."

"No, I mean, do you want to be with him permanently?"

Eva eyed her, feeling like Ingrid was trying to get her to divulge information she didn't want to. "I don't know."

"Come on, Eva. You aren't being honest with yourself. If you actually asked yourself that question, you would know the answer."

"Would I?"

"Yes, you would."

Eva narrowed her eyes at Ingrid. "Maybe I don't want to know the answer to that question right now. I think we both need something from each other. I believe I know what I need from him, but what does he need from me?" Eva questioned.

"Maybe you are what he needs?"

"That's ridiculous. He doesn't need me. I don't think he needs anyone. That man does just fine on his own."

Ingrid's face had an odd expression. "What are you going to do now?"

Eva pulled at the side of her dress to look at the tear. "Change and pack a bag for tonight, then go to work."

"How did you tear your dress?" Eva gave her a side glance. "Oh." She smiled.

"I'm going to change now." Eva went to her room and put on her uniform, then packed an outfit for tomorrow and some toiletries.

It was slow at the hospital, and she was glad. She needed some time to think things over. Like, what did he want to talk to her about? Was she prepared to answer whatever it was? She wasn't worried, but it did make her nervous. Ingrid's comment about him needing her kept surfacing. Of course, she often thought about what he was to her, but did she really consider what she was to him? What did he believe or hope would happen between them? Did she ask him or leave it unanswered? She wasn't sure and decided she would see what happened tonight.

After work, she went back to the apartment to get her bag. Ingrid was ironing clothes when she came in. "I'm going to get my bag and go."

"Alright." She stopped ironing and looked up at her. "Can I expect you to be gone a lot, then?"

She pursed her lips and thought about it. "I don't know. But I promise I will let you know if I am." Ingrid gave her a faint smile, and Eva felt bad. Ingrid liked having her there, but she spent so much time with Wilhelm when he was in Dieppe. Even when he wasn't, she still spent a lot of time with him, like going with him to Paris. She came over and wrapped her arms around Ingrid. "I think we should go to the beach tomorrow. What do you think?"

Ingrid didn't smile, but a spark lit in her eyes. "I think we should."

"Then that is what we will do." She gave her one arm a squeeze. "I have to go. I'll see you tomorrow."

She went to the cottage and was going to sit on the steps, but remembered that she was the last one there and didn't have a key to lock it. The knob turned when she tried it, and she pushed the door open. She went inside and put her bag on the floor beside the stairs, then went into the living room and sat on the couch to wait. It was almost nine, and she suspected she wouldn't have to wait long. She leaned back and looked up at the ceiling. What did she want from Wilhelm? Maybe she should have asked herself that question sooner?

While she was lost in thought, the front door opened, snapping her back to the moment. She got off the couch and went out into the hall by the front door. Wilhelm walked through the entryway, kicking the door shut behind him and tossing his hat on the floor by the closet. In two long strides, he was in front of her, then took her by the shoulders and backed her up against the wall, and kissed her. She thought about resisting for only a second, but it felt good to be held and touched.

She gripped his flexed upper arms and let him press her to the wall without any resistance. The heat of his body suffused with hers. She parted her lips, and he needed no other invitation. He tilted her chin up towards him and kissed her deeply. She didn't quite understand what was going on. Why he had this sudden need for her? She did understand, however, that all the times he held back were only for her sake. But after last night, she had given him permission to take her whenever he felt like it.

He pulled away, breathing heavily. "Hi," he said, his voice deep and husky.

She blinked a few times. "Hi."

She could tell he was trying to reign in his emotions. He stepped away from her a fraction, took her hand, and then pulled her into the living room. She wondered if he was going to have her on the floor again, but he sat her down on the couch and went to his usual chair.

"As I've told you, they have taken away half of my leave, but that's fine because I don't use most of it, anyway. However, I still have a couple of weeks of my leave. I thought I would go to Austria or maybe southern Germany for a few days and want you to come with me."

She had gone to Paris with him several times now and Berlin once, but for some reason, this felt different to her. More personal and intimate. Were they moving to another level in their relationship? Every evening they spent together added another link in her chain to him. She reconsidered spending tonight without him. After all, she had not told him she was, and he hadn't asked her to.

"When?" she asked.

"The day after tomorrow."

She looked down at her hands, thinking. "How many days would we be gone?"

"Three or four, probably."

She didn't want to say no, but to her, if she said yes, she would be committing herself to a relationship with him. But would that really be so bad? This went back to what Ingrid had asked her. Did she want to be his? She played with her fingers as she contemplated what to do, what she wanted to do. These thoughts went back and forth in her mind.

"Eva." She lifted her head to look at him. "I didn't think it would be this hard for you to decide."

"I'm just considering all my options."

He raised a brow. "Options?"

"Like work." She looked back down at her hands. "Yes, I will go with you." She brought her head back up to look at him, and his face relaxed, her answer seeming to relieve some tension he was feeling.

"I saw your bag in the hall. Were you planning on spending the night?"

She was embarrassed now. She hadn't even asked before she packed a bag and brought it over. "Well… I—"

"You can stay, Eva."

"I'm sorry. I should have asked you before assuming. Do you want me to stay?"

His expression softened. "Of course I want you to stay."

She gave a shy smile. "Maybe we should actually sleep in a bed tonight."

"That might be hard, with only twin beds in the house."

"Right. I'll sleep in my old room."

"Or we could sleep down here."

She looked around the room, the room they had sex twice in now. "We could. Do you want me to make dinner?" she asked, changing the subject from sleeping arrangements.

He gave her a look she couldn't read. "That would be nice."

She made a simple stew and set two bowls on the table, putting the pot in the middle. He came and stood just in the entryway, watching her.

"I have something for you."

She stiffened, and her heart skipped a beat. She didn't know if she liked the idea of him giving her things.

She cleared her throat. "Oh. You didn't have to do that." She tried hard not to sound upset.

He walked into the kitchen and laid something on the table. She looked down, and beside her bowl was a round, orange tin canister that read Scho-Ka-Kola Die Stärkende Schokolade. She traced her fingers over the top of it. "You brought me chocolate?"

"I thought you would enjoy some. They give this to the Luftwaffe to keep them awake and the U-boat crews and men in the army. It has a lot of caffeine in it, so I wouldn't recommend eating it at night."

"You spoil me." She felt guilty that he did these kinds of things for her. She never did anything like this for him.

"I am happy to."

He gave her a smile, and it tugged at her heartstrings. She needed to repay him for this somehow. It was just chocolate, a trivial thing, really, yet it meant so much. He had done so many things for her already. Like what he sacrificed, and she was indebted to him until she could somehow sacrifice something for him in return. But she could see no end to that obligation.

"Thank you."

"You're welcome."

After they ate, she did the dishes while he made a bed for them on the floor. When she was finished, she went into the living room, but he wasn't there. She walked into the hall and looked up the stairs. She could hear the water running in the bathroom. He was taking a shower, and she wondered why he didn't ask her to join him.

He doesn't have to, she chided herself. She was being overly sensitive, and she knew it.

She went back to the living room and waited for him to finish so she could shower. When he came into the living room, she stood up. He was just in his underwear and undershirt.

"I'm going to go shower."

He lowered himself onto the makeshift bed and laid down, putting his arm under his head as a pillow. "Alright."

She got her bag and went upstairs. She showered quickly, then brought her stuff back down, sitting it in the hall. She turned out the lights, then went to the blankets on the floor and laid down next to him, covering her legs up with the blanket. She scooted closer to him and laid her head on his shoulder. He put his arm around her and held her to him. After a few minutes, she lifted her head and kissed the side of his neck. He didn't move, but she could feel the muscles in his neck and jaw tighten. She planted another kiss on his neck, then ran her lips over his Adam's apple.

He placed his hand on her shoulder to stop her. "Not tonight, Eva."

She blinked in the dark, stunned. He was rejecting her, and she didn't know why. He once again flipped a switch. How was he so good at doing that? She didn't want him to see that it hurt her, so she stayed close to him and laid her head back on his shoulder. She lay awake listening to his slow, steady breaths and the feeling of his chest rising and falling with them. She wished it didn't hurt when he denied her. If she didn't love him, it wouldn't, or at least the sting of rejection would not be as painful.

They took the train instead of his car, and she preferred it. There was room to get up and move around whenever she wanted. Since the night he rejected her on the floor, he treated her as he did before they slept together the second time. Emotionally, she felt utterly cut off from him because he was shutting her out. She didn't know what was going on in his head, and she wished he would talk to her.

"What part of Austria are we going to, and where will we stay when we get there?"

"We are actually not going to be staying in Austria, but in Bavaria. It's called Berchtesgaden, and it's right on the border with Austria."

Why did that name sound familiar to her? She creased her brows, thinking hard. Finally, it came to her, and she remembered why it did. Berchtesgaden was the place the Nazis made their last stand. And Hitler, along with other members of the German high command like Hermann Göring, Joseph Goebbels, Martin Bormann, and Heinrich Himmler, frequented it as well.

"Why are we going there?"

He didn't seem to understand her sudden change in mood. "Because it's a good place to vacation."

"Really? So is that why Hitler goes here?"

His face hardened. "That is a strange question."

"Wilhelm, why did you not tell me the party was for Hitler's birthday?"

"I didn't think it was important. Did it matter what the party was for?"

"Yea, it did. I would not have gone if I had known."

"It was your idea to go." He was angry now.

"Jurgen told me while he had his hand around my throat, before the garden, I mean, that no one would care what he did to me there because of the kind of event it was. That the party was for Hitler and his loyal followers, and I wasn't one of them."

For a long while, he didn't speak, but when it came, it was low and indignant. "For starters, Jurgen did not represent everyone there. And you know, if I could go back and do things differently, I would. What happened to you will be with me for the rest of my life. I understand it is my fault. If I had not decided to go and agreed to let you come or arrived late, none of that would have happened. But I cannot undo what has been done," he said, on the verge of losing his calm composure.

It bothered her that he would defend anyone there, but she couldn't fault him for it, really. In his mind, the Germans were the good guys. And his distress over what happened to her affected her more than his anger did. She suddenly saw what she had failed to see before. She hadn't realized he blamed himself for what happened or that his feelings on the matter were a good deal more complex than she thought. She was always suspicious of him, didn't appreciate nearly enough all the things he had done for her, and felt like she was taking advantage of him. She hated who she had become.

She swallowed hard. "You should not blame yourself for what happened. None of it was your fault. You are right. I was the one who suggested we go."

He took a deep breath and closed his eye, and when he opened them, he was calmer. "Let's not sit here assigning blame."

"I never blamed you for that. But when I kissed you at the cottage, and you were not receptive to me, I wasn't sure you wanted me anymore. And I think that was almost more painful than anything Jurgen could have done to me. The only thing he could hurt was my body, but you can hurt all of me." This was her way of telling him she loved him without actually saying it. She wasn't ready to speak those words to him yet, even though she felt it. The way he looked at her, she could tell he was churning what she said over in his mind.

His eyes bore into her, then finally, he spoke, and his words were gentle. "I would never intentionally hurt you. I want you to know that."

"I do." She believed him. She wanted to believe him. But, if his rejections weren't intended to hurt her, then what was the reason? She never quite had him figured out. "I need to go to the lady's room."

"Sure."

She left the private compartment they were in and walked down the narrow hall of the train car. She went into the bathroom and closed the door, locking it behind her.

After she was finished, she remained in the bathroom for a bit. She sat on the toilet seat and bent down, putting her face in her hands.

"Eva, you are so stupid. Why do you let him get under your skin?"

She hated how he sometimes made her feel. He had so much control over her emotions, and she was angry at herself for wanting him like she did. She couldn't decide if she should wait for him to make the next move or try again. As disgusted as she was with herself, she knew she would let him take her now, in their compartment, if he wanted to.

"Get it together, Eva." She stood up and tapped her hands on her cheeks, then returned to their compartment.

They checked into the Hof Hotel, which was a three-story, white building on the edge of town. The dining area was extensive, furnished with small, round tables, each with four padded chairs. In the middle of the wooden panel ceiling hung two crystal chandeliers.

She was angry when she walked in and saw red flags with swastikas on the hotel's walls. She tried to ignore them and followed Wilhelm to the room after they checked in. It was a small room with a large set of window doors that opened onto a balcony overlooking the mountains. It had a small table in the middle of the room with two chairs, a couch along the wall next to it, and a single bed. She was glad there was a single queen bed and not two twin beds.

She sat her suitcase beside the bed and looked at Wilhelm. "Well, what are we going to do today?"

"I have made plans for us tomorrow, but I thought today we might hike up the mountain and have a picnic."

"I would like that. What's the plan for tomorrow?"

"If I tell you, it won't be a surprise."

"I didn't know it was a surprise." She cracked a smile. "I'm not sure I like surprises."

He smiled back and took off his jacket. He was in civilian clothing, and it looked strange to her not to see him in his uniform. "You'll like this one. Shall we go?"

She creased her brows. "Where is the food?"

"At the front desk. We'll get it on our way out. You will also need to put on better shoes."

She looked down at her feet, at the brown heels she was wearing. She had brought a pair of flat shoes that tied, the kind women used to wear with socks. "I have another pair." She slipped off the heels and went to her bag, retrieving the other shoes and a pair of socks. She sat on the end of the bed and put them on. "I'm ready."

They went to the front, and he collected a small wooden basket and a blanket, handing it to her. She took it from his outstretched hand and followed him out front. They walked around the back of the hotel and started up a narrow dirt path that led into the trees.

They hiked single file in silence for a while, him occasionally taking her hand to help her around some mud, up a hill, or over uneven ground. She, of course, didn't need his help, but he never accepted it when she told him no. The area was beautiful and green. Pine trees were everywhere, and the landscape was covered with flowers, mostly tall white ones she didn't know the name of. The pine trees reminded her of home, with the Wasatch Mountains in the east and north and the Oquirrh Mountains to the west of Salt Lake City, which lay in a valley at the base of them. A lump formed in her throat at the thought, but she tried hard to drive it away.

The ground finally leveled off, and they were now in a large, green meadow. A clearing opened before them, with haphazardly strewn atypical German-style farmhouse in the distance.

"We'll stop and eat here," he said.

She was glad because she was tired. The shoes were hurting her feet; she was thirsty and had to pee. She looked around, realizing she would have to pee in the trees. "I'll be right back. I need to find a place to go to the bathroom."

"You can just turn your back to me," he said mockingly, a smirk on his face.

She glared at him. "I would if it was as easy for me as it is for you."

He let out a little laugh, and she pulled up a handful of grass and tossed it at him. He batted it away with his hand, laughing harder. She turned and walked into the trees, vowing to get him back. When she returned, she saw he had the blanket spread out with the basket sitting beside it on the grass. He was lying on it, turned to his side, holding himself up on one elbow as he looked out across the land. She sat beside him and took the bottle with water, pouring some over her hands to clean them so she could eat. She put the basket on the blanket and opened it, dividing the food between them. It was just a little bit of cold-cut meat, cheese, bread, and some grapes.

She watched him watching her as they ate and wondered why he was staring. She was down to only her grapes now and ate them slowly, enjoying being in the sun. It wasn't hot, but comfortably warm, which was typical of mountain weather.

He looked off into the distance, watching something, and she threw a grape at him, hitting his shirt. When he turned back to her, she looked away, pretending she was watching something off in the distance too. She could feel his eyes on her and almost smiled, giving herself away. He turned his gaze back to the valley, and she tossed another grape, but this time he caught her trying to put her hand down before he saw her.

He narrowed his eyes at her, and she pretended she still knew nothing about it. She bit into a grape, looking at him from under her lashes. She waited a few minutes before throwing another one until he was looking at something other than her. She tossed it quickly, hitting him in the arm.

"That's it." He lunged for her, and she screamed. She managed to get to her feet, but he grabbed hold of her legs and pulled her down. He had her on her stomach, pinning her on the blanket, his full weight on top of her. She couldn't move and breathed heavily from the pressure on her lungs.

He leaned down, putting his lips to her ear. "You knew you were going to start a war when you threw those."

She closed her eyes and bit her bottom lip. She knew exactly what she was doing. "But the war isn't over. You haven't won yet."

He drew in a long breath, then let it out. "But I know who will win." His voice was low and threatening, and she couldn't mistake the desire in it.

"Do you?"

He reached down and tugged up her dress, but didn't let her up, then roughly pulled her underwear off. There was a clink from his suspenders as he undid his pants, then he pushed her legs apart and she sucked in a breath, a rush of warmth hitting between he thighs as a throb pulsed. He entered her from behind and it wasn't gentle. She cried out, but knew this was exactly how it would be, and she wanted him to do it to her.

He leaned back down and spoke in her ear. "No one can hear you scream out here." Then he forcefully thrust into her again, and she buried her face into the blanket, but to her surprise, he stopped, and she felt his weight gone from her.

"Turn over," he commanded.

She did as he said, and he undid the buttons of her dress and pulled it open, then slid it over her arms until it was at her waist. He removed her bra and threw it on the grass. He took his shirt off, leaving just his undershirt on, and tossed it on the grass with her bra and underwear. One of his fingers rubbed across her nipple, then he leaned over and entered her again. He hooked her legs around his, then drove deeper. Her pelvis rose from the blanket as if seeking something, and her breaths grew short and ragged. He brushed his lips across her breasts, taking one into his mouth; he was frantic now. She pressed him hard against her. It was strange to have someone already in your arms, to be so close to them and still be yearning for them. She kissed his shoulder and could taste him, salty in her mouth. She felt her wetness slipping on his skin as he moved in her.

While he had one nipple in his mouth, he cradled her other breast in his hand. It was velvet on the calloused skin of his palm. He drove into her hard, again and again, then all his muscles tightened, his body tensing as he came. A deep groan escaped his lips, and he pushed into her twice more before letting his body relax on top of her.

He lay there for a minute, breathing heavily before rising. Her whole body felt weak, and she looked up at him. He got back down on the blanket and rubbed her hips and between her thighs, then he leaned down and put his head between her legs, gentle at first. His whiskers were rough on the inside of her thighs. He placed his hands on her hips, and it didn't take long for her body to start shaking and the intensity of it to rise under his emphatic skill. She put one hand on the top of his head and reached out with her other, gripping the blanket.

She arched her back, and moaned. "Oh my God," she cried out, her eyes screwed shut, her mouth open. Quickly, she released the blanket, bringing her hand to her mouth, clasping it over it, suppressing another cry. Her body quivered several times and then went limp. She felt all her energy had left her, and she laid placidly on the blanket. She was drowsy, and her eyelids felt heavy.

He was over her now, then leaned down and kissed the tip of her nose. "I think I won." A triumphant note in his voice as he whispered in her ear.

"I think you did." But she smiled, knowing she had really won.

Chapter Twenty-Six

The sound of whistling chirps from birds outside the open window pulled her from a light sleep. She rolled onto her back and put her hand on the other side of the bed, but it was empty. For most of last night, she was cuddled against him. Their bodies merged and wrapped around each other. She had her head on his chest, and a leg draped over him.

She leaned up on her elbows and looked around the room. But he wasn't there, but she did see a tray of food on the table. She threw the blanket off and slid off the bed. She looked down at the tray, and beside it was a folded piece of paper. She picked it up and unfurled it.

Eva,

I will be back soon. I am at the place I will take you to later today. Try to be ready soon.

Wilhelm

She laid the note on the table and smiled. She sat in one of the chairs and ate a simple breakfast of eggs, cheese, and fruit. There was a cup of real coffee beside the plate, and it did not surprise her he got it. She sipped the delicious black liquid and closed her eyes, smiling.

After eating, she went to her bag, got out a fresh dress, brushed her teeth, and changed. She got out a pair of socks, deciding to wear the same shoes she hiked in yesterday. While putting up her hair, she heard the door close, and hurried and stuck the last pin in, then stepped out of the bathroom.

"Where did you go?"

"I left a note," he said, pointing to the table.

"I read it. What place did you go to?" He only smiled and went to the couch. "You should have taken me with you."

"You looked so peaceful laying there I didn't want to. I almost woke you by accident trying to move you off me, though. You rolled, opening your eyes briefly, and I waited, but then you closed them again and didn't move."

She rubbed her hands over the skirt of her dress and looked down at her shoes. "I'm ready."

"Alright," he said and stood up.

She followed him down to the lobby, then outside, and walked beside him down the narrow stone road. "How far is it?"

"Not far."

He wasn't going to give away anything. At the end of the paved road was a dirt road, and he started down it. "It's out here?" She had no idea what he was taking her to do.

"Yes."

The dirt road wasn't long, and at the end stood a large, sun-bleached brown barn, and beside it were two saddled horses tied to a log. She halted and looked at the animals. He stopped, too, and glanced back at her. She felt excitement rise inside. She loved horses and used to take riding lessons with her brother when they were kids. She remembered now him mentioning that he enjoyed riding horses.

He watched her staring at the animals but not moving any closer. "Can you ride?"

"A little. I used to take lessons as a child."

"Come on, I'll help you."

She went to the side of the white horse and Wilhelm gave her a leg up and she met his gaze from where she sat, the reigns in her hands. He untied the lead of her horse and wrapped it around the saddle horn. Then went over and untied the brown horse beside hers and did the same, then mounted it. He turned the horse around and waited for her to follow. Her horse seemed happy to trail along beside his with no prodding.

They rode through the valley they picnicked in the day before, then into the forest. He made sure to check on her often.

"Are you alright?" he called back.

"Yes. I forgot how much fun it was. But my butt and legs are going to feel it later." She gave a sheepish laugh.

"Do you need to take a break and get off for a while?"

"No. Let's keep going." He never rode his horse fast, not even to a trot, and she was glad.

They circled around and rode back towards the barn, and walked the horses up to the horizontal log. He swung his right leg over the top of the saddle and stepped down.

"Wait, and I'll help you off."

"I think I can manage." He tied up his horse and came around to the side of hers, just in case. Her legs felt shaky, but she got down without falling. "Ow." She put a hand on her butt.

He chuckled. "The walk back will help." He tied her horse up, then came to her side and took her hand, and they started back to the hotel.

She looked down at their joined hands and remembered what he told Jurgen before he beat him, that she was his and Jurgen made a mistake in trying to take something that belonged to him. She knew he believed what he said, that she was his. And for all intents and purposes, she was. Although she wasn't sure he would have said it out loud if he wasn't in the heat of the moment.

"Tomorrow, we will head back."

"I thought we were staying for three days?"

"No. I have to be back in Paris the day after tomorrow. It is out of my hands."

"Alright." She would have liked to stay one more day with him, but she knew he could not say no to orders or things that were pressing and needed his attention.

They spent the rest of the day walking around the town and looking in the shops. She lit a candle in the church as he waited outside for her, then they ate dinner in the hotel restaurant and returned to their room. She was sitting on the edge of the bed, thinking about the fact that he was going to be in Paris and she was going to be in Dieppe. She still wanted to chastise herself for caring, but she couldn't bring herself to. He had her on her knees, and she suspected he knew it.

The bedframe creaked, and the mattress sank as Wilhelm sat next to her. She didn't look at him, and he stayed within his restraints. But finally, his arm came around her, warm and strong, and she melted into him, the same way her body had been responding to him as of late. In her mind, she wanted to be strong and say no, but she didn't. Instead, she leaned into him, seeking his heat. She felt him tugging her down, laying her gently on the bed, then he tucked himself behind her. She would love to forget about the war and all the complications in her life right now, except for Wilhelm, he was a complication she wanted.

She woke up in the middle of the night, and at some point, he must have covered her up because there was a blanket between them. Only she was under the blanket, but she could still feel his body against hers, and she liked the pressure; it felt good against hers. While she stared into the dark room, she told herself that she needed to get used to him not always being around. She had gotten too used to having him near her, to his touch and affection. She liked his attention, but it was just an illusion. She knew having this with him was wrong, but what happened in the last two years changed her. She could no longer convince herself she hated him because she kept going back to him and it made her happy. She always felt something intense when they were together, and her only explanation for it was love. Lately she only thought of him, not Gerhardt. Every time she wanted to be touched, was turned on, or alone in the dark.

She lied for so long, telling herself it wasn't and that he didn't really love her. But in the garden, she saw the true monster inside him, one that he fought every day for her. And how could that be anything but love? She wanted to ask if she could stay with him tomorrow night at the cottage, knowing he would leave for Paris the day after, but she grappled with whether or not she should. She closed her eyes and drifted into a peaceful sleep.

June 24th, 1942

Wilhelm had been in Paris almost four weeks, but he had been sending her letters to let her know he was alright and some of what he had been doing. However, he didn't tell her when he would be returning to Dieppe because he didn't know.

It was her day off, and she was spending it at the beach with Ingrid. They had come several times in the last few weeks. The weather had been exceptional, and she wanted to get out of the house. She had caught a cold the week before, which kept her inside for several days. She still wasn't entirely over it, but she was tired of being inside. Mostly it was a lingering sinus pressure that caused her frequent headaches and an upset stomach.

They had found a spot with smaller rocks, and each brought three towels. Two were used to lie on, and the other one was to dry off with. Eva had just gotten out of the water and was lying beside Ingrid. Her eyes were closed, and she had her sunglasses on, listening the seagulls squawk overhead. Her skin felt so warm from the sun, and it was making her tired. She was having a hard time staying awake.

Her stomach growled, and she lifted her head, looking at Ingrid. "I'm going to have some chocolate; do you want some?" They brought a small basket, and she had put the chocolate Wilhelm gave her in with the food. It had been so long since she'd eaten chocolate that she craved it all the time now, but she ate it sparingly, trying to make it last. She pretended like she didn't want any more when this one was gone, but she did. She wanted it a lot. Although she didn't dare ask him for any more favors.

Ingrid sat up with a smile on her face. She also loved the chocolate and couldn't believe Eva wasn't asking for more. "Of course," she said matter-of-factly.

Eva opened the canister and held it out to Ingrid. She took a piece, then Eva sat it on her lap and got a piece for herself. She bit into it and her mouth watered. They watched the waves come in as they ate, and she realized the chocolate was only making her hungrier. She finished her piece and got one of the sandwiches they had brought. "Want one?" She held one out to Ingrid.

"No, thanks."

Should we go back after I eat? I didn't sleep well last night, and I am having a hard time staying awake."

"We can. You must not sleep well a lot of nights. The other day you feel asleep while sitting up in the middle of the day. I was talking to you and stopped for five minutes, and when I turned back you were already sleeping."

"I'm sorry. I have been struggling to sleep normally at night lately." Eva looked down at her pink skin. "Besides, I'm getting burned." She wished sunscreen was as easily accessible in the 1940s as it was in her time.

She finished her sandwich, then they picked up their things and walked back to the apartment. She took a shower, and told Ingrid she was going to take a nap. She lay down, feeling oddly cool, considering her skin was so hot. She pulled the blanket over her and fell asleep.

There were low, muffled voices coming from the living room. One from a man and one from a woman. Eva blinked a few times, trying to wake up. It was dark in her room, and she was a little confused by it because she thought she had only been sleeping for maybe an hour. She sat up, feeling the pressure in her forehead and under her eyes. She moved the blanket aside and swung her feet over the edge of the bed. She listened but couldn't quite make out who was talking or what they were saying. She went to the door and cracked it open, peeking through it.

Her eyes grew wide. Wilhelm was standing near the door but had not taken his cap off. It looked like he hadn't been here long. He hadn't mentioned he was coming in any of his letters. She watched them for a few seconds, then he said something to Ingrid and gave a perfunctory nod. He turned to the door and put his hand on the knob, and the sudden fear that he was going to leave rushed in. She pulled the door open all the way and practically ran to the living room.

"Wilhelm."

His hand paused on the knob, and he turned to look at her. His expression was grim, and it fixed her in place. She knew instantly something was wrong. Her eyes scanned him, but nothing seemed to be amiss. He let go of the handle and shot a quick glance at Ingrid before crossing the floor and coming to stand in front of her. She looked up at him, waiting for whatever it was that had him looking so somber. The seconds that passed between them were killing her.

"She put her hand on his arm. "Wilhelm, what is it?" Her voice was urgent.

"Why don't we go into your room? We can talk in there." He removed his cap and laid it on the back of the couch.

She looked past him at Ingrid, but she shook her head, indicating she didn't know what was happening.

"Alright."

He followed her into her room and shut the door. She turned to face him, and he came to stand in front of her, sitting her down on the bed. He put his hand in his pocket and pulled out a yellow slip of paper. He held it out to her, his eyes boring into her, but he didn't say anything. She looked at the piece of paper in his hand, feeling apprehensive. Slowly, she reached out and took it from him. She unfolded it, and her breath caught in her throat when she saw the bold, black writing at the top that read **Telegram**. There were only a few lines typed on it. Under the bold letters at the top was an address in Berlin, a time, and a date, which was June 14th, 1942. Then there was another address for Berlin above Gerhardt's parents' names.

The Secretary of War desires me to express his deep regret that your son, First Lieutenant Gerhardt Schulz, has been reported missing in action since twenty May, 1942 in Russia. If further details or other information are received, you will be promptly notified.

Underneath the lines in the right corner was an officer's name and rank and the time it was written. She could hardly breathe and had lost the feeling in her hand, dropping the paper to the floor. Wilhelm bent down beside her and picked it up, putting it back in his pocket. He took her hands in his and looked at her, waiting for her to tell him what she needed. She drew in a long, shuttering breath and could no longer hold back the tears. They ran down her face in streams dripping onto her legs. He didn't move to do anything other than hold her hands. She didn't understand how this could happen to Gerhardt. He was not an infantry soldier. She looked into Wilhelm's eyes and pleaded for him to tell her this wasn't true, that Gerhardt wasn't missing in action, but his eyes confirmed it was true. After several tries, she gained some control over her sobbing and steadied her breaths enough to speak.

"How? He isn't an infantry soldier?"

"I don't know. The frontline is dangerous for everyone, no matter your job or position."

"But it said he was missing in action, not dead." She squeezed his hand harder. "Maybe he is still alive?"

"He might be. I wish I could tell you he was, but I only know what the telegram said," he tells her soothingly.

"I think I'm going to be sick."

She bolted from the bed and ran to the bathroom, dropping to her knees in front of the toilet, but couldn't hold it in long enough to lift the lid, and some got on it and the floor. She felt someone pulling the hair from around her face, holding it behind her head as she vomited.

She heaved a second time into the toilet, then sat down on her feet. She sniffed and wiped her mouth with some toilet paper. Wilhelm was kneeling beside her. He was the one holding her hair. Her eyes filled with tears again, and her skin felt hot and clammy. She flushed the toilet and he helped her stand, then she went to the sink. She washed her hands and rinsed out her mouth, then got the cleaner that was on the floor under the sink.

He reached for the bottle and took it from her. "I'll clean it up. Go lay down."

His words were kind but had an undercurrent of severeness. She turned from him, walked to her room, and lay down, curling into a ball. Her head was spinning and hurt so bad. Her stomach cramped, and she felt like she might vomit again if she moved. He walked into the room and looked at her on the bed. She waited for him to say something or move closer, but he didn't.

"Would you lay with me?"

He sat on the bed and scooted next to her, and she leaned into him, putting her head on his chest. He wrapped her tight in his arms, and she cried into his jacket.

She dozed but jerked herself awake when she took a shuttering breath in her sleep. She had only been out for a couple of minutes and looked around, a little disoriented. Then she let herself drift back into sleep, feeling completely exhausted. She woke several more times through the night, feeling he was still in bed with her, holding her in his arms. They were both under the blanket now, and she felt warm and loved. She scooted her body as close to his as she could and gripped onto his shirt, holding on to him for dear life.

Her eyes slowly fluttered open, and she was looking at her hand resting on the bed near her face. Realizing that she didn't see Wilhelm, she frantically rolled onto her back and sat up. He was still on the bed beside her. He had his head on the pillow, but his eyes were open, looking at her. A sense of relief calmed her at the sight of him. She laid back down and curled up against him. He felt so inviting, and she wanted him to drown out the anguish inside, the ache in her heart. She knew it wasn't fair to ask him to help her forget another man or comfort her until she did, but she didn't think she could do this without him. She loved him too, and he was the one with her now. Gerhardt chose someone else, and Wilhelm chose her.

"I can only stay for a day before I have to go back to Paris. We should stay at the cottage while I'm here. It will be easier."

"We can." Her stomach rumbled, and she realized how hungry she was. She sat up and looked at him. "Why don't I make us some food, then we can go to the cottage?"

He pulled himself up and leaned against the wall. "Why don't I make the food so you can pack a bag?"

She remembered the last time he tried to make their food and how bad it tasted. She considered telling him no but didn't want to sound ungrateful. She gave a slight smile. "Sure."

She packed a bag then went into the kitchen and sat at the small table across from him. He made scrambled eggs this time instead of fried. She was glad because these tasted a lot better. She didn't think her stomach could handle his fried ones right now.

After breakfast, they went to the cottage, and Wilhelm had his orderly bring some food for them. She slept a lot of the day, and he built a small fire in the fireplace for her while she lay on the couch, covered with a blanket. She tried not to dwell on the strong emotions, and how she felt like a shell of herself. It was like a part of her had died.

Wilhelm sat in the chair he usually did, reading some papers with the lamp on. The sun was low on the horizon now, and it was dark in the cottage. She watched him from the couch, thinking how she didn't deserve him and how she wanted to get her mind off Gerhardt.

"What have you been doing in Paris?"

He laid the papers in his lap. "Mostly just work, which you know I can't talk about. But for the first time since they have stationed me in France, I went up in the Eiffel Tower."

"How come you never went up before now?"

"I never really had time. But I was having lunch with some other officers, and one suggested we go to the top. I figured, why not?"

The opera house, the city of Paris, everything about it tore her up inside. Every time someone talked about Paris, it would remind her of Gerhardt. She looked from him and stared into the fire, watching the flames lick the bricks.

"I am so sick of this war. What have they ever solved? Wars are an atrocity, and people feel it gives them the right to commit heinous, unspeakable acts. It is a waste of men's lives. Some aren't even that, so many of them are no more than boys." She thought about how many young men came into the hospital every day when she worked in Berlin and on the front.

He laid the paper in his lap. "Do you love your country?"

She turned her head on the pillow towards him. "Of course."

"And do you want it to stay as it is, free of foreign control?"

"Yes, of course."

"But you criticize your own countrymen, the very soldiers who fight for it?"

"No, I don't blame them for what they do. But too many men, whether they are leaders or soldiers, seem to love war. I'm not sure they would know what to do with peace.

"Lots of American men have perished, so your country can stay free. They have died, so you have a safe place to return home to. Maybe you shouldn't judge them so harshly. Perhaps they deserve your forgiveness for the so-called heinous, unspeakable acts you accuse them of instead of the resentment you feel towards them."

"I think you misunderstand me. I feel nothing but gratitude and respect for what they do. But it doesn't make it any less awful. No matter the reasons behind why they fight, people will always have to die. And that is a tragedy. Gerhardt is probably dead, and you could be next. When does it end?"

He studied her, something intense in his eyes she couldn't read. "It doesn't."

That wasn't the answer she had hoped to hear. She wanted him to say that he would be safe through the entire war and alive and well at the end. But how could he? He was a soldier of Germany, and she knew that meant he was at a higher risk of dying or being imprisoned than American soldiers.

"I know that I am a spectator and not directly involved in this war, but that is how I see it from my side."

"I know other people just like you, and I have heard their reasons before as well. You wonder why people fight, why sometimes wars must be waged. And you think men like me enjoy bloodshed and warfare, that we live to fight. I could sit here and try to convince you otherwise. That there is more to us than the need for violence and domination, but in all honesty, I can't. Sure, I could speak the words, but you would never understand, so why would I try?"

"Because you don't know if I'll understand, you have never given me a chance."

"Alright." He leaned forward, putting his elbows on his knees. "You said that wars were pointless and solved nothing, but that's not true. Germany needed saving. We were a nation in turmoil, and our identity shaken after the loss of the first war. But we are finally united under one symbol, under one man. He promised us what we needed the most. Low and order, a sense of purpose, stability, and most importantly, belief in ourselves, and he has given us that. And where you are an American, I know you won't agree with that or understand it, how could you. Besides, your opinion on the matter is unimportant. It's the opinion of the Germans that count."

She knew he was right, but his blanket disregard for her opinion and the intentional separation of them upset her. She felt like he always saw her on the other side, looking across at one another. There was him, and then there was her. He was a German, her an American, him male, her female, him a soldier, her a civilian. All three of these things served as a wall between them. He thought because she was American, she didn't understand the plight of the Germans and that because she was a civilian and a woman, she didn't understand the ins and outs of war.

She sat up. "You are right, I don't agree. I'm going to go take a bath." She hoped he got the hint that she wanted to be alone. She went upstairs and filled the tub, took off her clothes, and sank into the warm water. She hated being angry with him, but he always did this. He always pushed people away. He was the one that always kept them at arm's length, not her. Yes, they had slept together several times now, but that was only physical. And he was there for her when she needed him, but there was a part of him that was always closed off to her. A piece of his soul that he kept locked away, even from her, and it hurt.

She closed her eyes, exhaustion sweeping through her. She was just getting over a cold, and now the emotional agony over Gerhardt was killing her inside. She didn't have the energy for this.

After a long while, she drained the water and went back downstairs. On the table, Wilhelm had sat out some of the food his orderly had brought over. It looked like he had already eaten, and she didn't see him in the house and wondered where he had gone. She put some food on her plate and quickly ate, then filled it again and went to the living room. She would sit on the couch and eat it while enjoying the fire. It wasn't cold outside at night anymore and was already warm for late June, but it still felt nice.

The back door closed, and footsteps echoed on the kitchen tile. Then Wilhelm appeared in the living room doorway. He eyed her for a moment before coming to sit beside her on the couch.

"If I upset you, I'm sorry. Maybe we shouldn't talk about such things."

"It's alright. But for now, maybe it's better if we don't." She picked at her food, and the silence between them grew weighted. She cleared her throat. "How is your mom doing?"

"She is well."

"She is not feeling unwell anymore, then?"

"No."

"I bet she misses you a lot."

"She would like it if I was home more, yes."

"I'm sure she wishes she had something to divert her time." She was trying to keep the small talk going.

"I suppose," he said, becoming more suspicious of her questions.

She wondered if his mom knew about him and her or if he still hadn't told her. His mom no doubt wanted him to date a German woman, one that he would marry and have kids with.

"Your mom told me she would love to have grandchildren someday." She held her breath, waiting to see what he would say about that.

"I'm sure she would." He said each word slowly and deliberately. "But that's not going to happen."

She wanted clarification. "Why is that? I'm sure there are plenty of pretty, sweet German girls who you could marry now or after the war that your mom would like."

He narrowed his eyes at her. "Why are we talking about this?"

"I was just remembering my conversation about it with your mom. But you didn't answer my question. Why would it not happen?" She took another bit of her food, pulling the fork out slowly.

"Eva, oh Eva. Because I don't know what the war will develop into or if I would still be able to care for a wife by the end of it. I might be dead, in a camp somewhere, or Germany could be worse off in its stability than it had been before the war, and there would be no work for me. Having to worry about my mother is enough, but you add a wife to that, and it makes things a lot harder. Everything from that point would be more profound, the stakes would be higher, and any failure more painful. My life would be less certain. And I am not even talking about a child, just a wife. That is why I don't want to bring a baby into this uncertain time we find ourselves living in. I'm not sure I even want to have children."

Everything he said made perfect sense to her but sounded so sad. "That is a lonely life. That would be hard for me to do. To have no plans for a future of any sort."

"I can't afford to. If it was during a time of peace, I would consider it, but that's not a luxury I have now."

"You do not have the same opinion as other…" she paused, "Nazis then. The more German babies born, the better."

He looked appalled. "I do not, at least not me being one to help supply Germany with babies."

"I'm sure your mom knows your reasons and understands."

"She does."

"Why are you not sure you ever want children?"

"For reasons of my own."

She understood that door was now closed, and he would not reopen it.

Chapter Twenty-Seven

July 10th, 1942

When Wilhelm returned to Paris, she had asked to go with him, but he told her he would be gone long hours and couldn't spend time with her. He assured her that he would come and visit.

"Ingrid, hurry, or we are going to be late." They were headed to a gathering at another doctor's house. The doctor and his wife were kind enough to invite her, Ingrid, and Dr. Möller as well. He wasn't as hostile towards the Germans as some French people were.

"I'm done." Ingrid came out of the bathroom, putting her lipstick in her purse.

"Klaus said to meet him at the hospital, and we could all go together in his car. I guess they live on the edge of town. I'm sure he is already waiting for us." She glowered at Ingrid, then opened the apartment door.

"I'm sorry. I haven't been out in a long time and wanted to look pretty."

"You always look pretty."

"Well, I can improve on that. You look nice tonight."

"Thanks. If only I felt as good as I look. Ever since I got sick and then… well, I haven't been myself." She never said Gerhardt's name out loud anymore if she could help it.

"It will get better someday, Eva, I promise. But what about SS Obersturmbannführer Bauer? Are you and he still…?"

"Honestly, I don't know what we are. He continues to hold me at a distance. I can never completely close the gap between us."

"If you could, would you?"

She bit her lip, thinking. "Yea, I think I would. If only he would let me."

"Maybe you should tell him that."

Eva let out a long breathy laugh. "It wouldn't do any good."

They walked across the street to the hospital, and Klaus was waiting out front, pacing by his car. "I told you," Eva said, leaning into Ingrid.

"Sorry."

"There you are, ladies." He opened the back door for them, and once they were in, he climbed into the front seat with his driver. The car pulled away from the curb wasting no time, and made its way out of town. When the faint lights of the city were almost gone, they turned down a narrow, unlit dirt road. The car bounced around, and it made Eva feel sick. She closed her eyes, trying not to vomit on the floor.

"Are you alright?" Ingrid asked in a low voice.

"I guess I don't always do well in the back seat of a car, especially one that is bouncing around this much." Ingrid rubbed her arm to try to help in some way.

Finally, the driver pulled off on the side of the road in front of a house. It was a single-story house with a wooden fence separating it from the road. Even though it was only one floor, it was still a rather large house. Klaus opened the door for them, and Eva was happy to be out of the car.

When they got close to the house, she could hear laughing coming from inside. Klaus pulled the doorbell, and after a few seconds, a woman opened it. She still had a smile on her face as she stood in front of them.

"You must be Dr. Möller. Please, come in." Klaus removed his cap, and she led them into a large living room already full of people. "I'll take that for you." She held her hand out for his hat. He gave it to her, and she disappeared from the room.

"Klaus," Dr. Tremblay, who also worked at the hospital, called from across the room. "Come in here. Let's see if you can do any better." Klaus went to Dr. Tremblay's side and patted him on the shoulder.

"What are we playing?"

"Well, in this game, you have to balance a matchbox on your nose and pass it to the other person, but only using your nose, and if you drop it, you lose."

"Sounds intense," Klaus laughed. He motioned for Eva and Ingrid to join him. Eva always thought parlor games were funny. She and Ingrid came to stand beside Klaus, and one of the women in the room brought a matchbox.

"We will start with you," she told Ingrid. "We play in teams. The first two players on the team kneel opposite each other, with the matchbox between them. At your signal, the first player maneuvers the matchbox onto their nose then passes it to the next player's nose and moves out of the way. She will be on your team," she pointed to Eva, "along with him," she pointed to a man in the room Eva didn't recognize, "and her, and her," she said, pointing to two other women in the room." Eva and Ingrid got on their knees, and the woman laid the matchbox on the floor between them.

"You start," Eva said to Ingrid.

Ingrid picked up the box and balanced it carefully on her nose, almost dropping it as she tried to hold back a laugh. Eva lowered herself to Ingrid's level and lifted her head slightly, putting her face close. Ingrid held her breath and touched the tip of her nose to Eva's, then lowered her head. The matchbox fell, tipping onto the bridge of Eva's nose, and Ingrid pulled away and stood up. Eva managed to pass it to one of the women on her team, but the woman dropped it, passing it to the man.

This went on for a while, and Eva watched from the couch, smiling at the silliness of the whole thing. But she was happy to have a distraction. After the parlor games were over, they all ate finger food and then listened to music, some people dancing to it. They passed around alcohol, and Eva took a glass of wine, then, after finishing it, had a couple of schnapps with Ingrid and Klaus.

"Come and dance with me." She held her hand out to Klaus. He didn't get up, and she raised an eyebrow at him.

"Alright." He sat down his drink and took her hand. They went to the middle of the room, and faced one another.

The volume on the record player was turned up loud, and as they moved, Eva had the sensation that the room was spinning, even though she wasn't being spun around. With every passing second, her dizziness got worse. She abruptly stopped dancing and stared at the wall, panting. Her eyesight began to fade quickly, and then felt herself being caught by someone right before everything went black.

She opened her eyes and blinked several times. She turned her head and saw Ingrid and Klaus standing over her, and then she noticed other people in the room were also gathered around the couch. She tried to sit up, but Klaus put a hand on her shoulder.

"No, stay lying down."

"I think I had too much alcohol," she said, placing her hand on her clammy forehead.

"How much did you drink?"

"A glass of wine and the two shots of schnapps with you and Ingrid."

He pursed his lips. "That should not have made you pass out, but maybe you didn't have enough to eat and drank it on an empty stomach. Come on, let's get you to the car, and I'll take you home. You can get some rest, and I'll come by tomorrow."

Eva's head was still spinning as they drove back to Dieppe. She felt strange and was regretting drinking. She had her head on the window, going in and out of sleep.

When they go to the apartment, Klaus helped her upstairs and told her he would be by in the morning. Ingrid sat beside her on the couch once Klaus was gone.

"That was scary. You started falling, and Klaus caught you and carried you to the couch."

"I don't know why the alcohol affected me like that. It never has before, even at times when I drank more." She was puzzled.

"Maybe it's because of the cold you had?"

Eva's face tensed. Events were running through her head. She quickly stood up, pacing the length of the couch. "No," she said.

Ingrid stood up too. "No, what?" Eva paced some more, her hands on her hips, then she stopped. "Eva, what is it?"

"I… um…." She didn't know how to say it. She tried again. "I just now realized I haven't had my period in over a month. I have felt sick to my stomach for weeks. I'm tired all the time and hungrier than what is normal for me." She put her face in her hands. "It makes sense now."

Ingrid looked at her, comprehension registering on her face. "Eva, are you—"

Eva cut her off. "Yes, Ingrid, I think I'm pregnant."

Ingrid took her arm and pulled her down onto the couch. "But you said he used protection."

"Yes, the first time, not any of the other times. Oh my God, how did I not think this would happen? I was so caught up in the moment, so caught up in him." She groaned and covered her face again.

"Do you think he knows?"

Eva looked at her. "How could he? I only realized it now, and I am the one who is pregnant. It's not like I'm showing yet."

"Are you going to tell him?"

Eva leaned back on the couch. "I don't know. It doesn't even seem real yet. And I'm not a hundred percent sure I am pregnant, although now that I think about it, there have been all these signs. Me fainting tonight is just another one. I didn't have enough alcohol to do that."

"Do you think you will tell him later, then?"

"He doesn't want kids, Ingrid. He told me the last time he was in Dieppe. And I don't think I want to be a single parent."

"You should ask Klaus tomorrow. Maybe he can confirm if you are."

"I'm fairly certain I am, and I don't know if I want to tell Klaus. Besides, there is no accurate way to tell if a woman is pregnant. I will be the best judge of that because it is happening to me. Maybe I will go to Paris and see what happens. I can probe and see if he would be happy about it without directly telling him. Depending on how he reacts to what I do or say will determine if I tell him."

"You told me when I was pregnant that you thought the father has a right to know. Does that not apply to you too?"

She was going to have to eat her own words. "Yes, but I need some time. I at least want to see how he might take it. Like I told you, he doesn't want kids."

"Maybe that is because he doesn't know he is going to have one and would think differently if he did."

"Maybe, but I want to see him first."

Ingrid smiled at her. "I can't believe you are having a baby."

"But I shouldn't be. If I had never slept with him, this would not have happened. I'm going to go to bed and pretend this is a bad dream."

She said goodnight to Ingrid and went to her room. She lay on her bed, her mind racing. How could she have been so stupid? She is a nurse and a woman. She knew better. When he touches her and kisses her, all reason is gone. The pleasure he gave her pushed logic right out the window. She was afraid of her life now. What would he think if she told him, and would she be trapped in Germany forever because of it? And what about her own time? She was screwed.

She woke to Ingrid shaking her shoulder. "Eva, wake up. Klaus is here to check on you."

Eva sat up in bed. "He can't know, Ingrid."

"We won't tell him. But what if he knows without us even telling him anything?"

"Then he'll know." She threw the blankets off and got out of bed. She went to the bathroom first, then to the living room, and sat on the couch next to Klaus.

"How do you feel this morning?"

"Fine." She was lying. Her head hurt; she was nauseous, hungry, and still lightheaded. "I think it was just the alcohol on an empty stomach."

"It could be, but let's check you."

She suddenly was worried. "No, I don't think that's necessary. If I feel faint or unwell in the next few days, I'll let you know."

He eyed her suspiciously and pushed the glasses up on his nose with his index finger. "I don't think you are alright, Eva."

"The alcohol has worn off now, and I'm a lot better."

"I don't think it was the alcohol," was all he said. He stood from the couch. "If you feel at all unwell, let me know."

She smiled up at him. "I will." She loved this man, but she couldn't tell him. He thought of her as a father did but despised the man whose baby she was carrying. She stood and wrapped her arms around his large frame.

"Thank you for coming by to check on me."

He put a hand on her head and held her to his chest. "Just let me know if it gets worse?"

"I promise."

When he left, she sat back down on the couch and looked at Ingrid. "I can't believe I just lied to him."

"I think he suspects something. He just doesn't know what yet."

"I think you are right. What do you say about going to Paris with me?"

Her entire demeanor changed. "Really?"

"Yes, really."

She ran to the couch and sat next to Eva. "You would take me to Paris with you?"

Eva looked at her, wondering why it seemed so hard for her to believe. "Of course, I would. Paris is always a good idea, especially when you need to escape. I'm going to call him in Paris and ask if he will give us a pass, and if we can come. I must admit, I really want to see him. He's always in my thoughts, and I miss him a lot. It's almost painful, but I have to bear it every day."

Ingrid rubbed the hair on the side of Eva's head. "Go and call."

Eva patted her hand, then went to the phone in the kitchen. She dialed the operator, and when she picked up, she asked to speak with SS Obersturmbannführer Bauer at 84 Avenue Foch in the 16th arrondissement. The woman asked who was calling, and Eva gave her name. She told Eva to wait, then put her on hold. To Eva's surprise, she heard a man's voice on the other line, but it wasn't Wilhelm.

"Who is this?"

For some reason, Eva's pulse spiked. "Eva Abrams. I am calling for SS Obersturmbannführer Bauer."

"He is out of the office. I am his adjutant. You can leave a message with me if you want."

"Oh, um…" she looked at Ingrid for a second. "Can you just tell him I called and have him call me back?" She gave him her address and phone number.

"I will pass it on," was all he said, then hung up the phone.

She held the phone in her hand for a second before finally placing it back on the wall. "What happened?" Ingrid asked.

Eva shook her head. "Nothing, he was just in a meeting. The man on the phone said he would have him call me back."

"That's good. Do you want some breakfast?"

"I probably should eat. The nausea is always worse on an empty stomach."

Ingrid went into the kitchen to make food, and Eva lay on the couch. Now that she was aware she might be pregnant, she noticed everything that pointed to the fact that she was and wondered why she hadn't realized it sooner. She closed her eyes and dozed, but the loud ringing of the phone made her jump. It had startled her, and her heart was pounding, trying to beat out of her chest. She hopped off the couch, went to the phone, and picked up the receiver.

"Hello," she said in a breathless voice.

"Eva," Wilhelm's voice came from the other end. "They told me you called. Is everything alright?"

She swallowed hard. "It is, but I was hoping I could get a pass to go to Paris. Ingrid wants to come with me." She now realized how silly it was to have bothered him at work for this. There was silence on the other end for a while, and she wondered if they somehow got disconnected. "Hello," she said again into the receiver.

"I'm still here."

She covered her eyes with her hand. "I'm sorry I bothered you at work. Don't worry about it."

"It's not that I don't want you to come. It's just that a lot is happening right now. I wouldn't want you to feel lonely because I was always gone."

"I won't be alone. Ingrid would be with me." She could feel his hesitation over the phone.

"I will give you and Ingrid a pass for a few days, but no more. I'll have a room reserved for you at the Hôtel Lutetia. It is a hotel for German officers, and that is where you will stay. I don't want to hear any objection about it, or you will remain in Dieppe."

She couldn't understand why he was being stern and so demanding. "I didn't realize it would be trouble for you."

"Eva, I want to see you, and you do not know how nice it is to hear your voice. It is hard for me not to pick up the phone every day and call you, but that would interfere with my job." She heard an audible sigh on the other end. "Leave in the morning. The pass will be for three days. I have to go now. I'll see you tomorrow."

She didn't say anything, and he hung up the phone. Wilhelm acted as if he had all but forgotten about her. That she was just a passing fancy he no longer had time for. She hung the phone up and wiped tears of frustration out of her eyes.

"Eva, what happened?"

She sniffed. "We are leaving for Paris tomorrow, and we will be there for three days. But I don't think he wants to see me."

"What? Why do you say that?"

Eva huffed. "The way he acted, like I had annoyed him by calling. It was so obvious he didn't want me there."

"I don't think that is true."

"Stop sticking up for him, Ingrid," she yelled, immediately feeling bad about it. "I'm sorry, Ingrid. I shouldn't have hollered at you. It's not your fault. We'll have to see when we arrive if he truly wants me there."

The next morning, they picked up their passes and boarded the train to Paris. The whole time, she felt like she might vomit or pass out again. A lot of it was probably from nerves and that she hadn't eaten breakfast. She looked out the window and rubbed the top of her legs.

"Stop that. It will be alright." Ingrid had put her hand over Eva's, preventing her from nervously rubbing her legs.

"How can I ever tell him now? He doesn't want a baby, and he doesn't want me?"

"You don't know that."

"It sure seemed that way when I talked to him. He was dismissive and couldn't wait to get off the phone."

"Let's just see how he is when we get there."

Eva was on edge the whole ride, and her anxiety increased a couple of more notches when their train pulled into the Paris station. They got their bags and found which tram would take them to the Hôtel Lutetia. When they got off the tram and Eva saw the hotel, her jaw dropped. It was an amazing structure, a seven-story hotel made of tan stones, set at the corner of two joining streets. It was one of the fanciest hotels she had ever seen. No wonder it was a place they housed German officers.

She looked at Ingrid. "What if something goes wrong, and they won't let us have a room?"

"They will. You said that he had a room reserved for us."

"He did, but that doesn't mean something didn't go wrong."

"It didn't. Let's cross the street." Ingrid took her arm, and they stepped onto the road.

The inside of the building was just as impressive as the outside, and Eva strained her neck, trying to take it all in. She went to the desk and rang the little golden bell.

A man dressed in a suit turned around, looked at her, and then walked up to the counter. "May I help you?"

"Yes. SS Obersturmbannführer Bauer had reserved a room for me. My name is Eva Abrams."

He flipped through a large pad of paper in front of him. "I have two rooms reserved by him. One for an Eva Abrams and one for an Ingrid Braun." He looked up at her, waiting for her to confirm that was correct.

She looked back to Ingrid a little confused, then answered. "Yes, that is right."

"Let me get your keys." He went to the back wall, got two golden keys, and handed them to her. They were on large, round key chains with the room numbers on them. "You are both on the top floor. You say you are Eva Abrams?"

She looked at him, concern creeping in. "Yes."

"You have room 713. It is the suite. Ingrid Braun has the room across from it, room 714."

"Thank you." She started to walk away, then turned back. "Do you know if SS Obersturmbannführer Bauer is here?"

"I don't believe so."

"Thank you." She picked up her bag, and Ingrid followed her into the elevator. Eva handed Ingrid the key to her room. "We are in separate rooms."

"And you don't wonder why?" Ingrid asked caustically.

"Yes, I did wonder why. And yes, I have come to the same conclusion as you."

When they got to the top floor, they checked out both rooms, and Ingrid put her luggage in hers but stayed in Eva's room with her. It had a private balcony overlooking the Eiffel

Tower, and sitting on it was a small, blue cast iron table with two chairs and a vase of fresh hydrangeas in the middle. It was picturesque.

"He certainly gave you the better room," she said, appearing envious.

"Your room is fine. We can even switch if you want."

"Why, so he can come crawling on me in the middle of the night thinking I'm you? I don't think he would be pleased about that."

Eva's face flushed. "I don't think that is what he is going to do."

"How else did you make that baby with him, then?"

Eva put her hands up. "I'm going back inside. You stay out here and enjoy the view alone." Ingrid smiled and followed her into the room. Eva sat on the end of the bed. "This is so miserable. I feel like I never get any sleep. Yet I sleep all the time. I'm exhausted. I've decided pregnancy isn't enjoyable."

"That is how I felt, too. I understand. Maybe we can eat, then you can sleep."

"It's not even five o'clock."

"It doesn't matter. If you are tired, sleep."

She was torn between what she should do and what she wanted to do. "Alright, let's go eat, then I'll see about sleeping. That's something else I am all the time now, hungry. And food is in short supply. At least I don't have to buy sleep."

"He would not hesitate to help you with rations."

"I am not asking him for food or more ration coupons."

They went to a restaurant on the same street as the hotel and used some of the ration coupons they brought to buy a small meal each. Eva ate all her food and some of Ingrid's. She had insisted she didn't want it all, but Eva knew why she was really doing it.

They went back to the hotel, and Eva laid down to nap. The food made her even more tired, and she didn't have anything else to do. She told Ingrid she would come to her room after she slept for a few hours.

There was a light ticking feeling on her cheek. She jerked her head to the side and drifted back into sleep. Then it was there again. She slowly opened her eyes, blinking against the dry sleepy feeling in them, but the room was dim. Only a faint light permeated through the window. She turned her head to the right and saw the silhouette of a person sitting on the bed beside her. She jumped, instinctively scooting away.

"Ingrid?"

"It's not Ingrid," Wilhelm's deep voice cut through the silence.

"I didn't hear you come in. How long have you been here?"

"A while."

She sat up. "You should have woken me."

"I thought about it."

"And decided not to?" He didn't answer, so she asked, "what time is it?"

"Eight-thirty."

"That's late."

"Not really." He stroked her face with his fingers again, letting them linger on her cheek.

She honestly didn't know how to act around him at this moment. Ingrid was expecting her now, but how did she tell him she had to leave and go to her?

"Did you eat?" he asked.

"I did. Ingrid and I went out together a few hours ago." Again, he didn't answer but moved his hand from her face and placed it on her breast over her dress. She sucked in a breath, her heartrate spiking. He moved his other hand to her waist and pulled her across the bed to him, pressing his lips hard against hers. Right then, she stopped worrying about Ingrid wondering where she was or whatever the rest of the night would be.

Wilhelm didn't rush. He kissed her lips, her throat, her eyes, and held her gently, patiently waiting for her. She put her hands through his hair, kissing him now. She thought only a moment about what they were doing, but did it matter? She was already pregnant. She couldn't get pregnant again from what they did tonight.

He lifted her dress, rubbing up her thighs, his rough tanned hands on the smooth white skin of her hips. He pulled her dress over her head, then her slip, leaving her in only the bra and underwear she had on. His hands were insistent, running over her belly, and she flinched. His hand stopped moving, a finger resting just above her navel. She knew he felt it, and it wasn't because she didn't want him touching her. It was because she had an irrational fear that he could tell she was pregnant. But that was silly because she wasn't showing yet. He reached behind her, undid her bra's clasp, and slid it from her shoulders. She heard it drop to the bed. Then with both hands, he cupped each of her breasts with brazen knowledge of her body. She considered protesting, but the words wouldn't come out. She knew they were swollen from the pregnancy and wondered if he could tell too.

His lips were on her shoulder, her collarbone, then her throat. With lustful insistence, he kissed her, tracing his lips over her body. Then he laid her back on the bed, and she felt his teeth on her breast. He was biting them, sucking, and it hurt. They were tender, and she thought about saying something, telling him to stop, but she didn't want him to.

Her eyes drifted dreamily to the window as his lips and teeth worked against her. He removed her underwear and kissed just above her opening, then he removed his clothes, and he was on her. His lips softly against hers, then her cheek, her ear. She gladly moved her legs on each side of his hips, giving him permission to have her. She felt his smile against her cheek when she moved her legs apart for him. He entered her, and she inhaled, placing her hands on his sides. His skin was hot, the muscles in his back flexing as he moved in her. She missed this, being intimate with him, having him all to herself.

They weren't using protection, and she wondered if he even thought about it. He used it the first time, but it had been a little more planned than all the others times. He moved fast and hard against her, then let out a groan as he came.

He moved onto the bed beside her and pulled her to him. She turned in his arms to face him and kissed him. She rubbed his face, his chest, the curve of his side, and his hips. Her fingers trailed all along him, and she felt the goosebumps she made on his skin. They stayed this way for a while, and as the darkness surrounded them, he took her again. It was so sweet and tender it brought tears to her eyes. She didn't know exactly why she was crying, if it was because of his kisses, his tender caress, or the love he showed her. Maybe she was just emotional because of hormones, or perhaps she was happy he still wanted her when she was convinced he no longer did.

He cupped her face, kissed her, and felt the tears on her cheeks. "Why do women cry when they make love?" he asked in a low, gentle voice.

"They don't always, just sometimes."

He wiped a tear away with his thumb. "Why just sometimes?"

"Because sometimes it is more emotional than others."

"And if I asked, you would tell me why?"

"Maybe." She felt him rise on his elbow to look at her, even though it was hard to see in the dark. "After our conversation on the phone, I was convinced you didn't want me coming."

"I didn't, but not because of the reason you think. It is work-related, and I don't want you in Paris while it's happening. That is why you are only here for three days."

This worried her. "What stuff?"

He rubbed his finger along her jaw. "I can't tell you that, so don't ask."

She did not know what was happening in Paris in a few days. Her knowledge of history was better than most people in her time, and she could thank her interest in history, her two grandfathers, and one of her great grandfathers for that, but she still didn't know everything. Nothing was coming to mind, and it bothered her.

"I have to check in with Ingrid. I told her I would meet her in her room after taking a nap, but that isn't going to happen now, for obvious reasons. I think I'll take a shower, then go talk to her."

"I'll join you," he said.

She didn't know if that meant a shower or something else. He did shower with her, and they both cleaned off and washed their hair, but he, of course, could not keep his hands to himself or his mouth. His eyes scaled down her wet body, and touched and kissed her constantly, but she didn't object.

Once they were out of the shower, she dried off and put on a nightgown, then went across the hall and knocked on Ingrid's door.

She opened it, taking Eva in. "You showered already?"

"I'm going to go to bed."

"Did he not come?"

Eva couldn't suppress a smile. "He did."

Ingrid looked to Eva's door, then to Eva. "Oh, I see. So should I be worried to go to your room tomorrow morning, after he has taken you repeatedly?" Eva turned her eyes to the floor. "I'll talk to you in the morning, and you can tell me about it then."

"Some of it, maybe. Goodnight."

She went back to her room and closed the door. Wilhelm was already in bed, waiting for her. She crawled under the blankets and slid to his side. He curled up behind her and put his arm around her, pulling her tightly to his chest. She put her hand on his arm, and they fell asleep that way.

She opened her eyes and looked around the bright room, her feet hanging off the bed from under that blanket. She stretched and rolled onto her back, but the other side of the bed was empty. She raised up on her elbows and looked around the room, but he wasn't there. On the other pillow, she saw a piece of paper. She picked it up and read the words. He told her he had gone to work but would be back by five to take her and Ingrid to dinner. She smiled and laid back down, remembering last night. But then she also remembered he was doing something significant in Paris soon, and she had no idea what that was.

She got out of bed and went to Ingrid's room and knocked. Ingrid opened the door, sleep still heavy in her eyes, her hair a mess. "Do you want to go have breakfast with me?"

She looked a little confused. "Isn't um… Wilhelm here?"

"No, he left already. I thought after we ate we could walk around the city and see the sights. Maybe walk up to the Sacré-Coeur."

"We can. Let me change, and I'll knock on your door."

Ingrid closed the door, and Eva returned to her own room. She put on a dress and brushed her hair, leaving it down today. When a knock came on the door, she opened it, and Ingrid was waiting in the hall.

They left the hotel and returned to the same restaurant they had eaten at yesterday and had some breakfast. After breakfast they walked the streets arm in arm. It was a hot July day, but still a perfect for walking. The sky was blue, not a cloud in sight, and there was only a gentle breeze. They climbed the hill and the long steps to the Sacré-Coeur, walked around inside for a while, then sat to rest on the wall that surrounded the old church and looked down at the city.

"So, what happened last night?" Ingrid squinted against the sun as she looked at Eva.

"He came in while I was sleeping, and then we... you understand. Then I went to your room, and after we fell asleep."

"So, he does still want you?"

"At least in that way."

"Did he say why he acted that way on the phone?"

"He said that he doesn't want me, us, in the city for more than a few days because something is going to be happening in Paris soon, but he wouldn't say what it was. He said he didn't want me to come at all right now because of whatever this thing is that will be taking place."

"What do you think it is?"

"I don't know. This morning, he left a note saying he will be at the hotel at five to pick us up for dinner."

"Oh, good. We don't have to use our ration cards for dinner."

"Why would we not use our ration cards?"

"He isn't going to take us to dinner and make us pay for our own food with our rations. I thought that was obvious."

"I guess he wouldn't. Should we head back down and walk the Seine?"

"Alright." Ingrid stood up, and Eva linked her arm through hers again. It was busy around the Sacré-Coeur, with French people but also lots of soldiers. Men stationed here or men who came here on leave. Paris was always milling with Germans.

They walked along the river, watching the boats come and go. Eva looked at the brown water, thinking how nice it would be to put her feet in. They were hot and sweaty, sliding around in her shoes.

"Let's put our feet in the water."

"In that dirty water?"

"Ingrid, it will not hurt us. We're not drinking it." Eva sat on the stone walkway and removed her shoes, feeling the cool air on her feet. She hung them over the side, dipping them into the water. "Oh my God, this feels amazing."

Ingrid eyed her for a second, then sat down, took off her shoes, and put her feet in the water. "See, feels nice, doesn't it?"

Ingrid smiled. "It does."

Eva looked at her feet as she moved them gently up and down, splashing the water. "I wonder how long it will be before I have a hard time getting my feet in my shoes. I think the end of the second trimester, I hope, at least."

Ingrid watched her splash. "Are you not happy about this, baby?"

The question took Eva off guard. "I don't know yet. There are too many variables to consider. A simplified answer would be yes, but it's anything but simple, this situation I'm in." Eva took in a deep breath. "I have to pee again already, and this walking has taken it out of me."

"We can go back if you want."

"I think that would be best."

They made their way to the hotel, then Eva napped on Ingrid's bed. She didn't want to be alone, even though she would be sleeping. Ingrid woke her right before five, and they went to the lobby to wait. They weren't there long when Wilhelm walked through the front door at a brisk pace into the lobby, and Eva had to hop out of her chair and chase after him.

"Wilhelm," she called.

He stopped just before he was at the elevators and turned around. "Were you in the lobby?"

"Yes. Ingrid and I decided to wait for you there."

"Alright, let's go." He took her hand and pulled her along.

Eva motioned for Ingrid to follow as she walked by. They went out to a car that was waiting in front of the hotel and Ingrid got in the backseat first, then Eva, and lastly, Wilhelm. The car drove a couple of miles through the city and stopped in front of an upscale restaurant, people in fancy clothing leaving and coming.

Wilhelm got out and held his hand for each of them as they got out of the car, then linked Eva's through the elbow of his bent arm. They were seated at a table with a dark red, U-shaped cushion bench around it. Eva again sat in the middle and waited for the menus to be brought. Wilhelm looked at her, and she smiled, his severe expression softening some.

"Sorry for rushing. It has been a hellish day, and I still have more work to do before it is over."

She watched as he talked and noticed the circles under his eyes and a dark shadow on his face. "It's alright. I spent the day with Ingrid. We had fun exploring the city."

"I am glad."

The waiter passed out the menus, and they ordered their food quickly. Eva was famished, and couldn't wait to eat. When they brought the plates of food, her mouth watered from the smell. She took a bite and closed her eyes, and Wilhelm watched her. When she opened them and realized he had seen her do it she felt a twinge of embarrassment.

He looked away from her, and his gaze moved to a man who was coming toward their table.

"Son of a bitch," he said under his breath.

The man stopped beside the table and gave a salute to Wilhelm. He was a powerfully built, deep-chested man that was probably ten years Wilhelm's senior but of a lower rank.

"Hauptsturmführer Wittke, why are you here, interrupting me while I'm eating dinner? Can this not wait until I get back to my office?" There was no seemly deference in his tone. Wilhelm was in no mood to receive a delegation at dinner.

"I apologize, Obersturmbannführer, but I'm afraid it needs your urgent attention."

Wilhelm looked at Eva. "Excuse me. I'll be right back." He laid his napkin on the table, slid out of the booth, and followed the man through the restaurant.

Over fifteen minutes had passed, and he still hadn't returned. She looked to Ingrid. "I'm going to the bathroom. I have to pee, again, and this food isn't sitting well with me. If he returns before I'm back, just tell him where I went."

"I will."

Eva slid out of the booth and followed the hall to the back of the restaurant, where the bathrooms and smoking lounge were. She was almost to the door when voices of men talking in a nearby room carried into the hall, and one of them was Wilhelm. The man he was talking to did not sound like the one who came to the table. Instead of going into the bathroom, she stayed where she was and listened.

"It's not that easy," she heard Wilhelm say. "I am bound by this amalgamation of love. To me, it feels absolute. There is no turning back from it now. Which I don't mind, because being with her means everything to me. She is all that is clean and pure in my life. I am constantly surrounded shit in this world, and she almost makes me forget when I'm with her."

"So you are saying that you love her?"

Wilhelm gave a merciless bark of a laugh. "That word is so inadequate for what I feel. The truth is I'm drawing in her. I am completely mesmerized, utterly beguiled by that woman. The way she fixes me, the way she consumes me completely. The thought of being with her, the love I feel for her, I have lost myself to her entirely."

"This is a little surprising coming from you, the hardened, unregimented SS officer that strikes fear in people. To be taken down by a woman. And not just any woman, an American woman. This person you seem to have excessive love for."

"It isn't excessive love," Wilhelm answered sharply, but then stopped as if the other man had hit on the truth. "I know, I screwed up. I wanted her, and I wanted her to myself. It is done now and it can't be undone. So fuck it. I'm going to enjoy having her. I hadn't really planned on this happening. The first time I had her, feeling her body underneath mine and seeing the lust in her eyes, I was knocked on my ass. But it's not just that, I have never met anyone like her. She has rose to every challenge life has thrown at her and has handled it with grace. She does not deserve this, what this war puts her through, what I put her through."

"And you think it would be better if you had left her alone?"

"I had tried to ignore her over the years, but a fantasy or two crept in, unfortunately. And while having them made it more difficult to be around her, they had kept me angry, but also ready. I wanted to stop time. I have never been with a woman who feeds my soul like she does, or my lust. She said she doesn't trust me, but I know that is a lie. I'd be willing to bet I'm the one person she trusts the most."

"Well damn. How did you find her, such a rare jewel?"

"You know how I am after I've had a woman a couple of times?"

"I know you are not with them long."

"I get bored, so fucking bored. But the ironic thing is, I don't get bored of her. The frustrating, suspicious American woman. She is the whole package. Beautiful, clever, kind. The holy Trinity. Do you understand what I'm saying? Can you even understand?"

"Then what are you waiting for?" the other man asked. "Marry her."

His words hit Eva like a title wave, and she tensed, holding her breath. They were talking about her. He was being more honest and open about what he truly thought and felt because he didn't know she was listening?

"I'm afraid of what it would do to her if she stayed, what I would do to her if she stayed. I'm German and she is American. We have so little in common, but the thought of letting her go is too painful. I know to keep her here is selfish, but my need for her is stronger than my desire to give her what she wants, what she probably needs."

"So she wants to go home, then?"

"I believe she does."

"Well, this isn't her home, and she hasn't seen her family in years. Who wouldn't want to go back?"

"I know. But I can't let her. I want Germany to be her home, here with me, but I know I should really send her back to her country and away from all that is happening. She wouldn't have to suffer the effects of the war as much if she was back in America, and I would feel better knowing she was safely there with her family. But then I might never see her again, and I can't do that. I can't bear the thought of living every day without her, knowing she is so far away."

"That is the misery of being in love with a foreign woman, sometimes any woman, really." The man gave a small chuckle. "Women always make things more complicated."

Wilhelm let out a breath as he laughed. Then they changed the subject to something about work, and she hurried and went into the women's bathroom. She wanted to beat him back to the table. When she was done, she walked at a brisk pace back to the table and was relieved when she saw Wilhelm still wasn't there.

"You took a long time," Ingrid said as she slid back beside her.

"I was trying to keep my food down."

"He still hasn't come back."

"Hopefully, he will be back soon," Eva told her. "So tomorrow is our last day here, and he will be working, so maybe we can see a movie and visit a few more sites."

"Will you be sad to leave him?" Ingrid asked.

Eva forced a smile. "I will."

"And you still haven't told him you're pregnant?"

"No. I mean, you see how busy he is. He doesn't need anything else adding stress right now."

"When will you tell him?"

"That is the million-dollar question." Ingrid looked confused at her expression. "It means there is no way of knowing. Maybe I'll tell him next time he comes to Dieppe."

Ingrid tapped her arm. "He is coming back."

Eva looked up just as he was sliding in beside her. "Sorry, that took so long. I see you have finished your food."

"Oh, did you want me to wait until you returned?"

He grinned. "Of course not."

He ate quickly, not taking time to talk, then the car took them back to the hotel. He stepped out and helped Eva and Ingrid, then leaned in and placed a gentle kiss on her lips.

"Are you coming back here tonight?" she asked when he pulled away.

"I have to sleep somewhere, so why not with you?" A fiery look was in his eyes. "I mean, I could go back to my apartment and sleep alone in my empty bed, or I could come to the hotel and sleep in a bed with someone."

"I see your point." He gave her a quick second kiss on the cheek, then got back in the car. It was almost eight, and she felt tired enough to go to bed. She told Ingrid she was going to take a bath and wait for Wilhelm.

She took a long bath and then lay in bed, trying to stay awake until he got there, but it was getting harder to keep her eyes open, she was fading fast.

Her eyes opened when the mattress dipped with the weight of another person, then an arm came around her. She felt his body press against hers, and she smiled in the darkness. She knew he thought she was still asleep, and she didn't want to let him know she wasn't. Her stomach was upset from the food they ate at the restaurant, and she didn't want to have to tell him no if he tried to make love to her.

Chapter Twenty-Eight

July 14th, 1942

Again, Eva woke to an empty bed, and again there was a note. It said they could have dinner in the room tonight.

She and Ingrid ate breakfast at the hotel and then visited the catacombs first. They unsettled Ingrid, and she clung to Eva. "They are just bones. None of them are going to reach out and get you."

"It's still disturbing." Ingrid looked around, eyeing all the stacked bones.

"Do you care if we go see where Wilhelm works?"

"No, I would rather be there than here."

"I mean when we are done here, not that we are leaving the catacombs early."

"Sure, if you want." Ingrid eyed her surrounding nervously.

They made their way through the tunnels, then back to the surface. Eva had to ask some soldiers on the street how to get to the Gestapo headquarters. They seemed to find her question odd but told her anyway. As they got closer, Eva realized it was near the Arc de Triomphe. She remembered 84 Avenue Foch was the Parisian headquarters of the Sicherheitsdienst but wasn't sure how to get there. The Sicherheitsdienst, or SD, was the counter-intelligence branch of the SS during the German occupation of Paris. Avenue Foch was a wide residential boulevard in the 16th arrondissement that connects the Arc de Triomphe, with the Porte Dauphine on the border with the Bois de Boulogne. She remembered in high school, her history teacher showed them a video of the Germans marching down this street with the Arc de Triomphe in the background. It was right after the surrender of France.

She found 84 Avenue Foch, the address belonging to a four-story yellow stone building. She looked up at it, having a hard time believing this was the headquarters for the Gestapo. It was such a plain, unalarming-looking building.

"Eva," a man's voice called.

She turned to see who spoke her name, and coming towards them from across the street was Oberst Heinrich Schmitt. "Eva, what are you doing here?" He asked in an alarmed, hushed voice. There was an intense look of concern on his face.

Eva stared at him, not speaking. They had a history, a knowledge of each other's involvement with the resistance, and he had warned her in the past, and now here she was, standing in front of the Gestapo headquarters in Paris. She struggled several times to find her words. "I'm here, so see Wilhelm Bauer."

His eyes grew wide, and a consternation set in. "You cannot be here." He took her arm and pulled her along the sidewalk, and Ingrid followed. He stopped walking and looked at Ingrid. "There is something I need to tell you."

Eva saw how he was staring at Ingrid. "She's won't talk or say anything to anyone."

He gave her a strained look. "Follow me." He led them down several streets and then into an alley. Once they were far enough from the road he stopped and turned to Eva. "I have to tell you about Wilhelm Bauer. I don't think you understand. He had you followed. You are how he got to the resistance in Dieppe. You led him right to them. He used you, Eva. He knew you were with them again and took advantage of that, and it worked perfectly in his favor. Do you think it was just a coincidence that he brought you with him? Or that he had any genuine feelings for you? Men like him; they don't love. Their heart is made of stone. They use and discard the people around them without a second thought. Even now, I'm sure he is using you, seeing how you are obviously here with him or because of him."

Eva wanted to scream at him and tell him to stop saying those things, that they were only lies. "No, it isn't true. He had been searching for the resistance for a long time. Long before I got there."

"True, but ask yourself, how do you think he found them? And how did he capture all of them? There is something else too." He leaned on closer to Eva. "He is the one who reported

Hauptmann Gerhardt von Schulz. Wilhelm Bauer is the reason he is on the Russian front right now. And in a few days, on the 16th, the Gestapo will begin rounding up the Jews of Paris and send them East to camps. And I ask again, who do you think is overseeing this operation? You obviously have no idea what this man is capable of or what level he will stoop to ensure that the job gets done. I shouldn't have to remind you that the Gestapo doesn't have to give reasons for its orders."

He had lolled her into a false sense of security? Eva looked at Schmitt but wasn't really seeing him. So, that was what Wilhelm was talking about when he said he had something to do and why he didn't want her in the city while it was happening. Eva turned on her heels and walked out of the alley.

Ingrid and Schmitt chased after her. Schmitt grabbed hold of her arm and spun her around. "You cannot tell him anything that I just told you. He will know it came from someone high up, then it will only be a matter of time before they learn it was me."

Eva shook her head. "He only threatened to report Gerhardt. I just didn't realize he had actually done it. But not long before I came to Paris, there was a telegram saying he was missing in action. And he knew I was in the resistance. He told me he knew. But I won't say anything about the deportation of the Jews."

She turned away from him, but he retook her arm. "They will not just let you walk in and see him."

"I have to try." He let go of her, and she walked back to the building. She opened the front door and stepped inside but was quickly met by a stern-faced officer who came to stand in her path.

"You can't be in here."

"I'm here to see SS Obersturmbannführer Bauer."

"He can't see anyone right now. You need to leave." His tone was stern and menacing.

She knew it was no use, that she would have to confront him at the hotel tonight. She gave him a nod, then turned around and walked back out just in time to see a squad of German soldiers passing by on the street. She hurried back to Ingrid and Schmitt.

"They wouldn't let me see him."

"I told you they wouldn't. I can't be seen with you here, especially if you are going to go against my advice and talk to him. Take care of yourself, Eva." He tipped his hat to her, turned, and walked the opposite direction.

Ingrid looked at her. "What the hell is going on, Eva?"

"I'll explain later." She looked up and down the street. "I know what I have to do now. He has made the decision for me."

"You are scaring me, Eva."

Eva took her hand. "Help me find a hospital."

Ingrid creased her brows. "Why?"

"Because I cannot keep this baby. I know that now."

Ingrid's eyes widened, her mouth slightly ajar. "Eva, no!"

"I have to. That is the first step in getting away from him. The list of reasons why I can't have this baby is too long to explain it all here on the street."

Eva strode away, and Ingrid hastened after her. Eva asked a couple on the street where that nearest hospital was, and they gave her directions. She actually wasn't far, and it only took them a few minutes to get there. "Stay by the entrance, and I will get you on my way out."

"They won't give you an abortion at the hospital. It's illegal."

Eva felt like she was going to have a come apart. "I know that, but one of the doctors might know where I can get one."

She gave Ingrid a warning look, then went inside. She asked to speak to a doctor, and they had her wait in a room. After a while, a short, older man wearing a lab coat came into the and pulled the curtain closed.

"What are we here for today?"

"A pregnancy."

"Congratulations. And you want me to tell you how far along you are?"

"No, I want you to tell me how I can get rid of it."

He stood stock-still, his expression grave. "Abortions are illegal. If I perform one, I will be arrested."

"The baby's father is German, and I want to get rid of it. If you cannot help, point me in the direction of someone who can." She saw the change in him when she said the baby was part German.

He looked around, even though no one else was in the room. "I know of a woman in the Batignolles who does this for women." He took a pen from the pocket of his white lab coat and a small pad. He wrote something on the top sheet, then tore it off and handed it to her. "This is her name and address. Be careful, the Germans have these places watched, and they have arrested many of the women who perform the procedures already. They do it all the time."

"Thank you."

He nodded. "I understand your circumstance, and I sympathize."

It was then she realized he thought she had been raped or that she was coerced by a German. And she was going to let him continue to believe it. That might be the only reason he gave her the woman's information. "Thank you."

He pulled the curtain aside, and she gave him one last grateful look before putting the paper in her purse and walking to the front. Ingrid was waiting for her, biting her nails as she paced.

As soon as she saw Eva, she rushed over to her. "What happened?"

"He couldn't give me one." She saw the relieved look on Ingrid's face. "But he gave me the address of someone who can."

"You can't go through with this, Eva."

"I have to, Ingrid. He has left me with little choice."

"Look, I know it is not my decision, but I am pleading with you to reconsider. I would have given anything to keep my baby, but it was not meant to be. You still have that choice. A baby is not something to throw away because you don't want it. A baby is a blessing."

"It's not that simple, and you know why. A baby is a blessing when you planned for it, but this one was not planned."

"Didn't you conceive this baby with someone you love? So, wasn't it then made from love?"

"I thought it was with someone I loved and who loved me. But now I know he was just using me."

"Maybe if you told him, it would change things between you two."

"Trust me, it wouldn't help the situation. He can't take back what he has done, and he isn't incapable of being anything other than he is. There is no way we are ever going to be together. Not even if he came to me begging on his knees. This baby is not the solution to our problem. It is part of it."

"But you love him."

"I was in love with who I thought he was, not who he truly is. The minute I stepped foot into his cottage, I crossed a line."

"You didn't cross a line."

"I did. But unfortunately, you can't always see the line until you are on the other side of it. I have to do this, Ingrid, and I hope one day you will understand why." She looked at the clock on the wall. "Let's go."

They took the tram to the Batignolles area and followed the address on the paper and it led them to a row of townhouses. She went to the door with the black 12 on it and rang the doorbell. It buzzed, and a woman in a maid's uniform answered.

"Can I help you?"

"I am here to see Madame Lambert. A doctor at the hospital gave me this address."

Understanding registered on her face. "Of course. Come in." She ushered them in quickly and closed the door. "Which one of you is here for the procedure?"

"I am," Eva told her.

"Alright. You wait here," she said to Ingrid, pointing to a chair in the hall. "And you follow me." She led Eva to the back of the building and directed her to a room. "I will get Madame Lambert. Put that gown on and lay down on the table when you're done."

The woman disappeared, and Eva hurried and changed into the gown and laid back on the table. She looked around the room and her stomach twisted into knots. Her palms were already sweaty, and her heart was racing in her chest. She glanced at the foot of the table she was lying on and saw two stirrups that hold the legs apart, and beside it was a rollaway table with instruments on it like the ones they use in the hospital. But the room was nothing like the rooms in the hospital. The walls here were covered with pale yellow wallpaper, adorned with painted purple flowers that hung from vines.

She quickly sat up, feeling like she might faint and vomit at the same time. A strange sense of intense sadness filled her, and her eyes burned with the tears she fought to hold back.

There was a knock on the door, then it opened, and the maid who showed her to the room walked in, then another woman. "Hello. I'm Madame Lambert. My maid tells me a doctor sent you."

"Yes, he said you could help me."

"I can. Lay down." Eva laid back on the table, and the woman tenderly pushed on her stomach with her fingers. "Do you know how far along you are?"

"No, not exactly. I think maybe five or six weeks."

"I would say that is accurate from what I can tell from your stomach." She got a pair of gloves and put them on, and the other woman began to prep the things they would be using. "I have to warn you of the risks involved like I do all the women I help. You will be in a lot of pain after. There will be bleeding that can last for days or even weeks. You will probably experience episodes of sweating and dizziness, and the risk of sterility is high. There is also a risk of death."

Eva looked up at her. Could it really be that dangerous? "How is it performed?"

"You only being five or six weeks along; I can use this." She held up a long, skinny curved metal device with a slightly rounded end. "This is used for cleaning out the ear, but it is very similar to a tool that would have been made for abortions if those kinds of tools were made. It is not legal to make tools for abortions, so we use what we can." She then held up two curved, broad metal things. "This is a speculum, it is used for gynecological examinations, and I will insert it first, then I will use this," she held up something that looked like a small pair of pliers, "to dilate your cervix," then she held the first thing back up, "and this is what I will use to scrape the inside of your uterus and extract the embryo."

Eva looked at the tools, scared out of her mind. The room was spinning. "Is the procedure painful?"

"There will be some discomfort, but at this stage, it's not usually too bad."

"How long will it take?"

"Maybe ten minutes or so."

Eva laid her head down, resolute. "Let's get it over with."

Chapter Twenty-Nine

Eva came out of the room and walked the length of the hall back to Ingrid. She stood when she saw Eva. Worry and sadness clouded her face. Her eyes burning with the question. "Is it done?"

Eva shook her head and sat in the chair. Tears began to flow down her cheeks. "I didn't. I couldn't go through with it. I thought I could, but when she put that cold, metal thing inside me to dilate the cervix, I panicked and told her to stop. I knew I could not take this baby's life just because of who it's father is."

"What will you do now?"

She looked up at Ingrid. "Not tell him. But other than that, I don't know."

"How will you hide it from him?"

"Easy. I don't plan on seeing him again after today. We also need to switch our tickets from tomorrow to the last train of the evening, leaving for Dieppe today. Because after I talk to him, I want to leave. I will not stay another night in that hotel."

They rode the tram to the train station and had their tickets switched to a 9:30 pm train back to Dieppe. Then, they took the tram back to the hotel. Eva wasn't sure what time Wilhelm would be there, but she wanted to be ready to leave as soon as she told him what she had to say. She and Ingrid ate an early dinner at the café near the hotel, then Eva packed her suitcase and put it in Ingrid's room.

Eva went to her room, and Ingrid waited in hers until it was over. Eva paced, sat on the bed, threw up once from the nerves, looked out the window, then paced some more. The anxiety was almost unbearable, and she didn't know how much longer she could wait. It was already seven, and he still wasn't there. Finally, she heard the door open and froze, holding her breath, wanting to run now that it was time to confront him.

He closed the door and went to the table in the room, dropping his cap on it. He started unbuttoning his jacket when he noticed she hadn't moved from the spot she was standing in.

Their eyes me and his fingers stopped, pausing on a button, his fixed gaze firm on her. "Eva, what is it?"

Her hands and body were shaking, and she couldn't get them to stop. The urge to vomit was rising. Her heart pounded fast against her ribs, and she was lightheaded as sweat beaded on her forehead. She felt like she was having a stroke, which was actually the onset of an anxiety attack. She thought she would know what to say to him when the time came, but her mind was blank, and her body transfixed, paralyzed with fear.

He let go of his jacket and walked across the room, his eyes surveying her. It would be impossible for him not to know something was wrong. She watched him drawing nearer, and when he was close, he reached for her, his fingers barely grazing her hand, but she jumped back as if he poked her with a hot cattle prod.

"Don't touch me!"

He halted, his body becoming tense, but he made no move to come any closer, nor did he say anything. His self-control was well in check. They stayed this way, looking at one another. To her, it felt like an eternity. She understood that very soon, she was going to have to explain her actions and her words.

Fighting through tears and the searing anger she felt inside, she somehow managed coherent words. "When I learned of it I didn't want to believe it was true. I hoped that I was mistake, but clearly I was not. I trusted you, and you betrayed me. You lied and used me." Her eyes burned from angry hot tears. "I trusted you more than anyone else in this world and you broke that trust." A tear escaped her right eye. Her last three words seemed to strike a chord with him, and she knew he understood what she meant. He opened his mouth to speak, but she held up her hand to stop him. "No, don't talk. I don't want to hear your reasons, or how you love me, because you have no fucking idea what love is. That word has no meaning to you because you don't understand its power. You are supposed to be honest with the person you love, not lie to their face while you are hurting them in secret. I may not be as experienced in the world as you or know as much, which you love to point out, but I do know one thing. The way you have treated me is not love. You hurt me, Wilhelm. You, the person I thought would protect me from the pain, but you inflicted it. And that cuts so much deeper." She turned from him for a second, hardly able to speak because of her anger and the tears that she choked back.

She paced with her hands on her hips for a few seconds then turned back to him. "You," she pointed a finger at him, "wanted me so you could catch the resistance fighters in Dieppe. And you are responsible for the death of the man I love. You lied to me, and have been deceiving me for months," she shouted, putting her palm flat on her chest. "You said you wouldn't hurt me, but I guess what you said meant nothing to you. Your duplicity comes so naturally to you doesn't it?" His face was growing darker with every word. She had seen his rage before but never directed at her.

"I have no intention of telling you my reasons. And it doesn't matter if you think what I did was right or wrong. It's of no importance. What I would like to know is how the fuck you found out?" His voice was low, and the words were said deliberately apathetic, but beneath the exterior of calmness was the undercurrent of a terrifying storm of fury, and yet he was still the epitome of grace under fire.

His glare was so impassioned that she backed away. She had to get out of here. "This is over. You will never see me naked in your bed again. You will never have me in any kind of way. And I will never be yours. Being with you was a mistake, the biggest mistake of my life, one I will not make again. You never cared. I don't think you feel at all with that black heart of yours, because you are dead inside, and I never want to see your face again. I hope you go to hell where you belong you fucking bastard."

The muscles in his jaw clicked. "You are a terrible liar. And when this war is over, you will realize that I was the only one who was actually there for you."

She turned from him and walked to the door, trying to keep her legs from giving out. She opened it, stepped into the hall, and slammed it behind her. She pounded on Ingrid's door and hoped to God she hurried before he decided to come after her. When Ingrid opened it, she ran in, shutting it behind her. She leaned against it and slid down to the floor, struggling to breathe as moaning sobs escaped her lips. The tears blurred her eyes, and snot ran into her lips. She wiped at it, and Ingrid knelt beside her.

"What happened?"

When she got some control of her breathing, she spoke. "We-need-to leave," she said through hiccups.

They got their bags and made their way to the front of the hotel, turned in their keys and then walked to the tram stop. Eva didn't care that she had to wait over an hour at the train station. There was no way she was going to stay a minute longer at the hotel, knowing he was right across the hall from her. He could easily find out where she went, what train she was taking, and stop her from leaving, but she hoped he wouldn't.

She didn't have Gerhardt or Wilhelm anymore, so who was going to save her from being broken this time? Who was going to help her pick up the pieces of her shattered heart? It was hard knowing this was the end. Telling Wilhelm goodbye was one of the most challenging things she ever had to do. The heartache she was going to feel after this would be intense and prolonged. But it was time to dry her eyes and accept the fact that life would continue. For a while, she had the mistaken belief that they stood a chance, but that was a fantasy. Letting go of what she thought they had was breaking her heart, but she would find a way to ride the rest of the war out without him. First, though, she needed to make it through the rest of this day. Then she would learn how to face the world on her own. And someday, she would fall in love again in her own time and in her country. There would probably come a time she would grow to regret the things she said to him, but she couldn't imagine it would be soon.

She slept on the train, feeling emotionally and physically drained. Occasionally opening her eyes to see the shadows from outside the window move across her lap, before closing them again. The journey seemed to last forever, and she just wanted this day to end.

About the author

J.L. Robison is an American author who currently lives in western Pennsylvania with her husband and two daughters. She has recently finished the fourth and final book in the Edelweiss series and is now working on a new story in the world of dark fantasy. Before becoming a writer, J.L. Robison taught English as a second language. She has had the opportunity to live in many states and has been to over fourteen different countries, experiencing their unique cultures. She writes in multiple genres, spanning historical fiction, literary fiction, romance, and fantasy. When she is not sitting on the couch with her laptop, she is outside working in her garden, playing tennis, bowling, ice skating, traveling, or doing things with her kids. She also enjoys going on walks with her husband or drinking a glass of wine to relax in front of the TV. Most of her inspiration comes at night when she can't sleep, is listening to music, or when on a walk alone in nature.

Printed in Great Britain
by Amazon

59304958R00341